DRAGONSEYE
▼▼▼▼▼▼▼▼▼▼

DRAGONSEYE

ANNE McCAFFREY

BALLANTINE BOOKS • NEW YORK

A Del Rey® Book
Published by Ballantine Books

Copyright © 1997 by Anne McCaffrey

All rights reserved under International and Pan-American Copyright Con-
ventions. Published in the United States by Ballantine Books, a division of
Random House, Inc., New York, and simultaneously in Canada by Random
House of Canada Limited, Toronto.

http://www.randomhouse.com

Library of Congress Cataloging-in-Publication Data
McCaffrey, Anne.
Dragonseye / Anne McCaffrey. —1st ed.
p.   cm.
"A Del Rey book."
ISBN 0-345-38821-6
1. Pern (Imaginary place)—Fiction.   I. Title.
PS3563.A255D77   1997   96-44206
813'.54—dc20   CIP

Manufactured in the United States of America

First Edition: February 1997

10 9 8 7 6 5 4 3 2 1

This book is most respectfully
dedicated to
Dieter Clissmann,
who sorts out my various computers
and never fails to answer my pleas for *HELP!*

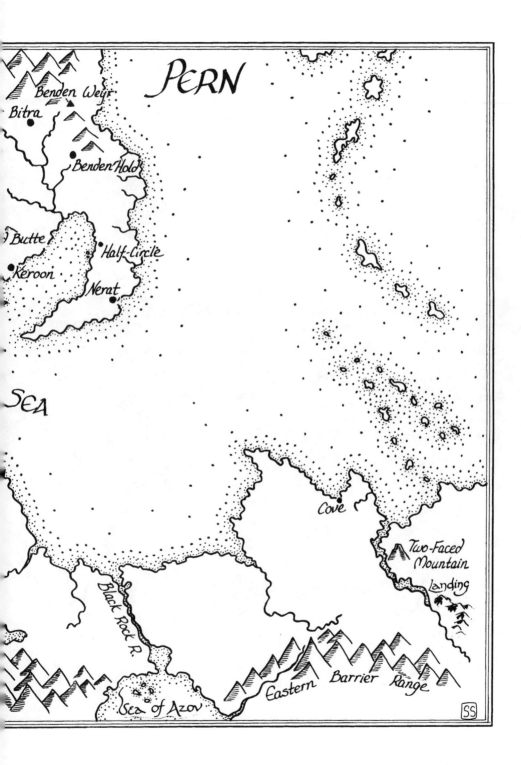

The Finger points
To an Eye blood-red.
Alert the Weyrs
To sear the Thread.
from Dragonflight

CONTENTS

DRAGONSEYE
▼▼▼▼▼▼▼▼▼

PROLOGUE

▼▼▼▼▼▼▼▼▼▼▼▼▼▼▼▼▼▼▼▼▼▼▼▼▼▼▼▼▼▼▼▼

Rukbat, in the Sagittarian sector, was a golden G-type star. It had five planets, two asteroid belts, and a stray planet it had attracted and held in recent millennia. When men first settled on Rukbat's third planet and called it Pern, they had taken little notice of the stranger planet, swinging around its adopted primary in a wildly erratic orbit—until the desperate path of the wanderer brought it close to its stepsister at perihelion.

When such aspects were harmonious, and not distorted by conjunctions with other planets in the system, the wanderer brought in a life form that sought to bridge the space gap to the more temperate and hospitable planet.

The initial losses the colonists suffered from the voracious mycorrhizoid organism that fell on them were staggering. They had divorced themselves from their home planet, Earth, and had already cannibalized the colony ships, the *Yokohama*, the *Bahrain*, and the *Buenos Aires*, so they would have to improvise with what they had. Their first need was an aerial defense against the Thread, as they named this menace. Using highly sophisticated bioengineering techniques, they developed a specialized variant of a Pernese life form which had two unusual, and useful, characteristics: the so-called fire-lizards could digest a phosphine-bearing rock in one of their two stomachs and, belching forth the resultant gas, create a fiery breath which reduced Thread to harmless char; and they were able both to teleport and to share an empathy that allowed limited understanding with humans. The bioengineered "dragons"— so called because they resembled the Earth's mythical creatures—were paired at hatching with an empathic human, forming a symbiotic relationship of unusual depth and mutual respect.

The colonists moved to the Northern Continent to seek shelter from the insidious Thread in the cave systems, new homes that they called "Holds." The dragons and their riders came, too, housing themselves in old volcanic craters: Weyrs.

The First Pass of Thread lasted nearly fifty years, and what scientific information the colonists were able to gather indicated that Thread would be a cyclic problem, occurring every 250 years as the path of the wanderer once again approached Pern.

During this interval, the dragons multiplied and each successive generation became a little larger than the last, although optimum level would take many, many more generations to reach. And the humans spread out across the Northern Continent, creating holds to live in, and halls in which to train young people in skills and professions. Sometimes folks even forgot that they lived on a threatened planet.

However, in both Holds and Weyrs, there were masses of reports, journals, maps, and charts to remind the Lords and Weyrleaders of the problem; and much advice to assist their descendants when next the rogue planet approached Pern and how to prepare for the incursion.

This is what happened 257 years later.

1

▼▼▼▼▼▼▼▼▼▼

EARLY AUTUMN AT FORT'S GATHER

Dragons in squadrons wove, and interwove, sky trails, diving and climbing in wings, each precisely separated by the minimum safety distance so that occasionally the watchers thought they saw an uninterrupted line of dragons as the close order drill continued.

The skies above Fort Hold, the oldest of the human settlements on the Northern Continent, were brilliantly clear on this early autumn day: that special sort of clarity and depth of color that their ancestors in the New England sector of the North American continent would have instantly identified. The sun gleamed on healthy dragon hides and intensified the golden queen dragons who flew at the lowest level, sometimes seeming to touch the tops of the nearby mountains as they circled Fort. It was a sight to behold, and always brought a thrill of pride to those who watched the display: with one or two exceptions.

"Well, that's done for now," said Chalkin, Lord Holder of Bitra, the first to lower his eyes, though the fly-past was not yet over.

He rotated his neck and smoothed the skin where the decorative embroidered border of his best tunic had scratched the skin. Actually, he had had a few heart-stopping moments during some of the maneuvers, but he would never mention that aloud. The dragonriders were far too full of themselves as it was without pandering to their egos and an inflated sense of importance: constantly appearing at his Hold and handing him lists of what hadn't been done and *must* be done before Threadfall. Chalkin snorted. Just how many people were taken in with all this twaddle? The storms last year had been unusually hard, but then that wasn't in itself unexpectable, so why were hard storms supposed to be a prelude to a Pass? Winter meant storms.

And this preoccupation with the volcanoes going off. They did periodically anyway, sort of a natural phenomenon, if he remembered his science orientation correctly. So what if three or four were active right now? That did not necessarily have to do with the proximity of a spatial neighbor! And he was *not* going to require guards to freeze themselves keeping an easterly watch for the damned planet. Especially as every other Hold was also on the alert. So what if it orbited near Pern? That didn't necessarily mean it was close enough to be dangerous, no matter how the ancients had gone on about cyclical incursions.

The dragons were just one more of the settlers' weird experiments, altering an avian species to take the place of the aircraft they had once had. He'd seen the airsled that the Telgar Foundry treasured as an exhibit: a vehicle much more convenient to fly in than aboard a dragon, where one had to endure the black-cold of teleportation. He shuddered. He had no liking for *that* sort of ultimate cold, even if it avoided the fatigue of overland travel. Surely in all those records the College was mustering folks to copy, there were other materials that could be substituted for whatever the ancients had used to power the vehicles. Why hadn't some bright lad found the answer before the last of the airsleds deteriorated completely? Why didn't the brainy ones develop a new type of airworthy vessel? A vessel that didn't expect to be thanked for doing its duty!

He glanced down at the wide roadway where the gather tables and stalls were set up. His were empty: even his gamesters were watching the sight. He'd have a word with them later. They should have been able to keep some customers at the various games of chance, even with the dragonrider display. Surely everyone had seen that by now. Still, the races had gone well and, with every one of the wager-takers *his* operators, he'd've made a tidy profit from his percentage of the bets.

As he made his way back to his seat, he saw that wine chillers had been placed at every table. He rubbed his beringed fingers together in anticipation, the black Istan diamonds flashing as they caught sunlight. The wine was the only reason he had been willing to come to this gathering: and he'd half suspected Hegmon of some prevarication in the matter. An effervescent wine, like the champagne one heard about from old Earth, was to have its debut. And, of course, the food would be marvelous, too, even if the wine should not live up to its advance notice. Paulin, Fort Hold's Lord, had lured one of the best chefs on the continent to his kitchens and the evening meal was sure to be good: if it didn't turn sour in his stomach while he sat through the obligatory meeting afterward. Chalkin had bid for the man's services, but Chrislee had spurned Bitra's offer, and that refusal had long rankled in Chalkin's mind.

The Bitran Holder mentally ran through possible excuses for

leaving right after dinner: one plausible enough to be accepted by the others. This close to putative Threadfall, he had to be careful of alienating the wrong people. If he left *before* the dinner . . . but then he wouldn't have a chance to sample this champagne-style wine, and he was determined to. He'd taken the trouble to go to Hegmon's Benden vineyard, with the clear intention of buying cases of the vintage. But Hegmon had refused to see him. Oh, his eldest son had been apologetic— something about a critical time in the process requiring Hegmon's presence in the caverns—but the upshot was that Chalkin couldn't even get his name put down on the purchase list for the sparkling wine. Since Benden Weyr was likely to get the lion's share of it, Chalkin had to keep in good with the Benden Weyrleaders so that, at the Hatching which was due to occur in another few weeks, he'd be invited and could drink as much of *their* allotment of wines as he could. More than one way to skin a wherry!

He paused to twirl one of the bottles in its ice nest. Almost perfectly chilled. Riders *must* have brought the ice in from the High Reaches for Paulin. Whenever he needed some, he couldn't find a rider willing to do him, Bitra's Lord Holder, such a simple service. Humph. But of course, certain Blood-lines always got preferential treatment. Rank didn't mean as much as it should, that was certain!

He was surreptitiously inspecting the label of a bottle when there was a sudden, startled intake of fearful breaths from the watchers, instantly followed by a wild cheer. Looking up, he saw he just missed some sort of dangerous maneuver . . . Ah, yes, they'd done another midair rescue. He saw a bronze dragon veering from under a blue who was miming a wounded wing: both riders now safely aboard the bronze's neck. Quite likely that Telgar Weyrleader who was such a daredevil.

Cheers were now punctuated with applause and some

banging of drums from the bandsmen on their podium down on the wide courtyard that spread out from the steps to the Hold down to the two right-angled annexes. Once again both the infirmary and the Teachers' College were being enlarged, if the scaffolding was a reliable indication. Chalkin snorted, for the buildings were being extended outward, wide open to any Thread that was purportedly supposed to start falling again. They really ought to be consistent! Of course, tunneling into the cliff would take more time than building outside. But too many folks preached one thing and practiced another.

Chalkin grunted to himself, wondering acidly if the architects had got Weyrleader approval for the design. Thread! He snorted again and wished that Paulin, chatting so cozily with the two Benden Holders as he and his wife escorted them back to the head table, would hurry up. He was dying to sample the bubbly white.

Rattling his fingers on the table, he awaited the return of his host and the opening of the tempting bottles in the cooler.

K'vin, bronze Charanth's rider, put his lips close to the ear of the young blue rider sitting in front of him.

"Next time wait for my signal!" he said.

P'tero only grinned, giving him a backward glance, his bright blue eyes merry.

"Knew you'd catch me," he bellowed back. "Too many people watching to let me swing and give Weyr secrets away!" Then P'tero waved encouragingly at Ormonth, who was now flying anxiously at Charanth's wing tip. Though unseen from the ground, the safety-tethers still linked the blue rider to his dragon. P'tero unbuckled his end of the straps and they dangled free.

"Lucky you that *I* was looking up just then!" K'vin said so harshly that the brash lad flushed to his ear tips. "Look at the fright you've given Ormonth!" And he gestured toward the blue, his hide flushing in mottled spots from his recent scare.

P'tero yelled something else, which K'vin didn't catch, so he leaned forward, putting his right ear nearer the blue rider's mouth.

"I was in no danger," P'tero repeated. "I used brand-new straps and he watched me braid 'em."

"Hah!" As every rider knew, dragons had gaps in their ability to correlate cause and effect. So Ormonth would scarcely have connected the new straps with his rider's perfect safety.

"Oh, thanks," the rider added as K'vin snapped one of his own straps to P'tero's belt. Not that they would be doing more than landing, but K'vin wished to make a point of safety to P'tero.

While K'vin approved of courage, he did not appreciate recklessness, especially if it endangered a dragon this close to the beginning of Threadfall. Careful supervision had kept his Weyr from losing any dragon partners, and he intended to maintain that record.

Spilling off his blue before K'vin had passed the word was taking a totally unnecessary risk. Fortunately, K'vin had seen P'tero dive. His heart had lurched in his chest, even if he knew P'tero was equipped with the especially heavy and long harness as a fail-safe. Even if he and Charanth had not accurately judged the midair rescue, those long straps would have saved the blue rider from falling to his death. Today's maneuver had been precipitous instead of well-executed. And, if Charanth had not been as adept on the wing, P'tero might be nursing broken ankles or severe bruising as a result of his folly. No matter how broad, those safety straps really jerked a man about midair.

P'tero still showed no remorse. K'vin only hoped that the

stunt produced the effect the love-struck P'tero wished. His mate would have been watching, heart in mouth, no doubt, and P'tero would reap the harvest of such fear sometime this evening. K'vin wished that more girls were available to Impress green dragons. Girls tended to be steadier, more dependable. But with parents keenly interested in applying for more land by setting up cotholds for married children—and no dragonriders, male or female, were allowed to own land— fewer and fewer girls were encouraged to stand on the Hatching Grounds.

The dragons who had taken part in the mass fly-by were now landing their riders in the wide road beyond the court. Then they leaped up again to find a spot in which to enjoy the last of the warm autumnal sun. Many made for the adjoining cliffs as space on Fort's heights filled up on either side of the solar panels. Dragons could be trusted not to tread on what remained of the priceless installations. Fort's were the oldest, of course, and two banks had been lost last winter to the unseasonably fierce storms. Fort, being the largest as well as the oldest northern installation, needed all its arrays in full working order to supply heat for its warren of corridors, power for air circulation units and what equipment still worked. Fortunately, a huge stockpile of panels had been made during the first big wave of constructing new Weyrs and Holds. There would be enough for generations.

Weyrleaders sought their tables on the upper level with Lord Holders and professionals, while riders joined whatever company they preferred at tables set up on the huge expanse of the outer apron. Not a sprout of vegetation anywhere on that plaza surface, K'vin noticed with approval. S'nan, Fort's Weyrleader, had always been fussy, and rightly so.

The musicians had struck up sprightly music, and couples were already dancing on the wooden floor set over the cobbles. Beyond the dance square were the stalls, tents, and tables where goods were being sold or exchanged. There'd been brisk business all day, especially for items needed during the winter months when there would be fewer big Gathers. The various Craftsmen would be pleased, and there'd be less for the dragons to haul back.

Charanth was now circling over the annexes, which had been started to increase living space for both Pern's main infirmary-research facility and teacher training. The dormitories were also going to house volunteers who were assiduously trying to save the records, damaged during last spring when water had leaked down the walls of the vast storage caverns under Fort. Riders had offered to spend as much time as possible from their training schedules to help in the project. Everyone who had a legible script was acceptable, and Lord Paulin had done a bang-up job in making the copyists comfortable. The other Holds had contributed material and workforces.

The exterior buildings of the College were designed to be Thread proof, with high peaked roofs of Telgar slate, and gutters that led into underground cisterns where errant Thread would be drowned. All the Craftsmen involved, including those destined to inhabit the facility, would have preferred to enlarge the cave system, but there had been two serious collapses of caverns, and the mining engineers had vetoed interior expansion for fear of undermining the whole cliffside. Even the mutant, blunt-winged, flightless photosensitive watchwhers had refused to go on further subterranean explorations which, their handlers insisted, meant dangers human eyes couldn't see. So build externally they did: stout walls more than two and a half meters thick at ground level, tapering to just under two meters beneath the roof. With the iron mines at Telgar going full-blast, the necessary structural beams to support such weight had posed no problem.

The new quarters were to be finished within the month.

Even today there had been a workforce, though they had taken a break to watch the aerial display and would finish in time for the evening meal and entertainment.

Charanth landed gracefully, with Ormonth right beside him, so that P'tero might remove the tethering safety straps before they could be noticed. As he was doing so, M'leng, green Sith's rider, came up to him, scolding him for "putting my heart in my mouth like that!" And proceeded to berate P'tero far more viciously than his Weyrleader would.

K'vin grinned to himself, especially as he saw how penitent P'tero became under such a harangue. K'vin rolled up his riding straps and tied them to the harness ring.

"Enjoy the sun, my friend," he said, slapping Charanth on the wide shoulder.

I will. Meranath is already there, the bronze dragon said, his tone slightly smug as he executed a powerful upward leap, showering his rider with grit.

Charanth's attitude toward his mate, Meranath, amused, and pleased, his rider. No one had expected K'vin to accede to Telgar's Weyrleadership when it fell open after B'ner's death nine months before. Who would have expected that the sturdy rider, just into his sixth decade, had had any heart problems? But that is what the medics said killed him. So, when Meranath was ready to mate again, Telgar's senior Weyrwoman, Zulaya, had called for an open flight, leaving it up to the dragons to decide on the next Leader. She'd insisted that she had no personal preference. She had been sincerely attached to B'ner and was probably still grieving for him. There had certainly been no lack of "suitors."

K'vin had sent Charanth aloft in the mating flight because all the Telgar Weyr wingleaders were expected to take part, as well as bronze riders from the other Weyrs. He had no real wish to lead a Weyr into a Pass. He considered himself too young for such responsibilities. He had observed from B'ner that the normal duties of an Interval were bad enough, but to *know* that a high percentage of your fellow riders would be injured, or killed: that the lives of so many people rested on your expertise and endurance was too much to contemplate. Some nights, now, he was wracked by terrifying dreams, and Threadfall hadn't even started. On the occasions when he was in Zulaya's bed, she had been understanding and calmly reassuring.

"B'ner worried, too, if that's any consolation, Kev," she said, using his old nickname and soothing sweat-curled hair back as he trembled with reaction. "He had nightmares, too. Comes with the title. As a rule, the morning after a nightmare, B'ner'd go over Sean's notes. I figure he had to have memorized them. I've seen you do the same thing. You'll do well, Kev, when push comes to shove. I know it."

Zulaya could sound so *sure* of something, but then she was nearly a decade his senior and had had more experience as a Weyrleader. Sometimes her intuition was downright uncanny: she could accurately predict the size of clutches, the distribution of the colors, the sex of babies born in the Weyr, and occasionally even the type of weather in the future. But then, she was Fort Weyrbred, a linear descendant of one of the First Riders, Aliana Zuleita, and *knew* things. It was odd how the golden queens seemed to prefer women from outside the Weyrs—but sometimes a queen had a mind of her own and chose a Weyrbred woman, defying custom.

However, just like his predecessor, he constantly reviewed accounts of the individual Threadfalls, how they differed, how you could *tell* from the Leading Edge of Fall that this would be an odd one. Most often the accounts were dry statements of fact, but the prosaic language did not disguise the presence of great courage: especially as those first riders had to figure out how to cope with Thread, easy or hard.

The fact that he was a several times great-nephew of Sorka

Connell, the First Weyrwoman—and Zulaya pointed this out more than once—constituted a secondary and subtle reassurance to the entire Weyr.

"Maybe that's why Meranath let Charanth catch her," Zulaya said, her face dead serious but her eyes dancing.

"Had you, I mean . . . did you think of me . . . I mean . . ." K'vin tried to summon appropriate words two weeks after that momentous flight. He had been overwhelmed by her response to him that night. But afterward she seemed very casual in her dealings with him, and she did not always invite him into her quarters, despite the fact that their dragons were inseparable.

"Who *thinks* at all during a mating flight? But I do believe I'm glad that Charanth was so clever. If there is anything in heredity, having a distant great-nephew of Fort Weyr's First Weyrwoman, *and* from a family that has put many acceptable candidates on the Hatching Grounds, as Telgar's Weyrleader gives us all a boost."

"I'm not my many-times-great-aunt, Zulaya . . ."

She chuckled. "Fortunately, or you wouldn't be Weyrleader, but Blood will tell!"

Zulaya had a disconcerting directness but gave him no real hint how she, the woman, not the Weyrwoman, personally felt toward him. She was kind, helpful, made constructive suggestions when they discussed training programs, but so . . . impersonal . . . that K'vin had to conclude that she hadn't really got over B'ner's death yet.

He himself was obscurely comforted that his great-great-aunt had managed to survive Fall and he would attempt to do the same. As, he was sure, would his two siblings and four cousins who were also dragonriders. Though no others were Weyrleaders . . . yet. Still, if his being of the Ruathan Bloodline, which had produced Sorka, M'hall, M'dani, Sorana, Mairian, offered reassurance to his Weyr, he'd reinforce that at every turn during the Pass.

Now, at probably the last large gather Pern would enjoy under Threadfree skies for the next fifty years, he watched his Weyrwoman leave the group of Telgar holders she had been talking to and stride toward him across the open courtyard.

Zulaya was tall for a woman, long-legged—all the better for bestriding a dragon's neck. He was a full head taller than she was, which she said she liked in him: B'ner had been just her height. It was her coloring that fascinated K'vin: the inky black curly hair that, once freed of the flying helmet, tumbled down below her waist. The hair framed a wide, high cheek-boned face, set off the beige of her smooth skin and large, lustrous eyes that were nearly black; a wide and sensual mouth above a strong chin gave her face strength and purpose which reinforced her authority with anyone. She strode, unlike some of the hold women who minced along, her steel-rimmed boot heels noisy on the flagstones, her arms swinging at her side. She'd had time to put a long, slitted skirt over her riding gear, and it opened as she walked, showing a well-formed leg in the leather pants and high boots. She'd turned the high-riding boot cuffs down over her calf, and the red fur made a nice accent to her costume, echoed in the fur trim of her cuffs and collar, which she had opened. As usual, she wore the sapphire pendant she had inherited as the eldest female of her Blood.

"So, did P'tero win M'leng's undying affection with that stunt?" she demanded, an edge to her voice. "They've gone off together . . ." and she looked in the direction of the two riders who were headed toward the temporary tents along the row of cots.

"You might have a word with both later. They're afraid of you," K'vin said, grinning.

"For that piece of stupidity I'll make them more afraid," she said briskly, hopping a step to match his stride. "You really should learn how to scowl menacingly." She glanced up at K'vin and then shook her head, sighing sadly. She had once teased him that he was far too handsome to ever look genuinely threatening, with the Hanrahan red hair, blue eyes, and freckles. "No, you just don't have the face for it. Be that as it may, Meranath's going to give out to Sith for allowing a blue to put himself in danger."

"Get 'em where it hurts," K'vin said, nodding, because Meranath was even more effective as a deterrent with the dragons than any human could be, even the dragon's own rider. "Damned fool stunt."

"However," and now Zulaya cleared her throat, "the Telgarians thought it was 'just marvelous!' " she added in a gushing tone. "Especially since they won't get much chance to see the dive in real action." Now she grimaced.

"Well, at least Telgarians believe," K'vin said.

"Who doesn't?" Zulaya demanded, looking up at him.

"Chalkin, for one."

"Him!" She had absolutely no use for the Bitran Lord Holder and never bothered to hide it.

"If there's one, there may be others, for all the lip service they give us."

"What? With First Fall only months away from us?" Zulaya demanded. "And why, pray tell, do we have dragons at all, if not to provide an aerial defense for the continent? Oh, we provide transportation services, but that's not nearly enough to justify our existence."

"Easy, lady," K'vin said. "You're preaching to the dedicated."

She made a disgusted sound deep in her throat and then they had reached the steps up to the Upper Court. She put her hand through his arm so that they would present the proper picture of united Weyrleadership. K'vin stifled a sigh that the accord was only for public display.

"*And* Chalkin's already into that new bubbling wine of Hegmon's," Zulaya said irritably.

"Why else do you think he came?" said K'vin as he deftly

guided her away from the Bitran who was smacking his lips and regarding his wineglass with greedy speculation. "Though today's also a chance for his gamesters to profit."

"One thing's sure, I hear tell he's not on Hegmon's list," she said as they reached their table, which the Telgarians shared, by choice, with the High Reaches Weyr and hold leaders and those from Tillek. The senior captain of the Tillek fishing fleet and his new wife completed the complement at their table.

"That was quite a show you put on," said the jovial shipmaster, Kizan, "wasn't it, Cherry m'dear?"

"Oh, it was, indeed it was," the girl replied, clapping her hands together. While the gesture was close to an affectation, the young wife was clearly awed by the company she kept at this Gather, and everyone was trying to help her cope. Kizan had let it be known that she came from a small fishing hold and, while a capable shipmaster, she had little experience with a wider world. "I've often seen the dragons in the sky, but never so close up. They are so beautiful."

"Have you ridden one yet?" Zulaya asked kindly.

"Oh, heavens, no," Cherry said, modestly lowering her eyes.

"You may, and soon," her husband said. "We came overland here to Fort for the Gather, but I think we'd better see how good our credit is . . ."

"Very good, Captain," said G'don, the High Reaches Weyrleader, "as you've never applied to us half as much as you're entitled to." Mari, his Weyrwoman, nodded and smiled encouragingly at Cherry's almost horrified reaction.

"What?" Kizan teased his bride, "the woman who sailed through a Force Nine gale without complaint is nervous about flying on a dragon?"

Cherry tried to respond but she couldn't find words.

"Don't tease," Mari said. "Riding a dragon *is* considerably different to standing on your own deck, but I don't know many people who refuse a ride."

"Oh, I'm not refusing," Cherry said hastily, startled.

Just like a child fearful of being denied a promised treat, K'vin thought, and struggled to keep from grinning at her.

"All of you, leave her alone," said the Telgar Lady Holder, scowling at them. "I remember my first ride a-dragonback—"

"Back that far, huh," said her husband, Lord Tashvi, eyeing her blandly. "And yet you can't remember where you put that bale of extra blankets . . ."

"Don't start on that again!" Salda began, scowling, but it was apparent to the others at the table, even young Cherry, that the Telgar Holders often indulged in such sparring.

"Have you not opened your wine?" asked an eager voice, and they looked round at Vintner Hegmon, a stout, gray-haired man of medium height with a flushed face and a reddened nose which he jokingly called an occupational hazard.

"Do us the honor," Tashvi said, gesturing to the chilled bottles.

Hegmon complied and, in his experienced hands, the plug erupted from the bottle neck with speed and a "plop." The wine bubbled up but he deftly put a glass under the lip before a drop could be spilled.

"I think we've done it this time," he said, filling the glasses presented to him.

"I say, it does look exciting," Salda said, holding her glass up to watch the bubbles make their ascent.

Thea, the High Reaches Lady Holder, did likewise and then sniffed at her glass. "Oh, my word," she said, putting a hand to her nose just in time to catch a sneeze. "The bubbles tickle."

"Try the *wine*," Hegmon urged.

"Hmmmm," Tashvi said, and Kizan echoed the sentiment.

"Dry, too," the captain said. "Go on, Cherry," he urged his wife. "It's quite unlike Tillek brews. They tend to be foxy and harsh. This'll go down easily."

"Ohhh," and Cherry's response was one of sheer delight. "Oh, I like this!"

Hegmon grinned at her ingenuousness and accepted the approving nods from the others at the table.

"I quite like it, too," Zulaya said after letting a sip slide down her throat. "Rather nice."

"I say, Hegmon, wouldn't mind a refill," and Chalkin appeared at the table, extending his glass under the mouth of the bottle the vintner held.

Hegmon kept the bottle upright and regarded the Lord Holder coolly. "There's more at your own table, Chalkin."

"True, but I'd rather sample different bottles."

Hegmon stiffened and Salda intervened.

"Leave off, Chalkin. As if Hegmon would offer an inferior bottle to anyone," she said and waved him off.

Chalkin hesitated between a scowl and a smile, but then, keeping his expression bland, he bowed and backed away from the table with his empty glass. He did not, however, return to his own table but moved on to the next one where wine was being poured.

"I could—" Hegmon began.

"Just don't supply him, Hegmon."

"He's already insisting that I give him vine starts so he can grow his own," Hegmon said, furious at such importunity. "Not that he'd do that any better than any of those other projects he starts."

"Ignore him," Zulaya suggested with a flick of her fingers. "M'shall and Irene do. He's such a toady."

"Unfortunately," said Tashvi with a grimace, "he's managed to find like minds . . ."

"We'll settle him at the meeting," K'vin said.

"I hope so," Tashvi said, "though a man like that is not easily convinced against his will. And he does have a following."

"Not where it matters," Zulaya said.

"I hope so. Ah, and here's food to soak up all this lovely stuff before we're too muddled to keep our wits about us this evening."

Zulaya waved at the wine cooler. "I doubt there's more than two glasses apiece, scarcely enough to muddle us, though it's lovely stuff." And she sipped judiciously. "Hegmon is generous but not overly so. And here's our dinner . . ."

She sat back as a swarm of men and women in Fort colors began to distribute platters of steaming food among the tables. And bottles of red wine.

"You spoke too soon about muddling, Zuli," K'vin said, grinning as he served her roast slices from the platter before passing it around the table.

They had finished their meal and all the wine before Paulin rose from his table and signaled those in the Upper Court to follow him into the Hold for the meeting. Dancing was well under way in the square and the music made a cheerful processional.

K'vin hoped the musicians would still be playing when the meeting ended. Despite the height of her, Zulaya was so light on her feet she was a pleasure to partner, and because he was so tall, she preferred him as hers. And a full orchestra of professionals was far more entertaining than the half-trained, if enthusiastic players currently in the Weyr. Different music, too.

"Ah," said Zulaya appreciatively as they filed into Fort's Great Hall, "they've done a great job of freshening the murals."

"Hmmm," K'vin agreed, craning his neck around and impeding Chalkin's entrance into the Hall. "Sorry."

"Humph," was Chalkin's response, and he glared sourly at Zulaya as he passed, shrugging his garments away from touching them.

"Consider the source," K'vin said when he thought Zulaya might fire a tart comment after the Lord Holder.

"I want to be at Bitra when the first Fall hits his hold," she said.

"Isn't he lucky, then, not to be beholden to us, but to Benden?" K'vin said wryly.

"Indeed," said Zulaya, and allowed herself to be guided to Telgar Weyr's usual seat at the big conference table. "I wonder did anyone get any sleep in this hold the past week," she said, stroking the banner of Telgar's colors, which clothed their portion of the table. "Makes such a nice display," she murmured as she pulled out the chair which also sported Telgar's white field and black grain design.

The table itself was made up of many smaller units hooked together, forming a multifaceted circle: Telgar's Weyr and hold leaders were between High Reaches and Tillek since they were the northernmost settlements. Across from them were Ista Weyr and Hold, and Keroon Hold, with their brilliant sun-colors. Benden Weyr was seated with Bitra on one side and Nerat and Benden on the other. The Chief Engineer, the Senior Medic, and the Headmaster were also included in the meeting. Fort, traditionally the senior hold, with Ruatha and Southern Boll on either side, was at table center, and this time was the "Chair."

"Now, if any of us still have our heads after Hegmon's fine new wine, let's get this over with so we can get in some dancing," said Paulin, smiling around the table.

Chalkin banged the table in front of him with a very loud "Hear, hear!"

K'vin stifled a groan. The man was half drunk, if not all drunk, his face flushed red.

"I'm sure we're all aware of the imminence of Threadfall—"

Chalkin made a rude noise.

"Look, Lord Chalkin," Paulin said, scowling at the dissident, "if you managed to get too much of the champagne inside your skin, you can be excused."

"No, that's exactly what he wants," said M'shall, Benden's Weyrleader, quickly. "Then he can claim anything decided today was done behind his back."

"If he can't shut up, we can always hold his head under the tap until he sobers enough to remember common courtesy," put in Irene, Benden's weyrwoman. "He doesn't like getting his Gather clothes wet." Her expression suggested she'd had experience enough to know.

"Chalkin!" Paulin said, his voice steely.

"Oh, all right," the Bitran said in a surly tone, and he settled himself more squarely in his chair, leaning forward on his elbows at the table. "If you're going to be that way . . ."

"Only because you are," snapped Irene. Paulin gave her a stern look and she subsided, though she kept narrowed eyes on Chalkin for a while longer.

"Three independent calculations were made, and there's no doubt that the Red Planet is getting closer . . . spatially speaking."

"Is there any chance of a collision?" asked Jamson of High Reaches.

"Fragit, Jamson," Paulin said, "let's not bring that up."

"Why not?" Chalkin said, brightening.

"Because that . . . improbability . . . has already been discussed to the point of nausea," Paulin said. "There isn't a hint in any of the information collected by our forefathers to indicate there is any chance of a collision between the two planets. Or that they considered the . . . improbability . . . for any reason."

"Yes, but does it say anywhere that there *can't* be?" Chalkin was obviously delighted with this possibility.

"Absolutely not," Paulin said simultaneously with Clisser,

who was not only the College Head but the senior of the trained astronomers. Paulin gestured for Clisser to continue.

"Captains Keroon and Tillek," and he paused in reverence, "both annotated the Aivas report, which included data from the *Yokohama*'s records. I have repeatedly reworked the relevant equations, and the rogue planet will Pass Pern on an elliptical orbit that *cannot* alter to a collision course with us. A matter of celestial mechanics and Rukbat's gravitational pull. I'd've brought the diagram of the orbits involved if I'd had forewarning." Clisser gave Chalkin a disgusted glare.

"Bad enough it brings in the Thread. Do you *want* to be blown to smithereens, Chalkin?" asked Kalvi, chief of the mechanical engineers. "And I checked the maths, too, so I concur with Clisser and everyone else who's done the equations. Why don't you, if you're so worried?"

Chalkin ignored the jibe since he had never been noted for scholarship in any field. He was also well pleased with the reaction to his remark. No matter what they said, there was no proof that they were really that safe.

"Now, calculations indicate early spring will bring the first Threadfall of this Pass. There are several falls that could be live, depending on the weather conditions, mainly the ambient temperature, at the time of Fall." Paulin reached under his table then and hauled up a board on which Threadfall areas had been meticulously delineated. S'nan cleared his throat, moving restlessly, as if he felt Paulin should not have usurped a Fort prerogative. "The first two will be in Fort Weyr's patrol area, the second two in High Reaches', and the third two in Benden's. These are due to occur in the first two weeks, about three days apart. The second Fall in Fort territory and the first one in High Reaches happen on the same day—different flows of the same Fall. Also, we know from the records that there will be live falls over the Southern Continent for about a week before they commence here in the North. S'nan," and Paulin turned to the Fort Weyrleader, "may we have your progress report?"

S'nan stood, holding up his ubiquitous clipboard. (Rumor had it that that item had been passed down from the Connell himself.) He peered down at it a moment. The oldest Leader of the premier Weyr on Pern resembled his several-times-great-grandfather, though his silvery hair was more sandy than red. Privately, K'vin didn't think Sean Connell had been such a martinet, even if he had promulgated the rules by which the Weyrs governed themselves. Most of these were common-sensible, despite S'nan managing to pursue them into the ridiculous.

"The First Fall," S'nan began, and there was a touch of pride in his voice, "will start over the sea east of Fort Hold and come ashore at the mouth of the river, passing diagonally across the peninsula and out into the sea in the west. The second two falls, which will occur three days later, will be over the southern tip of Southern Boll." He used his stylus and, at his most condescending, touched Paulin's chart. "This one may go south far enough to miss land entirely, and in any case will be over land for only a short while—and over the western tip of High Reaches, again proceeding out to sea, and so over land for only a short time. The third Fall will start on the south coast of the Tillek peninsula, east of the site of the hold, and proceed out to sea, again over land only for a short time."

"Thread giving us all a chance to get accustomed to fighting it?" asked B'nurrin of Igen.

"Your levity is ill-placed," S'nan said, but there were too many grins around the table for his reprimand to affect the irrepressible young Weyrleader. S'nan cleared his throat and launched once more into his discourse. "The next two falls will be the most dangerous for unseasoned wings," and he shot a stern glance at B'nurrin as he found the proper Thread path. "The first will start over the sea in the east and proceed over

Benden Weyr and Bitra Hold, ending almost at Igen Weyr. This would normally be flown jointly by Benden and Igen Weyrs. The second will start at the northern end of the Nerat peninsula and proceed across it, over the east coast of Keroon and the east tip of Igen, and end just offshore from Igen. This also would normally be a joint Fall, flown by Benden over Nerat, Igen over the northern part of Keroon, and Ista over the southern part of Keroon . . ."

"We really do know what falls we fly, S'nan," M'shall said.

"Yes, yes, of course," and S'nan cleared his throat again. "However," and his glance went to the Lord Holders seated around the table, "it was decided at the last meeting of the Weyrleaders that, since any of these would be the first Fall in our experience, every Weyr would supply a double-wing at the initial engagement. Thus each Weyr would have firsthand experience."

"I still think we could all get *that* by hitting those first southern falls," B'nurrin began. "If the dragons miss, it's not going to fall on anyone's head or ruin any farmland."

"B'nurrin!" M'shall said sternly before the startled S'nan could open his mouth.

K'vin privately thought B'nurrin had a good idea and had backed him, but they were overruled by the older Weyrleaders. K'vin suspected that if he were to take some wings down south for that first Fall there, he'd be likely to find B'nurrin "practicing" there, too.

"I still think it's a good idea," the Istan said, shrugging.

Pretending such an interruption hadn't even occurred, S'nan went on. "As was customary in the First Pass, Lord Holders will supply adequate groundcrews and have them assembled as directed by the Weyrleaders. In this case, Weyrleader M'shall." He inclined slightly toward the Benden bronze rider. "Master Kalvi," and he bowed courteously to the head engineer, "has assured me that his foundry has turned out sufficient HNO_3 cylinders to equip the groundcrews but the HNO_3 must be made up on site. As in the First Pass, the labor and material are supplied by the engineer corps as part of their public duty. You all should have received your full allotment of tanks by Year's End." S'nan, as always, was precise in his language, scorning the new word "Turn," which the younger generation had begun to use instead of "year."

Kalvi rose to his feet. "I've scheduled every major hold with three days of training in the maintenance and repair of the flamethrowers and a practice session, which, I think," and Kalvi grinned, "you will find comprehensive as well as interesting." He shifted his stance and would have gone on but S'nan held up his hand and gestured Kalvi to sit.

With a bit of a snort and a grin, Kalvi complied.

Now the Fort Weyrleader turned his glance to Corey. "I believe you also plan a three-day seminar to instruct major and minor hold personnel in burn control and Thread ... ah ... first aid."

Corey did not rise but nodded.

"Lord Holders must assign suitable medics with every ground control unit, or have one member of each trained in first aid and supplied with kits containing numbweed, fellis juice, and other first-aid medications.

"Now," and he flipped over the top sheet, "I have done pre-Pass inspections of all Weyrs and find them well up to strength, with sufficient cadet riders to supply the wings with phosphine rock during the Pass. I have discussed all aspects of flight tactics and Weyr maintenance with the respective Weyrleaders ..."

K'vin writhed a bit on his chair, remembering the exhaustive inspection carried out by S'nan and Sarai: they'd even inspected the recycling plant! Then he noticed that G'don, the oldest Weyrleader, was also squirming. So, the Fort pair had spared no one in their officious search for perfection. Well, they *were* heading into a Pass, and the Fort Weyrleaders were correct to want every aspect of dragon-riding at the highest possible standard and readiness. In the propagation of dragons, the pair had found no fault with Telgar Weyr: it had had the largest clutches of all the Weyrs in the last three years as the dragons themselves answered the tide of preparations for the coming struggle. K'vin was hoping that Charanth's first clutch would be larger than any that B'ner's Miginth had sired: maybe then Zulaya would warm to him. The two junior queens had done well in their latest clutches, producing more of the useful greens and blues. Telgar Weyr would soon be full! They might have to shift out some of the excess population to other Weyrs, but that could wait until the yearly review.

"And, in conclusion, let me state that we are as ready as we can be."

"Far more ready than the First Riders were," G'don remarked in his dry fashion.

"Indeed," said Irene of Benden.

K'vin contented himself with a smile. Unbidden, a little wiggle of fear shot up from his belly to chill him. He gave himself a shake. He came from a Blood that had produced First Riders and contributed many sons and daughters to the Weyrs.

And you ride me, Charanth said firmly. *I shall be formidable in the air. Thread will fly in the other direction when it sees my flame.* And that was not all draconic boast, for Charanth had racked up the Weyr record for the length he achieved in flaming practice. *Together we meet Thread, not just you on your own. I shall be with you and we shall overcome.*

Thanks, Charrie.

You're welcome, Kev.

"You've got that look in your eye, K'vin," Zulaya murmured for his ear alone. "What's Charanth's opinion of all this?"

"He's raring to go," K'vin whispered back, and grinned. Charanth was right to remind him that he did not fly alone.

They were together, as they had been from the moment the bronze had broken his shell in half and stepped directly toward a fourteen-year-old K'vin of the Hanrahans waiting on the hot sands of the Hatching Ground. And K'vin had realized that that was the moment all his life had been aimed at: Impression. He'd seen his older brother Impress, and his second oldest sister, and three of the four cousins currently riders. From the moment he was Searched out, part of him had been sure-sure-sure, with all the fervor of an adolescent, that he would Impress favorably. The negative side of his personality had perversely suggested that he'd be left standing on the hot sands and he'd never live down such a humiliating experience.

"In conclusion," S'nan said, "let me assure this gathering that the Weyrs are ready." With that, S'nan sat down to an approving applause. "I hope that the holds are, too?" Not only did his voice end on an up note, but he raised his thick brows questioningly at the Fort Holder.

Paulin stood up again, shuffling until he found the right clipboard and cleared his throat. "I have readiness reports in from all but two major holds," and he glanced first at Franco, Lord Holder of Nerat, and then tilted his head toward Chalkin. "I know you received the forms to fill in . . ."

The tall, thin, bronze-skinned Neratian raised his hand. "I told you the problem we have with vegetation, Paulin, and we're still *trying* to keep it under control . . ." He grimaced. "Not easy with the excellent weather we've been having and the restriction against chemical deterrents. But I can assure you that we'll keep at it. Otherwise, we have emergency roofing for the seedling nurseries and sufficient stores of viable seeds to replant when that's feasible. We're also continuing our research into dwarfing plants for indoor propagation. All minor Holders are fully aware of the problems and are complying. Everyone's signed up for the groundcrew course."

Paulin made a notation, nodding. "Agriculture's still working on the problem of an inhibitor for your tropical weed types, Fran."

"I hope so. Stuff grows out of pure sand without any cultivation at all."

Then Paulin turned to Chalkin, who had been polishing his rings with every evidence of boredom. "I've had nothing at all from you, Lord Chalkin of Bitra," Paulin said.

"Oh, there's plenty of time . . ."

"A report was required by this date, Chalkin," Paulin said, pushing the issue.

Chalkin shrugged. "You all can play that game if you wish, but I do not believe that Thread is going to fall next spring, so why should I bother my people with unnecessary tasks—"

He wasn't able to finish his sentence for the acrimonious reactions from everyone at the table.

"Now see here, Chalkin . . ."

"Hey, wait a bleeding minute . . ."

"Just where do you get off . . ." Bastom was on his feet with indignation.

Chalkin pointed one thick, beringed finger at the Tillek Holder.

"The Holds are autonomous, are they not? Is that not guaranteed in the Charter?" Chalkin demanded, rounding on Paulin.

"In ordinary times, yes," Paulin answered, waving a hand to the others to be quiet. He had to raise his voice to be heard over the angry remarks and protests. "However, with—"

"This Thread of yours coming. So you say, but there's no proof," Chalkin said, grinning smugly.

"Proof? What more proof do you need?" Paulin demanded. "This planet is already feeling the perturbation of the rogue planet . . ."

Chalkin dismissed that with a shrug. "Winter brings bad storms, volcanoes do erupt . . ."

"You can't so easily dismiss the fact that the planet is becoming more visible."

"Pooh. That doesn't mean anything."

"So," and Paulin first had to quell angry murmurs to be heard, "you discount entirely the advice of our forebears? The massive evidence that they left for our guidance?"

"They left hysterical—"

"*They were scarcely hysterical!*" Tashvi bellowed. "And they coped with the emergency, and gave us specific guidelines to follow when the planet came back. And how to calculate a Pass."

"Hold it, hold it!" Paulin shouted, raising both arms to restore order. "I'm Chair, I'll remind you," and he glared at Tashvi until the Telgar Lord resumed his seat and the others had quieted down. "What kind of proof do you require, Lord Chalkin?" he asked in a very reasonable tone of voice.

"Thread falling . . ." someone muttered, and subsided before he could be identified.

"Well, Chalkin?" Paulin said.

"Some proof that Thread will fall. A report from this Aivas we've all heard about . . ."

"Landing is under tons of volcanic ash," Paulin said, and then recognized S'nan's urgent signal to speak.

"Nine expeditions have been mounted to investigate the installation at Landing and retrieve information from the Aivas," S'nan said in his usual measured tones. As he spoke he searched for and found a sheaf of plastic and held it up. "These are the reports."

"And?" Chalkin demanded, obviously enjoying the agitation he had aroused.

"We have not been able to locate the administration building in which the Aivas was located."

"Why not?" Chalkin insisted. "I remember seeing tapes of Landing prior to the first Threadfall . . ."

"Then you will appreciate the size of the task," S'nan said. "Especially since the blanket of volcanic ash covers the entire plateau and we have not been able to locate any landmark by which we could judge the position of the administration building. And since the housing was similar, it's difficult to establish where we are when we have dug one out of twenty feet of ash and debris. Therefore we have not been able to establish the location of the administration building."

"Try again," Chalkin said, turning his back to S'nan.

"So you have done nothing to prepare your Hold at all for the onslaught?" Paulin asked calmly, reasonably.

Chalkin shrugged. "I don't perceive a need to waste time and effort."

"And money . . ." murmured the same heckler.

"Precisely. Marks are hard enough to come by to waste them on the off chance—"

"*Off chance?*" Tashvi erupted out of his chair. "You'll have a revolt on your hands."

"I doubt that," Chalkin said with a sly smile.

"Because you haven't bloody seen fit to warn your holders?" Tashvi demanded.

"Lord Telgar," Paulin said repressively, "I'm Chair." He turned back to Chalkin. "If the rest of us, however misguidedly, do believe in the forewarnings—backed by irrefutable astronomical evidence of an imminent Pass, how can you deny them?"

Chalkin's grin was patronizing. "A spaceborne organism? That drops on a large planet and eats everything it touches? Why wasn't Pern totally destroyed during previous visitations? Why is it every two hundred years? How come the Exploration Team that did a survey of the planet before it was released to our ancestors to colonize . . . how come they didn't see any evidence? Ah, no," Chalkin said, flicking the notion away from him with his beringed hands, "ridiculous!"

"My calculations were confirmed by—" Clisser said, feeling that he was being maligned.

"There was evidence of Threadfall," Tashvi said, bouncing once more to his feet. "I've read the report. There were hundreds of circles where vegetation was just starting to grow . . ."

"Inconclusive," Chalkin said with another flap of a hand. "Could have been caused by one of the many fungus growths."

"Well, then, when this inconclusive evidence comes dropping out of the skies onto your hold, don't bother us," Bastom said.

"Or come crying to my hold for help," added Bridgely, completely disgusted by Chalkin's attitude.

"You may be sure of that," Chalkin said, and with a mocking bow to Paulin, left the Hall with no further word.

"What are we going to do about him?" Bridgely asked, "because sure as night follows day, he will come running for aid to Franco and me."

"There is provision in the Charter," Paulin began.

Jamson of the High Reaches stared with wide and disbelieving eyes at Paulin.

"Only if he believes in the Charter . . ." Bastom said.

"Oh, Chalkin believes in the Charter all right," Paulin said sardonically. "The patent conferring the title of 'Lord Holder' on the original major northern stakeholders is what gives his line the right to hold. And he's already used the Charter to substantiate his autonomous position. I wonder if he also knows the penalty for failing to prepare his hold. That constitutes a major breach of the trust . . ."

"Who trusts Chalkin?" G'don asked.

". . . the trust that holders rest in the Lord of their hold in return for their labor."

"Ha!" said Bridgely. "I don't think much of his holders either. Useless lot on the whole. Most of 'em kicked out of other holds for poor management or plain laziness."

"Bitra's badly managed, too. Generally we have to return a full half of his tithings," M'shall said. "Half the grain is moldy, the timber unseasoned, and hides improperly cured and often rancid. It's a struggle every quarter to receive decent supplies from him."

"Really?" Paulin said, jotting notes down. "I hadn't realized he shorted you on tithes."

M'shall shrugged. "Why should you know? It's our problem. We keep at him. We'll have to keep at him over this, too, you know. Can't let him get away with a total disregard for the upcoming emergency. Not every holder in Bitra's useless, you know, Bridgely."

Bridgely shrugged. "Good apples in every basket as well as bad. But I'd really hate to have to cope with the problem come springtime and Thread falls. Benden's too near Bitra for my peace of mind."

"So what is the penalty for what Chalkin's doing? Or, rather, not doing?" Franco asked.

"Impeachment," Paulin said flatly.

"Impeachment!" Jamson was aghast. "I didn't know—"

"Article Fourteen, Jamson," Paulin said. "Dereliction of Duty by Lord Holder. Can you give me a printout on that, Clisser? Perhaps we all should have our memory refreshed on that point."

"Certainly," and the Head of the College made a note in his folder. "In your hands tomorrow."

"So your system's still working?" Tashvi asked.

"Copies of the most important official documents were made in quantity by my predecessor," Clisser replied with a relieved smile. "I've a list if you need any . . . handwritten but legible."

Paulin cleared his throat, calling them to order. "So, my Lord Holders, should we proceed against Chalkin?"

"You've heard him. What option do we have?" M'shall wanted to know, glancing about the table.

"Now, wait a minute," Jamson began, scowling. "I'd want to have incontrovertible proof of his inefficiency as a Lord Holder as well as his failure to respond to this emergency. I mean, impeachment's an extreme step."

"Yes, and Chalkin'll do everything he can to slide out of it," Bastom said cynically.

"Surely there's a trial procedure for such a contingency?" Jamson asked, looking anxiously about. "You certainly can't act without allowing him the chance to respond to any charges."

"In the matter of impeachment I believe that a unanimous agreement of all major holders and leaders is sufficient to deprive him of his position," Paulin said.

"Are you sure?" Jamson asked.

"If he isn't, I am," Bridgely said, bringing one fist down firmly on the table. His spouse, Lady Jane, nodded her head emphatically. "I haven't wanted to bring it up in a Council before—" Bridgely began.

"He's very difficult to confront at the best of times," Irene said, setting her lips in a thin line of frustrations long borne.

Bridgely nodded sharply in her direction and continued. "He's come as near to bending, or breaking for that matter, what few laws we do have on Pern. Shady dealings, punitive contracts, unusual harsh conditions for his holders . . ."

"We've had some refugees from Bitra with stories that would curl your hair," Jane, Benden's Lady Holder, said, wringing her hands in distress. "I've kept records . . ."

"Have you?" Paulin said. "I'd very much like to see them. Autonomy is a privilege and a responsibility, but not a license for authoritarianism or despotic rule. Certainly autonomy does not give anyone the right to deprive his constituents of basic needs. Such as protection from Threadfall."

"I don't know about going so far as to impeach him," Jamson said, his reluctance deepening. "I mean, such an extreme remedy could have a demoralizing effect on all the holds."

"Possibly . . ." Paulin said.

"Not being prepared for Thread will certainly demoralize Bitra!" Tashvi said.

Paulin held up his hand as he turned to M'shall. "Please give me specific instances in which Bitra Hold has failed to supply the Weyr. Jane, I'd like to look at the records you've kept."

"I've some, too," Irene added.

Paulin nodded and looked around the table. "Since his dereliction of primary duty in regard to preparation against Threadfall could jeopardize not only his own hold but those of his neighbors, I feel we must examine the problem as quickly as possible and indict him—" Jamson jammed an arm up in protest, but Paulin held up a placatory hand. "If, that is, we do find just cause to do so. Just now, he was acting as if he'd had too much of Hegmon's new wine."

"Ha!" was Irene's immediate response, a cynical response echoed by others around the table.

"We cannot allow personal feelings to color this matter," Paulin said firmly.

"Wait till you read my notes," was her wry answer.

"And mine," said Bridgely.

"But who could take his place?" Jamson asked, now querulous with anxiety.

"Not a task I'd like so soon to Thread," Bastom admitted.

Paulin grimaced. "But it may have to be done."

"Ah, if I may," and Clisser raised his hand. "The Charter requires us to find a suitable candidate from the incumbent's Bloodline—" he began.

"He *has* relatives?" Bridgely asked, mimicking surprise and consternation.

"I believe so," Franco said, "beyond his children. An uncle . . ."

"If they're of the same Blood as Chalkin, would that be an improvement?" Tashvi wanted to know.

"They do say a new broom sweeps clean," Irene remarked. "I heard that Chalkin did his uncle out of succession by giving him an isolated hold . . ."

"He got him out of the way fast enough, that's sure," Bridgely said. "Some mountain place, back of beyond."

"All of Bitra is back of beyond," Azury of Boll remarked, grinning.

"A replacement is not the most immediate concern," Paulin said, taking charge again, "if we can persuade Chalkin that all of us can't be wrong about Threadfall."

Zulaya this time snorted at that unlikelihood. "He'll admit he's wrong only when Thread is eating him . . . which might solve the problem in the most effective way. Bitra's in the path of the First Fall."

"Remiss as Chalkin appears to be," Jamson said, "Bitra Hold may be better off *with* than without him. You don't learn the management of a hold overnight, you know."

Paulin gave the High Reaches Lord a long look. "That is very true, but if he hasn't even told his people that Thread is coming . . ." and he opened up his hands to show dismay at such an omission. "That's a dereliction of duty right there. His prime duty and the primary reason for having a Leader during a crisis. As a group we also have a responsibility to be sure each of us is performing duties inherent to our rank and position."

Zulaya shrugged. "It'd serve him right to be caught out in the First Fall."

"Yes, well," and Paulin rattled papers. "I'll accept reports of malfeasance and irregularities in his conduct of Bitra Hold. We'll do this properly, gathering evidence and making a full report on the problem. Now, let's finish up today's agenda. Kalvi, you wish to broach the subject of new mines?"

The lean, hawk-nosed engineer sprang to his feet. "I sure do.

We've got fifty years of Fall and we're going to need more ore: ore that's closer to the surface than the Telgar deposits."

"Thought they would last us a millennium," Bridgely of Benden said.

"Oh, there's certainly more ore down the main shafts, but it's not as accessible as these mountain deposits, which could be worked more efficiently." He unrolled an opaque plastic map of the Great Western Range where he had circled an area beyond Ruatha's borders. "Here! High-grade ore and almost waiting to leap into carts. We'll need that quality if we're to replace flamethrower equipment. And we'll have to." He said that with a degree of resignation. "I've the personnel trained and ready to move up there—which I'd like to do to get the mines going before Threadfall starts. All I need is your okay."

"You're asking to start a hold up there? Or just a mine?" asked Paulin.

Kalvi scratched the side of his nose and grinned. "Well, it'd be a long way to travel after the shift is over, especially if the dragons are all busy fighting Thread." He unrolled another diagram. "One reason I've backed this site is that there's a good cave system available for living quarters, as well as coal nearby for processing the ore. The finished ingots could be shipped downriver."

There were murmurs among the others as the project was discussed.

"Good thing Chalkin left," Bridgely remarked. "He's got those mines in Steng Valley he's been trying to reactivate."

"They're unsafe," Kalvi said scornfully. "I surveyed them myself and we'd have to spend too much time shoring up shafts and replacing equipment. The ore's second rate, too. There isn't time to restore the mine . . . much less argue with Chalkin over a contract. You know how he can be, haggling over minor details for weeks before he'll make a decision." He contorted his long face into a grimace. "If you," and he turned to the others at the table, "grant this permission, I'll have a chance to noise it about the Gather this evening and see who'd be interested in going along in support capacity and necessary Crafts."

"I'll second it," said Tashvi magnanimously, raising his hand.

"Good. Moved and seconded. Now, all in favor of the formation of a mining hold?" Hands shot up and were dutifully counted by Paulin.

"Chalkin's going to say this was rigged," Bastom remarked caustically, "and we drove him out of the meeting before the subject came up."

"So?" Paulin said. "No one asked him to leave, and he has a copy of the agenda same as everyone else." He brought his fist down on the table. "Motion carried. Tell your engineer he may start his project. High Reaches Weyr," and he turned to G'don, "Telgar," and he included K'vin now, "can you supply transport?"

Both Weyrleaders agreed. If a new hold was to be established, as many riders as possible from their Weyrs should become familiar with its landmarks.

"There won't be that much extra to protect against Threadfall," Kalvi said with a grin for the dragonriders. "It's all underground or within the cliff caverns. We'll use hydroponics for fresh food from the start."

"Any more new business?" Paulin asked.

Clisser raised his hand, was acknowledged and stood, glancing at the assembled: falling into his lecture mode, K'vin thought.

"Lord Chalkin's attitude may not be that unusual," he began, startling them into attention to his words. "At least, not in times to come. We, here and now, are not too distanced from the events of the First Pass. We have actual visual records from that time with which to check on the approach of the rogue planet. *We* know it is a rogue because we know from the excellent and exhaustive reports done by Captains Keroon and Tillek that the planet was unlikely to have emerged from our sun. Its orbit alone substantiates that theory since it is not on the same elliptical plane as the rest of Rukbat's satellites.

"I am assiduous in training at least six students in every class in the rudiments of astronomy and the use of the sextant, as well as being certain that they have the requisite mathematics to compute declension and ascension and figure accurately the hour circle of any star. We still have three usable telescopes with which to observe the skies, but we once had more." He paused. "We are, as I'm sure we all must honestly admit, losing more and more of the technology bequeathed us by our ancestors. Not through mishandling," and he raised a hand against objections, "but from the attritions of age and an inability, however much we may strive to compensate, to reach the same technical level our ancestors enjoyed."

Kalvi grimaced in reluctant agreement to that fact.

"Therefore, I suggest that we somehow, in some fashion, with what technology we have left at our disposal, leave as permanent and indestructible a record as possible for future generations. I know that some of us ..." Clisser paused, glancing significantly to the door through which Chalkin had so recently passed. "... entertain the notion that our ancestors were mistaken in thinking that Threadfall will occur whenever the Red Planet passes Pern. But we can scarcely ignore the perturbations already obvious on the surface of our planet—the extreme weather, the volcanic eruptions, the other cosmic clues. Should it so happen in centuries to come that too many doubt—not wishing to destroy a flourishing economy and happy existence—that Thread will return, all that we have striven to achieve, all we have built with our bare hands," and dramatically he lifted his, "all we have around us today," and he gestured toward the music faintly heard outside the Hall, "would perish."

The denials were loud.

"Ah," and he held one hand over his head, "but it could happen. Lord Chalkin is proof of that. We've already lost so much of our technology. Valuable and skilled men and women we could ill-afford to lose because of their knowledge and skills have succumbed to disease or old age. We must have a fail-safe against Thread! Something that will last and remind our descendants to prepare, be ready, and to survive."

"Is there any chance we could find that administration building then?" Paulin asked S'nan.

"Too close to Threadfall now," M'shall answered. "And it's going into the hot season down there, which makes digging anything enervating. However, I most emphatically agree with Clisser. We need some sort of a safeguard. Something that would prove to doubters like Chalkin that Thread isn't just a myth our ancestors thought up."

"But we keep records . . ." said Laura of Ista Weyr.

"How much plasfilm do you have left?" Paulin asked pointedly. "I know Fort's stock is running low. And you all know what happened to our Repository."

"True. But we've paper . . ." and she looked over at the Telgar Holders, Tashvi and Salda.

"Look, how can we estimate how many forestry acres will survive Threadfall?" Tashvi asked, raising his hands in doubt. "I've the timberjacks working nonstop, cutting, and the mill's turning out as much lumber and pulp as it can."

"You know we'll do our best to protect the forests," K'vin

said, though privately he wondered how good their best could be since even one Thread burrow could devastate a wide swath of timbered land in minutes.

"Of course you will," Salda said warmly, "and we will stockpile as much paper as we can beforehand. Old rags are always welcome." Then her expression sobered. "But I don't think any of us can know what will or will not survive. Tarvi Andiyar's survey when he took hold indicated that most of the slopes were denuded. Ten years before Threadfall ceased, he had seedlings in every corner of the hold, ready to plant out. We were just lucky that natural succession also occurred in the three decades after the end of First Pass."

"That is yet another item we must record for future generations," Clisser said.

"The ultimate how-to," said Mari of High Reaches.

"I beg pardon?"

"What to do when Threadfall has Passed is even more important than what to do while it's happening," she said as if that should be obvious.

"We've got to first survive fifty years—" Salda began.

"Let's get back to the subject," Paulin said, rising to his feet. "The chair concurs that we ought to have some permanent, indestructible, unambiguous, simple way to anticipate the rogue planet's return. Has anyone any ideas?"

"We can engrave metal plates and put them in every Weyr, hold, and Hall, where they're too obvious to be ignored," Kalvi said. "And inscribe the sextant settings that indicate the Pass."

"So long as there's a sextant, and someone to use it accurately," Lord Bastom said, "that's fine. But what happens when the last of them is broken?"

"They're not that complicated to make," Kalvi said.

"What if there's no one trained in its use?" Salda put in.

"My fleet captains use sextants daily," Bastom said. "The instruments're invaluable on the sea."

"Mathematics is a base course for all students," Clisser added, "not just fishermen."

"You have to know the method to get the answers you need," said Corey, the Head Medic, speaking for the first time. "And know when to use it." Her profession was struggling to maintain a high standard as more and more equipment became unusable, and unusual procedures became erudite.

"There has to be some way to pass on that vital information to future generations," Paulin said, looking first at Clisser and then scanning the faces at the table. "Let's have a hard think. Etching on metal's one way . . . and prominently placing tablets in every Weyr and hold so they can't be stored away and forgotten."

"A sort of Rosetta stone?" Clisser's tone was more statement than query.

"What's that?" Bridgely asked. Clisser had a habit, which annoyed some folk, of dropping odd references into conversations: references with which only he was familiar. It would lead to long lectures from him if anyone gave him the chance.

"On Earth, in the late eighteenth century, a stone with three ancient languages was discovered which gave the clue to translating those languages. We shall, of course, keep our language pure."

"We're back to etching again," Corey said, grinning.

"If it's the only way . . ." Clisser began and then frowned. "No, there has to be some fail-safe method. I'll investigate options."

"All right, then, Clisser, but don't put the project aside," Paulin said. "I'd rather we had a hundred sirens, bells, and whistles going off than no warning at all."

Clisser grinned slowly. "The bells and whistles are easy enough. It's the siren that will take time."

"All right, then," and Paulin looked around the table. Toe-tapping dance music was all too audible and the younger holders and Weyrfolk were plainly restless. "No more new business?" He didn't wait for an answer, and used the gavel to end the meeting. "That's all for now. Enjoy yourselves, folks."

The speed with which the Hall emptied suggested that that was what all intended to do.

2

▼▼▼▼▼▼▼▼▼

GATHER AT FORT

"Cliss, what on earth possessed you?" Sheledon demanded, glowering. He was head of the Arts faculty at the College and constantly jealous of what free time he had in which to compose.

"Well," and Clisser looked away from Sheledon's direct and accusing glare, "we do have more records and are more familiar with the techniques of assessing them than anyone else. Information and training *are* what this College was established to provide."

"Our main function," said Danja, taking up the complaint— she wanted spare time in which to work with her string quartet, "is to teach youngsters who would rather ride dragons or acquire many klicks of Pernese real estate to use the wits they were born with. And to brainwash enough youngsters to go out and teach whatever they know to our ever-widely-spreading population."

Dance music swirled about them but Sheledon and Danja were so incensed that they seemed oblivious to the rhythms that were causing the other three at their table to keep time with foot or hand. Danja shot Lozell a peevish look and he stopped rattling fingers callused from harp strings.

"I don't think it'll be that hard to find some way to indicate a celestial return," he said in an attempt to appease the wrath of Sheledon and Danja.

"It isn't the 'hard' that bothers me," Danja said acidly, "but when will we have the *time*?" She stabbed her finger at the as yet unfinished extension to the teaching facility. "Particularly since there is a time limit," and she shot another dirty look at Clisser, "Winter Solstice."

"Oh." Lozell grimaced. "Good point."

"We're all working every hour we can spare from classes on what's *urgent* right now," Danja went on, gesturing dramatically and pacing up and down the length of their table. While Sheledon closed in on himself when threatened, Danja exploded into action. Now her nervous movements hit the chair on which she had placed her violin, and she reacted as quickly, to keep the valuable instrument from falling to the cobbles. She gave Lozell a second nasty look, as if he had been responsible.

Sheledon reached across and took violin and bow from her, putting them very carefully on the table, which had been cleared of all but wineglasses. Absently he mopped a wine spill near the precious violin, one of the few usable relics from Landing Days. He gave it a loving pat while Danja continued.

"Like today," she said, resuming her pacing, "we taught in the morning and managed to eat something before we spent an afternoon painting, so that there will be some finished rooms for the summer term. We had five minutes to change, and even then we missed the fly-past, which I, for one," and she paused to jab her thumb into her sternum, "wanted to see.

"We've played two sets," she went on earnestly, "and will undoubtedly still be playing when the sun rises, and tomorrow will be a repeat of today except no Gather, so we get a good night's rest to prepare us for more of the above, except maybe get a little work done on next term. Which starts in a week, and then we'll have no time at all since we now have to prepare the teachers who'll be graduated to carry the Word to the outer extremities of the continent." She gestured eastward in a histrionic fashion, then flounced down on the chair the violin had occupied. "So how are we going to find time to do yet more research, Clisser?"

"We always do find the time," Clisser said, his quiet rejoinder a subtle criticism of her rant.

"Use it as a history class project?" suggested Lozell brightly.

"There you have the answer," said Bethany, who had merely, as was her habit, watched the fireworks Danja was so good at sending up. "My juniors could use an independent project."

"So long as we have power to run the Library," Danja added sourly.

"We will, we will," Clisser said, with bright encouragement. "Kalvi had his engineers up on the heights during the fly-past, working on the sun panels. They'll hook them up to the main banks tomorrow. Other people worked today, you know."

"Well, that's a big consolation," Danja said acidly.

Clisser refilled her glass. "And we'll need some catchy tunes and good lyrics, too, I should think. Something to teach students from a very early age so that they learn all the signs of a Pass before they learn to ask questions about it."

" 'One and one is two, two and two are four?' " Danja sang the old multiplying song, then grinned wryly.

"The song remains an effective teaching aid," Clisser said, filling his glass. "Shel, would you put on your composer's hat and whip up some simple effective tunes?"

Sheledon nodded enthusiastically. "I've been saying for years that we ought to incorporate more basic stuff into a musical format. Jemmy's good at little popular airs."

Bethany's face lit up with a great smile. Jemmy was a favorite pupil of hers, and she was his staunchest champion. Even Danja looked mollified.

"So," Clisser went on, having solved one of his immediate problems, "what shall we do in the next set?"

"Just like that?" Danja demanded. " 'What'll we do in this set?' Clisser, will you get real!"

Clisser looked hurt. Bethany leaned over and patted his hand, smiling encouragingly.

"What did you mean by that, Danja?" Clisser asked.

"Don't you realize what a huge responsibility you just so casually . . ." and Danja lifted wide her arms, flinging her hands skyward in exasperation, "laid on us all?"

"Nothing we can't solve, dear," Bethany said in her gentle manner. "With a little thought and time."

"Back to time again. Do we *have* time?" Lozell was back in the discussion. "Especially if the winter's even half as bad as it was last year—and it's supposed to be, with that damned Red Planet leering down on us—how are we going to cope?"

"We will. We always do," Sheledon said with a sigh of resignation. "Paulin will help us out. And certainly the Weyrs do."

Danja glared at him. "We've changed tunes, haven't we? I thought you thought we didn't have time."

Sheledon shrugged diffidently. "I think Lozell's idea of making a survey a class project will solve that problem. And, if Jemmy can whistle up some lyrics, I can certainly churn out some tunes. Or maybe Jemmy can do both in his spare time." Sheledon's face softened into a wry grin. He had had a tussle with himself not to be jealous of Jemmy, whose brilliance was multifaceted. Though he wasn't officially "graduated" from the Hall, he already ran several smaller study groups and seemed able to do a bit of everything—on a high level. The Consummate Jack of all Trades, Clisser called him.

"And what if, by leaving it to the student body, who are, as most students, indifferent researchers, the best notion is *missed*?" Danja asked.

"That's why we're teachers, dear," Bethany said. "To be sure they don't miss an obvious solution. They can at least save us having to sort through pounds of material and present us with the most viable options. We can put Jemmy in charge. He reads the fastest and his eyes are younger."

Just then the instrumentalists on the stage wound up their last number and received an enthusiastic ovation from both the sweating dancers and onlookers drinking at the tables. They filed off the stage.

"All right, what set do we do, Clisser?" Sheledon asked, tossing off the last of his wine as he got to his feet.

"Those seniors did a lot of fast dance music," Clisser said. "Let's give everyone a chance to catch their breaths and do some slow stuff . . . the old traditionals, I think. Start with 'Long and Winding Road.' Put everyone in a sentimental mood."

"Hmmm . . . then we can get some supper while the juniors do what they so erroneously call 'music,' " said Danja, who had considerable contempt for the contemporary loud and dia-tonic musical fad.

"Can't please everyone all the time," Clisser said, collecting his guitar. He drew back Bethany's chair for her and offered her an arm. Smiling in her gentle way at the courtesy, Bethany picked up the flute in its worn hard case, her recorders in their leather sleeves, and the little reed whistle that had won its maker a prize that year. It had a particularly sweet clear tone that young Jemmy had been trying to reproduce with other reeds. Then she limped forward, seemingly oblivious to her clubbed foot and awkward gait, her head high, her gaze directed ahead of her.

Jemmy joined them from his table, automatically taking Bethany's flute case from her. He was the drummer for their group, though he had been playing guitar with others. Unprepossessing in physical appearance, with pale hair and skin and oversized features, he was self-effacing, indifferent to his academic achievements. While not in the least athletic, he had won the long-distance races in the Summer Games for the last three years. He did not, however, relate well to his peer group. "They don't think the same way I do," was his diffident self-appraisal.

That was, of course, accurate, since he had tested off the scale of the standard aptitude tests given prospective scholars. His family, fishers at Tillek Hold, didn't understand him at all and at one point thought him retarded. At fourteen he had followed his siblings into training in the family occupation. He lasted three voyages. Though he proved himself an able navigator, he had such constant motion sickness—never acquiring "sea legs"—that he had been useless as a deckhand: a source of much embarrassment to his family. Captain Kizan had interested himself in the lad, recommended the boy be trained as a teacher and sent Jemmy to Fort Hold for evaluation. Clisser had joyfully accepted him—finding such an avid learner was a real boost to his morale. And, when Clisser had seen how Jemmy galloped through even the hardest lessons, he set up an independent study program for him. Although Jemmy had perfect pitch, he couldn't sing, and started playing instruments to make up for that lack in himself. There was nothing he couldn't play, given a few hours of basic training.

Although his family, and indeed the Lord Holder Bastom, too, had expected him to return to Tillek to teach, Clisser argued hard that anyone could teach the basics to hold children. He would supply a suitably trained candidate, he said, but Jemmy must be allowed to continue at the College Hall, benefiting the entire continent.

What no one at the Hall mentioned beyond their most private sessions was that Jemmy seemed intuitively to know how to fill in the gaps left by improper copying or damaged records. His notations, short and concise, were models of lucidity. The College could not afford to do without his skills and intelligence. He wasn't a good teacher, being frustrated by mental processes slower than his own, but he could, and did, produce manuals and guides that enhanced the basic texts the settlers had brought with them. Jemmy translated "Earth" into "Pern."

If his peer group did not enjoy his company, he enjoyed that of his mentors, and was fast outstripping all of them in knowledge and practical applications. It was also well known, if tacitly ignored, that he idolized Bethany. She was consistently kind and encouraging to everyone but refused to accept any partner. She had long since decided never to inflict her deformity on offspring, and refused any intimacy, even a childless one.

Clisser wondered, though, as he and Bethany made their sedate way to the stage, if Jemmy might not breach the wall of her virginity. He was certain that Bethany cared more for the Tillek lad than anyone else in the thirty years he had known her—student and teacher. She was a lovely gentle woman: she deserved to be loved, and to love in return. Since there were ways of preventing conception, her prime concern could be taken care of. Clisser thought the age difference was immaterial. And Jemmy desperately needed the balance that a fully rounded life experience would give him.

Clisser and Jemmy provided support for Bethany to ascend the unrailed steps to the stage, and then, with a swirl of the long skirts that covered the built-up shoe she wore, she settled herself in her chair. She placed her flute case and the recorders where she wanted them, and the little reed flute on the music stand. Not that this group of musicians required printed sheets to read from, but the other groups did.

Danja lifted her fiddle to her chin, bow poised, and looked at Jemmy, who hummed an A with his perfect pitch for her to tune her strings. Sheledon softly strummed his guitar to check its tuning, and Lozell ran an arpeggio on his standing harp. The continent's one remaining piano—his preferred instrument—was undergoing repairs to the hammers: they had not yet managed to reproduce quite the same sort of felt that had been originally used.

Clisser nodded at Jemmy, who did a roll on his hand drum to attract attention, and then, on Clisser's downbeat, they began their set.

It was several days before Clisser had a chance to discuss the project with Jemmy.

"I've wondered why we didn't use the balladic medium to teach history," Jemmy replied.

"It isn't history we'll be setting to music."

"Oh yes, it is," Jemmy had contradicted him in the flat and tactless way he had. It had taken Clisser time to get used to it. "Well, it will be when the next generation gets it . . . and the next one after that."

"That's a point, of course."

Jemmy hummed something but broke off and sprang across to the table, where he grabbed a sheet of paper, turning it to the unused side. He slashed five lines across it, added a clef, and immediately began to set notes down. Clisser was fascinated.

"Oh," Jemmy said offhandedly as his fingers flew up and down the lines, "I've had this tune bugging me for months now. It's almost a relief to put it down on paper now that I've a

‹ 53 ›

use for it." He marked off another measure, the pen hovering above the paper only briefly, before he was off again. "It can be a showpiece anyhow. Start off with a soprano—boy, of course, setting the scene. Then the tenors come in ... they'll be the dragonriders, of course, and the baritones ... Lord Holders, with a few basses to be the professionals ... each describing his duty to the Weyr ... then a final chorus, a reprise of the first verse, all Pern confirming what they owe the dragons. Yes, that'll do nicely for one."

Clisser knew when he wasn't needed, and left the room, smiling to himself. Now, if Bethany was right and this term's students could perform the research satisfactorily, he could make good on his blithe promise to the Council. He did hope that the computers would last long enough for a comprehensive search. They had got so erratic lately that their performance was suspect at most times. Some material was definitely scrambled and lost among files. And no one knew how to solve the problem of replacement parts. Of course, the PCs were so old and decrepit, it was truly a wonder that they had lasted as long as they had. Was there any point these days in holding a course on computer electronics?

Which thought reminded him that he had interviews with two sets of parents who were insisting that their offspring be put in the computer course since that was the most prestigious of those offered. And the one involving the least work since there were so few computers left. Where would they practice the skills they learned? Clisser wondered. Furthermore, neither of the two students concerned had the aptitude to work with mechanical objects. They just *thought* it was what they wanted. There were always a few cases like that in an academic year. And one set of holder parents who did *not* like their daughter associating with "lesser breeds without the law" ... as Sheledon put it.

As if there was room, or facilities, for more than one

teachers' school. Or the private tutors some holders felt should be supplied them because of their positions. Ha! As it was, the peripatetic teachers were going all year long, trying to cover the basics with children in the far-flung settlements. Well, maybe one day they could site a second campus—was that the word?—on the eastern coast. Of course, with Threadfall coming, he'd have to revise all the schedules as well as instruct his travelers on how to avoid getting killed by the stuff. He had seen footage—when the projector still worked—of actual Threadfall. He shuddered. Accustomed as he had been all his life to the prospect of the menace, he still didn't *like* the inevitability. The reality was nearly *on them*.

The Weyrleaders could waffle on about how well-prepared hold and Weyr were, with dragon strength at max, and groundcrews and equipment organized, but did anyone really *know* what it would be like? He swore under his breath as he made his way to the rooms that still needed to be completed to receive occupants in five days. He'd work on the syllabus during his lunch break.

A sudden thought struck him so that he halted, foot poised briefly above the next step. What they really needed was a totally new approach to education on Pern!

What was the point of teaching students subjects now rendered useless here on Pern? Like computer programming and electronic maintenance? What good did it do the Pernese boys and girls to know old geographic and political subdivisions of Terra? Useless information. They'd never go there! Such matters did not impinge on their daily lives. What was *needed* was a complete revision of learning priorities, suitable to those who were firmly and irrevocably based on this planet. Why did anyone *now* need to know the underlying causes of the Nathi Space War? No one here was going to go into space—even the dragons were limited to distance that they could travel before they were in oxygen debt. Why not study the spatial maps of

Pern and forget those of Earth and its colonies? Study the
Charter and its provisions as applicable to the Pernese citi-
zenry, rather than prehistoric governments and societies. Well,
some of the more relevant facts could be covered in the course
to show how the current governmental system, such as it was,
had been developed. But there was so much trivia—no wonder
his teachers couldn't get through the lessons. Small wonder the
students got bored. So little of what they were presently
required to learn had any relevance to the life they lived and
the planet they inhabited. History should really begin with
Landing on Pern . . . well, some nodding acquaintance with the
emergence of Homo sapiens, but why deal with the aliens that
Earth's exploratory branch had discovered when there was
little chance of them arriving in the Rukbat system?

And further, Clisser decided, taken up with the notion, we
should encourage specialized training—raising agriculture and
veterinary care to the prestige of computer sciences. Breeding
to Pernese conditions and coping with Pernese parasites was
far more important than knowing what had once bothered animals back on Earth. Teach the miners and metalworkers where
the spatial maps showed deposits of ores and what they were
good for; teach not the history of art—especially since many of
the slides of Masterpieces had now deteriorated to muddy
blurs—but how to use Pernese pigments, materials, design,
and tailoring; teach the Great Currents, oceanography, fish-
conservation, seamanship, naval engineering, and meteo-
rology to those who fished the waters . . . As to that, why not
separate the various disciplines so that each student would
learn what he needed to know, not a lot of basically useless
facts, figures, and theories?

For instance, get Kalvi to take in . . . what was the old term—
ah, apprentices—take in apprentices to learn fabrication and
metalwork? And there'd have to be a discipline for mining, as

well as metalworking. One for weaving, farming, fishing. And one for teaching, too. Of course, education in itself was designed to teach you how to solve the problems that cropped up in daily living, but for specialties, you could really slim down to the essential skills required by each. As it was, that sort of apprentice system was almost in place anyhow . . . with parents either instructing their kids in the family's profession or getting a knowledgeable neighbor to do it. Kalvi had both sons now in supervisory capacities in his Telgar Works. And there should be provisions to save other kids, like Jemmy, and see that they were able to develop a potential not in keeping with their native hold's main business. Administer a basic aptitude test to every child at six, and the more specific one at eleven or twelve, and be able to identify special abilities and place him or her where he or she could learn best from the people qualified to maximize the innate potential.

Even in medicine, a new curriculum should be established, based on what was now available on Pern, rather than what the First Settlers had had. Mind you, Corey was constantly regretting the lack of this or that medicine, or equipment and procedures that would save lives but was no longer available. Clisser snorted: too much time was spent bitching about "what had been" and "if only we still had" instead of making the best of what was available in the here and now. What was that old saying?

Ours not to wonder what were fair in life
But finding what may be, make it fair up to our means?

Well, he couldn't remember who had said it or to what it applied. But the meaning definitely applied! Pern had great riches which were being ignored in the regret of the "what had been." Even Corey had to admit that the indigenous pharmacopoeia was proving to be sufficient for most common ailments, and even better in some cases now that the last of the carefully hoarded Earth chemicals were depleted.

Basic concepts of math, history, responsibility, duty could indeed be translated into music, easier to transmit and memorize. Why, anyone who could strum an instrument could give initial instruction in holds; teach kids to read, write, and do some figuring; and then let them apply themselves to the nitty-gritty of their life's occupation. And music had always been important here!

He put his foot down on the step, pleased with this moment's revelation. A whole new way of looking at the education and training of the young, and entirely suitable to the planet and its needs. He must really sit down and think it all through . . . when he found the time.

His laugh mocked his grandiose ideas, and yet they'd had to revise and reform so many old concepts here on Pern: Why not the method in which education was administered? Was that the word he wanted: administered? Like a medicine? He sighed. He did wish that learning was not considered an unavoidable dose. Certainly someone like Jemmy proved that learning was enjoyable. But then, insatiable appetites like his for knowledge, for its own sake, were rare.

Clisser trotted up the last of that flight in considerably better humor. He'd find the time, by all that's still holy, he would.

3

▼▼▼▼▼▼▼▼▼

LATE FALL AT TELGAR WEYR

Zulaya beamed at Paulin. "Yes, she rather outdid herself, didn't she?" She turned to regard her queen fondly as the golden dragon hovered proprietarily over the fifty-one eggs which would, by all the signs, hatch sometime this day.

All morning dragons had conveyed in guests and candidates.

"Aren't the Weyrs overproducing a trifle?" Paulin asked. Benden and Ista Weyrs had also had Hatchings in the past month. He had lost two very promising holder lads to the Weyrs: a felt loss, as riders would no longer be as free as they were during an Interval to journey easily between hold and Weyr, and to learn and practice other professions.

"Frequent clutches are one of the surefire signs that there will be a Pass," Zulaya said, obviously looking forward to the days when the dragons of Pern started the work for which they were engineered. "Have you heard that song the College sent out?"

"Hmmm, yes, I have," and Paulin grinned. "In fact, I can't get it out of my mind."

"Clisser says they have several more to play for us tonight."

"Just music?" Paulin asked, scowling. "It's a device we asked them for . . . something permanent so that no one can deny the imminence of a Pass."

Zulaya patted his hand encouragingly. "You can ask what progress he's made on that project."

K'vin, coming up behind them, casually laid a hand on his Weyrwoman's shoulder, acting as proprietary of her as her dragon was of her clutch. Amused, Paulin coughed into his hand and hurriedly excused himself.

"He's worried about that fail-safe," Zulaya said, almost amused by K'vin's show of jealousy but not about to remark on it.

"You're looking very beautiful in that new dress," he said, eyeing it.

"Do I? Why, thank you, Kev," she said, twisting her hips to make the skirt whirl. "Which reminds me . . ." and she held out a fold of the rich crimson-patterned brocade that she had had made for this Hatching. "Fredig suggested tapestries, hanging in every Weyr and hold, depicting the return of the Red Star—with the formulae in the borders. Make an interesting design, certainly."

"Colors fade and fabrics certainly deteriorate . . ."

"We've some that graced houses in Landing. That Earth-Moon scene . . ."

"Which was made, as I've been told, out of synthetic yarns which are more durable than what we have now—cotton, linen, and wool. And even they are looking worn and losing color."

"I'll have them washed . . ."

"You'll have them thread-worn . . . oops," and K'vin grinned at the pun.

". . . which is not what is wanted, but there's no reason, Kev, not to have a hundred different reminders."

"Something set in stone . . ." the Weyrleader said in a more sober tone.

"Even stones move . . ."

"Only prior to a Pass. Only *how* to perpetuate the critical information?"

"I think everyone's worrying too much. I mean, here we are," and Zulaya gestured broadly to include the Hatching Ground and the Weyr around them. "Why else have dragons? And Weyrs set apart to preserve them, if not for a very, very good reason. They're the planet's only sure defense."

A sound, subliminal, more than a real noise, alerted them. It issued from Meranath, who reared to her hindquarters, spreading her broad wings, her eyes glowing brightly green and beginning to whirl with excitement.

"Ah, it starts," Zulaya said, smiling in anticipation. "Oh, I love Hatchings!"

Hand in hand the two Weyrleaders raced to the entrance and called out the news, scarcely needed, for the Telgar dragons were already reacting to the queen's maternal croon with their deep masculine humming.

The Weyr Bowl became active with dragons a-wing in excitement, flipping here and there on seemingly unavoidable collision courses: with the Weyrlingmaster herding the candidates forward; with parents and friends of the lucky boys and girls rushing across the hot sands to take their places in the amphitheater: hustling to get the best seating for the Impression about to happen.

K'vin sent Zulaya back to keep Meranath company as he urged people inside, checking the nervous white-clad candidates who had been halted in a clump near the entrance until the spectators were all seated.

"You've long enough to wait on the hot sands as it is,"

T'dam, the Weyrlingmaster, told them. "Singe your feet, you could, out there . . ."

All this time the humming was rising in volume: Meranath joined by all the other dragons in a chorus of tones that Sheledon—and others—had tried to imitate without quite succeeding. Meranath's throat was swollen with her sound, which continued unabated and seemingly without her needing to draw breath. Soon, as the volume increased, her chest and belly would begin to vibrate, too, with the intensity of her humming. K'vin was aware of the usual response in himself, a jumble of emotions; a joy that threatened to burst his heart through his chest, pride, hope, fear, yearning—oddly enough, hunger was part of it—and a sadness that, on some occasions, could make him weep. Zulaya always wept at Hatchings—at least, until Impressions began. Then she was jubilant, picking up on her queen's acceptance of her clutch's partnering.

In Fort Hold's storage there were file boxes full of early psychological profiles about the effect of Hatching on riders, dragons, and the new weyrlings. The bonding that occurred was of such complexity and depth that no other union could be compared to it: almost overwhelming in the initial moment of recognition, and certainly the most intense emotion the young candidates had ever experienced. Some youngsters had no trouble at all adapting to the intense and intrusive link: some suffered feelings of inadequacy and doubt. Every Weyr had its own compendium of information about what to do in such-and-such a situation. And every weyrling was assiduously trained and supported through the early months of the relationship until the Weyrleaders and Weyrlingmaster deemed he/she was stable enough to take responsibility for her/himself and her/his dragon.

But then, a rider was the dragon, and the dragon the rider, in a partnership that was so unwavering, its cessation resulted in suicide for the dragon who lost his mate. The unfortunate rider was as apt to take his life as not. If he lived, he was only half a man, totally bereft by his loss. Female riders were less apt to suicide: they at least had the option of sublimating their loss by having children.

When the little fire-lizards, who had supplied the genetic material to bioengineer the larger dragons, had still been available, a former male rider found some solace in such companionship. Only three fire-lizard clutches had been found in Ista in the last five decades; though it was thought more might be found in the Southern Continent, that quest had so far been futile. The vets had decided that some sort of odd disease had infected the creatures on northern warm beaches, reducing their numbers and/or their clutches. Whatever the reason, no one had fire-lizard companions anymore.

As soon as most of the guests had crossed the hot sands, T'dam allowed the candidates to make a loose circle around the eggs. There was no golden egg in this clutch—a circumstance that had both relieved and worried the Weyrleaders. They had five junior queens, which was quite enough for Telgar's low-flight wing. In fact, there was no dearth of queens in any of the Weyrs, but there was safety in having enough breeders.

Five girls stood on the Hatching Ground. There should have been six, but the girl's family had refused to give her up on Search since they claimed a union had been arranged and they could not go back on that pledge. As K'vin thought that a good third or even half of this clutch might be greens, he hoped there'd be enough suitable candidates to Impress all the green hatchings. Green dragons were valuable to a Weyr for their speed and agility, even if they didn't have the stamina of the larger dragons. Still, they were perhaps the most problematic when it came to Threadfighting. Greens with male riders tended to be more volatile, apt to ignore their Weyrleaders' orders in the excitement of a Fall—in short, they tended to unnecessarily show off their bravery to the rest of the Weyr. Female riders, on the other hand, while more stable, tended to get pregnant frequently, unless they were very careful, since the greens were usually very sexually active. Even spontaneous abortions due to the extreme cold of *between* required sensible convalescence, so female green riders were all too often off the duty roster for periods of time. "Taking a short dragonride" was now a euphemism for ending an unwanted pregnancy. Still, K'vin had fallen on the side of preferring females when Search provided them.

The draconic humming—what Clisser called a prebirth lullaby—was reaching an almost unendurable level, climaxing when the first egg cracked open. The spectators were exhibiting the usual excitability, jumping about, weeping, singing along with the dragons. They'd calm down, too, once the Hatching had begun.

And it did. Three shells burst outward simultaneously, fragments raining down on nearby eggs and causing them to crack, as well. K'vin counted nine dragons, six of them wetly green, and revised his "third" of greens closer to "half."

The hatchlings were so dangerous at this stage, ravenous from their encapsulation, and some of the nearer candidates hastily avoided the bumbling progress of the newborn. Two greens seemed headed for Weyrbred Jule, but the blonde from Ista, already noted in the Weyr for her quick wits, stepped beside one and Impression was made for both. Three of the other greens made for lads who had demonstrated homosexual preferences in their holds. The remaining green, after lunging out of her shell, stood, weaving her head back and forth, crying piteously.

T'dam called out to the remaining girls to converge on her. The brunette girl from Ista made for her and instantly the little green covered the intervening distance, squeaking with relief.

K'vin swallowed against the emotional lump in his throat:

that instant of recognition always brought back the moment he had experienced the shock of Impression with Charanth. And the glory of that incredibly loving mind linking with his: the knowledge that they were indissolubly one, heart, mind, and soul.

We are, are we not? Charanth said, his tone rough with the memory of that rapture. Despite the fact that Charanth, like the rest of the Weyr's dragons, was perched up along the ceiling, K'vin could "hear" the dragon's sigh.

Zulaya grinned up at K'vin, aware of what was taking place within him, tears flowing down her face as the high emotional level of the Hatching affected her.

Absently K'vin thought that the glowing bulk of Meranath behind Zulaya made a great background for her beautiful new gown . . . red against gold.

Then another dozen or so eggs split wide open and the raucous screeching of starving little dragonets reverberated back and forth on the Ground. There was a piercing quality to these screams like lost souls. As each hatchling met its rider, the scream broke off and a mellow croon began. That quickly segued into a piteous "hungry" appeal which was almost more devastating than the earliest screech the weyrlings made. K'vin's stomach invariably went into empathetic hunger cramps.

The noise of a Hatching, K'vin thought, was unique. Fortunately, because human eardrums were not designed to deal with such decibels and cacophony, it didn't last too long. He always felt slightly deafened—certainly ear sore—by the end of a Hatching.

He was suddenly aware of another sort of babble and fuss going on just outside the Hatching Ground. K'vin tried to see what was happening, but noting T'dam striding over to investigate, he turned his attention back to the pairing of the last few Hatchings, two browns and the last green. Two lads were homing on the green, desperate expressions on their faces. Abruptly the green turned from them and resolutely charged across the sands to the girl who had just entered. K'vin gave a double take. There were only five girls, weren't there? Not that he wasn't glad to see another. And she was the one the green wanted, for the hatchling pushed aside the boy who tried to divert her.

Then three men strode into the Ground, furious expressions on their faces, with T'dam trying to intercept their angry progress toward the lately impressed green pair.

"Debera!" yelled the first man, reaching out and snatching her away from the green dragonet.

That was his first mistake, K'vin thought, running across sands to avert catastrophe. Damn it all. Why did this marvelous moment have to be interrupted so abruptly? Hatchings should be sacrosanct.

Before K'vin could get there, the green reacted to the man's attempt to separate her from her chosen one. She reared, despite being not altogether sure of her balance on wobbly hindquarters. Extending her short forearms with claws unsheathed, she lunged at the man.

K'vin had one look at the shock on his face, the fear on the girl's, before the dragon had the man down and was trying to open her jaws wide enough to fit around his head.

T'dam, being nearer, plunged to the rescue. The girl, Debera, was also trying to detach her dragonet from her father, for that's what she was calling him.

"Father! Father! Leave him alone, Morath. He can't touch me now, I'm a dragonrider. Morath, do you hear me?"

Except that K'vin was very anxious that Morath might have already injured the man, he was close to laughing at this Debera's tone of authority. The girl had instinctively adopted the right attitude with her newly hatched charge. No wonder she'd been Searched ... and at some hold evidently not too far away.

K'vin assisted Debera while T'dam pulled the fallen man out of the dragon's reach. Then his companions hauled him even farther away while Morath continued to squeal, and writhed to resume her attack.

He would hurt you. He would own you. You are mine and I am yours and no one comes between us, Morath was saying so ferociously that every rider heard her.

Zulaya joined the group and, bending to check the father's injuries, called for the medics who were dealing with the minor lacerations that generally occurred at this time. Fortunately, Morath had no fangs yet, and although there were raw weals on the man's face and his chest had been badly scratched by unsheathed claws—despite their newness—he had been somewhat protected by the leather jerkin he wore.

By now most of the newly hatched were out of the Grounds, being fed their first meal by their new life companions. The spectators, beginning to descend from the amphitheater's levels, managed to get a peek at the injured man. Undoubtedly they would recount the incident at every opportunity. K'vin hoped the embellishments would stay within reason. Now he had to deal with the facts.

"So, perhaps you would tell us what this is all about?" he asked Debera who, confronted by the Weyrleader and Weyrwoman, was suddenly overcome with remorse and doubt.

"I was Searched," she said, urgently stroking Morath, who was trying to burrow her head into the girl's body. "I had the right to come. I *wanted* to come," and then she waved an indignant hand at her prostrate father, "and they didn't even show me the letter telling me to come. *He* wants me for a union because he had a deal with Boris for a mining site and with Ganmar for taking me on. I don't want Ganmar, and I don't know anything about mining. I was Searched and I have the right to decide." The indignant words rushed out, accompanied by expressions of distaste, resentment, and anger.

"Yes, I remember seeing your name on the Search list, Debera," Zulaya said, ranging herself beside the girl in a subtle position of support. The alignment was not lost on the older of the two men attending their fallen friend. "You are Boris?" she asked him. "So you must be Ganmar," she said, addressing the younger one. "Did you not realize that Debera had been Searched?"

Ganmar looked very uncomfortable and dropped his eyes, while the scowl on Boris's face deepened and he jutted his jaw out obstinately.

"Lavel told me she'd refused."

At that point Maranis, the Weyr's medic, arrived to have a look at the wounded man. When he had, he sent a helper for litter bearers. Then he began to deal with the injuries, pulling back the tattered jerkin, provoking a groan from the dazed man.

"Well, Boris," Zulaya said at her sternest. "As you seem to be aware, Debera does have the right . . ."

"That's what you Weyrfolk always say. But it's us who suffer from what you call 'right.' "

"Making more trouble, Boris?" asked Tashvi, arriving just then with Salda.

"You agreed, Tashvi," Boris said with little courtesy for his Lord Holder. "You said we could dig that new mine. You were glad to have me and my son here start. And Lavel was willing for Ganmar to have his daughter . . ."

"Ah, but the daughter seems not to have been so willing," Lady Salda remarked.

"She was willing, all right, wasn't you, Deb?" Boris said, staring with angry accusation at the girl, who returned his look by lifting her chin proudly. "Till they came from the Weyr on Search . . ."

"Search has the priority," Tashvi said. "You know that, Boris."

"We had it all arranged," the father said, speaking up now that his pain had been alleviated by the numbweed Maranis had slathered on his wounds. "We had it *arranged*!" And the look he gave his daughter was trenchant with angry, bitter reproach.

"*You* had it all arranged," Debera said, equally bitter, "between yourselves but not with me, even *before* the Search." A wistful moan from Morath interrupted her angry rebuttal. "She's hungry. I have to feed her. Come along now," she added in a far more loving tone. Without a backward glance, she led her green dragon out of the Hatching Ground.

"I'd say that the matter was certainly not well arranged, then," Tashvi said.

"But it *was*," Lavel said, jabbing one fist at the dragonriders, "until they came 'round, putting ideas in her head when she was a good, hardworking girl who always did as she was told. Then you riders tell her she's fit for dragons. Fit! I know what you riders get up to, and Debera's a good girl. She's not like you lot—"

"That's quite enough of such talk," Zulaya said, drawing herself up, insulted.

"Indeed it is," Tashvi said, scowling angrily. "The Weyrwoman will realize that you're not yourself, wounded as you are . . ."

"Wounds got nothing to do with my righteous anger, Lord Holder. I know what I know, and I know we had it all arranged and you should stick up for your holders, not these Weyrfolk and all their queer customs and doings, and I dunno what'll happen to my daughter." At that point he began to weep, more in frustrated anger than from the pain of the now well-anesthetized injuries. "She was a *good* girl until they come. A good biddable girl!"

Tashvi gestured peremptorily to the two litter men to take the man out. Then he turned back to the Weyrleaders.

"I did approve the new mine, and Boris and Ganmar as owners, but I'd no idea that Lavel was in any way involved. He's a troublemaker from way back," Tashvi said, absently shifting his feet on the hot sands.

Zulaya gestured for them all to leave the Hatching Ground. Despite the extra lining she'd put in her boots this morning, she was uncomfortable standing there, and Tashvi was wearing light pull-ons.

"And it's not that he doesn't have other daughters," Salda said, taking her husband's arm to speed up his progress. "He's got upward of a dozen children and had two wives already. At the rate he's been making these arrangements of his, he'll have himself sufficient land among his relatives to start his own hold. Not that anyone in their right mind would want *him* as a Lord Holder."

They paused outside the Ground now. Adroitly, Zulaya and K'vin chose a position so that they could also keep a weather eye on the newly hatched who, with the help of their riders, were rapidly devouring the piles of cut meat prepared for their initial feeding.

Debera's situation was unusual. Most families were glad enough to have a child chosen on Search, because of the advantages of having a dragonrider in the family: the combination of the prestige accrued to the Bloodline as well as the availability of transport.

Listening to the vitriol in Lavel's criticism of Weyr life upset both Weyrleaders and Lord Holders. It was true that certain customs and habits had been developed in the Weyrs to suit dragon needs, but promiscuity was certainly not encouraged.

In fact, there was a very strictly observed code of conduct within the Weyr. There might not be formal union contracts, but no rider reneged on his word to a woman nor failed to make provision for any children of the pairing. And few Weyr-bred children, reaching puberty, left the Weyr for the grand-parental holds even if they failed to Impress.

By now the festivities had started in the Main Cavern, with the instrumentalists playing a happy tune, one that reflected the triumph of a successful Hatching. Although the new riders were still feeding their dragons or settling them into the weyrling barracks, once the sated dragonets fell asleep, the new dragonmen and women would join their relatives.

Zulaya wondered if she should remind Lavel that the female riders were housed separately from the males. He obviously had no idea at all how much care a new dragonet required from its human. Most days the weyrlings fell into bed too exhausted to do anything *but* sleep. And had to be rousted out of their bunks by the Weyrlingmaster when they failed to respond to their hungry dragons' summonses.

The young lad, Ganmar, sulked, looking decidedly uncomfortable in his present situation. Zulaya doubted that his heart was the least bit broken by this turn of events. Of course, if he had to work with that father of his building a new hold, maybe a pretty girl to bed at night would have been a major compensation.

"What I should like to know," Salda was saying, "is why Debera arrived here so late, on her own and you evidently in hot pursuit. You realize, of course," and the stern expression in Salda's eyes was one Zulaya knew well, "that we—Lord Tashvi and I—would not be at all pleased to find that Debera has been denied her holder rights."

"Holder?" Lavel snorted and then moaned as the injudicious movement caused him pain. "She'll not be a holder now, will she? She'll be lost to us forever, she will."

"And any chance of bagging her legal land allotment," Salda said with mock remorse. Lavel growled and tried to turn away from the Lady Holder. "You've claimed more than most as it is. I trust Gisa is in good health? Or have you got yet another child on her? You'll wear her out the same as you did Milla, you know. But I suppose there are women stupid enough to fall for your ever-increasing land masses. Sssh," and Salda turned from him in disgust. "Get him out of my sight. He offends me. And sullies the spirit of this occasion."

"He's not so wounded he can't travel," the medic said helpfully.

"Travel?" Boris exclaimed, pretending dismay as he had glanced in the direction of the Lower Cavern, where the roasts were being served.

"I could find him a place overnight," Maranis began hesitantly.

Just then four young Weyrfolk led up the visitors' horses, which they had recaptured.

"Ah, here are your mounts, Boris," Zulaya said. "Let us not keep you from a safe journey home. You should easily make it home before dark. Maranis, give Lavel enough fellis juice to see him to his hold. Lads, help him mount. Come, K'vin, we're overlong congratulating the happy parents."

She linked her right arm in K'vin's and her left with Lady Salda and hauled them along across the Bowl.

"A very good Hatching, I'd say," she began, without a backward look at the three dismissed holders. "Nineteen greens, fifteen blues, eleven browns, and seven bronzes. Good distribution, too. Good size to the bronzes as well. I do believe every clutch produces dragons just slightly larger than the last."

"Dragons haven't yet reached their design size," K'vin said, answering her lead. "I doubt we'll see that in our lifetime."

"Surely they're big enough already?" Salda asked, her eyes wide.

Zulaya laughed. "Larger by several hands than the first ones who fought Thread, which will make it all that much easier for us this time 'round."

"You know what to expect, too," Tashvi said, nodding approval.

Zulaya and K'vin exchanged brief glances. Hopefully what they could expect did not include unwelcome surprises.

"Indeed we have the advantage of our ancestors in that," K'vin said stoutly.

Zulaya gave his arm a little squeeze before she released him and strode to the first table, where the families of two new brown riders were sitting. K'vin continued in with Salda and saw her and Tashvi settled at the head table, where he and Zulaya would join them after they'd done their obligatory rounds of the tables. Then, making a private bet with himself, he started at the opposite end of the wide cavern.

By the fourth stop he had won his bet: news of the unusual Impression of the last green dragon was already circulating.

"Is it *true*," the holder mother of a bronze rider asked, "that that girl had to run away from her hold?" She, and the others at this table, were clearly appalled at such a circumstance.

"She got here in time, that's what's important," K'vin said, glossing over that query.

"What if she hadn't come?" asked one of the adolescents, her expression avid. "Would the dragon have—"

She stopped abruptly, as if she'd been kicked under the table, K'vin thought, suppressing a grin.

"Ah," he said, bridging the brief pause, "but I'm sure you saw that other lads crowded 'round, ready and willing. The dragonet would have chosen one of them."

That was not exactly true. Which was why every Weyr had

more than sufficient Candidates on the Ground during a Hatching. Early on, the records mentioned five occasions when a dragonet had not found a compatible personality. Its subsequent death had upset the Weyr to the point where every effort was then made to eliminate a second occurrence, including accepting the dragonet's choice from among spectators.

There were also cases where an egg did not hatch. In the early days, when the technology had still been available, necropsies had been performed to establish cause. In most of the recorded instances, there had been obvious yolk problems or the creature had been malformed and would not have survived Hatching. Three times, however, the cause of death could not be established, as the fetus had been perfect, with no apparent deficiency or disability. The message was handed down to dispose of such unhatched eggs *between* immediately: a duty performed on such rare occasions by the Weyrleader and his bronze.

"I saw her ride up," the girl said, delighted to recount this fact. "And then the men who tried to stop her."

"You must have had the best seat in the house," K'vin said, grinning.

The girl shot a vindictive glance around the table. "Yes, I did, didn't I? I saw it all! Even when the dragonet tried to eat someone. Was that her father?"

"Suze, now, that's enough of that," said her own father, and the older boy beside her must have pinched her for she shot straight up on the bench and glared at him.

"Yes, it was her father," K'vin said.

"Didn't he know any better than to strike a dragon's rider?" asked Suze's father, shocked by such behavior.

"I think he has perceived his error," K'vin said dryly and caught Suze's startled reaction. "What has your son"—and Charanth, as he always did, supplied the boy's name so quickly that the pause was almost unnoticeable—"Thomas, decided on for a rider name?"

"Well, I don't think Thomas dared to hope," his mother said, but her expression revealed both her pride in his modesty and her delight in his success.

"He never liked being a Thomas," Suze said, irrepressible. "He'll pick a new name," and she gave a snide sideways glance at her parents.

"And here he is, if I don't miss my guess," K'vin said, gesturing toward the lad making his way across the cavern floor. K'vin had lectured the candidates on their responsibilities to their dragonets, so he was familiar with many of them. This Thomas, or whatever, bore a strong enough resemblance to both sister and brother to make him easily identifiable. He hoped that a facial resemblance was all Thomas shared with his sister. She was a spiteful one.

"Well done, young man," K'vin said, holding out his hand. "And how shall we style you now?"

"S'mon, Weyrleader," the new bronze rider said, still flushed with elation. He had a good firm handshake. "I considered T'om but I never liked the nickname."

"You said you'd—" Suze got yet another kick under the table for she yipped this time and tears started in her eyes.

"It's easier to say," S'mon said. "Tiabeth likes it." Now he showed the delightful confusion of pride and proprietariness so many brand-new weyrlings exhibited while accustoming themselves to their new condition and duties. As K'vin remembered so vividly, that took time. "And there was a T'mas in the first group at Benden."

"He's long dead," his father said, not altogether pleased with his son's choice. "Thomas is a family name," he admitted to K'vin. "I'm Thomas, ninth of my line."

The boy looked at his father with that curious aloofness of

independence that came with being a newly paired dragon-rider: sort of "You can't tell me what to do anymore" and "This is my business, Dad, you wouldn't understand."

"Tiabeth and S'mon," K'vin said, lifting the glass he'd been carrying from table to table and drinking a toast to the partners. The others made haste to repeat it. "Eat, S'mon. You'll need every meal you get a chance to eat," he added, and left the boy to follow that very good advice.

At each subsequent table he heard more speculation about the late arrival of Debera. There had been embellishments: one had her father bleeding to death. Another variation suggested that Debera had been the reluctant one and her family had insisted that she try to Impress, having been Searched. Young Suze had had the best seat in the Hatching Ground after all, despite having been so far from the center that she hadn't had a good view of Impression, but a perfect one for what was happening outside. So K'vin edited the facts to keep the incident from getting out of hand. Fortunately, the music the band was playing, and the lyrics, provided a happy distraction. Most of the music was new. Clisser's musicians had done their job very well indeed.

He avoided having his glass filled too often, and used slices of the roast wherry and beef to sop up what was required by the obligatory toasting of the new riders.

He had almost completed his circuit when he saw the Telgar holders and T'dam leading Debera in, all moving toward the head table. Salda and Tashvi rose and went to meet her halfway. She still had a dazed look on her face, and glanced, almost wildly, around the crowded cavern. Someone had given her a green gown which showed off a most womanly body, and the style of it as well as the color suited Debera. The deep clear green set off her fine complexion and a head of curling bronze-colored hair which was attractively dressed, not straggling unkempt around a sweaty distraught face. No doubt

Tisha, the headwoman, had had a hand in the transformation. Zulaya had once said Tisha treated all the Weyrgirls like live dolls, dressing them up and fussing with their hair. Nor was Tisha herself childless, but her excess of maternal instinct was an asset in the Weyr.

Salda put an arm about Debera, her head inclined to the shorter girl as she chatted: evidently determined to make up for the lack of family members on what was generally a very happy occasion for holder or Crafter. Had Debera seen the last of her relatives? No matter, she was in the larger, extended family of the Weyr and could find more amiable and sympathetic replacements.

Zulaya was introducing Debera to Sarra, the sun-bleached blonde from Ista who was chatting away with such animation that Debera smiled—tentatively, K'vin thought, but with growing self-confidence.

"You got Morath to sleep all right?" he asked, joining the women.

"I thought she'd never stop eating," Debera said, a slightly anxious frown on her face. Her green eyes, K'vin saw, were also emphasized by the color of the gown. Tisha had done her proud.

"They're voracious," Zulaya said, with a kind laugh. "And so am I. Come, let's all be seated before there's nothing left for us."

Salda gave a good-natured snort, grinning down at Debera. "Not likely. We've been sending you the fatted calves for the past week in anticipation." She turned to the girl as she passed her over to K'vin. "One thing's sure, girl, you'll eat higher on the hog here in Telgar than you ever did at home. *And* not have to cook it."

Debera was so clearly startled by such jocularity that K'vin took her hand, guiding her to the steps up to the platform on which the head table was placed.

"I think you'll be very happy here, Debera," he said gently, "with Morath as your friend."

Immediately the girl's face softened with joy and her eyes watered. Her look of vulnerable wonder struck such a responsive chord in him that he stumbled in following her.

"Oh, and she is more than a *friend*," she said, more like a prayer than a statement of fact.

"Come, sit beside me," Zulaya said, pulling out the chair, and signaling K'vin to take the one beyond. They were not in their usual center table position, but quick eye contact with Salda and Tashvi had the holders pulling out those chairs as if such placement was normal. "Listen to that melody. How lovely . . ." she added, tilting her head as the music, not quite martial, but firm, was stopping conversation throughout the cavern.

"So are the words . . ." Salda said, eyes widening in surprise, as well as delight, at what she heard. When her husband started to say something, she hushed him.

K'vin was happy to listen, too.

Sheledon, who had insisted on using the Telgar Impression as the debut of some new music, was very pleased that conversation had trailed off and everyone was hearing what was being sung. Now was the time to spring the big one on them. As soon as the coda on what Jemmy called "Dragonlove" had finished, he held up the music to the Duty Ballad and then pointed it at his soprano spouse, Sydra, who would sing the boy soprano part. They hadn't found a lad with a suitable voice yet, but she could whiten her voice to approximate the tone. At Sheledon's signal, Bethany piped the haunting notes of the intro and Sydra rose to sing the opening verse.

All right, they didn't have enough trained voices to really sock the Ballad to this audience—in his mind, Sheledon "heard" what a *full* chorus would sound like—but the excellent acoustics in the cavern were a big help. And the music captivated. Sydra managed to sound very young and awed . . . Gollagee came in with his fine tenor as the dragonrider, Sheledon was right on cue with his baritone part, and then, with Bethany singing alto and the Weyr's own musicians adding their voices, they wound it all up.

There was just one split second's total silence—the sort that makes performers rejoice—and then everyone was standing, wildly cheering, clapping, stamping their approval. Even the dragons joined in from outside, caught up in their riders' enthusiasms. Sydra kept bowing and urging the rest of the musicians to stand and accept the accolades. Even Bethany stood, a few tears trickling down her cheek at such a unanimous reception.

They gave five encores of the Ballad—with people adding their voices to the chorus as they quickly picked up on the words. When Sheledon ruefully waved off a sixth repeat, there were calls for the "Dragonlove" song which was so appropriate for this evening.

All in all, Sheledon decided as he caught Sydra's smiling face, a very successful debut! Jemmy had outdone himself and Clisser would be delighted. Perhaps there was something to Clisser's notion of redesigning the educational system so less time would be wasted on unessentials and the Real Meaning of Life could be addressed sooner.

4
▼▼▼▼▼▼▼▼▼

TELGAR WEYR AND THE COLLEGE

I T was the Weyrwoman, Zulaya, who noticed Debera's increasing nervousness.

"Go on back to Morath, m'dear. You're exhausted and you'll need your sleep."

"Thank you . . . ah . . ."

"We make no use of titles in the Weyr," Zulaya added. "Just go. I've given you permission, if that's what you were so politely waiting for."

Debera murmured her thanks and rose, wanting to slip out as inconspicuously as possible. She'd felt so awkward and unsocial, even when everyone, even the Lord and Lady Holder, had been so incredibly kind and easy. She thought they would expect her to give an explanation of her unusual behavior, but they'd supported her instantly. Really, it was as if her *real* life had started the moment she and Morath had locked eyes.

It had, she decided as she made her way along the side of the cavern wall, head down so she needn't make eye contact with anyone. She saw only smiles from folks as she passed them, smiles and courtesy. And certainly none of the lascivious behavior that her father had often said was prevalent in the Weyr.

Of course, he'd told her a lot of things. And not told her others. Like the fact that an official announcement of Search, with her name on it, had been delivered to the hold so that she'd know when to come, to be available for the Hatching. No, she'd had to find that, stuffed in the cupboard where bits and pieces that could be reused were kept. No one at Balan Hold, especially her father and stepmother, Gisa, would have thrown out a whole sheet of paper that had a clean side that could be recycled. How she hated that word! Cycle, recycle. Use, reuse. The concept dominated every aspect of Balan Hold. And they were not "poor" in material possessions: not the way some holders were. But "poor" Balan Hold had been in spirit ever since her mother died.

She'd been looking for something else entirely when she found the sheet. Not that she knew the day's date, but it was obvious that the announcement must have come sometime before, the paper being soiled and the creases well set. Maybe even weeks. She had been ready to accept Ganmar as an alternative to continued living in her father's house. She knew that she'd have to work as hard, if not harder, setting up a new hold, chiseling it out of rock above the mine, but it would have been hers—and Ganmar's—and something she could design to her own wishes. Not that she'd been inclined to believe any of the blithe and extravagant promises Ganmar or Boris had made her. All they wanted was a strong body with lots of hard work in it.

But she had seen many dragons in the sky the day before, most of them carrying passengers. Balan Hold was not that far from Telgar Weyr—not even by surface travel. So, the moment she'd read the message, she made her plans right then, without any wavering. She'd been Searched. She had the right to be there. No matter how life in the Weyr might be, it couldn't be worse than what she now endured. And if she could be a dragonrider . . .

She had tucked the paper into her hip pocket and slammed the drawer shut. She was alone in the kitchen, and sun streamed in, almost as if adding light to her resolve. She didn't even go back to the room she shared with her three half sisters. Grabbing her jacket, she made for the paddock where the riding horses were kept. There was no one about in the yard: all were at work. Assignments had been given out over breakfast, and everyone had to show their father completed chores or there'd be no lunch break until they were.

She didn't even dare collect a saddle or bridle from the barn, because her eldest brothers were restacking hay—they'd done a sloppy job of it the first time around. She just grabbed up a leather thong. Since she'd had the most to do with the hold horses, she'd have little trouble managing any of them with just a lip rein.

Bilwil would be the fastest. She had probably three hours before the midday meal, when her absence would be noticed. By then she'd be well up the track to the Weyr.

With one look over her shoulder to see if she was being observed, Debera walked quickly—as if she were on an errand—to the paddock. Bilwil was not far from the fence that she climbed—the gate would be too near the vegetable garden where two half sisters were weeding. They loved nothing better than to report her "idling ways" to either their mother or her father. Two brothers were in the barn, the next pair out with her father in the forestry, and her stepmother in the dairy hold making cheese. Debera had been grinding wheat for flour when the cotter pin snapped. That's what she'd been trying to find in the drawer, a nail or something to replace the cotter pin so she could continue her task. So Gisa wouldn't miss her for a while to sound an alarm. For until flour had been made there'd be no bread, and Gisa wouldn't want to turn that heavy stone, not pregnant as she was.

Bilwil nickered softly when she approached him and grabbed his forelock. No one had bothered to groom him last night and his coat was rough with perspiration from yesterday's timber hauling. Maybe she should take one of the others. But Bilwil had lowered his head to accept the twist of thong around his lower jaw. She could scarcely risk chasing a better-rested, less amenable mount about the paddock, so she inserted the rein, grabbed a handful of mane, and vaulted to his back. Would she be vaulting to the back of a dragon tomorrow? She lay as flat as she could across his neck, just in case someone looked out across the paddock, and kneed him forward, toward the forest.

Just before they reached the intertwined hedging that marked the far boundary, she took one more look back at the hold buildings, its windows chiseled out of the very rock, the uneven entrance to the main living quarters, the wider one into the animal holding. Not a soul in sight.

"C'mon, Bilwil, let's get out of here," she'd murmured, and kicked him sharply into a trot, heading him right at the fence, a point not far from one of the tracks through the forest.

It was a good thing Bilwil liked to jump anyhow, because she'd given him only enough room to gather himself up. But he was nimbly over and had planted his left front foot, swinging left on it in response to her pull on his mouth and to her right heel as he brought his other feet down. In moments they were among the trees and quickly reached the track. Bilwil tried once to pull to the left, to go back to the hold, but she kicked him sharply and he went right. They were far enough from the hold so that his hoofsteps wouldn't be audible—not unless someone had their ear to the ground, which was unlikely.

Noses would be to the grindstones where hers no longer was. The thought made her grin, though she was not yet safe from discovery.

As soon as the track widened she set Bilwil to a canter, enjoying the one activity in which she took any pleasure.

She stopped several times, to rest her own backside as well as Bilwil's . . . and found late berries to eat. She really ought to have snatched up the last of the breakfast cheese or even an apple or two to tide her over on the way.

It wasn't until Debera reached the final leg of the journey up to the Telgar Weyr that she was aware of pursuit. Or at least spied three horsemen on the road. They could well be visitors, coming for the Hatching, but it was prudent to suspect the worst. Her father could be one, and possibly Boris and Ganmar the other two. She had to get to the safety of the Weyr before they caught up to her. How had they made such good time in pursuit of her? Had someone seen her, after all, and run to alert Lavel?

A long tunnel had been carved in the thinnest wall of the Telgar Crater as access for surface traffic. It was lit with glow baskets. Bilwil was tired from the last long steep climb on top of yesterday's work. She thought she heard male voices yelling at her and kicked Bilwil into a weary trot. No matter how she used her heels on his ribs, he wouldn't extend his stride. Then she heard the humming—as if it emanated from the walls around her. She knew what that meant. She gave a cry of despair.

After all this, she'd be too late and there wouldn't be a dragon left for her to Impress . . . even if she had been Searched. How could she possibly go back? She wouldn't. She knew her rights. She'd been Searched. She could stay at the Weyr until the next clutch. Anything was preferable to going back to what she'd just left. The union with Ganmar would not have been any real improvement, although she had been determined to establish a proper relationship with the young miner. He looked impressible. Her own mother had told her that there were ways of handling a man so he didn't even know he was being managed. But Milla had died before she could impart those ways to her daughter. And Gisa, who had probably given up all thought of a second union if she had been desperate enough to partner her father, was a natural victim who enjoyed being dominated.

More hoofsteps sounded in the tunnel and, desperate to reach her objective, Debera kicked Bilwil on. The gallant animal fell into a heavy canter that jarred every bone in her body, but they made it into the Bowl.

Debera could see that not only was the Hatching Ground full of people, but also new, staggering dragonets. But as she got close enough she saw there were still a few eggs. Her pursuers were catching up. She had no need to halt Bilwil at the entrance. He stopped moving forward the moment she stopped kicking him. She slid off and raced toward the Hatching Ground just as her father, Boris, and Ganmar caught up, yelling at her to stop, to come to her senses . . . She wrenched herself free of grasping hands . . . just in time to reach Morath. And finally came into her own.

Now, as she made her way back to the weyrling barracks, she was as tired as she had ever been in her life, and far happier! As she rattled the door in her nervousness to open it, T'dam poked his head out of the boys' barracks next door.

"Back, are you? Well, she hasn't moved so much as a muscle. And I don't think you will, either, will you?"

She shook her head, too tired to speak. She opened one side of a door wide enough to accommodate wing-trailing dragonets and slipped inside, turning to close it after her, but T'dam came in as well, reaching up to turn the glowbasket open. It was well he did because Debera would have knocked into the first of the dragonet beds.

These were basically simple wooden platforms, raised half a meter above the ground, ample for dragons until they were old enough to be transferred to a permanent weyr apartment. The rider's bed was a trundle affair to one side of the dragon's, with storage space underneath and a deep chest at the foot.

She skirted the bed, relieved she had not awakened the occupant, and got to Morath's, the next one in. And hers. There were several items of clothing on the chest.

"Tisha sent in some other things since you weren't able to bring any changes with you," T'dam said. "And a nightdress, I believe. Open the glow above the bed and then I'll shut this one."

When she had done so, he closed the larger one and the door behind him. As soon as he had, she examined Morath, curled tightly on her platform, wings over her eyes. Was that how dragonets slept? Wondering at the good fortune that had happened to her this day, Debera watched the sleeping dragonet as dearly as any mother observed a newborn, much wanted child. Morath's belly still bulged with uneven lumps from all the meat she had eaten. T'dam had laughed when Debera worried that the dragonet would make herself sick with such greed.

"They repeat the process six or seven times a day the first month," he'd warned her. "You'll end up thinking you've spent all your life chopping gobbets until she settles to the usual three meals a day. But don't worry. By the end of her first year she'll be eating only twice a week—and catch her own at that."

Debera smiled, remembering that conversation and thinking that T'dam had no idea what a relief it would be to have such an easy job, the doing of which would be a labor of love and so gratefully received. She held her hand over her beloved Morath, wanting to caress this so-beloved creature but not wishing to disturb her—especially when Debera was all but asleep herself. She lingered, though, despite weariness, just watching Morath's ribs rise and fall in sleeping rhythm. Then she could no longer resist fatigue.

She was the lone human in the weyrling barn . . . no, barracks. Well, the others had their families to celebrate with. Who'd've thought that Debera of Balan Hold would be sleeping with dragons this night? She certainly hadn't. She slipped out of the fine dress now, smoothing the soft fabric of the green gown one last time as she folded it. It had felt so good on her body and was such a becoming color: quite the loveliest thing she had ever worn. Gisa had got all her mother's dresses, which ought by custom to have come to her. Debera shrugged into the nightgown, aware of the subtle bouquet of the herbs in which it had been stored. She'd once had time to gather the fragrant flowers and leaves for sachets with her mother.

She pulled back the thick woolen blanket, fingering its softness, and not regretting in the slightest the overwashed and thin ones she had shared with her stepsisters. The pillow was thick under her cheek, too, as she put her head down, and soft and redolent of yet more fragrances. That was all she had time to think.

Back at the College, Sheledon, Bethany, and Sydra arrived a-dragonback, full of the ardent reception they'd had at Telgar Weyr.

"I don't know why we didn't think of Teaching Ballads before now," Sydra said, slightly hoarse from all the singing she'd done the night before.

"Too bad we hadn't the selections ready for the other two Impressions," Sheledon said, for he invariably saw disadvantages everywhere. "Are there any more upcoming?"

"Well, there're Year's End celebrations . . ." Bethany said.

"We tend to stay here for them," Sheledon replied, not wanting to miss the feasts that Chrislee generally provided for those holidays. The senior teachers at the College invariably were included on the Fort guest list and never missed such opportunities, even if they had the option of returning to their native hearths for the three-day celebration.

"Maybe this once," Sydra began, looking at Sheledon, "we should go home and spread the word."

Bethany frowned. "The full chorus and accompaniment is what makes the songs so effective . . ."

Sheledon frowned. "We can certainly organize substantial groups for the main Holds. The dragonriders always come as guests anyway, so they'd all get a chance to hear . . ." Then he smiled down at his wife, settling an affectionate arm across her shoulders. "You sure did the boy soprano bit well. But I think we'd best get the juvenile voice for Year's End. You're hoarse today."

"Halllooo down there," and they all looked up to see Clisser, bending far out an upper window and waving at them. "Did the ballads work?" he yelled, hands to his mouth.

The musicians looked at each other, Sheledon counted the beat, and they roared back, "THEY LOVED US!"

Clisser made a broad okay gesture with both hands and then waved them to go to his office in the original section of the facility.

They reached it first, still elated with the success of their performance, an elation that began to disperse when they saw Clisser's expression.

"What's the matter?" Bethany asked, half rising from her chair.

"The computers went down and Jemmy thinks they're totally banjaxed now," Clisser said glumly, flopping into the chair at his desk, his body slack in despair.

"What happened? They were working perfectly," Sheledon said, scowling. "What was Jemmy—"

Clisser held up one hand. "Not Jemmy . . ."

"One of those students hacking around . . ." Sheledon's expression suggested dire punishments.

Clisser shook his head. "Lightning . . ."

"Lightning? But we had no storm warnings . . ."

"Fried all the solar panels, too, although, at least we can replace *those*. Corey lost her system, what was left of it, including the diagnostics she's been trying so desperately to transcribe."

Made speechless by such a catastrophe, Sheledon sat down heavily on the corner of the desk while Sydra leaned disconsolately against the wall.

"How much is gone?" Bethany asked, trying to absorb the disaster.

"All of it," and Clisser flicked his fingers before he clasped them together across his chest, chin down.

"But . . . but, surely, it's only a matter—" Sheledon began.

"The motherboards are charcoal and glue," Clisser said dully. "Jemmy's gone through every box of chips we had left, and there aren't enough to rebuild even a few meg, and that wouldn't operate the system. Even part of the system. It's gone," and he waved his hand helplessly again.

There was silence for long moments as those in the room coped with such a massive loss.

"How much did the students—" Bethany began, cutting her sentence off as Clisser waved, almost irritably, to silence her. "Surely they saved something."

"Something, but nowhere near what we *need*, what was waiting to be copied, a mere fraction of what we need to know . . ."

"Look, Clisser," Bethany said gently, "what have we really lost?"

He jerked his head up, glaring at her. "What have we really lost? Why, everything!"

Sheledon and Sydra were regarding Bethany as if she had run mad.

"The history we are already seeing as irrelevant to our lives *now*?" she asked softly. "Descriptions of archaic devices and procedures that have no relevance on Pern since we no longer operate an advanced technological society? Isn't that what you were doing anyway, Clisser? Changing the direction of teaching in line to what is *needed* in this time, on this planet, and disregarding I don't know how many gigabytes of stored information that *is* irrelevant! Now that we don't have to worry about all that," and her hand airily dismissed the loss, "we can forge ahead and not have to concern ourselves with translating *useless* trivia for posterity. So I ask you, what have we really lost?"

Silence extended until Sheledon uttered a sharp laugh. "You know, she may be right. We've been knocking ourselves out copying down stuff that won't work here on Pern anyhow. Especially," and his voice hardened, "since no one back on Earth cares enough to find out what's happened to us."

Sydra regarded her husband with a blink. "Not that old Tubberman homing tube business again?"

Sheledon went defensive. "Well, we know from—"

"The records," Sydra said with a malicious grin, and Sheledon flushed, "that the message tube was sent *without* Admiral Benden's authority. Without the name of a colony leader on it, no one on Earth would have paid it any heed. If it even got to Earth in the first place."

"Someone could have come and had a look-see," Sheledon said.

"Oh, come now, Shel," Bethany said, as amused by his sudden switch, for he had always derided the Tubberman

Tube Theory. "Pern isn't rich enough for anyone to bother about."

"So the precious records said, but I think that was to save face. They should have checked on us to see how we were faring ... They got awfully proprietary about the Shavian colonies that were the basic reason for the Nathi Space War."

"That was over three hundred years ago, Shel," Bethany said in her patient teacher-tone.

"And it is totally irrelevant to *now*," Sydra added. "Look, the loss of the computers is undeniably a blow to us. But not something we cannot overcome ..."

"But all that information!" cried Clisser, tears coming to his eyes.

"Clisser dear," and Bethany leaned across to him, patting his hand gently, "we still have the best computers ever invented," she tapped her forehead, "and they're crammed full of information: more than we really need to operate."

"But ... but now we'll never find out how to preserve *vital* information—like early warning of the return of the Red Star."

"We'll think of something," she said in such a confident tone that it penetrated Clisser's distress. And briefly he looked a trifle brighter.

Then he slumped down in even deeper despair. "But we've failed the trust placed in us to keep the data available ..."

"Nonsense!" Sheledon said vehemently, crashing one fist down on the desktop. "We've kept them going past their design optimum. I've read enough in the old manuals to appreciate that. Every year for the past fifty has been a miracle. And we haven't, as Bethany says, lost all. A gimmick from the past has failed, like so many of them have. And we're now going to have to bypass the easy access to data they provided and sweat through books! Books! Books that we have in quantity."

Clisser blinked. He shook his head as if mentally rejecting a thought.

"We have been planning to ignore much of the old data," Bethany said gently. "What was most important to us," and her hand indicated the Pern of the present, "has been copied . . . well, most of it," she amended when Clisser opened his mouth. "If we haven't needed it up to now, we never will."

"But we've lost the sum total of human—" Clisser began.

"Ha!" Sydra said. "*Ancient* history, man. We've survived on Pern and it is *Pern* that's important. As Bethany said, if we haven't needed it up till now, we never will. So calm down."

Clisser scrubbed at his skull with both hands. "But how will I tell Paulin?"

"Didn't the lightning affect Fort, too?" Sheledon asked, and answered himself: "I thought I saw a workforce on the solar heights."

Clisser threw both hands up in the air. "I told him we were checking the damage . . ."

"Which is total?" Sheledon asked.

"Total!" and Clisser dropped his head once again to his chest in resignation to the inevitable.

"It's not as if you caused the storm, or anything, Cliss," Bethany said.

He gave her a burning look.

"Was the system being run at the time?" Sheledon asked.

"Of course not," Clisser said emphatically, scowling at Sheledon. "You know the rule. All electronics are turned off in any storm."

"And they were?"

"Of course they were."

Bethany exchanged a look with Sheledon as if they did not credit that assurance. They both knew that Jemmy would work until he fell asleep over the keyboard.

"I tell you," and Clisser went on, "everything powered went

down. It's just luck that the generators have all those surge protectors, but even those didn't save the computers. The surge came in on the data bus, not the power lines."

"The computers were dying anyway. They are now dead, really truly dead," Sheledon said firmly. "Rest in peace. I'll go tell Paulin if he's who you're worried about."

"I am not," and Clisser banged his fist on the table, "worried about Paulin. And it's my duty to tell him."

"Then also tell him that our new teaching techniques are in place and that we've lost nothing that future generations will need to know," Sydra said.

"But . . . but . . . how do we know what they might need to know?" Clisser asked, clearly still despairing with that rhetorical question. "We don't know the half of what we *should* know."

Bethany rose and took the two steps to the beverage counter.

"It's not working, either," Clisser said in a sharp disgusted tone, flicking one hand at it, insult on injury.

"I shall miss the convenience," she said.

"We all shall miss convenience," Clisser said and exhaled sharply, once again combing his hair back from his forehead with impatient fingers.

"So," said Sydra with a shrug of her shoulders, "we use the gas ring instead. It heats water just as hot, if not as quickly. Now, let's all go get a reviving cup, shall we?" She took Clisser by the hand, to tug him out of his chair. "You look as if you need reviving."

"You're all high on last night's success," he said accusingly, but he got to his feet.

"As well we are," said Sheledon. "The better to console you, old friend."

"Clisser," Bethany began in her soft, persuasive voice, "we have known from our reading of the Second Crossing that the artificial intelligence, the Aivas, turned itself off. We know why. Because it wisely knew that people were beginning to think it was infallible: that it contained all the answers to all of mankind's problems. Not just its history. Mankind had begun to consider it not only an oracle, but to depend on it far more than was wise. For us. So it went down.

"We have let ourselves be guided too long by what we could read and extract from the data left to us on computer. We have been too dependent. It is high time we stood squarely on our own two feet . . ." She paused, twisting her mouth wryly, to underscore her own uneven stance. ". . . and made our own decisions. Especially when what the computers tell us has less and less relevance to our current problems."

"You said it, Bethany," Sheledon said, nodding approval, his mouth in a wry twist.

Clisser smoothed back his hair again and smiled ruefully. "It would have been better if this could all have happened just a little," and he made a space between thumb and forefinger, "later. When we found what we need for the dragonriders."

"You mean, a fail-proof system to prove the Red Star's on a drop course?" Sheledon asked, and then shrugged. "The best minds on the continent are working on that problem."

"We'll find a solution," Bethany said, again with her oddly calm resolution. "Mankind generally does, you know."

"That's why we have dragons," Sydra said. "I could really murder for a cup of klah."

5

▼▼▼▼▼▼▼▼▼▼

WEYRLING BARRACKS AND BITRA HOLD

An insistent, increasingly urgent sense of hunger nagged Debera out of so deep a sleep she was totally disoriented. The bed was too soft, she was alone in it, and neither the sounds nor smells around her were familiar.

I really am most terribly hungry and I know that you were very tired but my stomach is empty, empty, empty . . .

"Morath!" Debera shot bolt upright and cracked her poll on the underside of the dragonet's head because Morath had been leaning over her bed. "Ouch! Oh, dearest, I didn't hurt you, did I?" Standing up in the bed, Debera wrapped apologetic arms about Morath, stroking her cheeks and ear knobs, reassuring her with murmurs of regret and promises to never hurt her again.

The little dragon refocused her eyes, whirling lightly but with only the faintest tinge of the red of pain and alarm, which dissipated quickly with such ardent reassurances.

Your head is much harder than it looks, she said, giving hers a little shake.

Debera rubbed underneath Morath's jaw, where the contact had been made.

"I'm so sorry, dearest," and then she heard a giggle behind her and swiveling around, half in anger, half in reflexive defense, she saw that she was not alone in the weyrling barracks. The blond girl from Ista—Sarra, that was her name—was sitting on the edge of her bed, folding clothes into the chest. Her dragonet was still curled up in a tight mound from which a slight snore could be heard.

"Oops, no offense intended ..." Sarra said, smiling with such good nature that Debera immediately relaxed. "You should have seen the looks on your faces. Morath's eyes nearly crossed when you cracked her."

Debera rubbed the top of her head, grimacing, as she descended from the bed.

"I was so deeply asleep ... I couldn't think where I was at first ..."

"Morath's been as good as she could be," Sarra said. "T'dam said to dress for dirty work. We're supposed to bathe and oil them after their first nap of the day."

That was when Debera remembered the pile of things she had not properly sorted the previous night.

Does dressing take long? Morath asked plaintively.

"No, it doesn't, love," and, turning her back in case Sarra might be embarrassed, Debera hauled off the nightdress and threw on the garments on the top of the pile—not new, certainly, but suitable for rough work.

The socks were new, knitted of a sturdy cotton, and she was especially grateful for them since the pair she had had on yesterday had already been worn several days. She stamped her feet into her own boots and stood.

"I'm ready, dear," she said to the little green, who stepped down off the raised platform and promptly fell on her nose.

Sarra jumped the intervening bed to help right Morath, struggling so hard to keep from laughing that she nearly choked. Once Debera saw that Morath had taken no hurt, she grinned back at the Istan.

"Are they always this . . . ?"

Sarra nodded. "So T'dam told us. You'll find a pail of meat just outside the door . . . We get a break this first morning," and she wrinkled her nose in a grimace, "but after today, it's up at the crack of dawn and carve up our darlings' breakfasts."

There was a long snorting snore from Sarra's green, and Sarra whirled, waiting to see if the dragonet was waking up. But the snore trembled into a tiny soprano "Ooooooh" and the snoring resumed its rhythm.

"Did she do that all night long?" Debera asked.

I am SO hungry . . .

Debera was all apologies, and so was Sarra, who sprinted ahead to fling open both leaves of the door. She made a flourishing bow for their exit. Morath immediately crowded against Debera, pushing her to the right, her young nose detecting the enticing smell in the two covered pails on the rack outside the barracks.

Debera lifted the pail down while Morath impatiently nudged off the cover and seemed to inhale the gobbets. Debera allowed her to fill her mouth and then started shielding the pail with her body.

"You will chew what you eat, Morath, you hear me? You could choke to death and then where would I be?"

Morath gave her such a look of pained astonishment and reproach that Debera couldn't remain stern.

"Chew," she said, popping a handful of pieces into Morath's open mouth. "Chew!" she repeated, and Morath obediently exercised her jaws before spreading them wide again for another batch. Debera had not tended the orphaned young animals of her hold without learning some of the tricks.

Whoever had decided on the quantity, Debera thought, knew the precise size of a dragonet's belly. Morath's demands had slowed considerably as Debera reached the bottom of the pail, and the dragonet sighed before she swallowed the last.

"I see she's had breakfast," said T'dam, appearing from behind so suddenly that Morath squawked in surprise and Debera struggled to get to her feet. T'dam's hand on her shoulder pushed her back down.

"We're not formal in the Weyr, Debera," he said kindly. "Now, lead her over to the lake there," and he gestured to the right, where Debera recognized the large mounds as sleeping dragonets. "Then, when she wakes up from this feed she'll be just where you can bathe and oil her." T'dam grinned. "Before you can feed her again, though . . ." and then he motioned to his left. "Are you squeamish?" he asked.

Debera took a good look in the direction he pointed and saw six skinned carcasses, swaying from butchering tripods. Weyrlings were busy with knives, carving flesh off the bones or at the table, chopping raw meat into dragonet morsels.

"Me?" Debera gave a cynical snort. "Not likely."

"Good," T'dam said approvingly. "Some of your peers are. Come now, Morath," he added in a totally altered tone, loving and kind and wheedling, "you'll need a little rest, and the sands by the lake are warm in the sun . . ."

Morath lifted her head, her eyes glistening bluey-green as she regarded the Weyrlingmaster.

He is a nice man, she said, and began to waddle toward the lake: her swaying belly bulged lumpily with her meal.

"When you've settled her, Debera, be sure to get your own breakfast in the kitchen. Good thing you're not squeamish," he said, turning away, but his chuckle drifted back to Debera's ears.

It's awfully far to the lake, isn't it, Debera? Morath said, puffing.

"Not really," Debera said. "Anyway, it's much too rocky underfoot right here to make a comfortable bed for your nap."

Morath looked down her long nose, her left fore knocking a stone out of her path. And sighed. She kept going, Debera encouraging her with every slow step, until they reached the sandier ground surrounding the lake. It had recently been raked, the marks visible between the paw and tail prints of the dragonets. Debera urged Morath farther onto the sand, to an empty spot between two browns who were tightly curled, with wings to shield their eyes from the autumn sun pouring down on them.

With a great sigh, Morath dropped her hindquarters to the sand with an I'm-not-going-a-step-farther attitude and sank slowly over to her right side. She curled her tail about her, curved her head around under her left wing and, with a sweet babyish croon rumbling in her throat, fell asleep.

Once again Debera could barely bring herself to leave the dragonet, lost in the wonder of having been acceptable to such a marvelously lovable creature.

She'd been lonely and lacking in love for so long—ever since her mother had died and her oldest full brother had left the family hold. Now she had Morath, all her very own, and those long years of isolation faded into a trivial moment.

She's perfectly safe here, Debera decided finally and forced herself to leave Morath and make her way across that quadrant of the Bowl to the kitchen caverns. Enticing smells of fresh bread and other viands made her quicken her steps. She hoped she'd have enough restraint not to bolt her food like her dragonet.

The kitchen cavern at Telgar Weyr was actually a series of

caves, each with an entrance, varying in size, width, and height. As Debera paused at the entrance of the nearest and smallest one, she saw that hearths or ovens were ranged against the outside wall, each with a separate chimney protruding up the cliff face. Inside, the many long tables where last night guests had been entertained were reduced to the number needed by the regular population of the Weyr. But the interior was busy as men and women went about the food preparation tasks.

"Breakfast's over there," a woman said, smiling at Debera and pointing. "Porridge's still hot and the klah's fresh made. Help yourself."

Debera looked to her left to the farthest hearth, which had tables and chairs set invitingly near it.

"There'll be fresh baked bread soon, too, and I'll bring some over," the woman added, and proceeded on her own business.

Debera had only just served herself a heaping of porridge— not a lump in it nor a fleck of burn—and a cup of klah when two boys, looking bewildered and not at all sure of how to proceed, wandered in.

"The bowls are there, the cups there," Debera said, pointing. "And use that hunk of towel to hold the pot while you spoon out the cereal. It's hot."

They sent her tentative smiles—they must just be old enough for Impression, she thought, feeling just a trifle older and wiser. They managed, but not without slopping gobs of porridge into the fire and jumping back from the hiss and smell, to get enough in the bowls and to pour klah into their cups.

"C'mon, sit here, I won't bite," she said, tapping her table. They were certainly not a bit sullen or grouchy, like her younger half brothers.

"You've a green, haven't you?" the first one said. He had a crop of black curls that had recently been trimmed very close to his skull.

" 'Course she has a green, stooopid," the other lad said, elbowing the ribs of the first. "I'm M'rak, and Caneth's my bronze," he added with a justifiable smirk of pride.

"My bronze is Tiabeth," the black-haired boy said, equally as proud of his dragon, but added modestly, "I'm S'mon. What's yours named?"

"Morath," and Debera found herself grinning broadly. Did all new riders feel as besotted as this?

The boys settled into chairs and began to eat, almost as eagerly as dragonets. Deliberately, Debera slowed the rhythm of her spoon. This porridge was really too good to gulp down: not a husk nor a piece of grit in it. Obviously Telgar tithed of its best to the Weyr, even with such a staple as oats for porridge. She sighed, grateful for more than Impressing Morath yesterday.

The boys suddenly stopped, spoons half lifted to their mouths, and warned, Debera turned quickly. Bearing down on their table was the unmistakable bulk of Tisha, the headwoman of the cavern. Her broad face was wreathed with a smile as generous as she was.

"How are you today? Settling in all right? Need anything from stores? Parents will pack your Gather best and you really need your weeding worst," she said, her rich contralto voice bubbling with good humor. "Breakfast all right? Bread's just out of the oven and you can have all you want." She had halted by Debera's chair, and her hands, shapely with long strong fingers, patted Debera's shoulders lightly, as if imparting a special message to her along with that pressure. "You lack something, come tell me, or mention it to T'dam. You weyrlings shouldn't worry about anything other than caring for your dragonets. That's hard work enough, I'm telling you, so don't be shy, now." She gave Debera a little extra pat before she removed her hands.

"I didn't think to bring with me the gown you lent me last

night," Debera said, wondering if that's what the subtle message was.

"Heavens above, child," Tisha said, big eyes even wider in her round face, "why, that dress was made for you, even if we didn't know you'd be coming." Her deep chuckle made her large breasts and belly bounce.

"But it's far too good a dress—" Debera began in protest.

Tisha patted Debera's shoulder again. "And fits you to perfection. I love making new clothes. My passion, really, and you'll see: I'm always working on something." Pat, pat. "But if I'd no one in mind when I cut and sewed it last year, I couldn't have worked better for you if I'd tried. The dress is yours. We all like to have something pretty to wear on Seventh Day. Do you sew?" she asked, eyeing Debera hopefully.

"No, I'm afraid not," Debera answered, lowering her eyes, for she remembered her mother with work in her hands in the evenings, embroidering or sewing fine seams in Gather clothes. Gisa barely managed to mend rips, and certainly neither of her daughters was learning how to mend or make garments.

"Well, I don't know what holder women are doing with their young these days. Why, I had a needle in my hand by the time I was three . . ." Tisha went on.

The boys' eyes were glazing over at the turn of the conversation.

"And you'll learn to sew harnesses, my fine young friends," she said, wagging a finger at them. "And boots and jackets, too, if you've a mind to design your own flying wear."

"Huh?" was M'rak's astonished reaction. "Sewing's fer women."

"Not in the Weyr it isn't," Tisha said firmly. "As you'll see soon enough. It's all part of being a dragonrider. You'll learn. Ah, now, here's the bread, butter, and a pot of jam."

Sure enough, another ample woman, grinning with the pleasure of what she was about to bestow on them, deposited the laden tray on the table.

"That should help, thank you, Allie," Tisha said as Debera added a murmur of appreciation and S'mon remembered his manners, too. M'rak made no such delay in grabbing up a piece of the steaming bread and cramming it into his mouth.

"Wow! Great!"

"Well, just be sure you don't lose it, preparing your dragonet's next meal," Tisha said, and moved off before the astonished bronze rider had absorbed her remark.

"What'd she mean by that?" he asked the others.

Debera grinned. "Hold bred?"

"Naw, m'family's weavers," M'rak said. "From Keroon Hold."

"We have to cut up what our dragonets eat, though, don't we?" S'mon said in a slightly anxious voice. "From the . . . the bodies they got hung up?"

"You mean cut it off the things that wore the meat?" M'rak turned a little pale and swallowed.

"That's what we mean," Debera said. "If you like, I'll do your carving and you can just cut up. Deal?"

"You bet," M'rak said fervently. And gulped again, no longer attacking the rest of the bread that hung limply from his fingers. He put the slice down. "I didn't know that was part of being a dragonrider, too."

Debera chuckled. "I think we're all going to find out that being a dragonrider is not just sitting on its neck and going wherever we want to."

A prophesy she was to learn was all too accurate. She didn't regret making the bargain with the two youngsters—it was a fair distribution of effort—but it did seem that she spent her next weeks either butchering or feeding or bathing her dragonet, with no time for anything else but sleeping. She had dealt with orphaned animals, true, but none the size nor with the appetite capacity of dragonets. Morath seemed to grow overnight, as if instantly transferring what she ate to visible increase—which meant more to scrub, oil, *and* feed.

"It's worth it. I keep telling myself," Sarra murmured one day as she wearily sprawled onto her bed.

"Does it help?" Grasella asked, groaning as she turned on her side.

"Does it matter?" put in Mesla, kicking her boots off.

"All that oil is softening my hands," Debera remarked in pleased surprise, noticing the phenomenon for the first time.

"And matting my hair something wicked," Jule said, regarding the end of the fuzzy plait she kept her hair in. "I wonder when I'll have time to wash it again."

"If you ask Tisha, she'll give you the most marvelous massage," Angie said, stretching on her bed and yawning. "My leg's all better."

She and her Plath had tripped each other up and she'd pulled all the muscles in her right leg so badly that at first they feared she'd broken a bone in the tumble. Plath had been beside herself with worry until Maranis had pronounced the damage only a bad wrenching. The other girls had helped Angie tend Plath.

"All part of being a dragonrider," T'dam had said, but he exhibited sympathy in making sure he was at hand to assist her, too. "Nothing you won't grin about later."

Although the room in which Lord Chalkin sat so that the newly certified Artist Iantine could paint his portrait of the Lord Holder was warmer than any other chamber in Bitra that Iantine had occupied, he sighed softly in weariness. His hand was cramped and he was very tired, though he was careful not to reveal anything to his odious subject.

He had to do a bang-up job of this portrait as fast as possible or he might not leave this miserable hold until the spring. Fortunately, the first snow was melting and, if he finished the painting, he'd leave before the paint was dry. And *with* the marks he'd been promised!

Why he had ever thought himself able to handle any problem that could occur on a commission, he did not know. Certainly he had been warned: more about not gambling with any Bitrans, to be sure, had he had any marks to wager. But the warnings had been too general. Why hadn't Ussie told him how many other people had been defrauded by the Bitran Lord Holder? The contract had *seemed* all right, *sounded* all right, and was as near to a total disaster as made no never mind. Inexperienced and arrogant, that's what he was. Too self-assured to listen to the wisdom of the years of experience Master Domaize had tried to get through his thick head. But Master Domaize had a reputation for letting you deal with your own mistakes—especially the ones unconnected with Art.

"Please, Lord Chalkin, would you hold still just a moment longer? The light is too good to waste," Iantine said, aware of the twitching muscles in Chalkin's fat cheeks. The man didn't have a tic or anything, but he could no more be still in his fancy chair than his children.

Impishly, Iantine wondered if he could paint a twitch—a muscle rictus—but it was hard enough to make Chalkin look good as it was. The man's muddy brown, close-set eyes seemed to cross toward the bridge of his rather fleshy, bulbous nose—which Iantine had deftly refined.

Master Domaize had often told his students that one had to be discreet in portraying people, but Iantine had argued the matter: that realism was necessary if the subject wanted a "true" portrait.

"True portraits are never realistic," his master had told him and the other students in the vast barn of a place where classes were held. "Save realism for landscapes and historical murals, not for portraits. No one wants to see themselves as others see them. The successful portraitist is one who paints with both tact and sympathy."

Iantine remembered railing about dishonesty and pandering to egos. Master Domaize had looked over the half spectacles he now had to wear if he wanted to see beyond his nose and smiled that gentle knowing smile of his.

"Those of us who have learned that the portraitist must also be the diplomat make a living. Those of us who wish to portray truth end up in a craft hall, painting decorative borders."

When the commission to do miniatures of Lord Chalkin's young children had been received at Hall Domaize, there had been no immediate takers.

"What's wrong with it?" Iantine demanded when the notice had stayed on the board for three weeks with no one's initials. He would shortly sit his final exams at Hall Domaize and had hopes to pass them creditably.

"Chalkin's what's wrong with it," Ussie said with a cynical snort.

"Oh, I know his reputation," Iantine replied, blithely flicking a paint-stained hand, "everyone does. But he sets out the conditions," and he tapped the document, "and they're all the ones we're supposed to ask for."

Ussie smothered a derogatory laugh in his hand and eyed him in the patronizing way that irritated Iantine so. He knew he was a better draughtsman and colorist than Ussie would ever be, and yet Ussie always acted so superior. Iantine *knew* his general skills were better, and improving, because, of course, in the studio, everyone had a chance to view everyone else's work. Ussie's anatomical sketches looked as if a mutant had posed as the life model . . . and his use of color was bizarre. Ussie did much better with landscapes and was a dab hand at designing heraldry shields and icons and such peripheral artwork.

"Yes, but you'll have to *live* in Bitra Hold while you're doing it, and coming into winter is not the time to live there."

"What? To do four miniatures? How long could it take?" Iantine had a sevenday in mind. Even for very small and active children that should be sufficient.

"All right, all right, so you've always managed to get kids to sit still for you. But these are Chalkin's and if they're anything like him, you'll have the devil's own time getting them to behave long enough to get an accurate likeness. Only, I sincerely doubt that an 'accurate' likeness is what is required. And I know you, Ian . . ." Ussie waggled a finger at him, grinning more broadly now. "You'll never be able to glamorize the little darlings enough to satisfy doting papa."

"But—"

"The last time a commission came in from Chalkin," Chomas said, joining in the conversation, "Macartor was there for nine months before his work was deemed 'satisfactory.' " Chomas jabbed his finger at the clause that began "on the completion of satisfactory work," and said, "He came back a ghost of himself and poorer than he'd started out."

"Macartor?" Iantine knew of the journeyman, a capable man with a fine eye for detail, now doing murals for the new Hall at Nerat Hold. He tried to think of a reason Macartor had not been able to deal well with Chalkin. "Great man for detail but not for portraiture," he said.

Ussie's eyebrows raised high in his long face and his gray eyes danced with mischief.

"So, take the commission and learn for yourself. I mean, some of us *need* some extra marks before Turn's End, but not so badly as we'd go to Bitra Hold to earn 'em. You know the reputation there for gambling? They'd sooner stop breathing than stop gambling."

"Oh, it can't be half as bad as they say it is," Iantine replied. "The sixteen marks, plus keep and travel expenses, is scale."

Ussie ticked the points off on fingers. "Travel? Well, you'd have to pay your own way there—"

"But he specifies travel . . ." Iantine protested, tapping that phrase impatiently.

"Hmmm, but *you* have to pay out for the travel there and account for every quarter mark you spent. Take you a few days to sort out right there. Chalkin's so mingy no decent cook stays with him, ditto for housekeeper, steward, and any other staff, so you may end up having to cook your own meals . . . if he doesn't charge you for the fuel to cook with. The hold's not got central heating, and you'd want a room fire this time of the year in that region. Oh, and bring your own bedfurs, he doesn't supply them to casual workers . . ."

"Casual? A portraitist from Hall Domaize is *not* classified as a casual worker," Iantine said indignantly.

"At Bitra, my friend, everyone's casual," Chomas put in. "Chalkin's never issued a fair service contract in his life. And read *every single word* on the page if you are foolish enough to take the commission. Which, if you had the sense of little green apples, you won't." Chomas gave a final decisive nod of his head and continued on his way to his own workstation, where he was doing fine marquetry work on a desk.

However, Iantine had a particular need for the marks the commission would bring him. With his professional diploma all but in his hand, he wanted to start repaying what he owed his parents. His father wanted to avail of Iantine's land allotment to extend his pasturage, but he didn't have the marks to pay the Council transfer fees: never a huge amount, but sufficient so that Iantine's large family would have to cut back on what few luxuries they had to save the sum. It was therefore a matter of self-esteem and pride for Iantine to earn the fee.

His parents had given him a good start, more than he deserved, considering how seldom he had been at the hold since his twelfth birthday. His mother had wished him to be a teacher, as she had been before her marriage. She had taught all the basics to him, his nine siblings, and the children in the other nearby Benden mountain sheep and farm holds. And because he had shown not only a keen interest in learning, but also discernible skill in sketching—filling every inch of a precious drawing book with studies of every aspect of life on the hillside hold—it had been decided to send him to the College. His help would be missed, but his father had reluctantly agreed that the lad showed more aptitude with pen and pencil than shepherd's crook. His next youngest brother, who had the temperament for the work, had been ecstatic to be promoted to Iantine's tasks.

Once at the College, his unusual talent and insights were instantly recognized and encouraged. Master Clisser had insisted that he do a portfolio of sketches: "animal, mineral, and floral." That had been easy to collect since Iantine constantly sketched and had many vignettes of unsuspecting classmates: some done at times he should have been doing other lessons. One in particular—a favorite with Master Clisser—was of Bethany, playing her guitar, bending over the instrument for intricate chording. Everyone had admired it, even Bethany.

His portfolio was submitted to several private Craft Halls which taught a variety of skills, from fine leather tooling to wood, glass, and stone workings. None of those on the West Coast had a place for another student, but the woman who was master weaver in Southern Boll had said she would contact Master Domaize in Keroon, one of the foremost portraitists on Pern, for she felt the boy's talent was in that direction.

To Iantine's astonishment, a green dragon had arrived one morning at the College, available to convey him back for a formal interview with Domaize himself. Iantine wasn't quite sure what excited him most: the ride on the dragon *between*, the prospect of meeting Master Domaize, or the thought of being able to continue with art as a possible profession. Afterward, Master Domaize, having set him the task of sketching himself, had accepted him as a student and sent off a message to his parents that very day, arranging terms.

Iantine's family had been astounded to receive such a message. Still more astonishing had been the information that Benden's Lord and Lady Holder were willing to pay more than half his fees.

Now he must earn as much as he could, as soon as he could, to show his family that their sacrifices had not been wasted. Undoubtedly Lord Chalkin would be difficult. Undoubtedly there would be problems. But the marks promised for the commission would pay the Land Transfer fee. So he'd initialed the contract, a copy was made for Master Domaize's files, and it had been returned to Lord Chalkin.

Chalkin had demanded, and received, a verification of Iantine's skill from his Master and then returned the signed contract.

"Best reread it, Ian," Ussie said when Iantine waved the document about in triumph.

"Why?" Iantine glanced down the page and pointed to the bottom lines. "Here's my signature, and Domaize's, alongside Chalkin's. That is, if that's what this scrawl is supposed to be." He held it out to Ussie.

"Hmm, looks all right, though I haven't seen Chalkin's hand before. My, where did they find this typewriter? Half the letters don't strike evenly." Ussie passed the document back.

"I'll see if there're any other examples of Lord Chalkin's signature in the files," Iantine said, "though how—and why—would he deny the contract when he himself proposed it?"

"He's a Bitran, and you know how they are. Are you sure that's your signature?" Ussie grinned as Iantine peered with a suspicious glare at his own name. Then Ussie laughed.

"Sure, I'm sure it's mine. Look at the slant of the *t*. Just as I always make it. What are you driving at, Ussie?" Iantine felt the first twinges of irritation with Ussie's attitude.

"Well, Bitrans are known to forge things. Remember those bogus Land Transfer deeds five years ago? No, I don't suppose you'd have heard about them. You'd've still been a schoolboy." With an airy wave of his hand, Ussie left a puzzled and worried Iantine.

When he brought the matter up to his master, Domaize could produce a sample of Lord Chalkin's signature on a document much creased and worn. Domaize also put his glasses up to his eyes and peered at his own name on the current contract.

"No, this is mine, and I recognize your slanting *t* bar." He put the document in the "to-do" tray. "We'll copy it into our Workbook. If you have any trouble, though, at Bitra Hold, let me know instantly. It's much easier to sort things out when they start, you know. And don't," and here Master Domaize had waggled a stern finger at him, "allow them to entice you into any games of chance, no matter how clever you think *you* are. Bitrans make their living at gaming. You can't compete at their level."

Iantine had promised faithfully to eschew any gaming. He'd never had much interest in such things, being far more likely to sketch the players than join the game. But gambling was not a "thing" that the Master would have meant. Iantine was learning what did fall into that category: especially the nuances of the word "satisfaction." Such a simple word that can be so misconstrued. As he had.

He had done not *four* miniatures, but nearly twenty, using up all the materials he had brought with him, so that he had had to send for more from Hall Domaize since the wood used in miniatures had to be specially seasoned or it would warp, especially in a damp environment like Bitra Hold. He had done the first four on the canvas he had brought with him for the job, only to discover, along with a long list of other objections from

Lord Chalkin and his wife, Lady Nadona, that canvas was not "satisfactory."

"If it isn't the best quality," and she ran one of her almost dragon-talon nails across one canvas, snagging a thread so badly the surface was unusable, "it doesn't last long. Sky-broom wood is what you should be using."

"Skybroom wood is expensive . . ."

"You're being very well paid for these miniatures," she said. "The least we can expect is the best grade of materials."

"Skybroom wood was not stipulated in the contract . . ."

"Did it *have* to be?" she demanded haughtily. "I made sure that Domaize Hall has the very highest standards."

"Master Domaize provided me with the best canvas," and he pushed his remaining frames out of her reach. "He said that is what he always supplies. You should have stipulated sky-broom wood in the contract if that's what you wanted."

"Of course it would be what I wanted, young man. The very best is none too good for *my* children."

"Is there any available in the Hold?" he asked. At least with skybroom, you could clean off "unsatisfactory" work without the risk of damaging the surface.

"Of course."

That was his first mistake. However, at that point he was still eager to do a proper job to the best of his abilities. And what skybroom was there turned out to be substantial lumber, being cured for furniture and not thin enough to be used for miniatures: "miniatures" which were now twice the ordinary size.

High on the list of "unsatisfactory" were the poses of the children, although these had been suggested by the Lady Holder herself.

"Chaldon doesn't look at all natural," Lady Nadona said. "Not at all. He looks so tense, hunching his shoulders like that. Whyever did you not tell him to sit up straight?" Iantine forbore to mention that he had done so frequently and within Lady Nadona's hearing. "And you've given him such an odious scowl."

Which had been Chaldon's "natural" expression.

"Standing?" he suggested, cringing at the thought of arguing any of them into standing for the "sittings." He'd had enough trouble getting them to sit still. They were, as Ussie had foreseen, not biddable, and had such short attention spans that he could never get them to strike the right pose or assume an even halfway cheerful expression.

"And why on earth did you paint on such a small canvas? I'll need to use a magnifying glass," Lady Nadona had said, holding Chaldon's likeness away from her as far as her arm would reach. Iantine had known enough about his patroness by then to suppress a remark about her farsightedness.

"This is the customary size for a miniature . . ."

"So you say," she replied repressively. "I want something I can see when I'm on the other side of the room."

As she was generally on the "other side of her room" whenever her children were in her vicinity, the need was understandable. They were the messiest preadolescents Iantine had ever encountered: plump, since they were indolent by nature; dressed in ill-fitting apparel, since the hold's seamstress was not particularly adept; and constantly eating: generally something that ran, smeared, or left crumbs on their chins and tunics. None of them bathed frequently enough and their hair was long, greasy, and roughly cut. Even the two girls showed no feminine interest in their appearance. One had hacked her hair off with a knife . . . except the long tress she wore down the back, strung with beads and little bells. The other had thick braids which were rarely redone unless whatever fastened the end of the plaits had got lost.

Iantine had struggled with the porcine Chaldon, and realizing that the child could not be depicted "naturally," tried to retain enough resemblance so that others would know which child had been depicted. But his portrait was "unsatisfactory." Only the youngest, a sturdy lad of three who said nothing beyond "No" and carried a stuffed toy with him from which he could not be parted, was deemed marginally "satisfactory." Actually, the dirty "bear" was the best part of Briskin's portrait.

Iantine had tried to romanticize Luccha's unusual hairstyle and was told that she'd look better with "proper hair," which he could certainly add in if he was any good at all. And why did she have such an awkward expression on her face when Luccha had the sweetest smile and such a lovely disposition? (Especially when she was busy trying to unite the hold's cats by tying their tails together, Iantine had said mentally. Bitra Hold did not have a single unscathed animal, and the spit boy said they'd lost seven dogs to "accidents" that year already.) Luccha's mouth was set aslant in her face, the thin lips usually compressed in a sour line. Lonada, the second daughter, had a pudding face, with small dark holes for eyes, and her father's nose: bad enough in a male but fatal for a female.

Iantine had also had to "buy" a lock from the hold steward to prevent his sleeping furs from walking out of the narrow little cubicle in which he was quartered. He knew his packs had been searched the first day; probably several times, by the variety of smeared fingerprints left on the paint pots. As he had brought nothing of real value with him—not having many possessions, he hadn't worried. Holds usually had one light-fingered person. And the hold steward usually knew who it was and retrieved what had gone astray from guests' rooms. But when Iantine found his paint pots left open to dry out, he protested. And "paid" for a lock. Not that he felt all that secure, for if there was one key to that lock, there could be duplicates. But his furs did remain on his bed. And glad he was to have them, for the thin blanket supplied was holey and ought to have been torn up for rug lengths long since.

That was the least of his problems at Bitra Hold. Having heard all that was wrong with the next set of miniatures he managed to produce, a third larger than the first, Iantine began to have a somewhat clearer grasp of just how the parents envisaged their offspring. On his fifth set he nearly won the accolade of "satisfactory." Nearly . . .

Then the children, one after another, succumbed to an infant disease that resulted in such a rash that they could not possibly "sit."

"Well, you'd better do something to earn your keep," Chalkin told his contract portraitist when Lady Nadona had announced the children were isolated.

"The contract says I will have room and board—"

Chalkin held up a thick forefinger, his smile not the least bit humorous. "*When* you are honoring that contract . . ."

"But the children are sick . . ."

Chalkin had shrugged. "That's neither here nor there. You are unable to honor the specific conditions of the contract. Therefore you are not entitled to be fed and housed at the hold's expense. Of course, I can always deduct your leisure time from the fee . . ." The smile deepened vindictively.

"Leisure . . ." Iantine had been so enraged, the protest burst from him before he could suppress it. No wonder, he thought, shaking with the control he had to enforce on himself, no one else at Hall Domaize would sign with Bitra.

"Well," Chalkin went on as if he were a reasonable man, "what else does one call it if you are not engaged in the labors which you are contracted for?"

Iantine had to wonder if Chalkin knew how necessary it was for him to earn the exact fee promised. Iantine had held no conversations with anyone in the hold: they were so sullen and uncommunicative a group at their best—which was usually at mealtimes—that he hoped he'd be spared them at their worst. He had steadfastly refused to "have a little game" with cooks or guards, which accounted for a good deal of the general animosity toward him. So how would anyone know anything about his personal life or his reasons for working here?

So, instead of already being on his way home with a satisfactory contract fulfilled and the marks of the transfer fee heavy in his pouch, Iantine spent his "leisure" time touching up the faces of Chalkin's ancestors in the main hall murals.

"Good practice for you, I'm sure," Chalkin had said, all too amiably, as he made his daily inspection of this project. "You'll be better equipped to do satisfactory portraits of this generation."

Pig faces, all of them, with the ancestral bulbous nose, Iantine noticed. Oddly enough, one or two of the ancestresses had been very pretty girls, far too young and attractive for the mean-mouthed men they had been contracted to. Too bad the male genes dominated.

Of course, Iantine had had to make up batches of the special paints required for mural work, having initially had no idea such would be required. He also found his supplies of the oil paints drastically reduced by the repeated unsatisfactory portraits. He had the choice of sending back to Hall Domaize for additional supplies—and paying transport charges plus having to wait for them to reach him—or finding the raw materials and manufacturing the colors himself. Which was the better option.

"How much?" he exclaimed in shock when the head cook told him how much he'd have to pay for the eggs and oil he needed to mix into his pigments.

"Yiss, an' that doan include cost of hiring the equipment," the cook added, sniffing. The man had a perpetually running nose, sometimes dripping down his upper lip. But not, Iantine devoutly hoped, into whatever he was in the process of preparing.

"I have to hire bowls and jars from you?" Iantine wondered how the cook could have become infected with Chalkin's greed.

"Well, if I aint using 'em, and you is, you should pay for the use, seems like." He sniffed so deeply Iantine wondered there could be any mucus left in his sinus cavities. "Shoulda brought yer stuff with ye if ye'd need it. Lord Holder sees you usin' things from his kitchen and one of us'll be paying for it. Won't be me!" And he sniffed again, shrugging one dirty white shoulder as emphasis.

"I came with adequate supplies and equipment for the work I was hired to do," Iantine said, curbing an intense desire to shove the man's face in the thin soup he was stirring.

"So?"

Iantine had walked, stiff-legged with fury, out of the kitchen. He tried to tell himself that he was learning, the very hardest way, how to deal with the client.

Finding the raw materials for his pigments had proved nearly as difficult since it was, after all, coming on to deep winter here in the Bitran hills. He discovered a hefty hunk of stone with a rounded end that would do as pestle and then a hollowed out rock that would act as a mortar. He had found a whole hillside of the sabsab bush, whose roots produced a yellow color; enough raw cobalt to get blue; and the pawberry leaves that boiled up one of the finest pure reds—with neither tint nor tinge of orange or purple. With the greatest of luck he also came across ochre mud. Rather than "rent" containers, he used chipped crockery he unearthed from the midden heap. He did have to pay the price of best oil for the substandard stuff that was all the cook would sell him. And that mark, he was sure, would never be passed on to Lord Chalkin as fee.

He managed to get enough saucers or mugs—they used a very cheap pottery in Bitra Hold—to hold the different colors he needed. He hadn't quite finished the repair work when Chaldon recovered sufficiently from the rash to be able to sit/stand—once more.

Chaldon had lost weight during the fever which accompanied the emergence of the rash. He was also lethargic, and as long as Iantine could think up funny stories to tell as he worked, he stayed reasonably still. Calling himself the worst kind of panderer, Iantine made the boy resemble the best looking of the ancestors he'd relimned. The boy was certainly pleased and ran off to find his mother, shouting that he did look like Great-granddaddy, just as she always said he did.

The same ploy did not quite work on Luccha's portrait when she had recovered. Her skin was sallower, she'd lost hair and too much weight to improve her undistinguished looks. While he had aimed for her great-grandmother thrice removed, she didn't have the right facial structure and even he had to admit the result was unsatisfactory.

"Her illness," he'd mumbled when Chalkin and Nadona recited the long catalog of dissimilarities between their daughter and the portrait.

He did better with Lonada and Briskin, who, several kilos lighter, had the look of his great-uncle—pinch-faced, lantern-jawed, and big-eared. Iantine had judiciously reduced the size of those even as he wondered what Artist had got away with such unflattering appendages on great-uncle.

He redid Luccha's after the other two: she'd put on some weight and her color was better. Not much, but better. And he set her eyes wider in her face, which improved her no end. Too bad it couldn't be done to the model. He vaguely remembered that the First Settlers had been able to remodel noses and bob ears and stuff like that.

So, grudgingly and after making him touch up each of the

four not-so-miniature paintings to the point where he was ready to break something—their heads for preference—the Lord and Lady Holder considered the four paintings satisfactory. The final critiquing had lasted well into the night, which was dark and stormy: the winds audible even through the three-meter-thick cliff walls.

So, as he descended wearily but in great relief to the lower-floor cubicle, he became aware of the intense chill in this level. The temperature in the big Hall had been somewhat warmed by the roaring fires in the four hearths, but there was no heating down here. In fact, it was so cold that Iantine did no more than loosen his belt and remove his boots before crawling onto the hard surface that was supposed to be a mattress. It looked and felt like something recycled from the ships of the First Crossing. He curled up in the furs, more grateful than ever that he'd brought his own, and fell asleep.

Arctic temperatures swirling about his face roused him. His face was stiff with cold and, despite the warmth of his furs, when he tried to stretch his body, his muscles resisted. He had a crick in his neck and he wondered if he'd moved at all during the night. Certainly it was cold enough to have kept in the warm of the furs. But he had to relieve himself.

He crammed his feet into boot leather that was rigid with ice and, wrapping his furs tightly about himself, made his way down the corridor to the toilet. His breath was a plume of white, his cheeks and nose stung by the cold. He managed his business and returned to his room only long enough to throw on his thickest woolen jumper. With half a mind to throw his furs around him for added warmth, he ran up the several flights of stone steps, past walls that dripped with moisture. He paused at the first window on the upper level: solidly snowed closed. He went up the next short flight and opened the door into what should have been the relatively warmer kitchen area.

Had every fire in the place gone out overnight? Had the spit boys frozen on their bed shelf? As he turned his head in their direction, his glance caught at the window. Snow was piled up against the first hand's breadth of it. He moved closer and looked out at the courtyard but it was all one expanse of unbroken snow. Indeed, where the courtyard should have stepped down to the roadway, the snow was even, concealing any depression where the road should have been. No one moved outside. Nor were there any tracks in the expanse of snow-covered court to suggest that anyone had tried to come in from one of the outer holds.

"Just what I needed," Iantine said, totally depressed by what he saw. "I could be trapped here for weeks!"

Paying for room and board. If only the kids hadn't come down with measles . . . If only he hadn't already freshened up the murals . . . How would he survive? Would he have any left of his original fee—that had seemed so generous—by the time he could leave this miserable hold?

Later that morning, when half-frozen people had begun to cope with the effects of the blizzard, he struck another bargain with the Holder Lord and Lady: and very carefully did he word it. Two full-sized portraits, each a square meter on sky-broom wood to be supplied by Lord Chalkin, one of Lady Nadona and one of Lord Chalkin, head and shoulder in Gather dress, with all materials and equipment to make additional pigments supplied by the hold; maintenance for himself and quarters on an upper floor with morning and evening fuel for a fire on the hearth.

He completed Lady Nadona's portrait without too much difficulty—she would sit still, loved nothing better than to have a valid excuse for doing nothing. Halfway through the sitting, though, she wanted to change her costume, believing the red did not flatter her complexion as well as the blue. It didn't, but he talked her out of changing and subtly altered her naturally florid complexion to a kinder blush and darkened the color of her pale eyes so that they seemed to dominate her face. By then he'd heard enough of the supposed resemblance between herself and Luccha so that he improved on it, giving her a more youthful appearance.

When she wanted to change the collar of her dress, he improvised one he remembered seeing in an Ancient's portrait—a lacy froth that hid much of the loose skin of her neck. Not that he had painted *that* in, but the lace softened the whole look of her.

He had not been as lucky with Chalkin. The man was psychologically unable to sit still—tapping his fingers, swinging one leg as he crossed and uncrossed them, twitching his shoulders or his face, making it basically impossible to obtain a set pose.

Iantine was nearly desperate now to finish and leave this dreadful place before another snowstorm. The young portraitist wondered if Chalkin's delays, and the short periods in which he would deign to sit, were yet another ploy to delay him—and rake back some of the original fee. Though Chalkin had even invited him to come into the gaming rooms—the warmest and most elegant rooms in the hold, Iantine had managed to excuse himself somehow or other.

"Do sit still, Lord Chalkin, I'm working on your eyes and I cannot if you keep moving them about in your face," Iantine said, rather more sharply than he had ever addressed the Lord Holder before.

"I beg your pardon," Chalkin said, jerking his shoulders about angrily.

"Lord Chalkin, unless you wish to be portrayed with your eyes crossed, *sit still for five minutes*! I beg of you."

Something of Iantine's frustration must have come across

because Chalkin not only sat still, he glared at the portraitist. And for longer than five minutes.

Working as fast as he could, Iantine completed the delicate work on the eyes. He had subtly widened them in the man's face and cleared up the edemic pouches that sagged below them. He had made the jowly face less porcine and subtracted sufficient flesh from the bulbous nose to give it a more Roman look. He had also widened and lifted the shoulders to give a more athletic appearance and darkened the hair. Further, he had meticulously caught the fire of the many-jeweled rings. Actually, they dominated the painting, which he felt would find favor with Lord Chalkin, who seemed to have more rings than days of the year.

"There!" he said, putting down his brush and standing back from the painting, satisfied in himself that he had done the best job possible: that is, the best job that would prove "satisfactory" and allow him to leave this ghastly hold.

"It's about time," Chalkin said, slipping down from the chair and stamping over to view the result.

Iantine watched his face, seeing that flash of pleasure before Chalkin's usual glum expression settled back over his features. Chalkin peered more closely, seeming to count the brush strokes—although there were none, for Iantine was too competent a technician to have left any.

"Watch the paint. It's not yet dry," Iantine said quickly, raising his arm to ward off Chalkin's touch.

"Humph," Chalkin said, shrugging his shoulders to settle his heavy jerkin. He affected diffidence, but the way he kept looking at his own face told Iantine that the man was finally pleased.

"Well? Is it satisfactory?" Iantine asked, unable to bear the suspense any longer.

"Not bad, not bad, but . . ." and Chalkin once again put out a finger.

"You will not smear the paint, Lord Chalkin," Iantine said, fearing just that and another session to repair the damage.

"You're a rude fellow, painter."

"My title is Artist, Lord Chalkin, and do tell me if this portrait is satisfactory or not!"

Chalkin gave him a quick nervous glance, one facial muscle twitching. Even the Lord of Bitra Hold knew when he had pushed someone too hard.

"It's not bad . . ."

"Is it satisfactory, Lord Chalkin?" Iantine put all the pent-up frustration and anxiety into that question.

Chalkin shifted one shoulder, screwed up his face with indecision and then hastily composed his features in the more dignified pose of the portrait before him.

"Yes, I believe it is satisfactory."

"Then," and now Iantine took Lord Chalkin by the elbow and steered him toward the door, "let us to your office and complete the contract."

"Now, see here—"

"If it is satisfactory, I have honored that contract and you may now settle with me for the miniatures," Iantine said, guiding the man down the cold corridor and to his office. He tapped his foot impatiently as Chalkin took the keys from his inside pocket and opened the door.

The fire within was so fierce that Iantine felt sweat blossom on his forehead. At Chalkin's abrupt gesture, he turned around while the man fiddled with wherever it was he had in his strongbox. He heard, with infinite relief, the turn of the metal lock and then silence. A slamming of a lid.

"Here you are," said Chalkin coldly.

Iantine counted out the marks, sixteen of them, Farmermarks, but good enough since he would be using them in Benden, which didn't mind Farmermarks.

"The contracts?"

Chalkin glared but he unlocked the drawer and extracted them, almost flinging them across the desk at Iantine. Iantine signed his name and turned them back to Chalkin.

"Use mine," Iantine said when Chalkin made a show of finding a good pen in the clutter on his desk.

Chalkin scrawled his name.

"Date it," Iantine added, wishing to have no complaint at a later time.

"You want too much, painter."

"Artist, Lord Chalkin," Iantine said with a humorless smile and turned to leave. At the door he turned again, "And don't touch the painting for forty-eight hours. I will not come back if you smear it. It was satisfactory when we left the room. Keep it that way."

Iantine returned to collect his good brushes, but left what remained of the paints he had had to make. Last night, in a hopeful mood, he had packed everything else. Now, he took the stairs up two and three at a time, stored his brushes carefully, stuffed the signed and dated contracts into his pack, shrugged into his coat, rolled up his sleeping furs, looped both packs in one hand, and was halfway down the stairs again when he met Chalking ascending.

"You cannot leave now," Chalkin protested, grabbing his arm. "You have to wait until my wife has seen and approved my portrait."

"Oh, no, I don't," Iantine said, wrenching free of the restraining hand.

He was out the main door before Chalkin could say another word, and ran down the roadway between the soiled snowbanks. If he was benighted on the road in the middle of a snowstorm, he would still be safer than staying one more hour at Bitra Hold.

Luckily for him, he found shelter during that next storm in a woodman's holding some klicks away from the main hold.

6

▼▼▼▼▼▼▼▼▼

TELGAR WEYR, FORT HOLD

"**G**uess what I found?" P'tero cried, ushering his guest into the kitchen cavern. "Tisha, he's half frozen and starving of the hunger," the young green rider added, hauling the tall fur-wrapped figure toward the nearest hearth and pushing him into a chair. He deposited the packs he was carrying onto the table. "Klah, for the love of little dragons, please . . ."

Two women came running, one with klah and the other with a hastily filled bowl of soup. Tisha came striding across the cavern, demanding to know what the problem was, who had P'tero rescued and from where.

"No one should be out in weather like this," she said as she reached the table and grabbed up the victim's wrist to get a pulse. "All but froze, he is."

Tisha pulled aside the furs wrapped about his neck and then let him take the cup. He cradled the klah in reddened fingers, blowing before he took his first cautious sip. He was also shivering uncontrollably.

"I spotted an SOS on the snow—lucky for him that the sun made shadows or I'd never have seen it," P'tero was saying, thoroughly pleased with himself. "Found him below Bitra Hold . . ."

"Poor man," Tisha interjected.

"Oh, you're so right there," P'tero said with ironic fervor, "and he'll never return. Not that he's told me all . . ." and P'tero flopped to a chair when someone brought him a cup of klah. "Got out of Chalkin's clutches intact," P'tero grinned impishly, "and then survived three nights in a Bitran woodsman's hold . . . with only a half cup of old oats to sustain him . . ."

Through his explanation, Tisha ordered hot water bottles, warmed blankets, and, taking a good look at the man's fingers, numbweed and frostbite salve.

"Don't think they're more than cold," she said, removing one of his hands from its fevered grip on the hot cup and spreading the fingers out, lightly pinching the tips. "No, no harm done."

"Thank you, thank you," the man said, returning his fingers to the warm cup. "I got so cold stamping out that emergency code . . ."

"And out of doors in such weather with no gloves," Tisha chided him.

"When I left Hall Domaize for Bitra Hold, it was only autumn," he said in a grating voice.

"Autumn?" Tisha echoed, widening her fine eyes in surprise. "How long were you at Bitra Hold, then?"

"Seven damned weeks," the man replied, spitting out the words in a disgusted tone of voice. "I thought a week at the most . . ."

Tisha laughed, her belly heaving under her broad apron.

"What under the stars took you to Bitra in the first place? Artist, are you?" she added.

"How'd you know?" The man regarded her with surprise.

"Still have paint under your nails . . ."

Iantine inspected them and his cold-reddened face flushed a deeper red. "I didn't even stop to wash," he said.

"As well you didn't, considering the price Chalkin charges for such luxuries as soap," she said, chuckling again.

The woman returned with the things Tisha had ordered. While they ministered to the warming of him, he clung with one hand or the other to the klah. And then to the soup cup. His furs, which had kept him from freezing to death, were taken to dry at one fire; his boots were removed and his toes checked for frostbite, but he had been lucky there, too, so they were coated with salve for good measure and then wrapped in warm toweling, while warmed blankets were snugged about his body. Salve was applied to his hands and face and then he was allowed to finish the hot food.

"Now, your name, and whom shall we contact that you've been found?" Tisha asked when all this had been done.

"I'm Iantine," he said, and then he added in wry pride, "portraitist from Hall Domaize. I was contracted to do miniatures of Chalkin's children . . ."

"Your first mistake," Tisha said, chuckling.

Iantine flushed. "You're so right, but I needed the fee."

"Did you come away with any of it?" P'tero asked, his eyes gleaming with mischief.

"Oh, that I did," the journeyman replied so fiercely that everyone grinned. Then he sighed. "But I did have to part with an eighth at the woodsman's hold. He had little enough to share but was willing to do so."

"At a profit, I'm sure . . ."

Iantine considered that for a moment. "I was lucky to find

any place to wait out the storm. And he did share ..." He
shrugged briefly, and a dejected look crossed his features as
he sighed. "Anyway, it was he who suggested I make a sign in
the snow to attract any dragonrider. I'm just lucky one saw
me." He nodded thanks to P'tero.

"No problem," the blue dragonrider said airily. "Glad I
came." He leaned toward Tisha across the table. "He'd've been
frozen solid in another day."

"Were you long waiting?"

"Two days after the storm ended, but I spent the nights with
ol' Fendler. If you're hungry enough, even tunnel snake tastes
good," Iantine added. How long had it been since he'd eaten a
decent meal?

"Ah, the poor laddie," Tisha said, and called out orders for a
double portion of stew to be brought immediately, and bread
and sweetening and some of the fruit that had been sent up
from Ista.

By the time Iantine had finished the meal, he felt he had
made up for the last four days. His feet and hands were tingling despite the numbweed and salve. When he stood to go
relieve himself, he wobbled badly and clutched at the chair for
support.

"Have a care, lad, filling the stomach was only half your
problem," Tisha said, moving to support him with far more
alacrity than her bulk would suggest. She gestured for P'tero to
lend a hand.

"I need to—" Iantine began.

"Ach, it's on the way to the sleeping cavern," Tisha said, and
drew one of his arms over her shoulder. She was as tall as he.

P'tero took up the packs again, and between them they got
him to the toilet room. And then into a bed in an empty cubicle.
Tisha checked his feet again, applied another coat of numbweed and tiptoed out. Iantine only made sure that his packs—

and the precious fee—were in the room with him before he fell deeply asleep.

While he slept, messages went out—to Hall Domaize and to Benden Weyr and Hold, since Iantine nominally looked to Benden. Although Iantine had taken no lasting harm, M'shall recognized yet another instance of Chalkin taking unfair advantage. Irene had already sent in a substantial list of abuses and irregularities in Chalkin's dealings—generally with folk who had no recourse against his dictates. He held no court in which difficulties could be aired and had no impartial arbiters to make decisions.

The big traders, who could be counted on for impartial comment, bypassed Bitra and could cite many examples of unfair dealings since Chalkin had assumed holding fifteen years before. The few small traders who ventured in Bitra rarely returned to it.

Following that Gather and its decision to consider deposing Chalkin, M'shall had his sweep riders check in every minor hold to learn if Chalkin had duly informed his people of the imminence of Thread. None had, although Lord Chalkin had increased his tithe on every household. The manner in which he was conducting this extra tithe suggested that he was amassing supplies for his own good, not that of the hold. Those in a more isolated situation would certainly have a hard time obtaining even basic food supplies. That constituted a flagrant abuse of his position as Lord Holder.

When Paulin read M'shall's report, he asked if Chalkin's holders would speak out against him. M'shall had to report that his initial survey of the minor holders indicated a severe lack of civic duty. Chalkin had his folk so cowed, none would accuse him—especially this close to a Pass—for he still had the power to turn objectors out of their holds.

"They may change their minds once Thread has started," K'vin remarked to Zulaya.

"Too late, I'd say, for any decent preparations to be made."

K'vin shrugged. "He's really not our concern, for which I for one am thankful. At least we rescued Iantine."

Zulaya gave a wry chuckle. "That poor lad. Starting his professional career at Bitra? Not the best place."

"Maybe that's all he could aspire to," K'vin said.

"Not if he's from Hall Domaize," Zulaya said tartly. "Wonder how long it'll take his hands to recover?"

"Thinking of a new portrait?" K'vin asked, amused.

"Well, he's down an eighth of what he needs," she said.

K'vin gave her a wide-eyed look. "You wouldn't . . ."

"Of course I wouldn't," she said with an edge to her voice. "He needs something in his pocket of his own. I admire a lad who'd endure Bitra for any reason. And Iantine's was an honorable one in wanting to pay the transfer fee."

"Wear that red Hatching dress when you sit for him," K'vin said. Then rubbed his chin. "You know, I might have my portrait done, too."

Zulaya gave him a long look. "The boy may find it as hard to leave Telgar Weyr as it was Bitra."

"With a much fuller pouch and no maintenance subtracted . . ."

"And soap and hot water and decent food," Zulaya said. "According to Tisha, he'll need feeding up. He's skin and bones."

When the singing woke Iantine, he was totally disoriented. No one had sung a note at Bitra Hold. And he was warm! The air was redolent of good eating odors, too. He sat up. Hands, feet, and face were stiff but the tingling was gone. And he was exceedingly hungry.

The curtain across the cubicle rustled and a boy's head popped through.

"You're awake, Artist Iantine?" the lad said.

"Indeed, I am," and Iantine looked around for his clothes. Someone had undressed him and he didn't see his own clothes.

"I'm to help you if you need it," the boy said, pushing halfway through the curtains. "Tisha laid out clean clothes." He wrinkled a snub nose. "Yours were pretty ripe, she said."

Iantine chuckled. "They probably were. I ran out of soap for washing three weeks ago."

"You was at Bitra. They charge for everything there." The boy threw up both arms in disgust. "I'm Leopol," he added. Then he lifted the soft slippers from the pile on the stool. "Tisha said you'd better wear these, not your boots. And you're to use the salve first . . ." He held up the lidded jar. "Dinner's ready." Leopol then licked his lips.

"And you must wait your meal until I'm ready, huh?"

Leopol nodded solemnly and then grinned. "I don't mind. I'll get more because I waited."

"Is food in short supply at this Weyr?" Iantine asked jokingly as he began to dress in the clean gear. Odd how important simple things, like freshly laundered clothing, assumed the level of luxury when you've had to do without.

Leopol helped him spread the salve on his feet. They were still tender to the touch. Even the act of applying the salve made them suddenly itchy. Fortunately, the numbweed, or whatever it was, reduced that sensation.

When he had relieved himself again and gingerly washed face and hands, he and Leopol made their way to the Lower Cavern, where the evening meal was in progress.

The lad led him to a side table near the hearth which had been set for two. Instantly, cooks descended with plates overflowing with food, wine for him and klah for Leopol.

"There now, Artist man," the cook said, nodding appreciation as Iantine attacked the roast meat, "eat first and then the

Weyrleaders would like a few words with you, if you're not too tired."

Iantine murmured thanks and understanding and addressed himself single-mindedly to his food. He would have had additional servings of the main course but his stomach felt uneasy: too much good food after several days of semifasting, probably. Leopol brought him a large serving of the sweet course but he couldn't finish it all because the back of his throat felt raw and sore. He would have gone back to his bed then but he saw the Weyrleaders advancing on him. Leopol made a discreet exit, grinning reassurance at him. Iantine tried to stand in courtesy to his hosts but he wobbled on his numbed feet and dropped back into the chair.

"We don't stand much on ceremony here," Zulaya said, gesturing for him to stay seated as K'vin pulled out one chair for her.

He carried the wineskin from which he filled all the glasses. Iantine took a polite sip—it was a nice crisp wine—but even the one sip made his stomach feel more sour.

"Messages have been sent, and acknowledgments received, that you've been rescued," K'vin said, grinning over the last word. "Master Domaize was becoming worried so we saved him a messenger to Bitra."

"That's very good of you, Zulaya, K'vin," Iantine said, thankful that part of his training at Hall Domaize had included knowing the important names in every hold, Weyr, and Hall. "I certainly appreciated P'tero's rescue."

Zulaya grinned. "He'll be dining on that one for the rest of the year. But it proves the wisdom of sweep riding even during the Interval."

"You should know," Iantine blurted out, "that Lord Chalkin doesn't believe there will be a Pass."

"Of course not," K'vin replied easily. "It doesn't suit him to.

Bridgely and M'shall would like a report from you, though, concerning your visit there."

"You mean, there's something that can be done about him?" Iantine was amazed. Lord Holders were autonomous within their borders. He hadn't known there'd be any recourse.

"He may *do* himself in," Zulaya said with a grim twist of her lips.

"That would be wonderful," Iantine said. "Only," and now honesty forced him to admit this, "he didn't really *do* anything to me . . ."

"Our Weyr Artist may not be trained," K'vin said, "but Waine informed me that it doesn't take seven weeks to do four miniatures . . ."

"I actually painted twenty-two to get four that they liked," Iantine said, clearing his throat grimly. "The hooker in the contract was the word 'satisfactory.' "

"Ah," Zulaya and K'vin said in chorus.

"I ran out of paint and canvas because I brought only what I *thought* I'd need . . ." He lifted his hands, then rubbed them because they were beginning to itch again. "Then the children all got measles, and so, rather than have anything deducted from the fee for room and board, I agreed to freshen up the hold murals . . . only I hadn't brought that sort of paint and had to manufacture the colors . . ."

"Did he charge you for the use of the equipment?" Zulaya asked, to Iantine's astonishment.

"How'd you know?" When she only laughed and waved at him to continue his telling, Iantine went on. "So I excavated what I needed in the midden."

"Good on you . . ." Zulaya clapped her hands, delighted by his resourcefulness.

"Fortunately, most of the raw materials for pigments are readily available. You only have to find and make the colors up. Which I'd have to do anyhow. Master Domaize was good about passing on techniques like that.

"Then I finally got them to accept the miniatures, which weren't exactly miniature size anymore, by the way, just before the first blizzard snowed me in." Iantine flushed. His narrative showed him to be such a ninny.

"So? How'd your contract go then?" Zulaya shot K'vin a knowing look.

"I was a bit wiser. Or so I thought," he said with a grimace, and then told them the clauses he'd insisted on.

"He had you on the drudges' level at Bitra?" Zulaya was appalled. "And you a diploma'd Artist? I would certainly protest about that! There are certain courtesies which most holds, Halls, and Weyrs accord a journeyman of a Craft, and certainly to an Artist!"

"So, when Lord Chalkin finally accepted his portrait, I made tracks away as fast as I could!"

K'vin clapped him on the shoulder, grinning at the fervor with which that statement came out.

"Not that my conditions improved that much," Iantine added quickly, and then grinned, "until P'tero rescued me." His throat kept clogging up and he had to clear it again. "I want to thank you very much for that. I hope I didn't keep him from proper duties."

"No, no," K'vin said. "Mind you, I'm not all that sure why he was over Bitra, but it's as well he was."

"How are your hands?" Zulaya said, looking down at him as he washed his itching fingers together.

"I shouldn't rub the skin, should I?"

Zulaya spoke over her shoulder. "Leopol, get the numbweed for Iantine, please."

The young journeyman hadn't noticed the boy's discreet presence, but he was just as glad he didn't have to walk all the way to his cubicle to get the salve.

"It's just the aftereffects of cold," he said, looking at his fingers, and noticing what Tisha had—pigment under the nails. He curled his fingers, ashamed to be at a Weyr table with dirty hands. And a deep shiver went down his spine.

"I was wondering, Iantine," Zulaya began, "if you'd feel up to doing another portrait or two. The Weyr pays the usual rates, and no extras charged against you."

Iantine protested. "I'd gladly do your portrait, Weyrwoman. It is of yourself you were speaking, isn't it?" That first shiver was followed by another, which he did his best to mask.

"You'll do it only if you are paid a proper fee, young man," Zulaya said sternly.

"But—"

"No buts," K'vin put in. "What with preparations for a Pass, neither Zulaya nor I have had the time to commission proper portraits. However, since you're here . . . and willing?"

"I'm willing, all right, but you don't know my work and I'm only just accredited—"

Zulaya caught his hands in hers, for he'd been wildly gesticulating in both eagerness and an attempt to disguise another spasm.

"Journeyman Iantine, if you managed to do four miniatures, two formal portraits, and refresh murals for Chalkin, you're more than *qualified*. Didn't you know that it took Macartor five months to finish Chalkin's wedding-day scene?"

"And he had to borrow marks from an engineer to pay off the last of his 'debt'?" K'vin added. "Here's Waine to greet you. But you're not to start work again until you're completely recovered from the cold."

"Oh, I'm recovered, I'm recovered," Iantine said, standing up as the Weyrleaders did, determined to control the next set of shiverings.

After they had introduced him to the little man, Waine, they left him, circulating to other tables as the Weyr relaxed. There was singing and guitar playing from one side of the room, cheerful noises, above a general level of easy conversation. That was something else Iantine only now realized had been totally absent at Bitra Hold: music, talk, people relaxing after a day's work.

"Heard you ran afoul a' Chalkin?" Waine said, grinning and ducking his head. Then he brought from behind his back a sheaf of large-sized paper sheets, neatly tied together, and a handful of pencils. "Thought you might need 'em, like," he said shyly. "Heard tell you used up all at Bitra."

"Thank you," Iantine replied, running his fingers appreciatively over the fine sheets and noticing that the pencils were of different weights of carbon. "How much do I owe you?"

Waine laughed, showing gaps in his teeth. "You been at Bitra too long. I've colors, too, but not many. Don't do more'n basics."

"Then let me make you a range of paints," Iantine said gratefully, gritting his teeth against yet another onslaught of ague. "You know where to find the raw stuff around here and I'll show you how I make the tints."

Waine grinned toothlessly again. "That's a right good trade." He held out a hand and nearly crushed Iantine's fingers with his enthusiasm. But he caught the paroxysm of almost uncontrollable shivering that Iantine could not hide.

"Hey, man, you're cold."

"I can't seem to stop shivering, for all that I'm on top of the fire," and Iantine had to surrender to the shaking.

"TISHA!"

Iantine was embarrassed by Waine's bellow for assistance but he didn't resist when he was bundled back into his quarters and the medic summoned while Tisha ordered more furs, hot water bottles, aromatics to be steeped in hot water to make breathing easier. He made no resistance to the medication that was immediately prescribed for him because, by then, his head had started to ache. So did his bones.

The last thing he remembered before he drifted off to an uneasy sleep was what Maranis, the medic, said to Tisha.

"Let's hope they all have it at Bitra for giving it to him."

Much later Leopol told him that Tisha had stayed by his bedside three nights while he burned of the mountain fever he had caught, compounding his illness by exposure on the cold slopes. Maranis felt that the old woodsman might be a carrier for the disease: himself immune but able to transmit the fever.

Iantine was amazed to find his mother there, when he woke from the fever. Her eyes were red with crying and she burst into tears again when she realized he was no longer delirious. Leopol also told him that Tisha had insisted she be sent for when his fever lasted so long.

To Iantine's astonishment, she didn't seem as pleased to receive the transfer fee as he was to give it.

"Your life isn't worth the fee," she told him finally when he was afraid she was displeased with the missing eighth mark he'd had to give the woodsman. "And he nearly killed you for that eighth."

"He's a good lad you have for a son," Tisha said with an edge to her voice, "working that hard to earn money from Chalkin."

"Oh yes," his mother hastily agreed as she suddenly realized she ought to be more grateful. "Though whyever you sought to please that old skinflint is beyond me."

"The fee was right," Iantine said weakly.

"Don't take on so, now, Ian," Tisha said when his mother had to return to the sheephold. "She was far more worried about you than about the marks. Which shows her heart's in the right place. Worry makes people act odd, you know." She patted Iantine's shoulder. "She wanted to take you home and nurse you there, you know," she went on reassuringly. "But couldn't risk your lungs in the cold of *between*. I don't think she liked us taking care of you!" She grinned. "Mothers *never* trust others, you know."

Iantine managed a grin back at Tisha. "I guess that's it."

It was Leopol who restored Iantine's peace of mind.

"You got a real nice mother, you know," he said, sitting on the end of the bed. "Worried herself sick about leaving until P'tero promised to convey her again if you took any turn for the worse. She'd never ridden a dragon before."

Iantine chuckled. "No, I don't think she has. Must have frightened her."

"Not as much," and now Leopol cocked a slightly dirty finger at the journeyman, "as you being so sick she had to be sent for. But she was telling P'tero how happy your father would be to have those marks you earned. Real happy. And she near deafened P'tero, shouting about how she'd always known you'd be a success and to get the whole fee out of Chalkin was quite an achievement."

"She did?" Iantine perked up. His mother had been bragging about him?

"She did indeed," Leopol said, giving an emphatic nod to his head.

Leopol seemed to know a great deal about a lot of matters in the Weyr. He also never seemed to mind being sent on errands as Iantine made a slow convalescence.

Master Domaize paid him a visit, too. And it was Leopol who told the convalescent why the Master had made such a visit.

"That Lord Chalkin sent a complaint to Master Domaize that you had skivved out of the hold without any courtesy and he was seriously considering lodging a demand for the return of some of the fee since you were so obviously very new at your Art, and the fee had been for a seasoned painter, not a young upstart." Leopol grinned at Iantine's furious reaction. "Oh, don't worry. Your Master wasn't born yesterday. M'shall himself brought him to Bitra Hold and they said that there was not a thing wrong with any of the work you'd done for that Lord Chalkin." Leopol cocked his head to one side, regarding Iantine with a calculating look. "Seems like there's a lot of people wanting to sit their portraits with you. Didja know that?"

Iantine shook his head, trying to absorb the injustice of Chalkin's objection. He was speechless with fury. Leopol grinned.

"Don't worry, Iantine. Chalkin's the one should worry, treating you like that. Your Master and the Benden Weyrleader gave out to the Lord Holder about it, too. You're qualified and entitled to all the courtesies of which you got none at Bitra Hold. Good thing you didn't get sick until after Zulaya and K'vin had a chance to hear your side of the story. Not that *anyone* would believe Chalkin, no matter what he says. Did you know that even wherries won't roost in Bitra Hold?"

Convalescence from the lung infection took time and Iantine fretted at his weakness.

"I keep falling asleep," he complained to Tisha one morning when she arrived with his potion. "How long do I have to keep taking this stuff?"

"Until Maranis hears clear lungs in you," she said in her no-nonsense tone. Then she handed him the sketch paper and pencils that Waine had given him his first night in the Weyr. "Get your hand back in. At least doing what you're best at can be done sitting still."

It was good to have paper and pencil again. It was good to look about the Lower Caverns and catch poses, especially when the poser didn't realize he was being sketched. And his eye had not lost its keenness, and if his fingers cramped now and then from weakness, strength gradually returned. He became unaware of the passage of time nor did he notice people coming up behind him to see what he was drawing.

Waine arrived with mortar, pestle, oil, eggs, and cobalt to make a good blue. The man had picked up bits of technique and procedures on his own, but picking things up here and there was no substitute for the concentrated drill that Iantine had had: drills that he once despised but now appreciated when he could see what resulted from the lack of them.

Winter had set in, but on the first day of full sun, Tisha insisted on wrapping him up in a cocoon of furs to sit out in the Bowl for the "good of fresh air." As it was bath time for the dragonets, Iantine was immediately fascinated by their antics and began to appreciate just how much hard work went into their nurture. It was also the first chance he'd ever had of seeing dragonets. He knew the grace and power of the adult dragon and their awesome appearance. Now he saw the weyr-lings as mischievous—even naughty, as one ducked her rider into the lake—and endlessly inventive. None of this last Hatching were ready to fly yet, but some of the previous clutch were beginning to take on adult duties. He had firsthand observation of their not-so-graceful performances.

The next day he saw P'tero and blue Ormonth in the focus of some sort of large class. As he wandered over, he saw that not only the weyrlings from the last three Hatchings were attending, but also all youngsters above the age of twelve. Ormonth had one wing extended and was gazing at it in an abstract fashion, as if he'd never seen it before. The expression was too much for the artist in Iantine and he flipped open his pad and sketched the scene. P'tero noticed, but the class was extremely attentive. What T'dam was saying slowly reached through Iantine's absorption with line and pose.

"Now, records show us that the worst injuries occur on wing

edges, especially if Thread falls in clumps and the partners are not sharp enough to avoid 'em. A dragon can fly with one-third of his exterior sail damaged . . ." and T'dam ran his hand along the edge of Ormonth's wing. "However," and T'dam looked up at Ormonth, "if you would be good enough to close your wing slightly, Ormonth," and the blue did so. "Thank you . . ." T'dam had to stand slightly on tiptoe to reach the area of the inner wing. "Injuries in here are far more serious, as Thread can, depending on the angle of its fall, sear through the wing and into his body. This," and he now ducked under the wing and tapped the side, "is where the lungs are and injury here can even be . . . fatal . . ."

There was a gasp around the semicircle of his students.

"That's why you have to be sharp every instant you're in flight. Go *between* the instant you even *suspect* you've been hit . . ."

"How do we *know*?" someone asked.

"Ha!" T'dam propped his fists on his thick leather belt and paused. "Dragons are very brave creatures for the most part, considering what we ask them to do. But," and he stroked Ormonth in apology, "they have exceedingly quick responses . . . especially to pain. You'll know!" He paused again. "Some of you were here when Missath broke her sail bone, weren't you?" and he pointed around the group until he saw several hands raised. "Remember how she squealed?"

"Went right through me like a bonesaw," a big lad said and shivered convulsively.

"She was squealing the instant she lost her balance and actually before she snapped the bone. She *knew* she would hurt even as she fell. Now, you don't have quite the same immediacy in Threadfall, since you'll be high on adrenaline, but you'll know. So, this brings up a point that we make constantly in all training procedures, *always*, ALWAYS, have a point to go to in your head. During Fall, it had better be the Weyr since everyone here," and now the sweep of his hand included those Iantine recognized as nonriders, "will be ready to help. *Don't* make the mistake of coming in too low. Going *between* will have stopped Thread burrowing farther into your dragon . . ." A muted chorus of disgust and fearfulness greeted that concept. ". . . so you can make as orderly a landing as injuries permit. What you don't need is a bad landing, which could compound the original Thread score. Start encouraging your dragon as soon as you know he's been hit. Of course, you may be hit, too, and I appreciate that, but you're riders and you can certainly control your own pain while seeing to your dragon's. *He's* the important one of you, remember. Without him you don't function as a rider.

"Now, the drill is," and once again he swept his glance around his students, "slather!" He picked up the wide brush from the pail at his feet and began to ply it on Ormonth's wing: water, to judge the way it dripped. The blue regarded the operation with lightly whirling eyes. "Slather, slather, slather," and T'dam emphasized each repetition with a long brush stroke. "You can't put too much numbweed on a dragon's injuries to suit him or her," and he grinned at the female green riders, "and the injury will be numb in exactly three seconds . . . at least the outer area. It does take time to penetrate through the epidermis to what passes for the germinative layer in a dragon's hide. So you may have to convince your dragon that he's not as badly hurt as he or she feels he or she is. Your injured dragon needs all the reassurance you can give him or her . . . No matter how bad you think the injury looks, don't think that at the dragon. Tell him or her what a great brave dragon they are and that the numbweed is working and the pain will go away.

"Now, if a bone has been penetrated . . ."

"Why, you've got P'tero to the life," said an awed voice

softly in Iantine's ear, and he shot a glance at the tall lad standing behind him: M'leng, green Sith's rider, and P'tero's special friend. Iantine had seen the two riders, always together, in the kitchen cavern. "Oooh, is there any chance I could have that corner?" And he tapped the portion that contained P'tero and Ormonth.

M'leng was a handsome young man, with almond-shaped green eyes in an angular face. The light breeze in the Bowl ruffled tight dark brown curls on his head.

"Since I owe P'tero my life, let me make a larger sketch for you . . ."

"Oh, would you?" And a smile animated M'leng's rather solemn face. "Can we settle a price? I've marks enough to do better than Chalkin did you." He reached for his belt pouch.

Iantine tried to demur, pleading he owed P'tero.

" 'Ter was only doing his duty for once," M'leng said with a touch of asperity. "But I really would like a proper portrait of him. You know, what with Threadfall coming and all, I'd want to have something—" M'leng broke off, swallowed, and then reinforced his pleading.

"I've to do a commission for the Weyrleaders," Iantine said.

"Is that the only one?" M'leng seemed surprised. "I'd've thought everyone in the Weyr would be after you . . ."

Iantine grinned. "Tisha hasn't released me from her care yet."

"Oh, her," and M'leng dismissed the headwoman, with a wave of his hand. "She's so fussy at times. But there's nothing wrong with your hand or your eye . . . and that little pose of P'tero, leaning against Ormonth, why, it's him!"

Iantine felt his spirits rise at the compliment, because the sketch of the blue rider was good—better than the false ones he had done at Bitra Hold. He still cringed, remembering how he allowed himself to compromise his standards by contriving such obsequious portrayals. He hoped he would never be in such a position again. M'leng's comment was balm to his psyche.

"I can do better . . ."

"But I like the pose. Can't you just *do* it? I mean," and M'leng looked everywhere but at Iantine, "I'd rather P'tero didn't know . . . I mean . . ."

"Is it to be a surprise for him?"

"No, it's to be for *me*!" And M'leng jabbed his breastbone with his thumb, his manner defiant. "So I'll *have* it . . ."

At such intransigence, Iantine was at a loss, and hastily agreed before M'leng became more emotional. M'leng's eyes filled and he set his mouth in a stubborn line.

"I will, of course, but a sitting would help . . ."

"Oh, I can arrange that, so he still doesn't know. You're always sketching," and that came out almost as an accusation. Iantine, thanks to the lecture he had been overhearing, was considerably more aware of the dangers dragons, and their riders, would shortly face. If M'leng was comforted by having a portrait of his friend, that was the least he could do.

"This very night," M'leng continued, single-minded in his objective, "I'll see we sit close to where you usually do. I'll get him to wear his good tunic so you can paint him at his very best."

"But suppose—" Iantine began, wondering how he could keep P'tero from knowing he was being done.

"You do the portrait," M'leng said, patting Iantine's arm to still his objections. "I'll take care of P'tero," and he added under his breath, "as long as I have him."

That little afterthought made the breath stop in Iantine's throat. Was M'leng so sure that P'tero would die?

"I'll do my best, M'leng, you may be sure of that!"

"Oh, I am," M'leng said, tossing his head up so that the curls fell back from his face. He gave Iantine a wry smile. "I've been watching how you work, you see." He extended a hand soft with the oils riders used to tend their dragons. Iantine took it and was astonished at the strength in the green rider's grip. "Waine said a good miniature—which is what I want," and he patted his breast pocket to show the intended site of the painting, "by a journeyman is priced at four marks. Is that correct?"

Iantine nodded, unable to speak for the lump in his throat. Surely M'leng was dramatizing matters. Or was he? In the background, Iantine could hear T'dam advising his listeners on the types and severity of injuries and the immediate aid to be given to each variety.

What a bizarre, and cruel, lecture to give to the weyrlings! And yet, the thought stopped him, was it not kinder to be truthful now and ease the shock of what could possibly happen?

"This evening?" M'leng said firmly.

"This very evening, M'leng," Iantine said, nodding his head.

When the green rider had left him, it took the journeyman some long moments before he could return to his sketching.

Well, this was one thing he could do as a gift to the Weyr for all the kindnesses to him—he could leave behind a graphic gallery of everyone currently living in Telgar Weyr.

7

FORT HOLD

Classes were also being held that same day in Fort Hold. In the College assembly room, Corey, as Head Medic, was conducting a seminar for healers from all over Pern, who had been flown in for a three-day clinic. This included a first-aid session dealing with both human and dragon injuries. She was assisted by the Fort Weyr medic, N'ran, who had originally studied animal medicine before he inadvertently Impressed brown Galath. Galath was, on this occasion, outside, enjoying the sun, while a green dragon, who was small enough to fit in the Hall, was being used for demonstration purposes much as Ormonth was at Telgar Weyr.

"Now we have been able to duplicate the records of Doctors Tomlinson, Marchane, and Lao, which include some fading photos of actual injuries. Lunch is fortunately sufficiently in the future," she said with a quirky smile. Then her expression turned sober. "The verbal descriptions are worse, but it's necessary to impress on all those who have to deal with ground injuries how incredibly fast," she ticked off one finger, "how horrendous Thread is," another and then with a sigh, "and how quickly we must act to . . ." Her pause was longer now. ". . . to limit suffering."

Murmurs answered her, and she could see that some of the audience had paled. Others looked defiant.

"From what I, and my staff," and she indicated those in the front seats, "have determined, there is little option. The alternative of getting into cold *between* as the dragons can is not available to us . . . Yes?"

"Why not? If that's an alternative . . ."

"For them, not us," she said firmly. "Because all the records emphasize the speed with which Thread . . . consumes organic material. Too swiftly to call a dragon, even if any were available in your locale. A whole cow goes in less than two minutes."

"Why, that's not even time to . . ." a man began, and his voice trailed off.

"Precisely," Corey said. "If a limb is scored, there's the chance it could be amputated before the organism spread over the body . . ."

"Shards! You can't just—" another man began.

"If survival means loss of just a limb, it can be done."

"But only if you're right there . . ."

Corey recognized him as a practitioner in a large hold in Nerat.

"And many of us will be right there," Corey said firmly, "with the groundcrews, sharing their dangers . . . and hopefully saving as many as we can." She managed a wry smile. "Any body of water handy is useful since Thread drowns. Quickly, according to reports. Depending on the site of the injury, water can impede the ingestion long enough for an amputation to be performed. Even a trough is sufficient." She glanced down at her notes. "Thread needs oxygen as well as organic material. It drowns in three seconds."

"What if it's burrowed into flesh?"

"Three seconds. Flesh does not have the free oxygen necessary for Thread life. Ice, too, can retard progress, but that isn't always available, either.

"Let us assume that we have, somehow, halted the organism's progress but we have a bad scoring and/or an amputation. Numbweed, numbweed, numbweed! And bless this planet for inventing something it didn't know we'd need so badly. In the case of an amputation, of course, proceed with standard practices, including cautery. That at least would eliminate any final vestige of Thread. There will be significant trauma so fellis is recommended . . . if the patient is still conscious."

She glanced down at her notes. "Tomlinson and Marchane also indicate that the mortality rate, due to heart failure or stroke, is high in Thread injuries. Lao, who practiced until the end of the First Pass, notes that often patients, who had received slight scores, successfully treated, died from the pathological trauma of being scored. In preparing our groups for this problem, do stress that Threadscore can be successfully treated."

"If we can move fast enough," a man said facetiously.

"That's why it's important for a medic to accompany as many groundcrew teams as possible. And why first-aid procedures must be taught to every hold and hall within your practice. There are only so many of us, but we can teach many what to do and cut down on fatalities.

"And," Corey went on, "we must emphasize that all nonessential personnel are to *stay* safely indoors until groundcrews report the area safe.

"Now, we will go on to dragon injuries since these, too, will occur and those of us on the spot may need to assist the dragon and rider. They will have the one advantage we can't provide—the chance to go *between* and freeze the attacking organism. But the score will be just as painful.

"The larger proportion of draconic injuries are to the wing surfaces ... if you please, Balzith," and she turned to the patient green dragon, who obediently extended her wing as the medic conducted that section of her lecture.

When they had adjourned for lunch, prior to discussing other problems—such as hygiene and sanitation within small and medium holds where the amenities were not as efficient as in the larger population centers—Corey was approached by Joanson of South Boll and Frenkal of Tillek Hold, both senior medics.

"Corey, what is your position on ... mercy?" asked Joanson in a very thoughtful tone.

She regarded the tall man for a long moment. "What it has always been, Joanson. We have, as you realize, quite a few persons in this audience who have not received full medical training. I cannot ask them to do what I would find very, very difficult to do: administer mercy." She gave Joanson a long stare, then glanced at Frenkal, who seemed to enjoy the ethical spot she was in.

"We are sworn to preserve life. We are also sworn to maintain a decent quality of life for those under our care." She felt her lips twitch, remembering that there were occasions when those two aims were in conflict. "We must, each of us, reflect on how we will face such a desperate situation: whether to cut short a final agony is necessary, even ethical. I don't think there will be much time to consider morals, ethics, kind or cruel, at the time we are forced to take ... action." She paused, took a deep breath. "I do remember seeing the tapes the Infirmary used to have, showing very graphically an animal being eaten alive by Thread . . ." She noticed Joanson's wince. "Yes, eaten alive because Thread caught the hind end of it. I think, if it was someone you knew, you'd opt for . . . the quickest possible end to *that*."

Since they were not the only two who approached her on that subject, she was almost glad when the lunch break ended and she could address the less vexatious matter of amputation. Everyone needed a refresher on that procedure, especially an emergency type of procedure when there might not be the time for all the preliminaries that made for a neat stump. She did have the new bonecutters—well, more axes than the traditional surgical tool—for distribution afterward. Kalvi had brought them with him.

"Best edge we've ever been able to make on a surgical tool, Corey," he told her with some pride. "Had them tested at the abattoir. Cut through flesh and bone like going through cheese. Gotta keep 'em honed, though. And I've made cases for the blades so no one slices off a finger by mistake."

Surgeons were not the only ones with a ghoulish sense of humor, Corey decided.

Meanwhile, in the Great Hall of Fort Hold, with Lord Paulin seated in the front row, Kalvi himself was demonstrating to those who would form the Fort groundcrews how to use and service the HNO_3 cylinders, taking his audience from assembly of the parts and then a quick rundown of common problems likely to be encountered in the field. Every small holder within Fort's authority was present: many had brought their elder children. All had come on foot, their own or a horse's. Fort Weyr, like the other five, was beginning to restrict dragon rides. Lord Paulin understood and approved.

"We've had it far too easy, using the dragons the way our ancestors would have used the sleds and airborne vehicles," he was heard to say when one of his holders had complained that he had been denied his right to a dragonride. "We haven't been breeding horses just to run races, you know. And the dragon-riders have been far too accommodating. Do us all good to walk or ride. You have, of course, extended your beast holds to shelter all your livestock?"

There had been moaning over that necessity, too, with complaints that the engineers should really have spent more time trying to replicate the marvelous rock-cutting equipment with which their ancestors had wrested living quarters out of cliffsides.

Kalvi had come in for considerable harangue over that, which he shrugged off.

"We have a list of priorities: that's not one. Nor could be. We still have two sleds in the North but no power to run 'em. Never did find out what they used," he said. "No way of duplicating such power packs, either, or I'm sure our ancestors would have. Otherwise why did they engineer the dragons? Anyway, renewable resources make more sense than erudite or exotic imports."

When the main lecture was concluded, everyone was told to reassemble after the noon meal for target practice. This was vastly more interesting than having to listen to Kalvi waffle on about how to adjust the wands of the HNO_3 throwers to give a long, narrow tongue of fire or a broader, shorter flame. Or how to clear the nozzle of clogged matter.

"You've got almost as much variation in flame as a dragon has . . ." Kalvi said as he slung the tanks to his back, his voice slightly muffled by his safety gear. "You, there, the hard hat has a purpose. Put it on your head! Lower the face screen!"

The offender immediately complied, Kalvi scowling at him.

"The effective range of this equipment is six meters on the narrowest setting, two on the broader. You wouldn't want it to get closer to you." He was fiddling with his wand. "Damn thing's stubborn . . ." He took out a screwdriver and made a slight adjustment. *"Always . . ."* he said loudly and firmly as he held the wand away from his body, "keep the nozzle of the wand pointed away from *you* and anyone in your immediate vicinity. We're flaming Thread, not folks. *Never . . .* never . . . engage the flow of the two gases without looking in what direction the wand is pointing. You can also burn, scorch, sear things without meaning to. *Can't you,* Laland?" he said, aiming his remark at one of his journeymen.

The man grinned and shifted his feet nervously, looking anywhere but at his Master.

"Now, signal the topside crews, will you, Paulin?" Kalvi said, setting himself firmly on both feet and aiming the wand up.

Paulin waved a red kerchief and suddenly a tangle of "something" catapulted off the cliff, startling everyone in the crowd behind Kalvi. Those with wands raised them defensively and others gasped as the tangle separated into long silver strands, some fine, some thick and falling at slightly different rates. As soon as they were within range, Kalvi activated his flamethrower.

There was a brief second when the fire seemed to pause on the ends of the launched strands before the flame raced along the material and consumed it so that only bits of smoking char reached the ground . . . and the rock that had been tied to the leading edge. There was a roar of approval and great applause.

"Not bad," Paulin said, grinning as he noted the new alertness in the crowd.

"Well, we tried for the effect we just delivered," Kalvi said, turning off both tanks. "Used a retardant on the rope, too. Had plenty of description of how Thread falls, and this is as near as we can get.

"Now," and he turned back to his students, "it's best to get Thread before it gets you or to the ground. We know there are two kinds: the ones that eat themselves dead—they're not a problem, even if they are in the majority and messy. Records tell us that the second kind find something in what they ingest that allows them to progress to the second step of their life-cycle: our ancestors could never do much with investigating this type. They only knew that it existed. We know it existed, too, because there are areas here in the North which are still sterile two-hundred-odd years since the last fall. If this type gets the nourishment it needs, above and beyond organic materials, then it can propagate, or divide or whatever it is Thread does. This is what we needed groundcrews for. This is the type we don't want hanging around and burrowing out of sight. Our ancestors thought Thread had to have some trace minerals or elements in the dirt, but as they never figured out what, we're not likely to now." Kalvi heaved a sigh of regret. "So," and with a wide sweep of his arm, "we incinerate all the buggers the dragonriders miss."

He paused and looked up the cliffside where the catapult crews were waiting.

"OKAY UP THERE?" he yelled, hands bracketing his mouth. Immediately in response, red flags were waved at intervals along the cliff.

"All right, in groups of five, range yourself parallel to the red flags you now see. When we're all in place—and out of range of anyone's wand," and Kalvi gave a wry grin, "I'll give the signal and we'll see how you manage."

The results were somewhat erratic: some men seemed to get the hang of their equipment immediately, while others couldn't even get the right mix on the gases to produce flame.

"Well, it happens," Kalvi said in patient resignation. "Should make 'em climb the thread back up the cliff . . ." he added.

"Do 'em good."

"Take too much time. THROW DOWN THE NETS," Kalvi roared, and then grinned at Paulin. "Thought we'd have some trouble. We'll get our mock Threads back up and in use."

"How much did you bring?"

"Yards," was all Kalvi said with another grin.

By the time the short winter afternoon was closing into darkness, all the holders had had a chance to "sear" Thread, despite hiccups and misses. The mock Thread supply ran out before they lost interest in the practice.

"Now I don't want you to overdo it on your own," Paulin said to those nearest him as they walked back to the hold. The practice area had been some distance up the North Road from Fort Hold, where there were neither beasts nor cotholds that could be affected. "HNO_3 isn't all that hard to manufacture, but the equipment is. Don't wear it out before it's needed."

During their practice, the main Hall had been rearranged for the evening meal, and the trainees were as hungry as gatherers.

"Tomorrow we'll clean the gear," Kalvi announced while klah was being served, "and you'll strip down and reassemble the units so I'm sure you know what you're doing. The man who does it fastest and best will get Lord Paulin's reward."

A loud cheer resounded through the Hall.

"Morale's good," Paulin said to Kalvi, who nodded, well satisfied with the way this first instruction session had gone.

If all of those meetings planned for the head engineer at the other major holds went as smoothly, Kalvi thought he might even get a chance for a few days off to fish in Istan waters. In the frantic search during the run-up to the Second Pass for materials long left in storage, some reels of stout nylon fishing line had been found. The bar-coding on the carton had been damaged, so there was no way of knowing how long ago the line had been manufactured, but Kalvi was eager to put it to the test with some of the big 'uns that swam in the tropical waters. This sort of synthetic material was extremely durable and would certainly take the weight of packfish, which was sometimes substantial.

A third group made up of teachers—novices and experienced—were gathered in the College's spacious refectory. Today this convocation had the happier task of learning and rehearsing the new ballads that were to be used in teaching the young. On the second day the Fort Weyrleader would instruct the peripatetic teachers on how best to shelter themselves if they should be caught out during Threadfall. Clisser had been inundated with complaints that the Weyrs were restricting rides that had been the accustomed mode of transport. Not all the teachers were familiar with nor competent enough to ride the sturdy horses that were bred for long-distance and mountain travel. He was going to have to reassign a lot of his older teachers, yet another headache.

But for this three-day period at least, the emphasis would be on the music and the new curriculum. Not that he hadn't had contentious reactions to *that*. He was beginning to think that Bethany had been right when she suggested that they, like the First Settlers, had relied too heavily on easy access to information. Oddly enough, some of the older teachers loudly approved the new curriculum.

"High time we brought things up to date, with relevance to the life we're leading here, not what folks had *there*," Layrence of Tillek said, "stuff we'll never have so what's the point of quizzing them on it?"

"But we have traditions we must uphold," Sallisha said, her brow creased in a frown. Which made Clisser realize once again that her reputation for being a "right wagon" was not without merit. "Traditions which they must understand to appreciate what we have . . ."

"Oh, Sallisha," and Bethany smiled in her soothing way, "we're incorporating all those traditions in the Ballads but *stressing* what they need to understand of the life they have here."

"But our glorious past—" Sallisha began.

"*Is* past," Sheledon said forcefully, scowling right back at her. "*All* past, *all* gone, and why dwell on contacts our ancestors severed for their own good reasons?"

"But . . . but . . . they should *know* . . ." Sallisha began again.

"If they wish to know more, they can read it," Sheledon said, "for advanced study. Right now, they have to cope with the problem of Threadfall . . ."

"And *that's* far more important than which planets outlasted the Nathi bombardments and who was World Leader in 2089," Shulse said. "Or how to plot a parabolic course around a primary."

Sallisha glared implacably at the maths teacher.

"Of course," Shulse went on, "I do approve of mentioning such history where it pertains to Emily Boll as governor, or Paul Benden as admiral of the fleet, because *they* are part and parcel of *Pernese* history."

"But you have to show students the overall picture . . ." Sallisha was persistence itself.

"And some students will be vitally interested, I'm sure," Shulse said, "but I agree with Clisser that we have to streamline the material to be studied to the point where it has relevance to *this* world and *our* civilization."

"Civilization?" Sallisha said at her most scornful.

"What? You don't call what we've made here 'civilized'?" Sheledon loved to tease the literal-minded Sallisha.

"Not in terms of what our ancestors had."

"And all that went with a high-tech society—like prepubescent addicts, city gangs, wild plagues, so much tech fraud that people were stuffing credits in their mattresses to protect their income, the—"

"Spare me," Sallisha said contemptuously, "and concentrate on the good that was done . . ."

Sheledon gave a chuckle. "D'you know how dangerous it was to be a teacher on old Earth?"

"Nonsense, our civilization," and she emphasized the word, "revered professors and instructors on every level."

"Only after they were allowed classroom discipline—" Sheledon began.

"And the use of stunners," Shulse added.

"That is not a problem on Pern," Sallisha said loftily.

"And we'll keep it that way," Clisser said firmly, "by adjusting what interests our classes and dispensing with irrelevancies."

Sallisha whirled on Clisser. "What *you* decide is relevant?"

Clisser pointed to the files along one wall of the library in which they were talking. "I sent out questionnaires to every teacher on the rolls, and to holders, major and minor, asking for input. I got it, and this curriculum," he lifted the thick volume, "is the result. You've all received copies. And the Teaching Ballads will be part of the package you receive during the conference."

Sallisha retired with poor grace, sulking as obviously as any intractable student would. He wondered if she saw the resemblance in attitude. Sallisha was, however, a very good teacher, able to impart knowledge at the level needed, and was therefore supervisor of southeastern Pern. But she had her little quirks—like everyone else in the world.

Making the children memorize the Teaching Ballads would improve their retention of words: a skill that Clisser realized he had lost with his dependence on technology. But then, one of the reasons the colonists had come to Pern with its limited resources was to revert to a society that was not so dependent on technology. He read accounts of persons who never left their home place, contacting others only by electronics, living as eremites. Not so much out of fear of the outside world, as out of indolence. No one could be indolent on Pern, Clisser told himself, and smiled. What a wasted life to remain in one place all one's days! Well, perhaps here on Pern events—like Threadfall—had forced them a little lower on the technological scale than the Settlers had anticipated, but they had adapted to Pern and were adapting it to their own use. And would meet the menace with a fully developed, renewable air defense force.

He hoped . . . Clisser sucked in his breath in a sort of reverse whistle. Everyone on the planet—with one notable exception—were girding their loins and securing their premises against that attack. Preparing was one thing, but enduring fifty years of an aerial attack was another. Briefly he reviewed the accounts published by the besieged colonists on Sirus III and Vega IV when the Nathi started bombarding the planets. Day after day, according to the history tapes, the worlds had been shelled with dirty missiles, rendering the surface uninhabitable. Whole generations had grown up on colonial planets, living in deep shelters . . . Clisser smiled to himself—not much different from the cave holds in which the Pernese now lived. And indeed those accommodations had benefited by the Sirian and Vegan experiences—using the magma core taps to provide heat, and solar panels for power. Humans had survived, under far worse conditions than pertained on this planet. At least on Pern you knew when and where Thread would fall and could mount effective defenses. And yet, the scale of Threadfall was awesome and failure had appalling consequences.

Failure usually did.

Therefore, Clisser hoped the music that had been composed as psychologically uplifting would have the desired effect: developing the morale and encouraging the effort. Briefly he wondered what would have happened on old Earth, during the National period, if there'd been a common extraterrestrial enemy to unite the diverse races.

Jemmy and Sheledon had certainly written some stirring music, martial as well as hopeful. Some of the less ambitious tunes had a tendency to stay with you so that you woke up in the morning whistling one or hearing it in your head: the mark of a good melody, to Clisser's way of thinking. And they had scored the music for various solo instruments or combinations of those readily available, so that even inexperienced players in the most isolated hold or hall would be able to accompany singers.

Jemmy's riddling song was a delight. Clisser hadn't quite got all the answers yet, but it would prove useful during the hours of Fall to distract folk from what was happening outside. Bethany's lament—the first song she had ever composed—was next on the program, and he settled back to listen to it.

But his mind, working overtime in anxiety over the success of his new program, refused to be caught up in the music. Among other things, *what* was he going to do about Bitra Hold? The last teacher he'd sent there had left, voiding his contract with Chalkin—not that Clisser blamed Issony when he'd heard the way the man had been humiliated and threatened by unruly Holder children—but children *had* to receive rudimentary education. You couldn't afford to let one whole province lapse into illiteracy.

To be sure, children learn at different rates: he knew that, and learning should be made as interesting as possible, to lay the foundations for further study, and for life itself for that matter. That was the purpose of education: to develop the skills required to solve problems. And to utilize the potential that existed in everyone—even a Bitran, he added sourly.

Maybe he should reappoint Sallisha to that area. Then he chuckled. Not much chance of that. She had enough seniority to refuse point-blank.

He made up his mind then, with the lovely phrases of Bethany's song soothing him, to bring the problem of Chalkin, Lord Holder of Bitra, up in the next Conclave. Something *had* to be done about the man.

D uring the final evening meal in which all three groups joined up on the Fort court for a dinner featuring three whole roasted steers, Clisser heard Chalkin's name come up and homed in on the group discussing the man.

"That's not all," M'shall was saying, a deep frown on his usually amiable face. "He's put up guards at the borders, and anyone who wants to leave can take only their clothes with them. Nothing else, not even the animals which they may have raised themselves."

Clisser had not realized that the Benden Weyrleader had arrived, but his presence was certainly fortuitous.

"You're speaking of Chalkin?" he asked when the others acknowledged his presence and made room for him in their circle.

M'shall gave a scornful laugh. "Who else would turn folks out of their holds right now?"

"I've just heard from one of my traveling teachers, Issony, and he's quit and nothing would persuade him to go back to Bitra. But even they have to grow up literate."

"Ha!" M'shall's scoffing was echoed by the others.

"School hours keep Bitrans from other jobs which earn their holder more marks. What did he do to Issony?"

"He'll give you chapter and verse if you ask him. In fact, it would do him good. I understand one of your riders rescued him."

"We do a lot of rescue work in Bitra," M'shall said, not at all pleased by the necessity. "But only non-Bitrans," he added.

"Now, look," and Bridgely seemed about to explode, "I will *not* succor all his refugees. And I will *not* lift a hand to help him when his hold is overrun by Thread."

"Ah," and M'shall raised one finger in a sardonic gesture, "but you see, he doesn't *believe* Thread's coming."

"Wouldn't we feel silly if he was right after all," said Farley, one of the other minor Fort holders. "Oops, wrong thing to say," he added when coldly repressive stares rejected his witticism.

"Chalkin has always been contrary by nature," Clisser said. "But never such an outright fool."

"Well, he's exceeded even 'damned fool,' " Bridgely said. "Is your teacher, Issony, here now? Well, then, bring him up to Fort. We're about to do something definitive about Chalkin."

"Right now?" and Clisser couldn't help looking over at the roasting carcasses and sniffing at the succulent odors they were producing.

"I expect to eat, too," Bridgely said, relenting.

"I just finished eating at Benden," M'shall said, but his nose was twitching at the aromas. "Ah, well, we could have a slice to allow you to enjoy your meal."

"Timed it just right, didn't you?" Farley said, with a grin for their obvious interest in the roasting meats. "*Can* something be done about an irresponsible Lord Holder?"

"Read your copy of the Charter, Farley," Clisser said.

"And how long have border guards . . ." Paulin paused, made indignant by such a measure. ". . . been in place?" He'd assembled those concerned in his office at the hold when they'd finished eating. Issony was on call if his testimony was required.

"As near as we can figure out, about seven days," M'shall said. "As you know, we've been canvassing all the holds, to see who, if any, of Chalkin's people has been told about the imminence of Thread."

"Surely they'd have heard that much at Gathers—" Paulin began.

"Ha!" Bridgely said. "Very few of his folk hear where or when Gathers are being held, much less attend them."

"That isn't right," Paulin said, shaking his head.

"Frankly, Paulin, I'd say his tithing of them is punitive. None of them ever seem to have a mark to spend even when they do bring work to sell at a Benden Gather. Not that they're encouraged to travel at all."

"Even to Gathers?" Paulin answered his own query. "No, he wouldn't encourage them, would he?"

"Not if he's afraid they'll compare conditions in another hold. Also he doesn't like Bitran marks to go past his borders."

"And gets every one those high rollers have when they attend those friendly little games he runs," M'shall said.

"I must confess I hadn't known how restrictive he is," Paulin said in a very thoughtful tone of voice.

"Well, how would you?" Bridgely replied, absolving him. "You're West Coast. We know because we see so few Bitrans at East Coast Gathers. Oh, his gamesters attend every one . . ."

"Hmm, yes, they're ubiquitous, you might say," Paulin murmured under his breath. "So, if he's had to close the borders, it would appear that some holders panicked when they learned Threadfall is indeed expected?"

"Indeed," Bridgely said with a grim expression, "and when a delegation got the nerve to approach him, he had them beaten out of the hold. I saw the lash marks so I know they aren't lying. They said they'd never seen him in such a temper. He announced that the dragonriders are trying to get extra tithing on false pretenses by spreading such rumors. He was also quite damning about the new mine being opened above Ruatha when good Bitrans could have worked the Steng Valley ones."

"The world is against Bitrans?" Paulin asked in a droll tone.

"You got it," M'shall said.

"Chalkin also refused to accept delivery of HNO_3 tanks . . ." Kalvi said.

"Wouldn't pay for them, you mean," M'shall said. "That's what Telgar riders told mine."

"Either way, there'll be no groundcrews. I think he's gone far enough to warrant impeachment," Paulin said with slow deliberation. "As a Lord Holder, it's his duty to inform, and prepare his folk, for Threadfall. That's why the Holder system was adopted: to give people a strong leader to supply direction during a Fall and to provide emergency assistance. By closing his borders, he's also abrogated one of the basic tenets vouchsafed in the Charter: freedom of movement. He's turned autonomy into despotism. I'll send all Lord Holders and Professional Heads particulars . . . Oh," and he glanced at Clisser in dismay, "we can't make quick copies anymore, can we?"

"One dragonrider could contact all the other Lord Holders," M'shall said. "Or one messenger on this coast and another on ours. That makes only two copies needed."

"I'll request a rider from S'nan," Paulin said, reaching for a pad.

"That'll please S'nan no end," M'shall said. "He's not been

the least bit pleased with Chalkin's defiance. Simply isn't done, you know," and M'shall grinned as he mimicked S'nan's rather prim tones.

"We must take action against Chalkin now," Paulin said, "rather than leave it until the next formal Conclave at Turn's End. Time's running out." Then Paulin turned to Clisser. "Which reminds me. Clisser, any luck on finding some method of irrefutably determining the return of Thread?"

Clisser jerked himself into alertness. "We've several possibilities," he said, trying to sound more positive than he was. "What with the loss of computer access, it's taking longer to sift through ways and means."

"Well, keep at it . . ." and then Paulin touched Clisser's shoulder and smiled, "along with everything else you're doing. By the way, the teaching songs are very good indeed." Then he put a finger in his ear, drilling it briefly as he grinned more broadly. "The kids sing 'em all the time, not just in class."

"That's what we intended," Clisser said with droll satisfaction. "Shall I wait for your message?"

"No need for that, my friend, but thanks for offering. This I will take pleasure in penning." Fort's Lord Holder grinned. "And I'll remember to keep a copy for the Archives. By the way, wasn't there some ancient way of making copies . . . something that would transfer the writing to the next page under?"

Clisser bowed his head briefly in thought. "Carbon copying, I think you mean. We don't have it, but Lady Salda might have some ideas. We've got to figure a way to make multiple copies or spend hours copying." He gave a heavy sigh of regret.

"I'll leave it to you then, Clisser," said Paulin. "Thank you all. Now get out of here, the lot of you," and he grinned at the Benden leaders and Kalvi, "and enjoy the rest of the evening while I get on with this task. Not that I won't enjoy it in some respects," he said, picking up his pen and examining the tip.

At that polite dismissal, they all filed out of the office. Clisser thought that Issony looked disappointed at not being able to recite his catalog of complaints against Lord Chalkin. So Clisser made sure that Issony had as much of the good wine as he wanted.

8

▼▼▼▼▼▼▼▼▼

TELGAR WEYR

Iantine asked to be allowed out again on the next sunny day, so he was in the Bowl when the traveling traders arrived. The entire complement of the caverns flocked out to greet them. Iantine furiously sketched the big dusty carts with their multiple teams of the heavy-duty ox-types which had been bred for such work. They had been one of the last bio-engineering feats from Wind Blossom, whose grandmother had done such notable work creating the dragons of Pern.

Iantine had seen traders come and go on their routes since childhood and fondly remembered the stellar occasions when the Benden trading group had arrived at their rather remote sheephold. More specifically, he recalled the taste of the boiled sweets, flavored by the fruits that grew so abundantly in Nerat, which the traders passed out by the handful. Once, there'd been fresh citrus, a treat of unsurpassed delight to himself and his siblings.

For a remote holding, having travelers drop by was almost as good as a Gather. To Iantine's surprise, Weyrfolk were equally delighted. Despite the fact they could usually find a dragon to convey them wherever they wanted to go, the arrival of the traders was even better than tithe trains. (The tithe wagons were a different matter, since everyone had to pitch in to store the produce given to the support of the Weyr.) And traders brought the news of all the holds and halls along the way. There were as many clusters of folks just talking, Iantine noticed, as examining goods in the stalls the Liliencamp traders set up. Tables and chairs were brought out from the kitchen cavern: klah and the day's fresh bread and rolls were being served.

Leopol, always on hand for Iantine, brought over a mid-morning snack and hunkered down to give the journeyman the latest news.

"They've been setting up sheltered halts," he said between bits of his own sweet roll, "along the road to here. They won't stop doing their routes just because Thread's coming. But they gotta prepare for it. Half of what they got on those big wagons right now is materials for safe havens. 'Course, they can use what caves there are, but no more camping out in the open. That's going to cramp their style," and he grinned broadly. "But if ya gotta, ya gotta. See," and one honey-stained finger pointed to a group of men and women seated with the two Weyrleaders. They were all hunched over maps spread out on the table. "They're checking the sites over so's everyone here'll know where they might be if they're caught out in a Fall."

"Who trades through Bitra?" Iantine asked with considerable irony.

Leopol snorted. "No one in their right mind. 'Specially now. Didja hear that Chalkin's closed his borders to keep his own people in? Didja know that Chalkin doesn't believe Thread's coming?" The boy's eyes widened in horrified dismay at such irreverence. "And he never told his holders it is?"

"Actually, I got that distinct impression while I was there," Iantine said, "more from what wasn't said and done than what was. I mean, even Hall Domaize was stocking food and supplies against Threadfall. They'd talk enough about odds and wagers at Bitra, but not a word about Thread."

"Did they sucker you into any gaming?" Leopol's avid expression suggested he yearned for a positive answer.

Iantine shook his head and grinned at his eager listener. "In the first place, I'd been warned. Isn't everyone warned about Bitrans at Gathers? And then, I didn't have any spare marks to wager."

"Otherwise you'd have lost your commission fer fair," Leopol murmured, his eyes still round with his unvoiced speculations of the disaster Iantine had avoided.

"I'd say Chalkin's gambling in the wrong game if he thinks ignoring Thread will make it not happen," Iantine said. "Shelters are going to have to be huge," he added, gesturing toward the solid beasts who were being led to the lake to drink.

Either the great beasts were accustomed to dragonets, or they were so phlegmatic they didn't care. However, the dragonets had never seen *them* before in their short lives, so they reacted with alarm at the massive cart beasts, squealing with such fright that dragons, sleeping in the pale wintry sun on their weyr ledges, woke up to see what the fuss was about. Iantine grinned. He did a rapid sketch of that in a corner of the page. At the rate he was going, he'd use up even this generous supply of paper.

"Well, they've had to use a lot of sheet roofing, I know," Leopol said. "The Weyr contributes, too, ya know, since the Liliencamps have to detour to get up to us."

Iantine had never given any thought to the support system required to serve a Weyr and its dragons. He had always assumed that dragons and riders took care of themselves from tithings, but he was acquiring a great respect for the organization and management of such a facility. In a direct contrast with what he had seen at Bitra, everyone in the Weyr worked cheerfully at any task set them and took great pride in being part of it. Everyone helped everyone else: everyone seemed happy.

To be sure, Iantine had recently realized that his early childhood had been relatively carefree and happy. His learning years at the College had also been good as well as productive: his apprenticeship to Hall Domaize had proceeded with only occasional ups and downs as he struggled to perfect new techniques and a full understanding of Art.

Bitra Hold had been an eye-opener. So, of course, was the Weyr, but in a far more positive manner. Grimly, Iantine realized that one had to know the bad to properly appreciate the good. He smiled wryly to himself while his right hand now rapidly completed the sketch of the Weyrleaders in earnest collaboration with the Liliencamp trail bosses.

That Bloodline had been the first of the peripatetic traders, bringing goods and delivering less urgent messages on their way from one isolated hold to another. A Liliencamp had been one of the more prominent First Settlers. Iantine thought he'd been portrayed in the great mural in Fort Hold, with the other Charterers: a smallish man with black hair, depicted with sharp eyes and a pad of some sort depending from his belt, and—Iantine had of course noted them—several writing implements stuffed in his chest pocket, and one behind his ear. It had seemed such a logical place to store a pencil that Iantine had taken to the habit himself.

He peered more closely at the trail bosses. Yes, one of them had what looked like a pencil perched behind one ear—and he also had an empty pouch at his belt: one that probably accommodated the pad on the table before him.

But even with such wayside precautions, would such traders be able to continue throughout the fifty dangerous years of a Pass? It was one thing to *plan*, and quite another, as Iantine had only just discovered, to put plans into operation. Still, considerable hardship would result in transporting items from Hall to hold to Weyr during Threadfall, especially since dragons would be wholly involved in protecting the land from Thread. They could not be asked to perform trivial duties. Dragons were not, after all, a transportation facility. They had been bioengineered as a defensive force: conveying people and goods was only an Interval occupation.

He wondered if the traders had any paper in their great wagons. Not that he had even a quarter mark left in his pouch. But maybe they'd take a sketch or two in trade.

As quick as he neatly could, he filled his last empty page with a montage: the train entering the Weyr Bowl, people rushing out to meet it, the goods being exhibited, deals being made, with the central portion the scene of the trail bosses discussing shelters with the Weyrleaders. He held the pad at arm's length and regarded it critically.

"That's marvelous," a voice said behind him, and he twisted about in surprise. "Why, you did it in a flash!"

The green rider, her dragon lounging beside her, smiled self-consciously, her green eyes shining with something akin to awe. Leopol had pointed this new rider out to him the other day and related the circumstances of her precipitous arrival at the Hatching.

"Debera?" he asked, remembering the name. She gasped, recoiling from him in her startlement. Her dragon came immediately alert, her eyes twirling faster with alarm. "Oh say, I didn't mean to—"

"Easy, Morath, he means me no harm," she said to the dragon and then smiled reassuringly up at him. "I was just surprised you'd know my name . . ."

"Leopol," and Iantine pointed his pencil to where the boy stood in earnest bargaining with a trader lad about the same age, "used to tell me everything that happened in the Weyr while I was recovering."

"Oh, yes," and the girl seemed to relax, and even managed a wider smile, "I know him. He's into everything. But kind-hearted," she added hastily, glancing up at Iantine. "You've had some adventures, too, or so Leopol told me." Then she indicated his sketch. "You did that so well and so quickly. Why, you can almost hear them bargaining," she added, pointing to the trader with his mouth open.

Iantine regarded it critically. "Well, speed is not necessarily a good thing if you want to do good work." He deftly added a fold to the head trader's tunic, where he now saw there was a bulge over the belt. "Let's see if the subject likes it." He was amazed to hear the edge in his voice. She glanced warily up at him.

"If that's what you can do quickly," she said reassuringly, "I'd like to see what you do when you take your time."

He couldn't resist, and flipped over pages to where he had made a sketch of her oiling Morath.

"Oh, and I didn't see you doing this . . ." She reached out to touch it, but he was flipping to the page where he had sketched her and Morath listening to T'dam at the lecture. She'd had one arm draped over her dragon's neck, and he thought he had captured the subtle bond that prompted the embrace.

"Oh, that's marvelous," and Iantine was amazed to see tears in her eyes. In a spontaneous gesture, she clung to his arm, feasting her eyes on the drawing and preventing him from turning the page over. "Oh, how I'd—"

"You like it?"

"Oh, I do," and she snatched her hands away from his arm and clasped them behind her back, blushing deeply. "I do . . ." and bit her lip, swaying nervously.

"What's the matter?"

She gave an embarrassed laugh. "I haven't so much as the shaving of a mark."

He tore the sketch out of the pad and handed it to her.

"Oh, I couldn't ... I couldn't," and she stepped back, although the look in her eyes told Iantine how much she wanted it.

"Why not?" He pressed the paper against her, pushing it at her when she continued to resist. "Please, Debera? I've had to get my hand back in after my fingers freezing, and it's only a sketch."

She glanced up at him, nervously and with some other fear lurking in the shadows of her lovely green eyes.

"You should have it, you know, to remind you of Morath at this age."

One hand crept from behind her back and reached for the sheet. "You're very good, Iantine," she murmured and held the sketch by fingertips as if afraid she'd soil it. "But I've nothing to pay ..."

"Yes, you do," he said quickly with sudden inspiration and gestured toward the traders still in their group about the table. "You can be a satisfied customer and help me wheedle another pad out of the traders in return for this drawing of them."

"Oh, but ..." She had shot a quick, frightened glance at the traders, and then, in as quick a change of mood, gave herself a shake, her free hand going to her dragon's head, as if seeking reassurance. The dragonet turned adoring eyes to her, and Debera's eyes briefly unfocused, the way Iantine had noticed in riders who paused to talk to their dragons. She let out a breath and faced him resolutely. "I would be glad to say a good word for you with Master Jol. He's by way of being a cousin of my mother's."

"Is he now?" Iantine said with fervor. "Then let us see if kinship is useful in trading."

"I can't, of course, promise anything," she said candidly as they moved toward the group. She found it hard to keep the sketch from fluttering. "Oh dear."

"Roll it up," he suggested. "Shall I do it for you?"

"No, thank you, I can manage." And she did, making a much tighter job of it than he would.

The conference was ending as they approached and the participants began to separate.

"Master Jol?" Debera said, her voice cracking a bit and not reaching very far. "Master Jol," she said, projecting a firmer tone. Iantine wondered if she was afraid the trader wouldn't recognize her at all.

"Is that Debera?" the trader said, peering at her as though he didn't believe his eyes. Then a broad smile of recollection covered his face and he strode rapidly across the distance between them, hands extended. Debera seemed to shy from such a warm welcome. "My dear, I'd heard that you'd Impressed a dragon."

Iantine put a reassuring hand at her waist and gave her an imperceptible forward push.

"Yes, this is Morath," and suddenly her manner became sure and proud. Dragon and rider exchanged one of those melting looks that Iantine found incredibly touching.

"Well, well, my greetings to you, young Morath," he said, bowing formally to the dragonet, whose eyes began to whirl faster.

Debera gave her a reassuring little pat. "Master Jol is my mother's cousin," she explained to Morath.

"Which makes me yours as well, my lass," Jol reminded her. "And very proud to have dragonrider kin. Ah, you're so like your mother. Did you know that?"

Iantine watched as Debera's expression turned sad.

"Ah, now, I didn't mean to grieve you, child," Jol said with instant dismay. "And how happy she would be to see you . . ."

He paused and cleared his throat, and Iantine knew the trader was hastily amending what he had started to say. ". . . here, a dragonrider . . ."

"And out of my father's control," Debera finished with droll bitterness. "Had you heard that, too, Master Jol?"

"Oh indeed," Master Jol said, grinning even more broadly, his eyes twinkling with a slight hint of malice. "I was right pleased to hear that, indeed and I was. Now, what can I do for you? Some Gather clothes, good lined boots . . . you'll have come with little if I know your father."

Such plain speaking momentarily made Debera uneasy, but her dragonet crowded reassuringly against her.

"The Weyr has furnished me with everything I need, Master Jol," she replied with quiet dignity.

"Master? Am I not cousin to you, young woman?" Jol said with mock severity.

Now her smile returned. "Cousin, but I thank you, though I do have a favor to ask . . ."

"And what might that be?"

Debera flipped open her sketch and showed it to the trader. "Iantine here did this of me, and he has one of you . . ." On cue, Iantine offered his sketch pad, open to the montage. "Only Iantine's used up his pad and, like me, hasn't a sliver to spend."

Master Jol reached for the pad, his manner altering instantly to a trader's critical appraisal. But he had only cast an eye over the sketch when he paused, peering more closely at the artist.

"Iantine, you said?" And when both Debera and Iantine nodded, his smile quirked the line of his generous mouth. "I place the name now. You're the lad who managed to escape unscathed from Chalkin's clutches." Jol offered his free hand to Iantine. "Well done, lad. I'd had wind of your adventure." He winked, his expression approving. "But then we traders hear everything and learn to sift the fine thread of truth from the chaff of gossip."

Then he turned back to the sketch, examining it carefully, nodding his head as his eyes went from one panel to the next. He gave an amused sniff as he took a longer look at himself, pencil cocked behind his ear.

"You've got me to the life, pencil and all," and he touched the tool to be sure it was in place. "May I?" he asked courteously, indicating a desire to look at the other pages.

"Certainly," Iantine said, making a courteous bow. He could have kicked himself when he swayed a bit on his feet.

"Here now, lad, I know you're not long recovered from your ordeal," Jol said, quickly supporting him. "Let's just take a seat so I can have a good look at everything this pad seems to have on offer."

Ignoring Iantine's protests, Jol led him to the table he had just left and pushed him onto a stool. Debera and Morath followed, Debera looking very pleased with this consideration.

Jol went through the pad as thoroughly as Master Domaize would have done, making comments about those Weyrfolk he knew, smiling and nodding a good deal. He also knew when Iantine had left a pose unfinished.

"Now, what is it you require, Artist Iantine?"

"More paper, mainly," Iantine said in a tentative tone.

Jol nodded. "I believe I do have a pad of this quality paper, but smaller. I bring some in for Waine from time to time. I can, of course, get larger sheets . . ."

"It's not as if I'll be staying around the Weyr until your next round . . ."

Master Jol dismissed that consideration. "I've stores at Telgar Hold and can forward what you need in a day or two." He gave Iantine a thoughtful glance. "You'll not be leaving here all that soon, I'd say." He took the pencil from behind his ear with one hand and the pad from its pouch at his belt with the other. "Now, what exactly are your requirements, Artist Iantine?"

"Ah . . ."

"He wants to make sketches of every rider and dragon in the Weyr," said Leopol, who had eased himself unnoticed close enough to hear what was being said.

"So you've many commissions already, have you?" Master Jol said approvingly, pencil poised over the fresh leaf of his pad.

"Well, no, not exactly, you see—" Iantine stammered.

"You've three I know of," Leopol said. "P'tero for M'leng . . . and the Weyrleaders . . ."

Iantine almost bit Leopol's nose off. "The Weyrleaders're different. I will do them in oils, but the sketches are to thank those in the Weyr who've been so kind to me."

"Doing portraits of an entire Weyr is quite an undertaking," and Master Jol scribbled a line. "You'll need a good deal of paper and plenty of pencils. Or would you prefer ink? I stock a very good quality. Guaranteed not to fade or blot." He looked at Iantine expectantly.

"But I've only this sketch to trade with you," Iantine said.

"Lad, you've credit with Jol Liliencamp Traders," Jol said gently, touching his pencil to Iantine's shoulder and giving it a little push. "I'm not Chalkin, mind you. Not any way, shape, or form." And he gave a burst of such infectious laughter that Iantine grinned in spite of himself. "Now, give me your requirements straight. But to ease your mind, if you'd finish off this," and the pencil end tapped the montage, "in watercolor, I'm ready to give you two marks for it. Oh, and I'd like this one of T'dam giving his lecture," he added, flipping to that page. "That'll show some folks that dragonriders do something beyond glide about the skies. A mark and a half for that . . ."

"But . . . but . . ." Iantine floundered, trying to organize his thoughts as well as his needs. Debera was grinning from ear to ear and so was her dragon. "I've no watercolors with me—" he began, wishing to indicate his willingness to finish the montage.

"Ah, but I just happen to have some, which is why I suggested them," Jol said, beaming again. "Really, this meeting is most serendipitous," he added, and his smile included Debera. "And this," he touched the montage again in a very proprietary fashion, "colored up a bit and with glass to protect it, will look very good indeed in my wagon office. Indeed it will. Advertising, I believe the ancestors called it."

"Ah, Master Jol?" called someone from one of the trade wagons. "A moment of your time . . ."

"I'll be back, lad, just you stay there. You, too, Debera. I've not finished with the pair of you yet, no I haven't."

As Iantine and Debera exchanged stunned looks, he trotted off to see what was required of him, tucking the pencil behind his ear again and folding up his pad as he went.

"I don't believe him," Iantine said, shaking his head, feeling weak and breathless.

"Are you all right?" Debera asked, leaning across the table to him.

"Gob-smacked," Iantine said, remembering a favorite expression of his father. "Completely gob-smacked."

Debera grinned knowingly. "I think I am, too. I never expected—"

"Neither did I."

"Why? Don't you trust traders?" Leopol asked, sounding slightly defensive.

Iantine gave a shaky laugh. "One can trust traders. It's just I never expected such generosity . . ."

"How long were you in Bitra?" Debera asked tartly, giving him a long look.

"Long enough," Iantine said, grimacing, "to learn new meanings to the word 'satisfactory.' "

Debera gave him a little frown.

"Never mind," he said, shaking his head and patting her hand. "And thank you very much for introducing me to your cousin."

"Once he saw that sketch, you really didn't need me," she remarked, almost shyly.

"I believe you ordered these," said a baritone voice. Rider and Artist looked up in astonishment as a trader deposited an armful of items on the table: two pads, one larger than the other, a neat square box which held a full glass bottle of ink, a sheaf of pens, and a parcel of pencils. "Special delivery." With a grin, he pivoted and went back the way he had come.

"Master Jol does pride himself on his quick service," Leopol said with a wide grin.

"There now! You're all set," Debera said.

"I am indeed," and the words came out of Iantine like a prayer.

9

▼▼▼▼▼▼▼▼▼

FORT HOLD AND BITRAN BORDERS,
EARLY WINTER

Lord Paulin's message to the other Lord Holders and Weyr-leaders received a mixed reception: not everyone was in favor of impeachment, despite the evidence presented. Paulin was both annoyed and frustrated, having hoped for a unanimous decision so that Chalkin could be removed before his hold was totally demoralized.

Jamson and Azury felt that the matter could wait until the Turn's End Council meeting: Jamson was known to be conservative, but Paulin was surprised by Azury's reservations. Those who lived in tropical zones rarely understood the problems of winter weather. To be sure, it would be more difficult to prepare Bitra Hold in full winter, which was Azury's stated concern, but some progress could be made to prepare the hold for the vernal onslaught of Threadfall. Preparations ought to have begun—as in every other hold—two years ago: larger crops sowed, harvests stored, and general maintenance done on buildings and arable lands, as well as the construction of emergency shelters on the main roads and for ground-crews. Not to mention training holders how to combat Thread burrows.

There was the added disadvantage that Chalkin's folk seemed generally dispirited anyhow—though that should not be used as an excuse for denying them news of the impending problem.

And who would succeed to the hold? A consideration that was certainly fraught with problems.

In his response, Bastom had made a good suggestion: the appointment of a deputy or regent right away until one of Chalkin's sons came of age; sons who would be specifically, and firmly, trained to hold properly. Not that the new holder *had* to be of the Bloodline, but following the precepts of inheritance outlined in the Charter would pacify the nervous Lords. To Paulin's way of thinking, competence should always be the prime decider in succession, and that was not always passed on in the genes of Bloodlines.

For that matter, Paulin's eldest nephew had shown a sure grasp of hold management. Sidny was a hard worker, a fair man, and a good judge of character and ability. Paulin was half tempted to recommend him up for Fort's leadership when he was gone. He had a few reservations about his son, Mattew, but Paulin knew that he tended to be more critical of his own Blood than others were.

He would definitely suggest Bastom's idea to the Council: good practice for younger sons and daughters to have actual hands-on experience in running a hold. Considering the state Bitra Hold was in, a team would be required. Such an expedient would certainly reduce the cry of "nepotism." And give youngsters a chance to display initiative and ability.

When the last of the replies came in, Paulin gave the young green rider a message for M'shall at Benden Weyr on the result of the polling. The Weyrleader was sure to be as disappointed as he was. He tried to convince himself that they could still get Bitra Hold right and tight in time for Threadfall. But the sooner it was done, the better. He hoped M'shall could get back to him about locating the Bitran uncle and whether he was competent to take hold. Otherwise a Search must be made of legitimate heirs to—

"Fragitall," Paulin muttered, pushing back from his desk and sighing deeply in frustration. One could no longer do a quick Search on the Bloodline program for a comprehensive genealogy. Surely that was one program Clisser had printed out and copied. "Well, we'll need a copy of whatever form that program's in," he told himself, sighing again. To cheer himself up he reviewed the progress report from the new mine.

They wanted permission to call the hold CROM, an acronym of the founders: Chester, Ricard, Otty, and Minerva. Paulin didn't see a problem with that but, as a matter of form—especially right now—the request should first be presented to the Council. During the Interval so many procedures had been relaxed, and the leniency was now coming back to plague them, as in the case of Chalkin becoming Lord Holder. At least Paulin was consoled by the knowledge that it was his father, the late Lord Emilin, who had voted Fort on that score. That evidence of bad judgment wasn't his own error, Paulin knew, even if it was now up to him to rectify the situation.

There was an abrupt rapping of knuckles on his door, and before he could respond it swung open: the Benden Weyrleader, M'shall, brushed past Mattew to enter.

"We've got to do something *now*, Paulin," the Weyrleader said, his expression grim as he hauled off his riding gauntlets and opened up his jacket.

"You got my message quickly enough . . . Bring klah, Matt," Paulin said, gesturing for his son to be quick. M'shall's face looked pinched with the cold of *between* . . . and more.

"I got it. And that's not the end of it. There's rough weather in Bitra and people freezing to death because they will not leave the border," M'shall announced.

"Will not? Or cannot?"

"More cannot than will not. Though Chalkin sent down orders that none of the 'ungrateful dissenters' could expect to reclaim their holdings—punishment for defying him— irrespective of the fact that he's putting their lives at risk by his notion of holding."

"How many are involved?" Paulin's sense of alarm increased.

M'shall ruffled thick graying hair that had been pressed down by his helmet. "L'sur says there must be well over a hundred at the main border crossing into Benden; women, children, and elderlies. There are as many or more at other border points, and no shelter at any, bar what the guards are using. The refugees have all been herded into makeshift pens. What's more atrocious, L'sur saw several bodies hung up by the feet that seemed to have been used as target practice. Benden Weyr cannot ignore such barbarity, Paulin."

"No, it can't, nor can Fort Hold!" Paulin was on his feet and pacing. "If that's what he calls hold management, he *has* to be removed."

"My thinking, too," M'shall said, running agitated hands through his hair again. "Another night like last and those people'll be dead of exposure and starvation. Bridgely concurs with me that something has to be done, now, today. And it's getting toward a cold night now there. I've come to you for Council authority since Bridgely says we'd better do this as properly as possible . . ." He paused, bitter. "Such a situation is not supposed to *happen*. Those people aren't defying *him*. They're just scared to death and desperate for security . . . which obviously they don't expect to find in Bitra." He hitched himself forward in the chair. "Thing is, Paulin, if we hand out supplies, what's to keep the border guards from just collecting them the moment we take off? So, I think I'll have to leave a couple of riders as protection ... which'll give Chalkin a chance to cry 'Weyr interference.' "

Paulin felt nauseous. That sort of thing was straight out of the ancient bloody history the settlers had deliberately left behind: evolving a code of ethics and conduct that would make such events improbable! This planet was settled with the idea that there was room enough for everyone willing to work the land that was his or hers by Charter-given birthright.

"There's no interference if your riders stay on your side of the border. Besides which, Bitra Hold looks to Benden Weyr for protection—"

"Thread protection," M'shall corrected.

"In a manner of speaking," and Paulin's smile was grim, "this is partly Thread protection. They're looking for what they should have had from their Lord Holder, and who else should they turn to but the Weyr? No," and Paulin brought one fist down sharply on the desk. "You're within your rights ... if you've riders willing to volunteer for such duty."

"L'sur's stayed on, or so his dragon told Craigath."

"But no firestone," and Paulin held up a stern finger, "much as some might like to show force."

"Oh, I've made myself clear on that point, I assure you," and M'shall gave a bitter twist to his lips. "And we haven't had any training at Benden recently so there's not a whisper of flame in any of the dragons. As for disciplining the guards, a short hop and a long drop *between* would be *my* preference, but ..." He held up both hands to assure Paulin of self-restraint.

At that point Mattew returned with a tray containing steaming cups of klah, soup, and a basket of hot breads. He deposited it on the table and left.

M'shall didn't wait for Paulin's invitation but grabbed up the soup and blew on its surface, sipping as soon as he dared.

"That hits the spot, and if you've a caldron of it, I'll take it back with me." He grinned, licking his lips. "It's certainly hot enough to survive a jump *between*."

"You may have it, caldron and all. L'sur has stayed on, you say? How about riders at other crossing points?" Paulin asked, stirring sweetener into his klah. M'shall nodded. "Good. Their presence ought to inhibit any further violence." But that presence was only a deterrent, not assistance. He would like to do more than send soup, but his position at this point, even as Council Chair, might be compromised. "At least the Weyr has a right to take action, and so does Bridgely," he added thoughtfully. He thumped his fist again. "But I will go personally to see both Jamson and Azury: especially since Chalkin has used such extreme measures. I'm hard-pressed to see the reason for them."

M'shall shrugged. "Fort holders have every reason to trust you, Paulin. Bitrans never have had any with Chalkin holding."

"What I'd like to do is haul the indecisive, like Jamson and Azury, and *show* them what's happening at Bitra. They probably think we've exaggerated the situation."

"Exaggerated?" M'shall was indignant, and it was as well the cup was empty of soup when he planted it hard on the table. "Sorry. What's wrong with them?"

"They wouldn't behave in such a manner. It's hard for them to believe another Lord Holder would."

"Well," and M'shall nearly growled, "he would and he has."

There was a more circumspect knock on the door, which Matt opened, showing in K'vin.

"I just heard about the border trouble, M'shall. Zulaya had Meranath bespeak Maruth, so Charanth and I thought to catch you here," the young Weyrleader said, his expression as grim as Benden's.

"So he's blocked the western borders as well?"

K'vin nodded. "Telgar has no grounds to object to his closing his borders, but he's deliberately killing people, turfing them out in this weather. I can't . . . and won't . . . permit people to be treated like that." He fixed an expectant stare on Paulin.

"M'shall and I have been discussing the intolerable situation. I've already polled the Lord Holders with a view to taking immediate action. The response was not unanimous, so even as Council Chair there is little I can do—officially, that is. But as M'shall pointed out, the Weyr has certain responsibilities to protect people. By stretching a point, you could say they're Thread-lost," and Paulin's smile was wry, "escaping a hold which is unprepared. So the Weyrs can move where the Council Chair may not."

"That's all I need to know!" K'vin slapped his riding gloves against his thigh to emphasize his approval.

"Of course," and Paulin held up one hand in restraint, "you must be careful not to give Chalkin due cause to cite an infringement against Hold autonomy . . ."

"Not if that includes deliberate mistreatment of people he's already misled," K'vin said, his voice rising in alarm.

"This is not the time to jeopardize the neutrality of the Weyrs, you know," Paulin said, looking from one to the other. "Thread hasn't started falling yet."

"C'mon, Paulin—" M'shall began in protest.

"I'm with you in spirit, but as Council Chair, I have to remind you—above and beyond my *private* opinion—that we don't have the *right* to interfere in the government of a hold."

"You may not, Paulin," K'vin said. "But M'shall and I do. There's truth in what you said about Weyrs protecting people from peril."

"From Threadfall . . ." Paulin reminded the younger Weyrleader.

"From peril," K'vin repeated firmly. "Freezing to death without shelter from inclement weather constitutes peril as surely as Threadfall does."

Paulin nodded approvingly. "I may even forget that you visited here this morning." He grinned. "M'shall, you don't happen to know where Chalkin's remaining uncle lives?"

"I already thought of that and he's not there," M'shall said. "Place was empty. Too empty. I know Vergerin was alive and well last autumn."

"How do you mean 'too empty'?" Paulin asked, jotting down the uncle's name.

"It had been cleaned out too thoroughly. Not," and M'shall held up one hand to forestall Paulin's query, "as if it had been set to rights after a man's death, but as if to prove no one had been there at all. But Vergerin had cleared vegetation back from his front court, as every smart holder should. Someone had thrown debris all around to disguise the clearance."

"Has Chalkin anticipated us?" Paulin asked in a rhetorical question. Then he looked from one dragonrider to the other. "Rescue those folks before either the weather or Chalkin's bullies kill them. And I'd like interviews from them, too, once they're not afraid to talk to outsiders." Just as M'shall had his hand on the doorknob, Paulin added, "And not so much as a trickle of flame, please. That could get magnified out of all proportion."

K'vin pretended wide-eyed shock at such a notion. M'shall glanced around.

"I didn't hear that, Paulin," the Benden Weyrleader said with stiff dignity.

"As if we would . . ." K'vin said to M'shall as they strode out of Fort Hold.

"I'd like to," M'shall said in a taut voice, "that's the problem. But then, I've known Chalkin longer than you."

Craigath and Charanth were already on the court, awaiting their riders.

"You'll take the western and northern crossings, K'vin?" M'shall asked as they separated to reach their bronzes. "Have you been checking on numbers for transport?"

"Yes, and had sweep riders checking in ever since Chalkin closed the borders. Zulaya will warn Tashvi and Salda that we're proceeding. We'll take all to the Weyr first. The entire Weyr is organized to help."

"You're a good man, K'vin," and M'shall grinned at his colleague. "So let's do it!" The Benden Weyrleader launched himself up his dragon's shoulder and swung neatly between the end ridges.

We go to help? Charanth asked K'vin.

Indeed we do. Tell Meranath to have Zulaya put our plan into operation. I'll meet my wing at the Falls road. And I think we'd better ask Iantine to come along.

When K'vin returned to Telgar, the first rescue wave was ready to take off at his signal. He paused long enough to haul Iantine behind him on Charanth.

"Get down as much in black and white as you can, Iantine. I want Chalkin nailed by the evidence."

Iantine was all too happy to comply with the request. It would be one way of paying back the arrogant Lord Holder for his snaking ways and meanness. But no sooner had Iantine dropped to the hard-packed snow of the border point than his attitude changed to horrified disgust. Using an economy of line, he sketched the "pen"—ropes looped around trees, and the shivering knots of people forced to stand, for there was not enough room to sit down—in the churned mud of an inadequate space. He drew the haggard faces, the chilled bodies bent inward from cold, or those clumped together to share what warmth they had. Some had been stripped of all but what covered private parts and were surrounded by their fellows in an attempt to keep them from freezing. Some were standing barefoot on the rough rags and boots of their neighbors, feet blue and dangerously white from frostbite. Children wandered weeping with hunger and fatigue or slumped in unconscious bundles in the mud at the feet of the adults. Three elderlies were stiff in death. Bloodied faces and bruised eyes were more common than the unmarked.

The guards, however, were warm with many layers of clothing, good fires with cooking spits turning to roast the meat of such animals as the refugees had brought with them. Others were tied or penned up for future use. Such belongings as the refugees had brought with them were now piled at the side of the guardhouse or in the barrows or carts lined up behind. Iantine faithfully recorded rings and bracelets, even earrings, inappropriately adorning the guards.

They had been alarmed at the arrival of the dragonriders, as many as could retreating into the shelter of the stone border facility. That had made it considerably easier to move the refugees. Of course many of them were in such a state of shock and fear that they were as frightened of the dragons and the riders as of the brutal guards.

Zulaya had brought Weyrfolk with her, and their presence reassured many. So did the blankets and the warm jackets. And the soup: the first sustenance many had had since they had left their holds.

What Iantine couldn't put down on paper were the sounds and the smells of that scene. And yet he did . . . in the open mouths of the terrified folk, their haunted eyes, the contortions of their abused bodies, their ragged coverings, the piles of human ordure because the guards had made no provision for that human requirement, and the abandoned belongings and carts.

Now that he had seen real privation, Iantine realized how

lucky he had been in his brief encounter with the Lord Holder of Bitra.

Iantine returned with the last group, letting his hand rest only in *between*, sketching as they flew, his pad propped against P'tero's back.

"You haven't stopped a moment," P'tero shouted over his shoulder. "You'll freeze your hand up here, you know."

Iantine waved it to prove its flexibility and continued to sketch. He was adding details to the men who had been hung by their heels and used as target practice. The men had been cut down—one of the first things the rescuers had done. Iantine had only had time enough to do an outline, but the details—despite all the other sketches he made that day—were vivid in his mind's eye, and he had to get every one down on paper or he would feel he had betrayed them.

When the young blue rider deposited him in front of the lower cavern, Iantine, still filling in substance, managed to get himself to a table near enough to the fire to get the good of the warmth—and increase the fluidity of his drawing. His fingers gradually thawed and his pencil raced faster.

A touch on his shoulder startled him half out of his chair.

"It's Debera," and the green rider placed klah and a bowl of stew in front of him. "Everyone else has eaten. You'd better," she said severely, wrenching the pencil out of one hand and taking the pad from the other. "You look awful," she added, peering closely at his face.

He reached for his pad but she slapped at his hand, swinging it out of his reach.

"No, you eat first. You'll draw better for it. Oh, my word!" Her eye was caught by the scene, and her free hand went to her mouth, her eyes widening in shock. "Oh, they couldn't have."

"I sketched what I saw," he said, exhaling in a remorse that came from his guts and then inhaling the tantalizing odor emanating from the stew. He looked down at it, thick with

vegetables and chunks of meat. They really could do miracles
with wherry here. He picked up the spoon and began to eat,
only then realizing how empty his stomach was. It almost hurt
receiving food, and that nearly made him stop eating altogether. Chalkin's prisoners had been without food for three or
four days.

"They're all fed now," Debera murmured.

Iantine gave her a startled glance and she patted his
shoulder reassuringly, as she often patted her Morath.

"I felt the same way when I ate earlier on." She sat down
across from him. "We'd been going flat out to feed them when
Tisha made us all stop to get something to eat, too." She started
turning the pages of his book, the look on her face becoming
more and more distressed at each new scene of the tragedy.
"How could he?"

Iantine reached over and gently pulled the sketch pad from
her, setting it down, closed between them.

"He gave the orders—" Iantine began.

"And knew just what would happen when he did, I know.
I've met some of his . . . 'guards.' Even my father wouldn't
have one about the hold." She tapped the pad. "No one can
ignore that sort of evidence."

Iantine gave a snort. "Not with dragonriders verifying
what's in here!" He finished the last of the stew and stretched
his legs out under the table, scrubbing at his face, still tingling
with his long hours in the unremitting cold of the border
crossing.

"Go to bed, why don't you, Iantine," Debera said, rising. She
glanced around the cavern, which was occupied by only a few
riders and folk finishing their evening meal. "They've all been
sorted out and you'll be lucky if you have your room to yourself. But I'd better get some sleep, too. That Morath of mine!
She wakes positively starved, no matter how much I give her."

Iantine smiled at the affection that softened Debera's voice.

He got to his feet, swaying a bit. "You're right. I need sleep. Good night, Debera."

He watched her striding purposefully out of the cavern, at the proud tilt to her head and the set of her shoulders. She'd changed a great deal since she Impressed Morath. He grinned, picked up his pad, and slowly made his way to his quarters.

He wasn't sharing with any refugee, but Leopol sprawled on a bed pad along one wall and didn't even stir as Iantine prepared himself for bed.

There were more refugees than originally estimated, and while the resources of the two Weyrs were stretched, the Lord Holders immediately sent additional supplies and offered shelter. Some of those rescued were in bad shape from the cold and could not be immediately transferred to the sanctuaries offered by Nerat, Benden, and Telgar Holds.

Zulaya had headed a rescue team of the other queens and the green riders. She came back, seething with rage.

"I knew he was a greedy fool and an idiot, but not a sadist. There were three pregnant women at the Forest Road border and they'd been raped because, of course, they couldn't sue the guards later on a paternity claim."

"Are the women all right?" K'vin asked, appalled by yet another instance of the brutality. "We arrived at the North Pass just in time to spare three lads from . . . very unkind attentions by the guards. Where does Chalkin find such men?"

"From holds that have tossed them out for antisocial behavior or criminal activities, of course," Zulaya replied, almost spitting in anger. "And that blizzard's closed in. We moved just in time. If we hadn't, I fear most of these people would be dead by morning. Absolutely nothing allowed them! Not even the comfort of a fire!"

"I know, I know," he said, as bitter about the sadistic behavior as she was. "We should have treated those guards to a taste of absolute cold. Like a long wait *between*. Only that would have been a clean death."

"We still can," Zulaya said in a grating tone. K'vin regarded her in astonishment. She glared at him, clenching her fists at her sides. "Oh, I know we can't, but that doesn't keep me from *wanting* to! Did you take Iantine with you? I thought of how useful on-the-spot sketches might be."

"In fact, he asked to come. He's got plenty to show Lord Paulin and the Council," K'vin said. He swallowed, remembering the stark drawings that had filled one pad. Iantine's quick hand had captured the reality, made even more compelling by the economy of line, depicting horrific scenes of deliberate cruelty.

The Weyrleaders introduced themselves to the first of the refugees and started off by interviewing the old couple.

"M'grandsir's grandsir came to Bitra with the then holder," the man said, his eyes nervously going from one Weyrleader to the other. He kept wiggling his bandaged fingers, though N'ran had assured him the pain and itch had been dulled by fellis and numbweed. "I'm Brookie, m'woman's Ferina. We farmed it since. Never no reason to complain, though the Holder keeps asking for more tithe and there's only so much comes out of any acre, no matter who tills it. But *he'd* the right."

"Not to take our sow, though," his mate said, her expression rebellious. "We needed that 'un to make more piggies to meet the tithe *he* set." Like her man, she laid a stress on the pronoun. "Took our daughter, too, to work in the hold when we wanted her land grant. Said we didn't work what we had good enough so we couldn't have more."

"Really?" Zulaya said, deceptively mild as she shot K'vin a meaningful glance. "Now that's interesting, Holder Ferina."

K'vin envied Zulaya's trick of remembering names.

You could've asked me, Charanth said helpfully.

You've been listening?

The people needed dragons' help. I listen. We all do.

When the pity of dragons has also been aroused, surely that's enough justification for what we've just done, thought K'vin, if the Council should turn up stiff. He must remember to tell Zulaya.

"But *he* says we got it wrong and we ain't had no teacher to ask," the man was saying. "An' thassa 'nother thing—we should have a teacher for our kids."

"At least so they can read the Charter and know what rights you all do have," Zulaya said firmly. "I've a copy we can show you right now, so you can refresh your memories."

The two exchanged alarmed glances.

"In fact," Zulaya went on smoothly, "I think we'll have someone read you your rights . . . since it would be difficult for you to turn pages with bandaged hands, Brookie. And you're not in much better shape, Ferina."

Ferina managed a nervous smile. "I'd like that real well, Weyrwoman. Real well. Our rights are printed out? In the Charter and all?"

"Your rights as holders are part of the Charter," Zulaya said, shooting K'vin another unhappy look. "In detailed paragraphs." She rose to her feet abruptly. "Why don't you sit over there, in the sun, Ferina, Brookie?" and she pointed to the eastern wall, where some of the Weyr's elderlies were seated, enjoying the warmth of the westering sun. "We'll make sure you hear it all, and you can ask any questions you want."

She helped the two to their feet and started them on their way across the Bowl as K'vin whistled for Leopol.

"Go get the Weyr's copy of the Charter, will you, lad?"

"You want me to read it to them, too?" the boy asked, eyes glinting partly in mischief and partly because he enjoyed second-guessing errands.

"Smart pants, are we?" K'vin said. "No, I think we need T'lan for this." He pointed toward the white-haired old brown rider who was serving klah to the refugees. "Just get the Charter now. I'll request T'lan's services."

Leopol moved off at his usual sprint, and K'vin went over to speak to the elderly brown rider. He had exactly the right manner to deal with nervous and frightened holders.

Bridgely arrived in Benden Weyr, his face suffused with blood, torn between fury and laughter.

"The nerve of the man, the consummate nerve!" he exclaimed and threw down the message he carried.

It landed closer to Irene than M'shall so she picked it up.

"From Chalkin?" she exclaimed, looking up at Bridgely.

"Read it . . . and pour me some wine, would you, M'shall?" the Lord Holder said, slipping into a chair. "I mean, I know that man's got gall, but to presume . . . to have the effrontery—"

"Ssssh," Irene said, her eyes widening as she read. "Oh, I don't believe it! Just listen, M'shall. 'This hold has the right to dragon messengers. The appropriate red striped banner has been totally ignored, though my guards have seen dragons near enough to see that an urgent message must be delivered. Therefore I must add . . .' " She peered more closely at the written page. "His handwriting's abominable . . . Ah, 'dereliction' . . . really, where does he get off to cry 'dereliction' . . . 'of their prime duty to the other complaints I am forced to lay at their door. Not only have they been interfering with the management of this hold, but they fill the minds of my loyal holders with outrageous lies. I demand their immediate censure. They are not even reliable enough to perform those duties which fall within their limited abilities.' Limited abilities?" Irene turned pale with fury. "I'll unlimit him!"

"Especially when we've had an earful of how he treats his loyal holders . . ." M'shall said, his expression grimmer than ever. "Wait a minute. What's the date on his letter?"

"Five days ago," Bridgely answered, with a malicious grin. "He had to send it by rider. From what the fellow told me, Chalkin's also sent messengers to Nerat and Telgar as well. He wants me, you'll see in the last paragraph, Irene," and Bridgely pointed to that section of the missive, "to forward it by a reliable messenger to Lord Paulin, registering his complaint with the Council Chair. I suppose," and his grin was droll, "I'll get another one when he finds out about yesterday's airlift rescue."

"The man . . ." Irene paused, unable to find words. "When I think of how he's treated those poor people . . ."

"And when he's called to account, he'll probably whinge that his guards exceeded their instructions . . . and he's fired them all," said Bridgely with a cynical shrug.

"Oh," M'shall said brightly, "not all of them." He scratched the back of his head. "Ah . . . they wanted to know why they couldn't get to ride a dragon if the riffraff could."

"You didn't, M'shall?" Irene exclaimed, her eyes wide with delighted anticipation, "drop them off on the way, did you?"

"No," and M'shall shrugged with mock regret. "But I felt it might be wise to . . . ah, sequester? Yes, that's the word, sequester certain of them should they be required to stand before the Council and explain exactly what orders they received."

"Oh." Bridgely turned pensive.

"Oh, I was select, you might say," and M'shall's face was grim. "I found out which had had a hand in those killings and took testimony from bereaved witnesses. Not even guards, acting under a Lord Holder's orders, may execute without trial, you know."

"Oh, indeed, and you've acted circumspectly," Bridgely

said, nodding with understanding. "Really, I don't think this can wait until Turn's End. And I shall so inform Jamson and Azury."

"I'd be happy to take you myself," M'shall said, "and speak for the Weyr. In fact," and the Weyrleader reached for Chalkin's written message, "you could deliver this at the same time, Bridgely."

"You are all consideration, Weyrleader," Bridgely said, gesturing grandly and looking exceedingly pleased.

"My pleasure at any time, Lord Holder." M'shall swept his arm in an equally grand gesture.

"Whenever you can spare a moment from your duties, Weyrleader?"

"Why, I do believe I can spare an hour or two now, since I perceive that it is an appropriate time to visit the western half of the continent . . ."

"Oh, will you two stop your nonsense and *go!*" Irene said, laughter in her voice though she tried to look reproving. But their antics relieved the tension in the Weyr.

10

HIGH REACHES, BOLL, ISTA WEYRS; HIGH REACHES WEYR, FORT, AND TELGAR HOLDS

"Now, really, M'shall, Bridgely," said Jamson, fussing with his robes as he shifted uneasily in his chair. High Reaches was invariably a cold place, and today, in Jamson's private office, was no exception. The Benden Holder was glad he had riding furs on, and made no attempt to open his jacket nor unglove his left hand after the usual handshake with Jamson. He noted M'shall did the same. "I cannot believe that a Lord Holder would treat the very people he depends on in such a way. Not in midwinter."

"With my own eyes I saw it, Lord Jamson," M'shall said in an unequivocal tone. "And I thought it wise to ask several of the guards to stay in the Weyr so you may learn what their orders were."

"But here, Chalkin complains that you have not accorded him the courtesy of conveyance." Jamson frowned.

"If you had seen what I have, Lord Jamson, you might find it hard to oblige him," M'shall said, his face stark.

"Really, Jamson, don't be such a prick," Bridgely said, under no similar restraint of courtesy with his peer. "Nerat and Telgar are taking in refugees as well as Benden. You can speak to any you wish to determine the extent of Chalkin's perfidy . . ."

"I'll gladly convey you where you wish to go," M'shall offered.

"I've my own Weyr," Jamson said stiffly, "if I need transport. But it's not the weather to be traveling about in unnecessarily at all."

Which was true enough since the High Reaches Hold was cloaked in snow crusted as hard as ice on the ground.

"Agreed," Bridgely said, trying hard not to shiver and wondering at Jamson's parsimony with fires, or if the heating system in the hold was another victim to technological obsolescence. "So you will grant that only a dire need would bring me out, asking you to change your mind about taking immediate action against Chalkin. People would have frozen to death on Bitra's borders last night!" And he pointed vigorously eastward.

"He doesn't mention that in this," Jamson said, peering at the letter on the table.

"Doubtless he'll circulate a longer letter on that score," Bridgely said with deep irony. "But what I saw required me to give aid without any delay."

"As you know, Lord Jamson," M'shall put in, "Weyrs are also autonomous and may withhold services with sufficient justification. I feel perfectly justified in refusing him basic courtesies. Come, Bridgely. We're wasting Lord Jamson's valuable time. Good day to you."

Before the astonished High Reaches Holder could respond to such peremptory behavior, the two men had left the room.

"My word! And I always considered M'shall to be a sensible man. Thank goodness G'don is a solid, predictable Weyrleader . . . One simply does *not* impeach a Lord Holder overnight! Not this close to Threadfall." He buried his hands more deeply into the sleeves of his fur-lined jerkin.

Azury was so shocked he did not even comment on M'shall's "dereliction" of services. "I'd no idea, really," he said.

In direct contrast to High Reaches, Southern Boll's weather was hot enough for Bridgely to wish he'd worn a lighter shirt. Although they were well shaded from the morning sun on a porch decorated by a blooming plant with fragrant pink blossoms tangling in clusters, he had to open his collar and roll up his sleeves to be comfortable. Azury had ordered a fruit drink, and by the time it came, Bridgely's throat was dry enough to appreciate the cool tang.

"I know Chalkin's not exactly . . . reliable," and Azury then grinned wryly. "And I've lost sufficient marks in his little games of chance to wonder about his basic honesty. But . . ." He shook his head. "A holder simply doesn't keep his folk in the dark about something as critical to their survival as Thread. Does he really think it won't come? That we're all foolish or stupid?"

"*He* is both foolish and stupid," Bridgely said. "Why else did our ancestors bioengineer the dragons? And develop a totally unique society to nurture and succor the species if not for future need?" He glanced at M'shall, who merely raised his eyebrows. "It isn't as if we didn't have graphic proof of the existence of Thread, which was part of our education. Nor tons of records annotating the problem. It's not something *we* thought up to inconvenience Chalkin of Bitra."

"Preaching to the converted, Bridge," Azury said. "He's ten times the fool if he thinks to brace the rest of the planet on this score. But," and he leaned forward on his wickerwood chair, which creaked slightly, "holders can spin great lies . . ."

"And I can spot a whinge and a bitcher as fast as you can, Azury," Bridgely said, moving to the edge of his chair, which also reacted noisily to the weight shift. "Like this chair. You can interview any of those we've taken in . . . and the sooner the better so you can judge the condition they were in before we rescued them."

"I think I'd better have an eyes-on at that," Azury said. He raised one hand quickly. "Not that I doubt you, but impeaching another Lord Holder . . . Nervous-making."

"That's as may be, but having a hold that is totally unprepared for the onslaught of Thread—one that's adjacent to me," and Bridgely jabbed a thumb in his chest, "is far more nervous-making."

"You've a point there," Azury admitted. He looked over his shoulder and beckoned one of the attendants, asking him to bring his riding gear. "You said that Jamson's reluctant? Doesn't impeachment require a unanimous verdict?"

"It does," Bridgely said and set his lips in an implacable line.

Azury grinned, thanking the attendant, who had quickly returned with his gear. "Then you also need me to add weight to a second delegation to High Reaches?"

"If you feel you can turn Jamson's opinion?"

Azury stamped into his boots. "That one's just perverse enough to hold out, but we'll see. Tashvi, Bastom, and Franco are involved, and I know Paulin is agitated . . . Who does that leave? Richud of Ista? Well, he will go along with a majority." He rose. "Now, let's leave before I swim in my own sweat . . ."

Azury interviewed each of the fourteen refugees still housed in Benden Weyr as unfit to be transferred elsewhere. He had a chat with three of the guards.

"Not that they were in a chatting mood," he said, his light blue eyes vivid with anger in his tanned face, "but they may soon have second thoughts on how much their loyalty is worth to Lord Chalkin. They do claim," and, as he grinned, his teeth were very white against his skin, "that they were outnumbered by the influx of so many ranting, raving maniacs and had to use force to restrain them until they could receive orders from the hold."

"That conflicts with what the ranting raving maniacs say, doesn't it?" M'shall replied.

"Oh, indeed," Azury said, grinning without humor. "And I do wonder that the guards came out of the ranting and raving mass unscathed while all of the maniacs seem to have a variety of injuries. Clearly the truth is being pulled in many directions. But it lies there, limpid as usual, to the eye that sees and the ear that hears."

"Well said." Bridgely nodded.

"So let's speak with Richud."

It was harder to find the Lord Holder of Ista because he had taken the afternoon off to fish—his favorite occupation.

The Harbormaster was unable to give any specific direction for a search.

"The dolphins went with him . . . circle your dragon, and see if he can spot them. Small sloop with a red sail but a lot of dolphins. Richud claims they understand him. He may be right," and the elderly man scratched his head, grinning with amusement at the notion.

"They do—according to the records," Azury said. "My fishers always watch out for them in the Currents."

"Wal, as you wish," the Harbormaster said, and went back to his tedious accounting of creel weights lifted ashore the previous seven days.

Craigath flew his passengers in a high-altitude circle, spiraling outward from Ista Harbor. It was he who spotted the craft and, with mighty use of his pinions, dove for it.

Despite the broad safety band securing him to his position, Azury grabbed frantically at Bridgely, who was sitting in front of him, and Bridgely worried lest his own grip bruise the dragonrider.

M'shall merely turned his head to grin back at them. The words he spoke—for his mouth moved—were lost in the speed of their descent. Bridgely watched the sea coming nearer and nearer and arched himself slightly backward. He'd ridden often enough not to be alarmed by dragon antics, but never at such an angle or speed. He tightened his hold on his safety straps and argued himself out of closing his cowardly eyes. Just as it seemed as if Craigath would impale himself on the mast of the sloop—which wasn't all that small to Bridgely's mind—the bronze went into hover, startling the two crewmen who were watching Richud struggle with a pole bent almost double by his efforts to land the fish he'd hooked.

"Any time you're free, Lord Richud," shouted M'shall between his cupped hands.

Richud glanced once over his shoulder, then again, and lost control of pole and fish—the reel spinning wildly as pressure ended.

"Don't creep up on me like that! Lookit what you made me do! Fraggit. Can't I ever get an afternoon off? Oh well, what catastrophe's hit us now? Must be something bad to bring the three of you this far south."

He handed his pole to a crewman and came to the starboard side. There was still some distance between him and his visitors.

"I'd ask you aboard but the bronze would sink us," he said.

"No problem," M'shall said, and his eyes unfocused as he spoke to his dragon. *Can you get us a little closer, Craigath?*

Craigath, eyes gleaming bluely and whirling with some speed, set himself down in the water, wings neatly furled to his backbone while, with his left forearm, he took hold of the safety rail, pulling himself, and his passengers, closer to the hull of the ship. The sloop began to heel over at the strength of the dragon's hold.

The wind left the sail and the boom started to whip around when, just as abruptly, the sail caught wind again and the ship resumed her forward motion and speed.

M'shall laughed, thumping Craigath on the neck in appreciation of the completed maneuver.

"What'd he do? How'd he do that? What under the sun?" Richud was looking at the dragon, back at the ship, and then at M'shall in confusion.

"He's paddling to keep up so you won't lose headway," the Benden Weyrleader said.

This is fun. I like it, Craigath informed his rider.

"He's enjoying himself," M'shall said.

"He won't snap the rail, will he?" Richud asked, staring with some apprehension at the huge forepaw clutching the metal upright.

The dragon shook his head. *It is fragile so I don't hold it hard.*

M'shall paused a moment. "Good lad. He says he's well aware of its fragility."

"He didn't say that," Richud replied, shaking his head in denial. "Fragility?"

"His very word. Craigath's got quite a vocabulary. You know how Irene speaks ... well, he has to keep up with Maruth, doesn't he?"

The dragon nodded.

"Well, I never. Never seen Ronelth or Jemath swim like this, either," Richud murmured. "So, what urgent matters bring you here?"

"Chalkin must be impeached as soon as possible. A hold is autonomous until it exceeds its rights," Bridgely said, and went on to give the Istan Lord Holder details of Chalkin's heinous behavior.

"I'd no idea he'd evict so many. Surely it's winter up there and they'd be in danger of freezing."

"They would be and have been," M'shall said.

"Their condition was appalling, Richud," Azury said. "I went to Benden myself to see. And the guards . . ." He dismissed them with a wide gesture. "You know the sort Chalkin hires . . ."

"Yes, toughnecks, layabouts, ruffians, and scoundrels like those Gather artists of his." Richud paused in thought. "Has that impeachment clause ever been used?"

"No, but it was put there as a safeguard. And there're a lot of people in Bitra who need their safety guarded . . . especially this close to Fall."

"Agreed. I'll go along with you. Only," and his tone turned entreating, "but not when I have an afternoon off to fish?"

Craigath let go of the rail and the two groups drifted apart. Suddenly the bronze shuddered from pate to tail.

I like that. Do it again.

Who are you talking to, Craigath? M'shall demanded, having had to clutch the neck ridge and lift his legs high above sudden waves sloshing Craigath's sides. His passengers had reacted as well to keep from a wetting.

Doll-fins rubbed me.

Playful, are they? Well, another time, my friend. We still have work to do. "Sorry about that. The dolphins were tickling Craigath."

"Dragons are ticklish?" Bridgely asked, startled.

"Their bellies, yes."

Dolphins flowed from under the dragon now, leaping up in the air and diving neatly back into the water as they sped off after the sloop.

"So, what do we do now? Beard Jamson again?" asked M'shall, stroking the bronze's neck affectionately. He was amused to see that Richud had retrieved his pole and was evidently baiting his hook.

"We'd probably have to drag Jamson down to Benden so he can see for himself, as you had to, Azury," Bridgely said, shivering as he thought of having to return to the frigid High Reaches.

Take the pictures, suggested Craigath, to his rider's astonishment. Dragons did not often offer unsolicited opinions, but then M'shall considered Craigath very intelligent.

"What pictures?" he asked.

"Pictures?" echoed Bridgely. "What pictures?"

Maruth says there are pictures. At Telgar.

"At Telgar?"

"Oh, that young painter," M'shall and Bridgely said in unison.

"What painter?" Azury wanted to know.

Bridgely explained.

"Very good idea, if Jamson will accept the proof as genuine," the Southern Boll Holder said skeptically.

Which was exactly what happened.

"How can you be sure these are accurate?" the High Reaches Lord Holder said when he had leafed through the vivid and detailed drawings on Iantine's pad. "I think the whole matter has been exaggerated out of proportion." He closed the pad halfway on the stark sketch of the hanging men.

"And you won't even accept my word, Jamson?" Azury said. "I've just been there and spoken to these people . . ." He riffled through the pages and came to one of a holder he'd interviewed. "That fellow, for instance. I spoke to him myself and I've no trouble accepting the truth of his story. He was four nights in an animal pen with no food and only the moisture he could get from snow, with his wife and elderly parents. Incidentally, they died of exposure despite all that Benden Weyr could do to try to revive them."

"I do not see why, Azury," Jamson said at his most pomp-ous, "you do not content yourself with running your own hold. Leave Chalkin to run his. He has the right."

"But *not* the right to inflict atrocities on any of his people." Azury's reply was heated.

Jamson regarded him coldly. "A few lazy holders—"

"*A few?*" Bridgely exploded in frustration, which, even as he did so, he knew defeated his purpose. "A few hundred is more like it, Jamson. And for that many we should all stir ourselves!"

"Well, I for one shall not, Bridgely. And that's final." He folded his arms across his chest and sat there, glaring at his visitors.

"Jamson," Azury said in a very controlled, calm voice as he pushed Bridgely to one side and leaned across the desk toward Jamson, huddled in his furs. "I, too, was skeptical when Bridgely came to me, unwilling to believe his report, much less his solution to the problem. One does *not* lightly impugn the honor of a peer, and I could not understand why Bridgely was so agitated over a *few* insignificant holders. Then, too, Bitra is too far to affect anything in *my* hold. Though I quite took his point that Thread must not be allowed to burrow unchecked anywhere on the Northern Continent. So I conceived that it was my duty, my responsibility, to personally investigate the allegations.

"I have the witness of my own eyes and ears now. As well as the disparity between what the guards told me and the evidence of my own eyes. The Bitran situation is dire and must be rectified. We cannot, as intelligent, responsible leaders, allow such a situation to fester and spread. It affects the very roots of our society, the strength of the Charter, the fundamentals on which this whole society is based. We cannot ignore it as the internal problem of an autonomous holding. You as an honorable Lord Holder owe it to yourself to investigate the situation. Then you can come to a considered judgment. At least, set your own doubts to rest by going, as I did, to Benden and gather firsthand information."

"I have no doubts," Jamson said. "The Charter clearly states that a Lord Holder has autonomy within his borders. What he does is his business and that's that. I should certainly protest anyone poking his nose in my business. So I suggest you take your meddling noses and spurious charges out of here, right now!"

This time he rang a handbell, and when his oldest son opened the door in response, said, "They're leaving. See them out."

Bridgely took in a deep breath, but a sudden short blow to his midriff by Azury robbed him of wind to speak and he was helpless as the Southern Boll Holder dragged him out of the room.

"No matter what you say, he's not in a mood to listen," Azury told him, straightening Bridgely's jacket in a tacit apology.

"Lord Azury's right, I'm afraid," M'shall said.

"You came about Bitra?" the son asked, leaning against the heavy office door to be sure it was tightly closed. "I'm Gallian, his eldest and acting steward."

"You've heard?"

"Hmmm, the door was a bit ajar," Gallian said, not at all penitent about eavesdropping, "and during your last visit. Father's memory's slipping a bit so one of us tries to be nearby for important visits. He sometimes gets details muddled."

"Any chance you can unmuddle this visit to get his cooperation?"

"May I see the sketches?" He held one hand out.

"Certainly," Bridgely said and put the pad in his hand.

"Awful," Gallian said, shaking his head as he viewed the distressing scenes and peering briefly with intent gaze at one or two. "And these are accurate?" he asked Azury.

"Yes, inasmuch as I verified the condition of some of these people now at Benden Weyr," Azury said.

The bell jangled. Gallian thrust the pad at Azury.

"I'll do what I can. And not because I already consider Chalkin a thief and a cheat. I must go. See yourselves out, can you?"

"We can and will."

"What could the boy *do*?" M'shall wanted to know as they ran quickly down the steps to the front door and out into the icy air.

"One can never tell," Azury admitted. "Shards, but it's colder than *between* here. Get me back to my sun as fast as possible."

"Would a stop at Fort Hold be too much to expect from you?" Bridgely asked, grinning at the southerner's chattering teeth.

"No, and I expect it's a tactical necessity in this struggle with Chalkin."

M'shall nodded approvingly and, vaulting to Craigath's back, lent a hand to the other two to mount.

The ambient temperature at Fort Hold was not warm but a decided improvement over High Reaches. Warmer still was the greeting Paulin gave them, insisting on a hot mulled wine when he heard of their adventures.

"I don't expect Jamson will change his mind, especially now that he has been specifically asked to do so," Paulin said when his guests were settled near the good fire he had on his office hearth. "Jamson's always been perverse."

"Then the son is unlikely to be able to alter him?" Bridgely asked, depressed that they had obviously only polarized Jamson's opposition.

"Gallian's a good man," Paulin said, temporizing, "but the truth is Jamson's getting old, as well as odd, and Gallian has taken over a great deal of the management."

"Really?" Bridgely was surprised, for, despite his regret for Jamson's intransigence, the High Reaches Holder had a good reputation and his Hold showed his skill as a manager.

"Hmmm, yes. In confidence, now, my friends, but Gallian and his mother came to me a year or so ago when they noticed Jamson was having spates of memory loss. Even countermanded orders he had written out himself."

"But something like this—impeachment, I mean—Jamson would have to be present. Wouldn't he?"

Paulin rubbed his chin thoughtfully.

"And there is some urgency to our taking action," Bridgely added. "How could we wait until such time as Gallian thinks he can persuade his father that he said opposite to what he just told us?"

"We can wait a few weeks . . . now that we've removed the refugees from Chalkin's, ah . . . benevolent management," Paulin said, but there was a glint in his blue eyes when he turned them on Bridgely that was reassuring.

Bridgely opened his mouth and then closed it. It would be as well to keep his thoughts—and questions—to himself rather than queer Paulin's plans.

"Let me have a look at that pictorial evidence Iantine was clever enough to make," the Fort Holder asked, and Azury passed him the pad. He went carefully through the sketches. "Remarkable talent the boy has. So few lines to express so much: the cold, the squalor, the agony and the pathetic endurance of these poor folk. Issony mentioned that one of Chalkin's restrictions over his lessons was that the Charter wasn't to be included."

"He didn't!" exclaimed Azury, looking up from the pleasurable sipping of the well-spiced wine.

"That would explain why so few of his holders even knew it existed," M'shall said in a tense voice. "And didn't know they had rights, too."

"By the way, Clisser's new teaching program handles that very nicely, indeed," Paulin said, rising to refill cups from the beaker kept hot by the fire. "Children will learn their rights from the moment they learn to sing 'em."

"Really?" Bridgely looked intrigued.

"With this new Pass upon us, it's appropriate to redefine quite a few parameters, including the education we give our young folk," Paulin said. "Rote learning from an early age—and music is a great help in that—has much to commend it, now that we no longer have information at our fingertips."

Iantine was painting Zulaya when his sketchbook was returned to him by K'vin.

"M'shall stopped by with this, and says to tell you it's been an enormous help," the Weyrleader said, but his attention was more on Zulaya, posing for her portrait.

She was seated on the edge of Meranath's stone couch, where the sleeping dragon lay, her head resting on her forepaws and turned toward her rider. K'vin was very pleased to see that his weyrmate was wearing the red brocade Gather dress, which was artistically draped so that the rich design was displayed. Zulaya had her hair up in an intricate style, held in place by the combs he had given her last Turn's End, the black diamonds in them sparkling when she moved her head. As she did just then, opening her mouth to speak.

"Stay still . . . please," Iantine said, stressing the last word as if he was tired of repeating the order. She snapped her mouth shut and returned to the pose.

K'vin stepped back, well behind Iantine as he worked,

making delicate brush strokes on Zulaya's painted face. K'vin couldn't see any difference, but Iantine seemed to be satisfied and started working on highlights for her hair.

The young man certainly had caught the spirit of his weyr-mate, slightly imperious, though the upcurve of her lips suggested humor. K'vin knew that Zulaya found it amusing to be sitting for a portrait at all, and was twitting him about what he should wear to be immortalized. K'vin also knew about Iantine's project to do miniatures of all the riders. Ambitious, considering there were close to six hundred in the Weyr at the moment. On the one hand, K'vin was grateful there would be the gallery, while on the other hand, he dreaded those who would become casualties.

"Will it make it any easier *not* to have pictures?" Zulaya had asked the other night when she had required him to tell her why he was so preoccupied. "We have nothing to remind us of the first occupants of this Weyr. I think I would have liked that. Gives a continuity to life and living."

K'vin had supposed it did and decided that he had to have a more positive attitude.

"It's not as if we knew who will not be here next year this time," she added. "But it'd be nice to know that they *were* here."

"How much longer, Iantine?" Zulaya said plaintively. The fingers of the hand she had resting on her thigh twitched. "I can't feel my feet or my left hand anymore."

Iantine gave an exaggerated sigh and laid down the palette, scratching his head with the now free hand as he swished the fine brush in the jar on the table. "Sorry, Zulaya. You should by rights have had a break some time ago. But the light's perfect and I didn't want to stop."

"Oh, help me up, K'vin," Zulaya said, holding out a hand. "I don't usually get a chance to sit still so long . . ."

K'vin was glad to assist her, and she was stiff enough so that her first steps were awkward. Then she recovered her mobility and walked firmly to the easel.

"My word, you did do yards today, didn't you? Filled in that whole panel of the dress and ... have you got my eyes crossed?"

Iantine laughed. "No, step a little to this side. Now back again. Do the eyes seem to follow you?"

Zulaya gave a little shake, widening her eyes. "They do. How do you contrive that? I must say, I'm not so sure I like me watching everything I do."

K'vin chuckled. "You won't, but your presence hanging in the Lower Cavern may spur the lazy to complete their tasks more quickly."

"I'm not sure I like that idea any more than having me leering at me up here." She turned to the table, mostly covered by Iantine's paraphernalia. "I had klah sent up not too long ago," and she cast an accusing eye on Iantine. "It should still be hot." She unscrewed the lid and steam obediently rose. "It is. Shall I pour for all of us?" Which she was doing even as she spoke.

"Maybe I should leave now?" Iantine said, looking from one to the other.

"No," she said quickly.

"I wanted to be sure your sketches were safely in your possession," K'vin said, taking a chair.

"And did they solve the problem?" Zulaya asked, spooning sweetener into the cups and passing him his. "Come, sit, Iantine. You must be more tired than I am. I've been sitting the whole time."

Iantine grinned as if, K'vin noted with a twinge of jealousy, totally at his ease with the Weyrwoman. Few were, except Tisha, who treated everyone like an errant child, or Leopol, who was impudent with everyone.

"So? What's the result?" She indicated with a wave of her hand that he should speak out in the portraitist's presence.

"M'shall's disgusted. They still don't have a unanimous decision about impeachment. Jamson's the holdout."

"He's not always dealing with a full deck," Zulaya said succinctly, "at least so Mari of High Reaches Weyr told me. And he's getting worse. Thea takes charge when she can, and that older lad of his—"

"Gallian's my age," K'vin exclaimed. "Can't they get around that?"

"Short of making Jamson abdicate, no. At least according to my understanding of the Charter. And it just got refreshed." She gave K'vin a droll smile. "As well I listened in to what T'lan was reading. I'd forgotten the half of it myself. Have you reread it recently?"

"I did," K'vin said, nodding and glad that he had. "Mind you, it isn't as ironclad as we used to think. Far more autonomy granted . . ."

"Where it can be abused by misdirection," Iantine said. "I borrowed the copy. It's going the rounds in the Weyr."

"No matter how Chalkin tries to interpret a Lord Holder's privilege, he can't deny that he's abrogated almost every right the holders are supposed to have . . . such as removal only after a jury of their peers had been convened. Which he certainly ignored in turfing them out . . . and *then* constraining them in unsuitable conditions. There certainly was no collusion or organized mutiny. They hadn't even presented him with a list of their grievances."

"Didn't know they could," Iantine said, his expression uncompromising. "Had to have the word 'mutiny' explained to them, and then denied that they'd do such a thing."

"And Jamson won't budge?" Zulaya asked.

K'vin shook his head.

"Won't he even come and speak to some of the refugees?"

"Doesn't feel it's his right to interfere in the autonomy of another Lord Holder," K'vin said.

Iantine growled in disgust. "I'll bet he really didn't believe my drawings were accurate."

K'vin nodded. "Even after Azury informed him that he thought you had glossed over *some* of the more gruesome injuries."

"Or some of the unseen ones, like those pregnant women," Zulaya added, her eyes flashing with outrage.

"How are they?" K'vin asked.

"One has delivered prematurely, but she and the babe will be all right. The others . . . well, Tisha's doing what she can . . . getting them to talk it all out before it festers too much in their minds."

"They can swear out warrants against the guards—" Iantine began.

"They have," Zulaya said in a harsh tone, her smile unpleasant. "And we have the guards. As soon as the women feel strong enough to testify, we're convening a court here. And M'shall wants to try the murderers he's holding at Benden."

"Two trials, then?"

"Yes, one for rape and one for murder. Not at all our usual winter occupation, is it?" Zulaya said in a droll tone.

"Is Telgar Hold joint with us?" K'vin asked, for the Weyr's Hold should be represented in such a process. He'd been surprised at how detailed the Charter was. His recollections of the Charter's contents were entirely too hazy. In this particular instance, they were also dealing with another holder's employees for a matter that had come up within that hold, not an incident in Telgar Weyr, or within the jurisdiction of Telgar Hold. "But the men are Bitran. Are *we* allowed to?"

"Indeed we're within our rights," Zulaya answered firmly. "Justice can be administered anywhere, provided the circumstances warrant. As the victims are currently in this Weyr and so are their attackers, we may legally hold trial here. However, we'll make sure to invite representatives of other holds and Weyrs to oversee that justice is done."

"How about making sure Jamson attends?" K'vin asked with some malice.

Zulaya gave him a broad smile. "That might alter the old fool's ideas about autonomy."

"And Chalkin?" Iantine asked, an intense expression of anticipation in his eyes.

K'vin chuckled. "We'll see about that. His attendance might just solve the problem."

"Or compound it," Zulaya said, shaking her head. "He's too clever to be caught out over what his men do. Or to come when he hears what it's about."

"No one's going to tell him, are they?" K'vin said.

"I wouldn't count on that, sir," Iantine said mournfully. "It's amazing what he does hear that he shouldn't."

"Then we keep what we've just discussed here," and Zulaya pointed her finger firmly down, "and not a whisper to anyone else. Right, Iantine?"

"Right!" Iantine nodded sharply.

11

▼▼▼▼▼▼▼▼▼▼

THE TRIALS AT TELGAR AND BENDEN WEYRS

As it happened, a blizzard covered most of the eastern mountain ranges and all of Bitra when the trial was convened. The winds were too fierce over Bitra for even a dragon to penetrate. Fortunately, the storm had not yet reached Benden, so representatives from every Weyr and hold were able to attend—with the exception of Lord Jamson of the High Reaches, who was very ill of a respiratory fever. The Lady Holder Thea came, annoyed that Jamson had a legitimate excuse for his absence and had sent Gallian in his place.

"It might have done that stubborn streak of his some good to hear just how Chalkin conducts his hold. Oh, he'd've spouted on about autonomy but he most certainly is against any harm coming to unborn children." Thea gave Zulaya a significant nod, reminding those around her that she had borne fourteen children to Lord Jamson in the course of her fertile years: sufficient to substantially increase the borders of the hold when the children were old enough to claim their land grants.

Held in the capacious Lower Cavern at Benden Weyr, the first of the two trials was a sobering, well-conducted affair. At one time there had been trained legists on Pern, but the need for such persons had waned. Most arguments were settled by negotiated compromise or, when all negotiation efforts failed, by hand-to-hand combat. Consequently, a spokesperson for the accused guards had to be found. One of the teachers from Fort Hold who specialized in legal contracts and land deeds reluctantly agreed to officiate.

Gardner had not been very enthusiastic about involving himself, however briefly, with rapists, but he recognized the necessity of representation and did his best. He had perfunctorily questioned the victims as to the identity of their alleged assailants and tried to shake their testimony. The three women were no longer the frightened, half-starved wretches who had been so abused. Their time in the Weyr had done wonders for their courage, self-esteem, and appearance. Gardner even insisted that they had been rehearsed in their testimony, but that did not mitigate the circumstances of the grievous bodily and mental harm inflicted on them.

"Sure I rehearsed," the oldest of the women said loudly. "In me mind, night and night, how I was flung down and . . . done by dirty men as wouldn't have dared step inside a decent woman's hold with such notions in their head. I ache still rehearsing," and she spat the word at him, "what they did, again and again and again." For emphasis she slammed one fist into the other hand. Gardner had ceased that line of questioning.

In the end he managed one small concession for the accused: the right to be returned to their Contract Hold, following the trial, rather than have to make their own way back to Bitra.

"Fat lot of good that'll do them," Zulaya muttered under her breath when he won that point. "Chalkin hates losers, and those guys have lost a lot more than their contract."

"I wonder what sort of tone Chalkin's next letter of protest will take," Irene said with a malicious chuckle.

Paulin had received a thick screed from the Bitran Holder when Chalkin discovered the "unmitigated interference of assorted renegade dragonriders in his affairs and the abduction of loyal holders from their premises."

"If he dares protest . . . Oh, why did it have to snow so hard?" Paulin lamented. "I'd love to have had him here when his guards said 'they was only following orders to keep the holders from leaving'! M'shall would have had gathered him up in a ball and rendered him spitless!"

M'shall had assumed the role of prosecutor, claiming that right since his riders had been first on the scene. He was exceedingly precise in manner and in his questioning.

"Poring over the Charter and what books Clisser could send him on legal procedures," Irene told Zulaya with a broad grin. "It's done him a world of good. Taken his mind off . . . the spring, you know."

Zulaya had nodded approvingly. "He'd have been a good legist . . . or did they call them lawyers? No, barristers."

"Yes, barristers stood before the judge and handled the trial procedures," Irene replied.

"Gardner wasn't half bad, you know. He tried," Zulaya remarked. "I'll even forgive him asking for mercy for those miserable clods. After all, he had to appear to work *for* his clients," she added tolerantly. "I'm glad we had Iantine sit up close. I want to see his sketches of the trial. I wish he could work as fast with my portrait."

"Your portrait is scarcely the same thing as annotating a trial. And he's to come to Benden when he's finished with you two, you know."

Zulaya was pleased to hear the pride in Irene's voice when she mentioned Iantine. He was a Bendenian.

"You mean, when he's finished sketching our riders."

Irene gave a wistful smile, tinged with sadness. "You'll be glad he did. I wonder will he do the same thing for us at Benden?"

"Whatever he can fit in, I'm sure. That young man's got himself more work than he can handle."

"If he can get it all done before . . . oh, the jury's back."

The twelve men and women, picked at random by straw from those who had come to observe, had listened to all the evidence. Tashvi, Bridgely, and Franco had sat as judges. Now a silence descended over the room, so intense that a cough was quickly muffled.

The three rapists were accounted guilty as charged, and three more were sentenced as accessories, since they had helped pin the victims down. The penalty for the rape of a pregnant woman was castration, which was to be carried out immediately. The others were to receive forty lashes, well laid on by Telgar's large and strong stewards.

"They were lucky there isn't Fall," Zulaya remarked to Irene, Lady Thea, and K'vin. "Otherwise they could also have been tied out during the next Fall."

Despite herself, Thea gave a shudder. "Which is probably why there are so few cases of rape recorded in our hold's annals."

"Small wonder," K'vin said, crossing his legs again. Zulaya had noticed his defensive position and her lips twitched briefly. He turned away. His weyrmate had nearly cheered aloud when the verdict was delivered.

"You can't do that to me," one of the guards was roaring now as he belatedly realized the significance of the verdict. He had been the leader of the men stationed at the eastern border crossing. The other defendants were too stunned, their mouths moving in soundless protest, Morinst being loud enough to drown out any complaint they could voice. "You're none of you my Lord," he'd railed at three Lord Holder judges. "You've got no right to do this."

"And you had no right to rape a pregnant woman!"

"But Chalkin ain't even here." The man writhed in the grip of his guards.

"Chalkin's presence would have had no effect on the trial or the verdict," Tashvi said at his most repressive.

"But he should've been here!" Morinst protested.

"He was invited to attend," Tashvi said without regret.

"He's gotta know. You can't do nothin' without him knowing. I gotta contract with *him*."

"To rape, torture, and humiliate?" Bridgely asked in too soft a voice.

Morinst clamped his lips shut. He struggled more violently as the bailiffs aimed him toward the exit. And his punishment. Not that he could escape either the sentence or the Weyr. The other two were still too stunned to resist their removal to the infirmary where the verdict would be carried out. Those to be lashed were brought outside, though not all the audience followed to witness the corporal punishment.

When that, too, had been completed and the men removed to have their wounds treated, the observers filed back into the Lower Cavern. While this was scarcely an occasion for celebration, except that justice had been served, a substantial meal had been prepared. Wine was the first item sought and served.

"You were superb, M'shall," Irene said when her weyrmate joined her, a newly opened skin of Benden wine on his shoulder, "and do please give me a glass. Though I'm sure you need one more than I. Nice of Bridgely to supply it," she added to Zulaya.

"I think we all need it," the Telgar Weyrwoman said,

glancing over to where the three plaintiffs were celebrating with considerable enthusiasm. Well, let them. "Now what do we do?"

"Well, we've the second trial to get through. I hope it goes as well," M'shall said.

"*No*, with *them*," and his weyrmate pointed to the three women.

"Oh. That them. They say they just want to go back to their homes. Not going to let Chalkin take it because they're not there holding their places." He made a grimace. "Some of them don't really have much to go back to. Chalkin's bullies burned what was flammable and pulled down what they could. I'd say the storms kept more damage from being done. But," and he altered the grimace to a grin, "give 'em credit. They do own what they hold and now they know it. It may give them a tad more backbone next time they're chivvied, and more pride in what they do. They've also asked for groundcrew training."

"Nothing like losing something—however briefly—to value what you have," Thea said. "On the practical side, though, I think High Reaches can supply some basic items. Anyone organizing that?" She glanced about at others in the group. "D'you have numbers yet?"

"Actually we do," Zulaya said, including Irene in her nod. "Three hundred and forty-two—no, forty-three with that premature baby. It's very good of you to offer, Thea."

Thea snorted. "I've reread the Charter, too, and know my duty to my fellow creatures. You wouldn't also happen to know how many poor wretches hold in Bitra?"

M'shall had that answer. "Of course, you can't tell if Chalkin doctored the last census or not, but he's supposed to have 24,657 inhabitants."

"Really?" Zulaya was surprised.

"But then, Bitra's one of the smaller holds and doesn't have any indigenous industry—apart from some forestry. The mining's down to what's needed locally. There're a few looms working but no great competition for Keroon or Benden."

"And the gaming," Thea said with a disgusted sniff.

"That's Chalkin's main industry."

"Well, he's lost a lot on this gamble," Zulaya said.

"Has he?" K'vin wanted to know.

The second trial was almost anticlimactic. Gardner again represented the seven defendants accused of "allegedly causing grievous bodily harm and death" to five innocent men and women.

While Gardner again stipulated that the men had only been following orders to "restrain by any means" anyone trying to cross the border out of Bitra Hold, their putative domicile, it was claimed that unnecessarily severe restraint had been used and caused the deaths of persons who should not have been denied "lawful" exit and a usurpation of their basic Chartered Right to freedom of movement.

The subsequent mutilation and/or torture of the seven, the prosecution said, was not inherent in the order to "restrain by any means." Chalkin had no right to take the lives of any holders without due cause and/or trial by jury.

The day's jury retired and, within half an hour, unanimously rendered a verdict of guilty. The men were sentenced to be transported to the Southern Islands by dragonback with a seven-day supply of food, which was the customary punishment for murderers.

"Are there many on the islands?" Thea asked. "I mean, there have been others sequestered there. Even families, I read, but that was years ago."

Zulaya shrugged. "Telgar's never had to take anyone there, so I wouldn't know."

"Benden hasn't," Irene said, "at least not as long as we've been Leaders."

"My father sent two," Paulin said. "And I do believe that both Ista and Nerat have sent killers there."

"Chalkin did, too," Gallian surprised them by saying. "About four years ago. I don't know where I heard about them. Some sort of real trouble down in his hold and he had Ista transport them since the men originated from that hold."

"Oh, I remember now," Irene said. "M'shall only mentioned he was glad he hadn't had to do the transport."

"Maybe we should send Chalkin's men there when they can travel," Zulaya said.

"No, let him see that we won't tolerate his methods of holding," Irene said, her tone implacable. "Maybe he'll come to his senses."

"That'll be the day!" Zulaya said facetiously.

When snow had melted sufficiently to allow any travel out of Bitra, Chalkin did send another blistering note of protest to Paulin, making it plain that he intended to demand compensation at the Turn's End Conclave for the "ritual disfigurement of men only doing their duty." This time, however, an elderly green rider collected the message when the urgent banner was seen flying from the panel heights of Bitra Hold. F'tol endured a long harangue from Chalkin that the letter had better be delivered, that dragonriders were parasites on the face of Pern, that there'd be some changes made or . . . F'tol was neither intimidated nor impressed. Stoically, he took the letter and responsibly delivered it.

Whether Chalkin knew, or cared, that the refugees had been returned to their holdings was not known. F'tol was reasonably sure that would have been included in the tirade since Chalkin seemed to have included every other shortcoming, mistake, and venial sin ever committed by a dragonrider.

Both Telgar and Benden Weyrs made daily checks on the

returned, to reassure them as well as those concerned with their welfare. Of course, the conditions in Bitra, with dragon-high drifts blocking major roads and tracks, made it improbable that any of Chalkin's men would have been able to move, much less go the distance to the far-flung properties.

Benden Hold and Weyr became the latest winter victims as the blizzards which had hovered over Bitra made their way eastward, coating the eastern seaboard, even down into the northern section of Nerat, which hadn't seen any snow since the settlement of the Bendens in the early decades of the First Fall.

The dragons were the only living creatures who didn't mind the snow, since their tough hide was impervious to its cold as well as *between*. They much enjoyed the snow battles that the Weyrfolk indulged in, and then the warmth of sun intensified by the white landscape, so they lounged in reflected glory.

Despite the more northerly position, Telgar Weyr got only a hand's span of snow and made do with that. The young dragonets were fascinated by the stuff and by having to crack the ice of the lake to bathe. Bathing a dragon had become a hazard, but T'dam allowed the weyrlings to suds up a dragonet and allow it to rinse itself off in the frigid water. But daily washings resulted in some distress for the rider.

"I've chilblains again," Debera complained to Iantine, showing him her swollen fingers when he came out to watch her tend Morath.

The little green was a favorite subject of his because, he told Debera, "She has a tremendous range of expression on her face and gets in the most incredible positions."

Debera was far too besotted with her dragon to disagree with such an impartial opinion. If she herself figured in every sketch Iantine did, she did not wonder about it. But the other green riders did.

"You should get some of Tisha's cream. It stopped my fingers from itching," Iantine snapped his fingers, "like that!"

"Oh, I have some of that," she replied.

"Well, it doesn't do you any good in the jar, you know."

"Yes, I know," she said, ducking her head, her tone low and apologetic.

"Hey, I'm not scolding," he said gently, putting one finger under her chin and lifting her head. "What'd I do wrong?"

"Oh, nothing," she said and pushed his finger away, giving him a too-bright smile. "I get silly notions sometimes. Don't pay me any mind."

"Oh, I don't," he replied so blithely that she gave him a startled look. "Just go on with lathering up that beast of yours . . ." He turned to a new page and removed the pencil from behind his ear. "Go on . . ."

"Iantine's gone on you, Debera," Grasella said, eyeing her barrack mate shrewdly.

"Iantine? He's sketch mad. He'd do his big toe if he had nothing else to pose for him," Debera replied. "Besides, he'll leave soon for Benden . . ."

"Will you miss him?" Jule asked, a sly look on her face.

"Miss him?" Debera echoed, surprised at the question.

I will miss him, Morath said in such a mournful tone that the other dragonets turned toward her, their eyes whirling in minor distress.

"What did she say that's got them all upset?" Jule demanded.

"That she'd miss him. But, love, he's not Weyrbred," Debera told her dragon, stroking her cheek and then her headknob. "He can't stay here indefinitely."

"If anyone asked me, I'd say Iantine would like to," Sarra put in.

"No one's asked you," Angie replied tartly.

"Has he ever done anything . . . I mean, beyond sketching you, Deb?" Jule asked with an avid glint in her eyes.

"No, of course not. Why would he?" Debera said, annoyed and flustered. That was the trouble with having to sleep in with the others. They could be terribly nosy, even if they weren't as mean as her stepmother and sisters had been. She didn't pry into where they were when they were late in at night.

"I give up on her," Jule said, raising her hands skyward in exasperation. "The handsomest unattached man in the Weyr and she's blind."

"She's Morath-besotted," Sarra put in. "Not that any of us are much better."

"Most of us . . ." and Jule paused significantly, "know that while dragons may now be a significant factor in our lives, they are not *everything*, you know. Even ol' T'dam-damn-him has a weyrmate, you know."

"We don't have weyrs yet," Mesla said, speaking for the first time. She took everything literally. "Couldn't have anyone in here with you gawking."

Debera knew she was blushing: her cheeks felt hot.

"That hasn't held *you* back, I noticed," Sarra said to Jule, cocking her head knowingly.

Jule smiled mysteriously. "From the only Weyrbred resident in this barracks, let me assure you that our wishes can influence our dragons' choices."

"They won't rise for another eight or ten months," Angie said, though she had obviously taken heed of Jule's remark. "But, Jule, suppose your dragon fancies a dragon whose rider you can't stand?"

"You mean, O'ney?" and she grinned at Angie's discomfort.

The girl overcame her embarrassment and snapped back quickly enough. "He's impossible, even for a bronze rider.

Have you ever *heard* him go on about how his wing is always tops in competitions! As if that was all that mattered!"

"To him it probably does," Grasella said, "but, Jule, I'm more worried about the blue riders. I mean, some of them are very nice guys and I wouldn't want to hurt their feelings, but they don't generally like girls."

"Oh," and Jule shrugged indolently, "that's easier still. You make an arrangement with another rider to be on hand when your green gets proddy. Then the blue rider gets his mate, if he's got one, or anyone else who's willing—and you'd better believe that anyone's willing when dragons are going to participate. So you bed the one you like, and the blue rider his choice, and you *all* enjoy!"

The girls absorbed this information with varying degrees of enthusiasm or distaste.

"Well, it's up to yourselves what you do, you know," Jule went on. "And we're not limited to this Weyr, either. Oh!" and she let out a gusty sigh. "I'll be so glad when we can fly out of here anytime we want."

"But I thought you were arranging matters with T'red?" Mesla said, her eyes wide with consternation.

"Well, so I am, but that doesn't mean I might not find someone I like better at another Weyr. Greens like it, you know."

"Ah, but can we go to other Weyrs?" Sarra said, waggling a finger at Jule. "In four, five months, we'll have Fall and *then* we'll really work hard, ferrying firestone sacks to the fighters." Her eyes gleamed brightly in anticipation and she hugged herself. "We'll be doing *something* a lot more exciting than having just one mate and plenty of kids."

Debera averted her face, not wanting to take part in such a ridiculous discussion.

Something bothers you, Morath said and slowly lowered her

head to her rider's lap. *I love you. I think you're wonderful. Iantine does, too.*

That confidence startled Debera. *He does?*

He does! And Morath's tone was emphatic. *He likes your green eyes, the way you walk, and the funny crackle in your voice. How do you do that?*

Debera's hand went to her throat and she felt really silly now. *Can you talk to him, too? Or just listen to what he's thinking?*

He thinks very loud. Especially near you. I don't hear him too good far away. He thinks loud about you a lot.

"DEB'RA?" and Sarra's loud call severed that most interesting conversation.

"What? I was talking to Morath. What'd you say?"

"Never mind," and Sarra grinned broadly. "Have you got your Turn's End dresses finished yet?"

"I've one more fitting," Debera said, although that subject, too, caused her embarrassment. She had tried to argue with Tisha that the beautiful green dress was quite enough: she didn't need more. Tisha had ignored that and demanded that she choose two colors from the samples available: one for evening and another good one for daytime wear. Everyone in the Weyr, it seemed, had new clothes for Turn's End. And yet, something in Debera had delighted in knowing she'd have two completely new dresses that no one had ever worn before her. She had, she admitted very very quietly to herself, hoped that Iantine would notice her in them. Now, with Morath's information, she wondered if he'd notice at all that she was wearing new clothes.

"Speaking of weyrs . . ." Mesla said.

"That was half an hour ago, Mesla," Angie protested. "Well?"

"There aren't that many left, and the bigger dragons would have first choice, wouldn't they?" she said.

"Don't worry," Jule said, "some'll come free by the time we

need them." Then she covered her mouth, aware of what she had just implied. "I didn't mean that. I really didn't. I mean, I wouldn't think of moving in . . ."

"Just shut up, Jule," Sarra said in a quiet but firm voice.

There was a long moment of silence, with no one daring to look at anyone.

"Say, who has the salve?" Grasella asked softly from the bunk beyond her, breaking the almost intolerable silence. "My fingers are itching again. No one told me I'd have to cope with chilblains dealing with dragons."

Angie found it in her furs and passed it on.

"After you," Debera said softly as she gave it to Grasella.

The easy laughing chatter was over for the night.

"I haven't had much time," Jemmy told Clisser in his most uncooperative tone of voice when Clisser asked how he was coming on the last of the history ballads. "Had to look up all that law stuff. Why'd you have to take so much trouble with those fragging guards? They shoulda all been dropped on the islands, right away. None of this trial farce."

"The trials were not farces, Jemmy," Clisser said, so uncharacteristically reproving that Jemmy looked up in a state of amazement. "The trials were necessary. To prove that *we* would not act in an arbitrary fashion . . ."

"You mean, the way Chalkin would have," and Jemmy grinned, his uneven teeth looking more vulpine than ever in his long face.

"Exactly."

"You're wasting too much time on him," and Jemmy turned back to reading.

"What are you looking up?"

"I don't know. I'm looking because I *know* there's something we *can* use to check on the Red Planet's position . . . something so simple I'm disgusted I can't call it to mind. I know I've seen it somewhere . . ." Irritably, he pushed the volume away from him. "It'd help a great deal if the people who copied for us had had decent handwriting. I spend too much time trying to decipher it." Abruptly he reached across the cluttered worktop to the windowsill and plonked down in front of him a curious apparatus. "Here's your new computer." He grinned up at Clisser, who regarded the object—bright colored beads strung on ten narrow rods, divided into two unequal portions.

"What is it?" Clisser exclaimed, picking it up and finding that the beads moved stiffly up and down on the rods.

"An abacus, they called it. A counter. Ancient and still functional." Jemmy took the device from Clisser and demonstrated. "It'll take the place of a calculator. Most are down now. Oh, and I found the designs for this, too." He fumbled around his papers and withdrew an instrument consisting of a ruler with a central sliding piece, both marked with logarithmic scales. "You can do quite complicated mathematical calculations on this slide rule, as they called it. Almost as fast as you could type into a digital pad."

Clisser looked from one to the other. "So that's what a slide rule looks like. I saw one mentioned in a treatise on early calculators, but I never thought we'd have to resort to ancient devices. And mention of an abacus, too, actually. You *have* been busy reinventing alternatives."

"And I'll find that other device, too, if you'll leave me alone and don't dump more vitally important, urgent research on me."

"I'm hoping," Clisser said at his most diplomatic, "that you can give me something to show before the Winter Solstice and Turn's End."

Jemmy shot straight up in his chair, cocked his head and

stared at Clisser so that Clisser leaned forward hopefully, holding his breath lest he disrupt Jemmy's concentration.

"Fraggit," and Jemmy collapsed again, beating his fists on the table. "It has to *do* with solstices."

"Well, if you've gone back to abaci and slide rules, why not a sundial clock?" Clisser asked facetiously.

Jemmy sat up again, even straighter. "Not a sundial," he said slowly, "but a cosmic clock ... a star dial like ... stone ... stone *something* ..."

"Stonehenge?"

"What was that?"

"A prehistoric structure back on Earth. Sallisha can tell you lots more about it if you'd care to ask her," Clisser said slyly, and was rewarded by Jemmy's rude dismissal of the suggestion. "It turned out to be rather an astonishing calendar, accurately predicting eclipses as well as verifying solstice at dawn."

Clisser stopped, looking wide-eyed at Jemmy, whose mouth had dropped open to form a soundless O as what he said astounded them both.

"Only that was a stone circle ... on a plain ..." Clisser stammered, gesturing dolmens and cross beams. Muttering under his breath, he strode across to the shelves, trying to find the text he wanted. "We must have copied it. We *had* to have copied it ..."

"Not necessarily, since you've been interested only in relevant historical entries," Jemmy contradicted him. "I remember accessing it once. It's only that we'll have to adapt it to fit *our* needs, which is framing the Red Planet when the conjunction is right." He was scrabbling among the litter on his desk for a clean sheet of paper and a pencil. The first three he found were either stubs or broken. "That's another thing we've got to re-invent ... fountain pens."

"Fountain pens?" Clisser echoed. "Never heard of fountain pens."

"I'll do them tomorrow. Leave me to work this out, but . . ." Jemmy paused long enough to grin diabolically up at Clisser's befuddlement. ". . . I think I'll have something by Turn's End. Maybe even a model . . . but only if you leave . . . *now*."

Clisser left, closing the door quietly behind him and pausing a moment.

"I do believe I've been kicked out of my own office," he said, pivoting to regard the door. His name, which had recently been repainted, was centered in the upper panel. "Hmm." He turned the sign hung there on a nail to DO NOT DISTURB and walked away whistling the chorus from the Duty Song.

He'd catch Sallisha before she climbed up the stairs to his office. That would please her. Well, it might.

He hurried down the steps and met up with her coming in the door.

"I'm not late," she said, at her most caustic, her arm tightening convulsively on the bulging notebook she carried.

He was in for it.

"I didn't say you were. Let's take the more comfortable option of the teachers' lounge."

"My conclusions are not something you'll wish to discuss in public," she said, recoiling. She might be one of his best teachers—though the rumor was that children learned their lessons to get out of her clutches—but her attitude toward him, and his proposed revitalization program, was totally hostile.

Clisser smiled as graciously as he could. "It's empty right now and will be for at least two hours."

She sniffed, but when he courteously gestured for her to precede him, she tramped in an implacable fashion. Like Morinst to his . . . Clisser shuddered and hurriedly followed her.

The lounge was empty, a good fire crackling on the hearth. The klah pitcher rested on the warmer, and for a change there were clean cups. He wondered if Bethany had done the housekeeping. The sweetener jar was even full. Yes, it would have been Bethany, trying to ease this interview.

As he closed the door he also turned the DO NOT DISTURB sign around and flipped the catch. Sallisha had seated herself in the least comfortable chair—the woman positively enjoyed being martyred. She still held the notebook, like a precious artifact, across her chest.

"You cannot exclude Greek history from study," she said, aggressively launching into an obviously prepared speech. "They've got to understand where our form of government came from to appreciate what they have. You have to include—"

"Sallisha, the precedents can be covered in the outline, but not the entire culture," he began.

"But the culture determined the form of government . . ." She stared at him, appalled by his lack of comprehension.

"*If* a student is curious enough to want to know more, we shall have it to give him. But there is no point in forcing hill farmers and plains drovers to learn something that has absolutely no relevance to their way of life."

"You demean them by saying that."

"No, I save them hours of dull study by replacing it with the history of Pern . . ."

"There is scarcely enough of that to dignify the word 'history.' "

"Yesterday is history today, but do you want to repeat it? 'History' is what happened in the life or development of a people . . . we," and he tapped his chest, "the Pernese. Also a systematic account of us," he tapped his chest again, "with an analysis and explanation. *From* . . . the beginning of the *Pern* colony . . . that is history, grand and sweeping, surviving against incredible odds and an implacable menace, derring-do, ingenuity, courage, and *of* this planet, not of a place that's only a name. It's better than our ancient history—if it's taught right."

"Are you impugning my—"

"Never, Sallisha, which is why I particularly need your complete cooperation for the new, enriched, relevant curriculum. On average, your students rank higher in their final examination papers than any other teacher's . . . and that includes the hill farmers and the plains drovers. But they never again *use* the information you imparted. Pern is difficult enough . . . with an external menace to contend with . . . Let them be proud of the accomplishments of their ancestors . . . their most recent ancestors. Not the confused and tortured mindlessness the Pern colonists left behind. Furthermore," he went on relentlessly as she opened her mouth to speak, "the trials at Telgar and Benden have proved that not enough time is spent teaching our people their rights under their Charter . . ."

"But I spend—"

"*You* certainly have never been remiss, but we must emphasize," and he slapped one fist into the other palm, "holder rights under their Lord: how to claim Charter acreage, how to prevent what happened in Bitra . . ."

"No other Lord Holder is as *wicked*," and her mouth twisted with disgust as she enunciated the last word, "as that awful man. Don't you think you can get me to teach there now that Issony's left!" She waggled her index finger at him and her expression was fierce.

"Not you, Sallisha, you're far too valuable to waste on Bitra," he said, soothing her. Bitra would need a more compassionate and flexible teacher than Sallisha. "But I'm amazed at just how many people were unaware of the Charter Rights. And that's wrong. Not that I think the cowed folk up in Bitra would have dared cite the clauses to him . . . even if they had known about them. I mean, it was appalling to realize just how few people who attended the trial *knew* that ordinary holders had the *right* to freedom of movement, and lawful assembly, or to appeal for mediation for crippling tithes."

"Why haven't the Lord Holders impeached him?" she wanted to know, her fierceness diverted toward a new victim. "It's patently obvious he is unfit to manage a hold, much less one during a Fall. I cannot see why they have been waffling about over the matter."

"Sallisha, it takes a unanimous decision to impeach a Lord Holder," he said with a light admonishment.

She regarded him blankly for a moment. Then flushed. "Who's holding out?"

"Jamson."

She clicked her tongue irritably. "And that's another place you mustn't send me. The cold would exacerbate my joint problem."

"I'm aware of that, Sallisha, which is why I wondered if you'd consider Nerat South this year?"

"How much traveling?" she demanded, but not unappeased.

"Six major holds and five smaller units but all within reasonable distance. And, of course, your journeys would fall on Threadfree days. Excellent accommodations and a very good contract. Gardner made sure that everything complies with your wishes as regards conditions." He reached into his jerkin pocket and pulled out the document. "I thought you might like to see it today."

"Sweetening me up, are you?" she said with an almost coquettish smile, hand half outstretched to the sheets.

"You are my best teacher, Sallisha," he said and extended his hand until her fingers closed around the contract.

"This won't make me approve your butchery of pre-Pernese history, Clisser."

"It's not intended to, but we can't have you in danger on the plains of Keroon . . ."

"I did promise to come back . . ."

"They will understand . . ."

"There are some really fine minds there . . ."

"You will find them wherever you go, Sallisha, you have the knack." Then he hauled out the larger sheaf of papers, the new syllabus. "You may find this much easier to impart to your students."

She eyed it as she would a tunnel snake.

12

HIGH REACHES AND FORT HOLDS

"So," Paulin said to Thea and Gallian in the comfortably warm High Reaches solarium where the Lady Holder received her guest, "is there *any* way we can get him to change his mind?"

Thea shrugged. "Not by reasoned argument, that's for certain. He was indignant that 'a Lord Holder's right to deal with his own folk' had been set aside for the two trials. Not that he objected to the sentences . . ."

" 'That was only right and just, and they should have been sent to the islands as well for they'll only make trouble of a different sort now,' " Gallian added, mimicking his father's thin wheezing voice. "If he would only give me authorization to deal with *all* hold matters . . ." and he raised his hands in helplessness. "He's too sick . . ."

"Wait a minute. He *is* sick," Paulin interrupted, "and your weather here is only aggravating the respiratory problem, isn't it?"

Thea's eyes widened as she jumped to a conclusion.

"If he was sent to Ista, or Nerat to recuperate, why, he'd have to authorize Gallian—" she began.

"Precisely . . ."

"What happens when he recovers and finds out what I did, knowing, as he's made sure I do, his views on impeachment," Gallian asked his mother, "and finds out I've gone against him? I could very likely lose my chance of succession."

"That's not likely, dear. You know how he carries on about your 'stupid' younger brothers," Thea said reassuringly, laying a hand on her son's arm. "You just know when to stand up to him. You've always had a flair for dealing with people. As for the nephews . . ." She threw up her hand in despair. Then her face clouded. "I really am worried about these constant chest infections. Frankly, I don't think he's going to last much longer." She sighed in regret. "He's been a good spouse . . ."

"Can you get your medic to recommend the warmer climate?" Paulin asked sympathetically.

"He's been doing so constantly," Thea said, setting her mouth in a firm line. "I'll make it so. Somehow! I couldn't live with myself if I didn't. For his sake as well as those poor wretches."

Gallian looked uncertain.

"Don't worry, lad," Paulin said. "You've already got full marks in my book for cooperation. And, as long as I'm Chair, you've my support. The Conclave doesn't necessarily have to abide by the deceased's wishes as to successor. But we've got to take action *now*. Even waiting until Turn's End is dangerous. We rescued those people, their rights were upheld in a duly assembled court, and Chalkin's in some state of mind over that." Paulin's laugh was mirthless. "We can't let him take his vengeance out on them or we've spent a lot of time and effort to no avail. With this thaw setting in, he'll be able to move about. And I think we all have a good idea that he'll retaliate in some fashion."

Thea shuddered, her comfortably plump body rippling under her thick gown. "I won't have *that* on my conscience, no matter what my Lord Jamson says." She rose. "Jamson spent such a poor night, I'll catch him now, before he can put up any more objections. One thing is certain, he doesn't *want* to die. He likes Richud more than Franco. I'll suggest Ista Hold. I wouldn't mind the winter there myself. In fact ..." She straightened her shoulders. "I think I'm gomig dowd wif a gold, too," she said, sniffing. "He might just humor me, where he wouldn't do a thing for himself. If you'll excuse me."

Both men had stood when she did, and now Gallian strode to open the door for her as she sailed gracefully out, grinning mischievously as she left. Gallian returned to his guest, shaking his head.

"I've never gone against my father before," he said anxiously, his expression unhappy.

"Nor would I urge you to do so, lad. I appreciate your doubts, but can you *doubt* what Chalkin will do?"

"No, I can't," and Gallian sighed, turning back to the Fort Lord Holder with a resolute expression. "I suppose I should get accustomed to *making* decisions, not merely carrying them out."

Paulin clapped him on the shoulder encouragingly. "That's it exactly, Gallian. And I'll guarantee, not all the decisions you'll be called upon to make will be the right ones. Being a Lord Holder doesn't keep you from making mistakes: just make the right wrong ones." Paulin grinned as Gallian tried to absorb that notion. "If you are right most of the time, you're ahead of the game. And you're right in this one for the good reasons which your father declines to see."

Gallian nodded his head. Then asked more briskly, "Will you have some wine now, Paulin?"

"You've your mother's way with you," Paulin said, accepting the offer. "Which you will find is an advantage. . . . Not, mind you, that I in any way imply a lack in your father's manners."

"No, of course not," Gallian said, but he smiled briefly, then cleared his throat. "Ah, what happens to Chalkin when he's removed? I mean, it's not as if he could be dropped on the Southern Islands, is it?"

"Why not?" Paulin replied equably. "Not," he added hastily when he saw Gallian's consternation, "that he would be placed on the same one as the murderers. There is a whole chain . . . an archipelago of isles . . ."

"Aren't they volcanic?"

"Only Young Island, otherwise they're tropical and quite habitable. But one is certain then that the . . . ah, detainee cannot leave and cause ructions. Which Chalkin would certainly do if he was allowed to remain on the mainland. No, the most sensible and most humane solution is to put him where he can't do any more harm than he's already done."

"Then who's to take over managing Bitra?"

"His children are too young, certainly, but there's an uncle, not much older than Chalkin at that. I heard a rumor, though, that Vergerin and Chalkin had played a game, the stakes being an uncontested succession."

"My father mentioned that, too, early on when impeachment first came up. Said he ought to have insisted that Vergerin stand in spite of what the old Neratian Lord wanted. Chalkin's spouse is Franco's sister, you know."

"I'd forgot that. Amazing," Paulin added. "Franco's totally different, but then his mother was Brenton's first spouse."

They were discussing the ever-interesting problem of heredity when the door suddenly opened and Thea came in, almost bent double.

"Great stars, Mother!" Gallian rushed to assist her. "Why, what's the matter? You're so flushed . . ."

She slammed the door shut, waved aside her son's help, and collapsed in her chair with laughter.

"What's so funny?"

"Oh, your father, dear . . ." She wiped tears from her cheeks and some of the 'flush' came away, too. She looked at the handkerchief and rubbed her cheeks more vigorously, still laughing. "We did it. He's going to the warm. I left him writing to ask for Richud's hospitality. I said I'd have the message pennon flown, but your rider would take it, wouldn't he, Paulin? When he takes you back to Fort?"

"Indeed, he will . . . or rather I'll take it to Richud myself and ask him to connive with us to keep Jamson from knowing what's happening off the island," Paulin said, grinning with relief.

"But why are you laughing, Mother? And why the face paint?" Gallian demanded.

"Well," and she flitted her handkerchief, beaming at the two. "What he wouldn't do for himself, he'd do for his ailing mate," she said, again assuming a stuffed-nose voice. "So first I had your sister go in and fetch Canell, as if there were an emergency. I primed Canell to back me up and it was he who suggested the rouge. So when I came into your father's room, I arrived moaning over my aches and pains, which had developed so rapidly overnight. And sneezing constantly . . . Fortunately, I have a small sneeze so I can imitate it . . . Then Canell took over—really, the man was quite convincing. He got alarmed over my rapid pulse and flushed face. He made much of worrying about the condition of my lungs and the strain on my heart. So, between us, why, Jamson agreed to take me south to Ista until I'm completely recovered. So there!" She beamed from one to the other, quite delighted.

"Mother! You are the living end."

"Of course," she said patronizingly. Then she surprised both men by sneezing. "Oh, good heavens!"

"Hmm," said Gallian with mock severity, "that's what happens when you tell stories. You *get* what you pretended you had."

"He's sent someone looking for you, too. So—"

There was a polite tap at the door. Gallian went immediately to answer it, opening only wide enough to be seen. "Yes, tell Lord Jamson that I'll be there directly," he said, and closed the door again.

"I'll wait with Lord Paulin until you can get the letter, Galli," she said, pouring herself some wine. "This is to fortify myself against my cold and any relapse I might have taken ... Another small glass for yourself, Paulin? To toast my debut as an actress?"

"I wish you'd thought of that ploy earlier."

"So do I," she said with a little sigh. "But I hadn't such an overwhelming *need* to before. Those poor people. Who will take over from Chalkin once you get him out? And what will happen to him, for that matter?"

"That has to be decided."

"We were just discussing that, Mother," Gallian said. "There's Vergerin, the uncle on the father's side."

"But Vergerin gambled his succession rights away," Thea said sternly.

"You heard that, too?" Paulin said.

"Well, you know that Bloodline," Thea said. "Always gambling. On the most ridiculous things, too, and for the most bizarre wagers. But to gamble on the succession?" Her expression showed her disgust over that wager.

"Perhaps Vergerin learned a lesson," Gallian remarked—a trifle condescendingly, Paulin thought.

"Perhaps," Paulin said. "If we find him alive."

"Oh no!" Thea's hand went to her throat in dismay.

"If the Council votes to impeach—"

"Not if, Gallian, *when*," Paulin said, raising his hand in correction.

"*When* they do, how do they go about getting Chalkin out of Bitra Hold?" Gallian asked.

"I think that will require thought and planning," Paulin said. "But go now and see your father, Gallian. Mustn't keep him waiting. He might change his mind."

"Not when Mother's health is at stake," Gallian said, and, with a final grin, left the room.

"Promise me, Paulin, that Gallian's chance at succession won't suffer because of this?" Thea said, earnestly gripping his arm.

"I do promise, Thea," he said, patting her hand.

F our days later, when Lord Jamson and Lady Thea had been safely conveyed to Ista Hold, the rest of the Lord and Lady Holders and the Weyrleaders convened an emergency meeting at Telgar Hold and formally impeached Lord Chalkin for dereliction of his duties and responsibilities to Benden Weyr, for the cruel and unusual punishment of innocent holders (Iantine's drawings were submitted as well as the proceedings of the recent trials), for refusing to allow the Charter to be taught so that all would know their rights as well as their responsibility (Issony gave testimony on that account), and for denying these rights to his holders without due reason.

Gallian soberly voted yea in his turn, having duly exhibited his authorization to act in all matters concerning High Reaches Hold.

"So, now what do we do?" Tashvi said, clasping his hands together with an air of relief at a difficult decision completed.

"Obviously, we inform Chalkin and remove him," Paulin said.

"No other trial?" Gallian asked, startled.

"He just had it," Paulin said. "Judge and jury of his peers."

"It would be against all precedent to employ dragonriders to effect his removal," S'nan said flatly.

Everyone turned to the Fort Weyrleader, showing varying degrees of surprise, disgust, anger, or incredulity at such a fatuous statement.

"Impeachment is also against all precedent, too, S'nan," M'shall said, "because this is the first time that clause has been invoked since it was written two-hundred-and-fifty-odd years ago. But it's now a matter of record. However, I disagree that the dragonriders should bow out. Fragit, S'nan, one of the main reasons for getting rid of him is that he has not helped to prepare his hold, which *we* are honor bound to protect. I'll drag him out of there myself if need be."

Irene beside him nodded vehemently in his support and then glared at S'nan. Sarai, S'nan's Weyrwoman, regarded Irene in horrified dismay.

"If you don't grab him first, he'll just flit out of that warren of a hold of his, and who knows what he might do then," Irene said. Then she blinked and cocked her head, puzzled. "You know, I don't know enough about the interior layout of Bitra Hold to know where to find him, much less grab him with all those bodyguards he has around him. Franco?"

"What?" The Nerat Lord Holder responded nervously. "I can't tell you what Bitra's like. I've never been in more than the reception rooms, even if Nadona is my sister."

"How curious," Bastom said.

"What will we do when we do get him out?" Franco asked. "Who's to hold? Those kids of his are too young."

"The uncle, Vergerin—" Paulin began.

"What about a regency till they're of age?" Azury suggested, cutting across the Fort Lord's beginning.

"Or a promising younger son from a well-conducted hold?" Richud of Ista asked, looking about brightly.

"We know the Bloodline's tainted with the gambling addiction," put in Bridgely.

"That trait can be remedied by strict discipline and a good education," Salda of Telgar said firmly. "As the seed is sown, so will it ripen."

"Vergerin . . ." Paulin said again, raising his voice to be heard above the various arguments.

"Him? He gambled his rights away," Sarai of Fort Weyr said at her most severe.

"Chalkin cheated . . ." M'shall said. "He did in every high-stake game I ever heard of."

Irene gave him a very thoughtful stare.

"So I *heard!*" M'shall repeated.

"VERGERIN," and Paulin roared the word, stunning everyone into silence, "must be considered first, since he is of the Bloodline. That's a stipulation of the Charter which I intend to follow to the letter. He is missing from the property where he has quietly resided since Chalkin took hold."

"Missing?"

"Chalkin do it?"

"Where? Why?"

"Vergerin would have had training from his brother in hold management," Paulin went on, "and I believe that the records state that Kinver was a capable and fair Lord Holder."

"He gambled, too," Irene said in an undertone.

"But he didn't cheat," M'shall said, giving his weyrmate a stern look.

"We all adhere, do we not," Paulin went on, "to the Charter Inheritance Clause which stipulates that a member of the Bloodline must be considered first. Now, if Vergerin is available . . ."

"And willing . . ." M'shall added.

"And *able*," G'don of the High Reaches Weyr amended in a firm voice.

"Able and willing," Paulin echoes, "we would then be following the Charter . . ."

"We've set one precedent today," Bastom said, "why not give Bitra a break and put in someone *trained* and competent. Especially since there's so much to be done to get that hold cleared for the spring action."

"Good point. How about a team? Give some young eager scions some practice in day-to-day management?" Tashvi suggested.

"All those with younger sons and daughters available for the job, raise your hands," said M'shall, not quite as facetiously as he sounded.

"No, you have to replace Chalkin with a member of the Blood-line," S'nan said loudly, pounding the table with both fists.

"Then it has to be Vergerin."

"If we can find him . . ."

"ORDER! ORDER!" and Paulin banged his gavel forcefully until silence prevailed. "There. Now, we can think again. First, we must remove Chalkin . . ."

"What good does that do if we've no one to put in authority in a hold that will be totally demoralized to find itself leaderless?" S'nan said, so incensed that he was speaking faster than anyone had ever heard him talk.

"Ah, but we could put in a new holder so quickly no one will have time to become demoralized," Tashvi suggested.

"I suspect that we will," Paulin said. "Vergerin is not in his known holding and indeed the place looks to have been deserted for some length of time."

S'nan was aghast. "Chalkin has removed him?"

"Probably to that cold storage he's said to have in his lower levels," M'shall said grimly.

"He couldn't have." One would think from S'nan's distressed expression that this latest evidence of Chalkin's complicity and dishonor was his final disillusionment. Sarai leaned over to pat his hand soothingly.

"We do not know that such suspicions are any more than that," Paulin said tactfully. "So, let us all be calm for a moment. Chalkin must be removed . . ."

"What do you do with him, then?" asked S'nan in a shaking voice.

"Exile him," Paulin said, glancing around the table and catching complete agreement with that decision. "That's the safest measure, and also the kindest. There are so many islands in that archipelago that he can have one all his own." Others chuckled at Paulin's droll tone.

"Yes, that would be fitting and proper," the Fort Weyrleader said, brightening somewhat from his gloom.

"We find Vergerin—" When others started to interrupt Paulin once more, he cracked the gavel hard once. "And to start preparing the hold for Thread and reassuring the holders right now, each of you will send a member of your family: one already competent in hold management. It's going to take a lot of work and time to get Bitra prepared. Too much responsibility for just one man or woman. If we find Vergerin and he's willing, he would in any case need assistants."

There was considerable murmuring at that, but the notion seemed to please all, even S'nan.

"We're back again to removing Chalkin," M'shall said. "And Bitra has more exits than a snake tunnel. If Chalkin suspects what we've just done, he'll make a break for it."

"Well, he can't! He's been impeached," S'nan said.

"He doesn't know that yet, S'nan," D'miel of Ista Weyr said, his tone tetchy.

"Considering how often he *knows* things he shouldn't," B'nurrin of Igen Weyr said, "we ought to *do* it now! He mightn't suspect me of anything devious," the young bronze rider said, grinning around the table. "I barely know the man. I'll volunteer."

"At the moment, I don't think any dragonriders are welcome at Bitra Hold," Bridgely said with a cynical lift of one eyebrow.

"You may be right," Irene said, "but only a dragonrider could get into Bitra easily right now. All the roads are snowbound. So it has to be one of us. I'll go."

"No, you won't," M'shall said firmly. "I don't want you anywhere near that lecher."

"Ah, but I could transport others in, you know, and drop them off quietly. He wouldn't be quite so upset at a queenrider coming." Irene gave a nasty chuckle. "He doesn't consider us dangerous, you know." She winked at Zulaya.

"If the snow's so bad at Bitra, where could he escape to anyhow?" Zulaya wanted to know.

"A good point, but he could also hide within the hold and impede progress when our deputies try to get things working again," Bastom said.

"Iantine was there for several weeks," Zulaya said. "Maybe he would know more about Bitra's levels and exits."

"Issony's been in and out for the past few years as teacher," M'shall said as he rose. "They're both still outside, aren't they? I'll just bring them in."

When the problem was explained to Iantine and Issony, they both hauled out writing implements, but it was Iantine who had paper.

"I did some explorations on my own," Iantine said, blocking out an irregular figure on the clean sheet.

"He didn't catch you?" Issony asked, his eyes on Iantine's fingers as the interior levels of Bitra were delineated in swift, sure strokes.

"I had a perfect excuse—I got lost. He lodged me down on the scullery level when I first got there," Iantine said.

Issony looked surprised. "Didn't anyone warn you about his contracts?"

"Yes, but not strongly enough. I learned."

"I could never do this!" Issony said in admiration. "And you've got the dimensions right, too."

"Master Domaize insisted that we learn the rudiments of architectural drafting," the young portraitist said.

"There's another level," Issony said, tapping the right-hand corner of the paper. "You were lucky not to visit it." He gave a snort. "Chalkin calls it his cold storage." The teacher glanced around the table. "A lot of small cubicles, some horizontal, some vertical, and none of them long enough or wide enough for the poor blighters shoved in 'em."

"You can't be serious?" S'nan's eyes protruded in dismay.

"Never more," Issony said. "One of the kitchen girls spilled a tub of sweetener and she was immured for a week. She died of the damp cold of the place." Then, as Iantine's pencil slowed, "There're steps down from his rooms here. They come out in the kitchen. He's always complaining that delicacies disappear from storage, but I know for a fact he's the one snitching." Issony grinned. "I was trying to get some food one night and he nearly caught me at it."

"There's an upper level over this section," Iantine said, his pencil poised. "But the door was padlocked."

"Supposedly due to subsidence," Issony said with a bit of a snort. "But there wasn't as much dust in the hall as usual in his back corridors. I think it could be an access to the panel heights."

"We'll have a dragon up there, too," Paulin said. He wasn't the only one to stand behind the artist to watch him work. "Quite a warren. Glad you looked about you when you were there, Iantine." He patted the young man's shoulder in approval. "So how many . . . ah, discreet exits are there?"

"I know of nine, besides the front one and the kitchen door," Issony said, pointing out the locations.

Paulin rubbed his hands together and, waving everyone to resume their seats at the table, stood for a long moment, looking at the floor plan.

"So, let us not waste time and agree on the . . . ah, strategy here and now. Irene, I appreciate your willingness to be bait, but let us use surprise instead. Issony, Iantine, when would the hold be at its most vulnerable?"

The two men exchanged glances. Issony shrugged. "Early morning, about four, five o'clock. Even the watchwher's getting tired. Most of the guards would be asleep." He glanced toward Iantine, who nodded.

"So, we will need dragonriders . . ."

"Let's stick to those of us in this room, if we can," M'shall said.

"It's totally improper to hound a man in his own hold," S'nan began, starting to rise from his seat.

G'don of High Reaches, seated just beyond him, pulled his arm to reseat him. "Give over, S'nan," he said wearily.

"You're excused from the force, S'nan," Paulin said, equally exasperated.

"But . . . but . . ."

Even his weyrmate shushed him.

"There're more than enough of us quite willing," Shanna of Igen said with a withering glance at the dismayed Fort Weyrleader.

"Good. Then we'll cover all the exits . . ."

"There's one window in the kitchen that they always forget to lock," Iantine said. "And I don't think they ever feed the watchwher enough. He's all bones. Something juicy might occupy him. And I think the window's beyond his chain's reach."

"Good points, Iantine," Paulin said. "Through the window,

then, and we'll infiltrate immediately up to Chalkin's private quarters through the back stairs."

"The hidden door's the panel next to the spice cupboard. If you take me along, I can find it in a jiffy," Issony said, his eyes bright with anticipation.

"If you're willing . . ." Paulin said.

"I am, too," Iantine added.

"I rather thought you might be," Paulin said, and then rapidly issued the details of the plan.

With the exception of S'nan, all the Weyrleaders were involved, and even young Gallian was persuaded to come.

"I might as well be hanged for the sheep as the lamb," he said with a fatalistic shrug.

"You'll not suffer from this day's work, Gallian," Bastom assured him. "It's a unanimous decision and our presence there will make that plain to Chalkin. He has no allies among us," the Tillek Lord said, with a reproving glance at S'nan, who sat with face set in such a mournful expression that Bastom was nearly sorry for the punctilious Weyrleader.

"So we are agreed, Lords, Ladies, and Leaders?" Paulin said when he was sure everyone had grasped their roles in the deposition. "Then let us refresh ourselves and rest until it's time to depart."

13

▼▼▼▼▼▼▼▼

BITRA HOLD AND TELGAR WEYR

Except for the fact that the watchwher did not succumb to the choice bits of meat brought to lure it from its duty, and M'shall had to have Craigath speak sharply to it, entry was obtained easily. Whoever should have heard the watchwher's one bellow did not. Issony had no trouble entering by the unlocked window and opening the kitchen door to that contingent. Those who were assigned to watch the various other exits from the hold were by then in place. Iantine sped through the kitchen and up into the main reception rooms, where he opened the front entrance for the rest of the group. Meanwhile, Issony had found the hidden door in the kitchen. Although the stairway was lit by dying glows, there was enough illumination for Paulin and the "arresting" Lords, Ladies, and Leaders.

Paulin opened the access door at the top and entered Chalkin's private apartments first. Behind him came eight Lord and Lady Holders and M'shall, who insisted on representing the Weyrs. To their surprise, the room was brightly lit, glows shining from wall sconces so that the sleeping figures in the massive fur-covered bed were quite visible. All three of them. Chalkin's portly frame bulked the largest under the soft sleeping furs, though his head was covered by a fold of the fine white bedsheet.

One of the girls woke first. She opened her mouth to scream and did not when she saw Paulin's abrupt gesture for silence. Instead, she slithered across the mattress, sheet held up to her chin, to the edge of the bed and grabbed a discarded dress from the pile on the floor. Paulin indicated that she could clothe herself. As smoothly as she moved, or perhaps because she had the sheet up to her chin and let cold air in, the other girl was awakened. She did scream.

"As loud as a green in season," M'shall said later, chuckling at the memory. "At that, Chalkin didn't rouse."

His guards had been alerted, though, and charged into the room, to be flabbergasted by the sight of so many armed folk in Chalkin's most private apartment.

"Chalkin has been impeached for failure to prepare this hold for Threadfall, for abuse of his privilege as Lord Holder, and for denying his holders their Charter-given rights," Paulin said in a loud voice, sword drawn.

"Unless you wish to join him in his exile, put up your weapons."

To a man they did, just as the reinforcements, led by Iantine, burst in from the hall.

That was what finally roused Chalkin from a drunken sleep.

Later Paulin remarked that he'd been disappointed at such an anticlimactic outcome of their dawn invasion.

"S'nan will be reassured," K'vin said. "I think he was certain we intended to humiliate Chalkin."

"We have," Tashvi said with a chuckle.

Chalkin showed every fiber of his cowardice, trying to bribe one Lord Holder after another, with hints of unusual treasure if they assisted him. If anyone had been in the least bit tempted, their resolve was strengthened when the broken, shivering wrecks were released from "cold storage."

"The place was full," Issony said, looking shattered by what he had seen on that level. "Border guards, most of them, but they didn't deserve that from Chalkin!"

Even the hardiest of them would bear the marks of their incarceration for the rest of their lives.

"Iantine? Did you bring . . . ah, you did. Do a quick sketch of them, will you," Issony said, pointing to the two so close to death: the two who had been castrated for rape. All that could be done for them was to ease their passing with fellis juice. "To show S'nan. In case he has lingering doubts as to the justice of what was done here today."

"Any sign of Vergerin?" Paulin asked when all the cells had been emptied.

"No," M'shall said grimly. "That shouldn't reassure you any." He jerked his thumb at some of the stretcher bearers who had previously been the "cold storage" guards. "They said there were four dead ones who were slipped into the lime pits day before yesterday. We may have moved too late for Vergerin."

Paulin cursed under his breath. "Did you ask if any had heard the name?"

M'shall grunted. "No one down there *had* a name."

Paulin winced. "We'd best send for the holder team."

"I have already dispatched riders to collect the deputies. They should be here . . ."

There was a commotion in the hall, with cheering and shouts of welcome.

"They can't have got here this soon," M'shall said, surprised. Both men went to investigate.

A tall man was shrugging out of thin and dirty furs and smiling at the riders clapping him on the back or whatever part of him they could touch.

"Guess who just walked in?" B'nurrin of Igen cried, seeing Paulin and M'shall.

"Vergerin?" Paulin asked.

"Optimist," M'shall muttered, and then, taking a second hard look at the face no longer hidden by a big furred hat, exclaimed, "It is!"

"It is?" Paulin hastened across the broad hall.

"Has the family eyebrows," M'shall said with a chuckle. "Where've you been hiding, Vergerin?"

"M'shall?" Vergerin peered around, a hopeful smile breaking across his weather-beaten face. He did bear a facial resemblance to Chalkin: as if Chalkin's features had been elongated and refined. "You don't know how glad I was to see all those dragons on the heights. I figured you had to come to your senses and get rid of him ..." He jerked his thumb ceiling-ward. "You've no idea ..."

"Where did you hide? When did you hide?" Paulin asked, clasping Vergerin's hand and shaking it enthusiastically.

Vergerin's grin turned wry. "I figured the safest place was under Chalkin's nose." He gestured in the general direction of the cotholds. "He houses his beasts better than his folk, so the smell of me is at least clean horse manure. I've been earning my keep at the beasthold."

"But your holding has been empty ..."

"By my design, I assure you," Vergerin said, running a grubby hand through greasy hair and smiling apologetically. "I've a strong survival streak, my Lord Holders, and when I realized my nephew really was not going to do a single thing about the imminence of Thread, I knew I had better disappear before he thought of possible retaliation . . . and me as his only too obvious replacement."

He had unwound the layers that clothed him and stood with a quiet dignity in the midst of the warmly dressed riders and Lord Holders. It was that innate dignity that impressed Paulin. Nor was he alone in noticing it.

"Admittedly, my Blood claim to the hold was squandered foolishly, but then, I should have known that Chalkin was likely to cheat that night, if ever, with such stakes. It took me quite some while to figure out *how* he managed it, for I'm not without knowing a few tricks myself, and most of those that can be played on the unwary." He gave a self-deprecating little smile. "I forgot just how hungry Chalkin was for a Lord Holder's power."

"But you kept your promises," Paulin said, nodding approval.

"The least I could do to restore self-esteem," and Vergerin executed a little bow to Paulin and the others. "Dare I hope that you wish to keep this Bloodline in Bitra Hold?" He cocked one of his heavy dark eyebrows, his glance candid and accepting.

Paulin did a quick check of the expressions on the other four Lord Holders who had arrived on the scene.

"You will certainly be considered by the Conclave when it meets at Turn's End," Paulin said, nodding. The others murmured.

Loud protestations of innocence suddenly broke up the tableau as Chalkin, bracketed by Bastom and Bridgely, was walked down the main stairs. The tears of his wife and the frightened shrieks of his children added to the tumult.

At the last landing Chalkin halted, wrenching his arms free from the two Lords as he flung himself down the stairs at Vergerin.

"You! *You!* You betrayed me! You broke your word! You did it. You did it all!"

Bastom and Bridgely, moving with creditable speed, managed to recapture Chalkin and restrained him from physically attacking Vergerin, who did not so much as recoil from his nephew.

"You did it to me. You did it all," Chalkin said and shrieked louder than his children when Vergerin, with an expressionless face, slowly pivoted away from him.

Then Lady Nadona saw Vergerin and her cries turned raucous with hatred.

"You've taken my husband and now you stand there to take my hold, my children's inheritance . . . Oh, Franco, how can you let them do this to your sister?" She fell against the Neratian's chest.

Franco's expression was far from repentant as he quickly unwound her plump arms from his neck with the help of Zulaya and the Istan Laura. Nadona was still in her nightdress with a robe half closed over the thin garment. Richud had the two boys by the arm, and his spouse had the two weeping little girls, who certainly didn't understand what was happening but were hysterical because their mother was. Irene took some pleasure in applying the slaps that cut Nadona's histrionics short.

Paulin took Vergerin by the arm and led him toward the nearest door, which turned out to be Chalkin's office. Decanters and glasses were part of the appointments, and Paulin hurriedly poured two glasses. Vergerin took his and drank it down, the draught restoring some color to his face. He exhaled deeply.

Paulin, impressed by the man's control in a difficult situation, clapped his shoulder and gripped it firmly.

"It can't have been easy," he said.

Vergerin murmured, then straightened himself. "What was hardest," and his smile was wry, "was knowing what a consummate idiot I had been. One can forgive almost anything except one's own stupidities."

Despite the thick stone walls, the screams and bellows continued, the sound altering slightly as Chalkin was hauled out of the hold and down the courtyard steps.

Lady Nadona was markedly absent. Despite her hysterics, she had decided quickly enough that she could not leave her darling children to the mercies of unfeeling men, and women, and would sacrifice herself to remain behind, while Chalkin went into exile. She was exceedingly well acquainted with her own rights as granted by the Charter, to the clause and relevant subparagraphs.

More shouting and confused orders! With an exasperated sigh, Paulin went to the shuttered window and threw it open on the most extraordinary scene: five men struggling to lift Chalkin to Craigath's back while the dragon, eyes whirling violently with red and orange, craned his neck about to see what was happening. Abruptly Chalkin's body relaxed and was shoved into position on Craigath's neck. M'shall leaped to his back and waited while two other Weyrmen roped first Chalkin to M'shall and then the collection of sacks and bags which would accompany the former Lord Holder into exile.

Craigath took off with a mighty bound and brought his wide wings down only once before he disappeared *between*.

"An island exile?" Vergerin asked, pouring himself another glass of wine.

"Yes, but not the same one we sent the guards to. Fortunately, there's a whole string of them."

"Young Island would be the safest one," Vergerin said dryly, sipping the wine. Then he made a face, looking down at the glass. "Wherever does he get his wines?"

Paulin smothered a laugh. "He's got no palate at all. Or did you like the idea of your nephew on an active volcanic island?"

"He's quick-witted enough to survive that. Does Nadona stay on?"

"Her children are young, but you would be perfectly within your rights to relegate her to a secluded apartment and take over the education and discipline of the children."

Vergerin gave a shudder of revulsion.

"Oh, there might be something worth saving in them, you know," Paulin said magnanimously.

"In Chalkin and Nadona's get? Unlikely." Then Vergerin walked to the cabinet where hold records should be kept and, on the point of opening the doors, turned back to Paulin. "Should I start right in? Or wait for the Conclave's decision?"

"Since we didn't know whether or not you had escaped Chalkin's grasp, we decided to let competent younger sons and daughters see what order they could contrive. However, since you would know a lot more about this hold than they could, would you take overall charge?"

Vergerin exhaled and a smile of intense relief lit his features. "Considering what I know of the state of this hold and the demoralization of its holders, I'll need every bit of assistance I can muster." He shook his head. "I don't say my late brother was the best holder in Pern, but he would never have countenanced the neglect, much less Chalkin's ridiculous notion that Thread couldn't return because it would reduce the gaming he could do."

There was a polite rap on the door, and when Paulin answered, Irene poked her head in.

"We managed to get the kitchen staff to prepare some food. I can't vouch for more than that the klah is hot and the bread fresh made."

Vergerin looked down at himself. "I couldn't possibly eat anything until I've washed."

Irene grinned. "I thought of that and had a room, and a bath, prepared for you. Even some clean clothing."

"Fresh bread and good hot klah will go down a treat," Paulin said, gesturing for Vergerin to precede him out of the room.

"No, my Lord Holder, after you," Vergerin said with a courtly gesture.

"Ah, but my soon to be Lord Holder, after you . . ."

"I didn't realize I smelled that bad," Vergerin said ruefully and led the way out.

He was looking about him now, Paulin noticed, as if assessing the condition of the place. He stopped so short that Paulin nearly bounced off him. Pointing to the inner wall where Chalkin's portrait by Iantine was ostentatiously illuminated, he pivoted, eyes wide, his expression incredulous.

"My nephew . . . never . . . looked . . . like that," he said, laughter rippling through his tone.

Paulin chuckled, too, having his first good look at the representation.

"I believe it took the artist some time to paint a . . . satisfactory portrait of your nephew."

"With so little to work on . . . but I can't have that hanging there," Vergerin exclaimed. "It's . . . it's . . ."

"Ludicrous?" Paulin suggested. Poor Iantine, to have had to prostitute his abilities to create *that*!

"That will do for starters."

Paulin leaned close to Vergerin, trying not to inhale because the warmth of the Hall was increasing the pong of manure emanating from Vergerin's clothing.

"I don't think you'll hurt the artist's feelings by removing it from such a prominent place."

"Would he consider repainting it to a closer likeness to the model?" Vergerin asked. "That would remind me of my youthful follies as well as how *not* to manage a hold."

"Iantine's here. Helped us get in, in fact. You can ask him yourself."

"*After* I've had that bath," Vergerin said, and continued on his way to the stairs and cleanliness.

Younger sons and daughters were conveyed in from every major hold, dressed and prepared to work hard. If some were disappointed that Vergerin had been found, they hid it well, which did them no disservice. By the time a substantial breakfast had been served, Vergerin had spoken to each of the eight young men and women about what area of responsibility they should assume.

Irene put a wing of Benden riders at Vergerin's disposition to use in contacting the larger holdings in Bitra to announce Chalkin's impeachment and exile.

By then M'shall had returned. "I dumped him and his packages on Island Thirty-two. You'll need to know that for the records. It's rather a nice place. Too bad *he* gets it."

"Did you have any trouble with him?" Paulin asked.

M'shall looked amused as he unbuckled his flight gear. "With the wallop Bastom gave him? He was still unconscious when I left him. Near a stream." He made a face. "I should have dumped him in it. Serve him right for what he did to those he had in cold storage."

By mid-morning matters seemed to be in Vergerin's complete control and the Council members felt able to leave Bitra Hold.

Iantine begged a ride from K'vin for himself and Chalkin's portrait.

"When are you coming to Benden Hold?" Bridgely wanted to know, catching the young portraitist coming down the courtyard steps.

"Lord Bridgely, I am sorry not to be ready quite yet," Iantine said.

Bridgely jabbed his finger at the painting. "You're not letting *that* take precedent, are you?" And he scowled.

"No, never," Iantine said, recoiling slightly. Then he grinned. "Not that it will take me long to change the face on it. But it's last on my list. I've to finish K'vin's portrait and a few more of the Telgar riders and then I'll come. I can probably make it after Turn's End."

"Well, I'll give you until then, young man, but no longer," Bridgely said, sounding aggrieved. Then he smiled to allay Iantine's obvious anxiety. "Don't worry about it, lad. I just want to know where my lady and I fit into your appointment calendar."

With that he walked away.

K'vin was hiding his grin behind his gloved hand. "One can be too successful, you know," he said, then gestured for Iantine to mount Charanth while he held the painting, which he passed up to the artist when he was settled. "I'm glad you're going to fix this."

"Lord Holder Vergerin specifically requested me to. And I must say, I'm glad to do the sitter . . . justice."

"Justice?" K'vin laughed as he landed neatly between the bronze neck ridges. "I think that's possibly a dirty word to Chalkin now."

Iantine grunted as the dragon suddenly launched himself. Not only was Iantine going to be able to set right that inaccurate portrait—he felt he had demeaned himself and Hall Domaize by succumbing to Chalkin's coercion in spite of having no viable alternative—but he had given himself more time at Telgar Weyr. And Turn's End was nearing. Turn's End and the festivities that the midwinter holiday always incurred. Maybe then he could come to some agreement with Debera.

Dragonriders *could* and often did take mates from nonriders. It would have been easier if his profession was one that he could offer the Weyr in return for staying on in Telgar. But once Morath was able to fly, Debera could fly him wherever his commissions took him.

That is, if she felt anywhere near the same about him as he did about her. Never in his wildest dreams had he thought he'd be *in* a Weyr at all. He could almost have thanked Chalkin for being the catalyst on that score: almost. Until he remembered the stark horror of what Chalkin had done at the borders and in the cold storage cells. He shuddered.

"Thought you'd be used to this by now," K'vin said, leaning back to speak into Iantine's ear.

"It isn't this," Iantine said, shaking his head and grinning. He thoroughly enjoyed flying and, after the first experience with the utter cold and nothingness of *between*, had not been nervous about that transfer. He took a firmer grip on the strings about the painting. Charanth was now high enough above Bitra Hold to go *between*. Meranath, bearing Tashvi and Salda as well as Zulaya, zoomed up beside his right wing, the dragon's golden body gleaming in the bright morning sun as her riders waved at him.

As he waved back Iantine was surprised to think it *was* still morning. The invasion of Bitra Hold had begun in such early hours that the day was not that old. So much happened these days!

Blackness! Iantine couldn't feel the cord on the painting, his butt on Charanth's neck, and then they were out in the sun, hanging over Telgar's familiar cone.

Far below, above the prow of Telgar Hold, a sparkle announced Meranath's arrival. The big bronze now turned gracefully on one wing and headed down toward the Weyr.

For Iantine this happened all too swiftly, for he saw so much more from this vantage point than he did from the ground: the dragons sleeping in the sun on their weyr ledges, the younger riders practicing catch and throw with firestone sacks, even the weyrlings getting their morning scrub around the lake. Debera would be among them. He tried to see if he could identify her and Morath, but at that height details were lost. Two dragons, browns both, were eating their kill farther down the valley. Another rider burst into the air above the watchrider, who gestured broadly for him to land. Then Charanth had spiraled close enough to be identified, too, and welcomed back. Iantine could feel a rumble in the bronze's body. Did dragons speak out loud to each other? He had to tighten his hold on the painting or have the wind of their descent pull it free.

As they dropped, K'vin turned his head. "At the cavern?"

"Please," and Iantine nodded, struggling to keep a grip on the painting. Not that losing it would bother him, but then he'd have to waste another board.

He swung his leg over and slid down Charanth's shoulder as quickly as he could.

"My thanks, K'vin," he said, grinning up, having to shield his eyes from the sun.

"Not needed. You more than earned it with today's doings."

Charanth rumbled again, his gently whirling blue eyes focused on Iantine, who saluted him in gratitude. Then the bronze leaped up, flapped his wings twice and was landing on the ledge of the Weyrwoman's quarters.

"You're back, you're back, and safe," and Leopol came racing out of the Lower Cavern, leaping toward Iantine, who put out a restraining hand so the boy wouldn't carom off the edge of the painting.

"What have you done now?" Leopol demanded, taking care not to batter it.

"It's to be redone," Iantine said, knowing the uselessness of avoiding Leopol's interest.

"Oh, the Chalkin portrait?" Leopol reached for it and Iantine pivoted, putting his body between it and the lad's acquisitive hands.

"You're clever, aren't you?"

"Yup," and Leopol's grin bore not a single trace of remorse. "So? What happened when you deposed him?"

Iantine stopped in his tracks and stared at him. "Deposed whom?"

Leopol planted his fists on his belt, cocked his head and gave Iantine a long and disgusted look, finally shaking his head.

"One, you rode away on a Fort Weyr dragon. Two, you've been gone overnight so *something* was up. Especially when the Weyrleaders are gone, too. Three, we all know that Chalkin's for the chop, and four, you come back with a portrait and it isn't one you've done here." Leopol spread his hands. "It's obvious. The Lords and Leaders have got rid of Chalkin. Impeached, deposed, and exiled him. Right?" He grinned at the summation, cocking his head over the other shoulder. "Right?" he repeated.

Iantine sighed. "It's not my place to confirm or deny," he said tactfully, and started again for his quarters.

Leopol dodged in front, halting him again. "But I'm right about Chalkin, aren't I? He won't get ready for Threadfall, he's been far too hard on his people, and half the Lord Holders owe him huge sacks of marks in gambling debts."

Iantine stopped. "Gambling debts?" He brushed past Leopol, determined to get to the dubious safety of his room without giving anything away to such a gossip as Leopol.

"Ah, Iantine." Tisha caught sight of him and moved her bulk with surprising speed and agility through the tables to intercept him. "Did they catch Chalkin all right? Did he struggle?

Did that spouse of his go with him? Which frankly would surprise me. Did they find Vergerin alive? Will he take hold or does he have to wait till the Conclave at Turn's End?"

Leopol bent double with laughter at Iantine's expression.

"Yes, no, no, yes, and I don't know," he said in reply to her rapid-fire questions.

"You see? I'm not the only one," Leopol said, hanging onto a chair with one hand to keep his balance while he brushed laugh tears from his eyes with the other, thoroughly delighted with himself and Iantine's reaction.

"I'd like to hear all, Iantine," Tisha said, and deposited the klah mugs and the plate of freshly baked cookies on the table nearest him. "Do. Sit. You've had a hard day already and it's not noon yet."

"I'll take it and put it very carefully in your room," Leopol said, grabbing hold of the wrapped painting and then snatching it out of Iantine's unconsciously relaxed grip. "And I won't look until you tell me I can."

"No, wait, Leo," Tisha said. "I want to see what Chalkin considered 'satisfactory.' "

"Do I have no privacy around here?" Iantine demanded, raising his hands in helplessness. "Is there no way to keep secrets?"

"Not in a well-run Weyr there isn't," said Tisha. "Eat. Drink. And, Leo, take the basket I made ready for K'vin up to his weyr. I didn't see Zulaya and Meranath so she may have stopped over at Telgar Hold."

His knees weakened, as did his resolve, and Iantine collapsed into the chair Tisha had invitingly pulled out for him.

"Shall I?" Leopol asked in his best wheedling tone, one hand on the cord knot.

"I'm not sure I could stop you," Iantine said, and caught the pad he had stuffed inside the wrapping as Leopol made short work of opening it.

Iantine put the pad to one side. He didn't really want to show the latest drawings he'd done. The two castrated rapists had died shortly after he finished the sketches. He intensely regretted how pleased he had been with their sentences. Had they had any idea of what additional torment Chalkin would inflict on them when they asked to be returned to their hold? No, or they wouldn't have gone. Then Iantine caught Tisha's sharp eye on his face and wondered if she had read his expression, which he had tried to keep blank. Fortunately, the much glamorized Chalkin stared out of the painting at them, and Tisha's first good look sent her into gales of laughter, with Leopol whooping nearly as loud.

The headwoman had an infectious laugh under any condition: a mere chuckle from her would have anyone in her vicinity grinning in response. Iantine was in sore need of a good laugh, and if his inner anxieties kept him from joining in wholeheartedly, at least he was made to grin.

Tisha's amusement alerted the rest of the Weyrfolk to Iantine's return, and the table was shortly surrounded by people having a good laugh over what Chalkin had considered to be a "satisfactory portrait" of himself. Iantine sated their curiosity by giving a brief report of what had happened. Everyone was much relieved that Chalkin was not only no longer Bitra's Lord, but also that he had been exiled far from the mainland.

"Too good for him, really," someone said.

"Ah, but he's lord of all he surveys, ain't he? Suit him!"

"No one was hurt?"

"Who's going to take hold there now, with so much to do so close to Fall?"

Iantine answered as circumspectly as he could, though he was amazed at how accurately the Weyrfolk had guessed what had happened. They also seemed to know a great deal about a hold that was not beholden to Telgar Weyr. He didn't think he'd talked much about his uncomfortable stay at Bitra, so they must have had their information from other sources. Weyrfolk did get to travel more than holders, so perhaps their level of information was more comprehensive.

Riders drifted in, early for the noontime meal and just as interested in what had happened at Bitra Hold. Some of the older ones remembered the wager that had cost Vergerin the holding, and knew other details about that Bloodline that certainly showed them well informed.

Iantine was grateful for the klah and cookies Tisha had brought and equally pleased to have Leopol bring him bread, cheese, and the sliced wherry meat that was being served for lunch. He did have a moment's anxiety when he saw K'vin, at the edge of the crowd, gesturing for his attention. Maybe he shouldn't have said a thing.

He told Leopol to take the notorious portrait to his quarters, bundled his pad under his arm—because he knew nothing would keep Leopol from looking at it—and then made his way to K'vin. Since he had obviously told all he was going to tell, he was allowed to pass, with good-natured mauling on his way.

"I'm sorry, Weyrleader, if I was speaking out of turn . . ."

K'vin regarded him with widened eyes. "Speaking out of turn? Ha, they probably had figured out everything on their own. What could you possibly tell them that they didn't know?"

"How many people Chalkin had in those appalling cells," Iantine said, blurting out the words before he realized what he was saying.

K'vin put a sympathetic arm around his shoulders. "I think I'll have a few bad dreams over that myself," and he gave a deep shudder. "Perhaps you'd best get some rest . . ."

"No, I'd rather not, if you've something else for me to do," Iantine said truthfully. He didn't even need to stop off at his quarters, as his tubes of oil and brushes were already in the Weyrleaders' quarters.

K'vin's solicitous expression brightened. "I've some time now, and you've the painting to finish of me . . . unless you'd rather redo Chalkin . . . but Bridgely made it very plain to me that he'd like you at Benden to do his commissions by Turn's End. You're much sought after, you know."

Iantine made a disparaging noise in his throat, embarrassed by his notoriety. K'vin, grinning at his reaction, slapped his back lightly in affection.

"So what's it to be?" the Weyrleader asked.

"You, of course. Did you . . ." He hesitated, not wanting to be thought pushy. "Did you like Zulaya's portrait?"

K'vin gave a low laugh and turned his face away. "You've done her proud, Iantine. Proud."

"She's easy. She's beautiful," Iantine said.

"Yes, isn't she?"

Something about the tone of his voice made Iantine wonder at such a response. They were Weyrleaders, together, weren't they? They always made such a stance of a good partnership. But Iantine was getting as good at hearing things that weren't expressed as he was at seeing all that could be seen. Not his place to comment, though, despite a growing admiration for K'vin as Weyrleader. Zulaya was a bit reserved, he knew from having spent so much time painting her, but she was much older than Iantine. And older than K'vin, too, for that matter.

"That gown was perfect for her," Iantine said to break an awkward silence.

"Yes, she had it made for the last Hatching," K'vin said, and the smile he turned toward Iantine was easy, relaxed.

Iantine wondered if all he'd seen that morning hadn't skewed his judgment. They were at the weyr stairs now and climbed up. At the top of the steep flight Iantine was glad he wasn't even out of breath.

"You're in good shape," K'vin said, with another friendly

slap to his back to push him on into the high-ceilinged entrance to the weyr.

"I'd need to be, wouldn't I?" Iantine replied with a droll laugh. He paused briefly, his eyes seeking the weyrlings at the lake. Yes, Debera was there, oiling Morath. He'd have a chance to talk to her later: maybe even take dinner with her and show her Chalkin's portrait before he made the changes. Could he add to Chalkin's face what went on in that man's miserable soul? he wondered as he watched K'vin change into the Gather clothes he wore for his portrait. Was he good enough to attempt such a portrayal?

Amid all the frantic preparations for Turn's End, Clisser braved S'nan's displeasure to request transport to the Telgar Engineering Hall to discuss the feasibility of the Stonehenge installation for Pern's purposes. All he told S'nan, however, was that he needed to discuss something vital with Kalvi; S'nan would not approve, believing that such bells, whistles, and signals should be unnecessary if the Weyrs were kept on their toes during Intervals.

Jemmy had meticulously drawn a replica of the prehistoric stone circle, plus another of a reconstruction of what it had originally looked like, and such description as might be valuable to Kalvi and his team.

Kalvi took one quick, almost derisive glance at the drawings, and then a second more respectful one.

"Eye Rock? Finger Rock? Solstice?" He gave Clisser a broad smile. "I do believe it will suffice, and rather neatly." Then he frowned. "Couldn't you have given me a little more time? Solstice is only two weeks off!"

"I—" Clisser began.

"Sorry, friend," Kalvi said with a self-deprecating smile,

"you'd be busy with rehearsing and all that. Hmmm. Just leave it with me. I think we can contrive something . . ." He riffled through Jemmy's sketches. "Hmm, yes, the lad has real talent."

"Don't you dare seduce him away from the College," Clisser said, assembling as fierce a frown on his face as he gave to wayward students.

Kalvi grinned, pretending to recoil in terror, but his eyes were on the drawings. "We'll manage." He gave an exaggerated sigh. "It's what we're good at."

Clisser left, reassured that he would not fail the Conclave on this matter.

14

▼▼▼▼▼▼▼▼▼

TURN'S END AT FORT HOLD AND TELGAR WEYR

Traditionally, the Lord Holders and the Weyrleaders—and the invited heads of the various professions—met in Conclave the day before Turn's End—the Winter Solstice—to discuss what matters should be brought to those who would assemble for the festivities. Should a referendum figure on the agenda, its details would have been previously circulated. It would also be read out that evening in every main hold and Hall. If voting was required, votes were cast the morning of the first day of Turn's End, the results counted and returned to the second traditional sitting of the Conclave on the day after Turn's End, when the new year started.

The tradition was even more important in this 258th year after Landing with the Pass so imminent. Although Vergerin had been in charge but twenty days before the Conclave, it was obvious that he was taking a firm but just hold on Bitra. He was also working his assistants hard but fairly. None of them had any complaint to register when adroitly queried by their fathers or mothers. Vergerin's first official act had been to send riders to every single known holding and announce Chalkin's removal and that as many as could attend Turn's End at Bitra Hold would be made welcome. Vergerin paid for additional supplies out of his own funds. (No one had found Chalkin's treasury: nor had he taken it with him into exile. Nadona had denied any knowledge of its whereabouts and moaned that he had left her without a mark to her name.)

Altering a previously made decision, the Teachers' College planned now to supply a Turn's End concert to Bitra. They would bring copies of the Charter, which Vergerin had requested, to be given to each small holder. That would deplete to a few dozen the printed copies left in the College Library, but Clisser felt it to be in a very good cause. Since the Turn's End music featured Sheledon's ambitious "Landing Suite"—which made mention of the Charter—the audience would have a better understanding of what the music, and indeed the printed Charter, was all about. Bitran holders would no longer be kept in abysmal ignorance of their Charter-given rights.

Consequently, when the Conclave sat, the first business was to confirm Vergerin as Lord Holder of Bitra. He was not abjured to train his young relatives, Chalkin's sons, to succession, although he was in conscience bound to see them well taken care of, educated, and prepared to make their own living as adults. He was relieved of his promise to forgo having legitimate heirs and promptly installed at Bitra a nine-year-old son and a five-year-old daughter. No one knew who their mother had been. Vergerin made it plain that he was interested in acquiring a spouse suitable to hold as his Lady.

Clisser was called on to report on the matter of an indestructible and unambiguous method of confirming a Pass, and he said that Kalvi and he had agreed on the device and it would be installed on the eastern face of every Weyr. Kalvi, looking suitably smug, nodded wisely, so Paulin allowed himself to be reassured. He wanted no more problems like Chalkin to arise again! Ever! And now was the moment to prevent them.

The matter of a new hold being established and named Crom came up and there was considerable discussion.

"Look, they are entitled to use their Charter-granted acres, and that amounts to a fair whack of land," Bastom said, coming unexpectedly down on the side of the applicants. "Let 'em call it a hold . . ."

"Yes, but they want autonomy, and besides, they're too far from any other hold up there in the hills," Azury put in.

"It'll have to prove it's self-sufficient . . ." Tashvi said, looking reluctant to admit that much. Which was understandable since Telgar was also a mining hold.

"They have to follow the rules, same as everyone else," Paulin said in a neutral manner. "And supply basic needs to Contract workers."

"They're in good shape to do so," Azury remarked dryly, "what with the profit they can expect from supplying high-grade ore at the start of a Fall."

"Consider them on probation," was Bridgely's suggestion, and that motion was carried.

There were a few more minor details to be discussed, but they were carried as well. This year there was no referendum to be presented to the population.

"However, I want every one of you to give a *full* report of the trials and Chalkin's impeachment to the assembled," Paulin reminded the Lord Holders. "We want the truth circulated and believed: not a mess of rumors."

"Like the cannibalism!" Bridgely had been highly indignant over that one. "Sadistic Chalkin was, but let's squash that one *now!*"

"How under the sun did such a rumor ever get started?"

Paulin asked, appalled. S'nan looked in a state of shock, staring incredulous at the Benden Lord Holder.

"The 'cold storage' I suspect," Bridgely said, disgusted.

"We didn't coin the term," Azury said with a shrug.

"Well, we don't want it circulated," M'shall said angrily. "Bad enough having to live with the facts without having to debunk the fantasies."

"We do want the swift justice meted out to the rapists and the murderers to be well publicized, though," Richud said.

"That, yes! Speculation, no," Paulin said. He rose, tapped the gavel on its block. "I declare this session of the Conclave dismissed. Enjoy Turn's End and we'll meet in three days' time."

He intended to enjoy every moment of it for the year he'd put in. He noticed a similar determination on other faces, especially young Gallian's. Apart from the Chalkin affair, Jamson had no need to fault his son's management of High Reaches. Though maybe that bit about "cannibalism" could be whispered in Jamson's presence. That would certainly alter his opinion about impeachment. Somehow Thea was still "ailing" and had persuaded her spouse to stay on in Ista for Turn's End. That gave more opportunity for the Chalkin affair to die a natural death.

Turn's End was a holiday for everyone except those involved in the ambitious "Landing Suite" debut at all the Weyrs and the major holds. Clisser was run ragged with rehearsals and last-minute assignments, and understudies for those with winter colds. Then he had the extra burden of preparing for the precise calculations needed to set up the fail-safe mechanism to predict a Pass. Clisser, torn between the musical rehearsals and observing the installation of a permanent Threadfall warning device, opted for the latter. Of course, his role was supervisory, as the more precise location had to be conducted by teams of astronomers, engineers, and Weyrleaders on the eastern rim of all six facilities. He, Jemmy, and Kalvi were to set the apparatus at Benden, the first Weyr to "see" the phenomenon, then they would skedaddle on dragonback to each of the other five Weyrs to install the others.

It was imperative that the first installation, at Benden, had to be accurate in case there might be a distortion at any other. Though Clisser doubted it, not with Kalvi fussing and fussing over the components. Clisser'd been over and over the requisite steps to pinpoint the rise of the Red Star. Once that circular "eye" was set on the rim, they could install the pointer, the finger. But the eye had to be right on it! The teams had been in place for the past week, with predawn checks on the Red Planet's position at dawn. All that was necessary now was a clear morning, and that seemed to be possible across the continent, which had enjoyed some bright, clear, if wintry, skies. Fine weather was critically important at Benden, for the other Weyrs could take adjusted measurements from that reading if necessary.

Kalvi was still fiddling with the design of what he was calling the Eye Rock, which would bracket the Red Planet at dawn on Winter Solstice. His main problem was adjusting the pointer ... the position at a distance from the eye itself at which the viewer would stand to see the planet. The pointer had to accommodate different physical heights. Old diagrams of Stonehenge and other prehistoric rings had surfaced. Actually, Bethany's students had found them after an intensive search of long unused documents. Fortunately, for Clisser's peace, Sallisha had gone to Nerat for the Turn's End celebration, ready to start her next year's teaching contract. He was spared any reminder from her of how important it was to keep such ancient knowledge viable. He had rehearsed arguments, in case he had a letter from her, about the fact that, in the crunch, someone *had* remembered.

He was quite excited—if freezing—to be on Benden Weyr's rim with the others, telescopes set up, aimed in the appropriate direction while Kalvi and Jemmy fiddled with their components. Kalvi had put up a cone for the pointer. The notion being that a person, resting their chin on the cone's tip, would see the Red Planet bracketed just as it cleared the horizon. They'd have to try it with folks of various statures to be sure the device worked, but technically, Clisser thought it would work. Kalvi was the shortest, he was tallest, M'shall was a half head shorter, and Jemmy between the Weyrleader and Kalvi. If all could see the Red Planet in the eye, the device would be proven.

Well, it would really be proven in another 250 years or so with the Third Pass.

But this moment was exciting. Clisser slapped his body with his arms, trying to warm himself. His feet, despite the extra lining, were frozen: he could barely feel his toes, and his breath was so visible he worried that it might cloud his chance to see the phenomenon.

"Here it comes," Kalvi said, though Clisser could see nothing in the crepuscular dawn light. Kalvi was looking at his instrument, not the sky.

A tip of red appeared just over the bottom of the Eye a breath or two later. A redness that seemed to pulsate. It wasn't a very large planet—from this distance, it wouldn't be, Clisser thought, though they had the measurements of it from the *Yokohama* observations. It was approximately the same size as Earth's old sister, Venus. And about as hospitable.

Somehow, Clisser thought—and told himself to breathe—as he watched, the wanderer managed to look baleful in its redness. Hadn't one of the other Sol satellites been called the "red planet"? Oh, yes, Mars. Suitable, too, since it had been named after a war god.

And equally a suitable color for a planet about to wreak

havoc on them. How could such an avaricious organism develop on a planet that spent most of its orbit too far away from Rubkat's warmth to generate any life form? Of course, he was aware that very odd "life" forms had been found by the early space explorers. Who had blundered into the Nathi, to name another vicious species!

But the reports on this mycorrhizoid gave it no intelligence whatsoever. A menace without malice. Clisser sighed. Well, that was *some* consolation: it didn't really *mean* to eat everything in sight—people, animals, plants, trees—but that was all it could do.

Which was more than enough, Clisser thought grimly, remembering the visuals of recorded incidents. That's another thing he ought to have done—a graphic record—even a still picture would make vividly plain how devastating Thread could be. Iantine's sketches done at the Bitran borders had impressed the teacher immensely. Though it was a shame to waste Iantine's talents on a copy job. Anyone could copy: few could originate.

Meanwhile, the red edge crept up over the rim of Benden Weyr.

"THAT'S IT!" Kalvi cried. He made a final twitch to the iron circle on its pedestal. "I got it. Cement it in place now. Quickly. You there at the finger rock. Eyeball the phenomenon. All of you should see it bracketed by this circle."

The viewers had lined themselves up, and each took a turn even as Kalvi raced back to grab a look from this vantage point.

"Yup, that'll do it. You got that solidly in place? Good," and the energetic engineer turned to M'shall. "As you love your dragon, don't let anyone or anything touch that iron rim. I've used a fast-drying cement, but even a fraction out of alignment and we've lost it."

"No one'll be up here after we leave," M'shall promised, eyeing the metal circle nervously. Though he knew the ring was iron, it looked fragile sitting there, the Red Planet slowly rising above it. "But that's going to be replaced, isn't it? With stone?"

"It is, and don't worry about *us* messing up the alignment later. We won't," Kalvi said, blithely confident, rubbing his hands together, grinning with success. "Now, we've got some more dawns to meet."

"Yes, surely, but take time for breakfast."

"Ha! No time to pamper ourselves. But I was indeed grateful for the klah." Kalvi was gathering up his equipment, including five more iron circles, and gesturing to his crew to hurry up. "Not with five more stops to make this morning. The things I talk myself into." He looked around now in the semidark of false dawn. "Where's our ride?"

"That way," M'shall said, pointing to the brown dragons and riders, waiting well around on the rim.

"Oh, good. Thanks, M'shall." And, rings clanging dully where they rode on his shoulder, Kalvi gathered up his packs and half ran, his crew trailing behind. Clisser sighed and followed.

Well, he thought, he'd be well inured to the cold of *between*. They'd have an hour and a half between Benden and Igen but then only half an hour from Igen to Ista to Telgar, where they'd have a little over an hour, and time for something hot to eat before going on to Fort. High Reaches was actually the last Weyr to be done, which really didn't salve S'nan's pride all that much, but sunrise came forty-five minutes later in the northernmost Weyr due to the longitudinal difference. S'nan couldn't argue the point that Benden had to have its equipment installed first since it was the most easterly.

Clisser had heard the talk about S'nan's continued distress over Chalkin's impeachment. The Fort Weyrleader was not the oldest of the six: G'don was, but no one worried about his competence to lead the Weyr. S'nan had always been inflexible, literal, didactic, but that wouldn't necessarily signify poor leadership during the Pass. Clisser sighed. That was a Weyr problem, not his. Thank goodness. He had enough of them.

He'd catch some rest when they finished at Fort Weyr, so he'd be fresh for the final rehearsal at the Hall. If Sheledon had altered the score again during his absence, he'd take him to task. No one would know what to play with all the changes. Get this performance over with and then refine the work. It was, Clisser felt, quite possibly Sheledon's masterpiece.

"You're riding with me, Teacher," a voice said. "Don't want you walking off the rim!"

Clisser shook himself to attention. "Yes, yes, of course." He smiled up at the brown rider, who extended a hand.

Clisser reached up to grasp the proffered hand. "Oh, thank you," he said to the dragon, who had not only turned his head but helpfully lifted his forearm to make an easier step up.

Then he was astride the big dragon, settling himself, snapping on the safety strap.

"I'm ready."

Clisser did catch his breath, though, when the dragon seemed to just fall off the rim into the blackness of Benden's Bowl. He grabbed at the security of the safety strap and then almost cracked his chin on his chest as the dragon's wings caught the air and he soared upward.

They were facing east, and the malevolence of the Red Star was dimmed by the glow of Rukbat rising, altering the rogue planet's aspect to one of almost negligible visibility, almost anonymity, in the brightening sky.

Amazing! thought Clisser. *I must remember to jot that down.* But he knew he never would. And Pernese literature was thus saved another diarist, he amended. Clisser saw that the rider, too, had his eyes fastened on the magnificent spectacle. He must savor this ride. The dragon veered northward, pivoting slowly on his left wing tip. The dragons would soon have more important journeys to make. Clisser did observe the majestic snowcapped mountains of the Great Northern Range, tinted delicate shades of orange by the rising sun. What Iantine could make of such a scene! Then abruptly all he could see was the black nothingness of *between*.

"What happens if you wear your fingers out?" Leopol asked Iantine.

The Artist hadn't even been aware of the lad's presence, but the comment—because Iantine was sketching the scene of the dragonets so fast that his elbow was actually aching—caused him to burst out laughing, even though he didn't pause for a moment.

"I don't know. I've never heard of it happening, though, if that's any consolation."

"Not to me, but for you," Leopol said, cocking his head in his characteristically impudent fashion.

"I'll miss you, you know," Iantine said, grinning down at the sharp expression on Leopol's face.

"I should hope so, when I've been your hands, feet, and mouth for months now," was the irrepressible answer. "You could take me with you. I'd be useful," and Leopol's expression was earnest, his gray eyes clouded. "I know how you like your paints mixed, your brushes cleaned, and even how to prepare wood or canvas for portraits." His pathetic stance could have persuaded almost anyone.

Iantine chuckled and ruffled the boy's thick black hair. "And what would your father do?"

"Him? He's winding himself up for Threadfall." A discreet question to Tisha had produced the information that a bronze rider, C'lim, was the boy's father; the mother had died shortly after Leopol's birth. But he, like every other child of the Weyr, had become everyone's child, loved and disciplined as the need arose. "He doesn't half pay attention to me anymore."

Which was fair, Iantine thought, since Leopol had become *his* shadow. "Tisha?"

"Her? She'll find someone else to mother."

"Well, I will ask but I doubt you'd be allowed. The other riders think you'll Impress a bronze when you're old enough."

Leopol tossed off that future with a shrug. What he could do *now* was more important than what might be three or four years in the future. "D'you *have* to go?"

"Yes, I *have* to go. I'm in grave danger of overstaying my welcome here."

"No, you're not," and Leopol looked significantly toward the lake, where the weyrlings were having their customary bath. "And you haven't drawn *all* the riders yet."

"Be that as it may, Leo, I'm due at Benden to do the holders, and that's a commission I've been owing since I started my training at Hall Domaize."

"When you do those, will you come straight back? You haven't done Chalkin's face like he really is, you know, and it isn't as if you were doing anyone else out of a place to sleep." Leopol's face was completely contorted now by his dismay. "Debera really wants you to stay, you know."

Iantine shot him an almost angry look. "Leopol?" he said warningly.

"Aw," and the boy screwed his boot toe into the dirt, "everyone knows you fancy her, and the girls say that she's gone on you. It's only Morath who's the problem. And she doesn't have to be. Soon as she can fly, she'll have a weyr and you'll have some privacy."

"Privacy?" Iantine knew that Leopol was precocious, but . . .

Leopol cocked his head and had the grace not to grin. "Weyrs're like that. Everyone knows everyone else's secrets."

Iantine hung amid irritation: relief in the information about

Debera, and amusement that his carefully hidden interest was so transparent. He had never thought about loving someone so much that their absence could cause physical discomfort. He never thought he would spend sleepless hours reviewing even the briefest of conversations; identify a certain voice in a crowded cavern; have to rub out sketches of imagined meetings and poses which his fingers did of their own accord. He kept close guard on his sketch pads because there were far too many of Debera—and the ever-present Morath. Morath liked him, too. He knew that because she'd told him she did.

That, actually, had been the first encouraging sign he'd had. He had tried, adroitly, to figure out how significant that might be, as far as Debera's awareness of him was concerned. He'd ask while he was sketching a rider, as if only politely inquiring about what was closest to his model's heart anyway. It appeared that a dragon could talk to anyone he or she wished. They did so for reasons of their own, which sometimes they did not discuss with their riders. Or they did. None of the other weyrlings, even the greens with whom Iantine was now quite familiar, spoke to him. It was Morath who counted. Not that the green dragon—who was the largest of that color from that clutch—ever explained herself. Nor did Iantine ask. He merely treasured the immense compliment of her conversation.

She did ask to see his sketch pad once. He noticed the phenomenon of the pad reflected in every one of the many facets of her eyes. They'd been bluey-green at the time, their normal shade, and whirling slowly.

"Do you see anything?"

Yes. Shapes. You put the shapes on the pad with the thing in your hand?

"I do." How much could a dragon see with that kind of optical equipment? Still, Iantine supposed it would be useful when Thread was falling from all directions. As the dragon eye protruded out from the head, it obtained overhead images, too.

Good design. But then, dragons *had* been designed, though no one nowadays could have managed the genetic engineering. It was one thing to breed animals for specific traits, but to begin from the first cell to create a totally new creature? "Do you like this one of Debera oiling you?" He tapped his pencil on the one he'd done that morning.

It looks like Debera. It looks like me? and there was plaintive surprise in Morath's contralto voice. That was when Iantine realized that Morath sounded very much like her rider. But then, that was only logical since they were inseparable.

Inseparable! That's what bothered him most. He knew that his love for Debera would be constant. But any love left over from Morath for him could scarcely match his commitment. Did it have to? After all, he was totally committed to his work. Could he fault her for being equally single-minded? There was, however, a considerable difference between loving a dragon and loving to paint. Or was there?

Maybe it was as well, Iantine thought, tucking his pencil behind his ear and closing his pad, that he was going to Benden after Turn's End. Maybe if Debera—and Morath— were out of sight, they might also go out of mind and his attachment would ease off.

"You got your Turn's End clothes ready? Need ironing or anything?" Leopol asked, his expression wistful.

"You did 'em yesterday and I haven't worn 'em yet," he said, but he ruffled the boy's thick hair again and, looping his arm over the thin shoulders, steered him to the kitchen. "Let's eat."

"Ah, there's not much to eat," Leopol said in disgust. "Everyone's getting ready for tonight."

"They've been getting ready all week," Iantine said. "But there's bread and cold meats set out."

"Huh!"

Iantine noticed that Leopol had no trouble making himself

several sandwiches of what was available and had two cups of soup and two apples. He noted that he had no trouble eating, either, though some of the smells emanating from the ovens—and all were in use—were more appetizing than lunch. He intended to enjoy himself this evening.

Then Leopol, eyes wide with excitement, leaped from the table. "Look, look, the musicians are here!"

Glancing outward, Iantine saw them dismounting from half a dozen dragons. They were laughing and shouting as instruments were carefully handed down from dragonbacks and carisaks were passed around. Tisha sailed out, her assistants with her, and shortly everyone was in the cavern and being served a lunch considerably more complicated than soup and sandwiches. Leopol was in the thick of it, too, the rascal, and the recipient of a huge wedge of iced cake. Iantine selected a good spot against the wall, sharpened his pencil with his knife, and opened his pad. This was a good scene to preserve. If he got them down on paper now, maybe he could listen to the music this evening without itchy fingers. As he worked he realized that Telgar had rated some of the best musicians, called back from wherever their contracts had taken them, for Turn's End celebrations. He'd finish in time for the concert and that would be that for the day!

It wasn't, of course. But then, he found it hard not to sketch exciting moments and scenes. Especially as he didn't want to leave this pad anywhere that it could be casually opened. And he could listen to the music just as well while drawing. Sketching also kept his hands where they should be and not itching to go around Debera's shoulder or hold her hand. Sketching did allow him some license, for he could always apologize that he didn't realize his leg was against hers, or that their shoulders were touching or he was bending his body close to hers. After all, he was so busy sketching, he wouldn't be noticing externals.

If Debera had found the contact unpleasant or annoying, she could have moved her leg away from his, or moved about on the bench. But she didn't seem to mind him overlapping her from time to time in the zeal to get this or that pose. Truth was, he was totally conscious of her proximity, the floral fragrance that she used that didn't quite hide the "new" smell of the lovely pale green dress she was wearing. Green was her color and she must know that: a gentle green, like new leaves, which made her complexion glow. Angie had told him the color of Debera's Turn's End gown, so he'd bought a shirt of a much deeper green so that they'd go together. He liked the way she'd made a coronet of her long hair, with pale green ribbons laced in and dangling down her back. Even her slippers were green. He wondered if there'd be dancing music, too, but there usually was at Turn's End. Although maybe not, what with the "Landing Suite" first. He bent to ask her to reserve dances for him but she shushed him.

"Listen, too, Ian," she said in a soft whisper, gesturing to his pad. "The words are as beautiful as the music."

Iantine glanced forward again, only now realizing that there were singers, too. Had he been that rapt in being next to Debera without Morath?

I'm here. I listen, too.

Morath's voice startled him, coming into his head so unexpectedly. He gulped. Would the dragon always be able to read his mind?

He asked the question again, more loudly, in his own head. There was no reply. Because there *was* no reply? Or because there was none needed to such an obvious question?

But Morath hadn't sounded upset that he was luxuriating in Debera's proximity. She had sounded pleased to be there and listening. Dragons liked music.

He glanced over his shoulder to the Bowl and could see

along the eastern wall the many pairs of dragon eyes, like so many round blue-green lanterns up and down the wall of the Weyr where dragons made part of the audience.

He began then, obediently, to listen to the words, and found himself drawn into the drama unfolding, even tho' he'd known the story from childhood. The musicians called it the "Landing Suite," and this verse was about leaving the great colony ships for the last time. A poignant moment, and the tenor voice rose in a grateful farewell to them where they would orbit over Landing forever, their corridors empty, the bridge deserted, the bays echoing vaults. The tenor, with creditable breath control, let his final note die away as if lost in the vast distance between the ships and the planet.

A respectful pause followed, and then the ovation which his solo had indeed merited burst forth. Quickly Iantine sketched him, taking his bows, before he stepped back into the ensemble.

"Oh, good, Ian. He was just marvelous," Debera said, craning her head to watch what he was doing. She kept right on clapping, her eyes shining. "He'll be delighted you did him, too."

Iantine doubted that and managed a smile that did not echo the stab of jealousy he felt because Debera's interest had been distracted from him.

She likes you, Ian, said Morath as if from a great distance, though she was ranged with the other still flightless dragonets on the Bowl floor.

Ian? he echoed in surprise. Other riders had told him that while dragons would talk to people other than their own rider, they weren't so good at remembering human names. Morath *knows* my name?

Why shouldn't I? I hear it often enough. And Morath sounded sort of tetchy.

Morath may never know just how much that remark means to me, Iantine thought, taking in a deep breath that swelled his chest out. Now, if he could just get her by herself alone . . .

But she's never alone, now that she's my rider.

Iantine stifled a groan that he wanted neither dragon nor rider to hear and compressed his thoughts as far down in his head as he could. Would it all be worth it? he wondered. And tried to divorce himself from Debera for the rest of the concert.

He didn't pay as close attention to the second and third parts of the "Landing Suite," which brought events up to the present. A cynical section of his mind noticed that Chalkin's impeachment was not mentioned, but then it was a very recent incident which the composer and lyricist would not have known about. He wondered would it ever make history. Chalkin would love it. Which might well be why no one would include him. That'd be the final punishment—anonymity.

Dinner was announced at the conclusion of the suite, and the big cavern was efficiently reorganized for dining. In the scurry and fuss of setting up tables and chairs, he got separated from Debera. The panic it caused him made it extremely clear that he could not divorce his emotions from the girl. When they found each other again, her hand went out to him as quickly as his to her, and they remained clasped while they waited in line to collect their food.

Iantine and Debera finally found seats at one of the long trestle tables where everyone was discussing the music, the singers, the orchestration, how lucky they were to be in a Weyr that got preferential treatment. There was, of course, a tradition of music on Pern, brought by their ancestors and encouraged by not only the Teaching Hall but also Weyr and Hold. Everyone was taught how to read music from an early age and encouraged to learn to play at least one instrument, if not two or three. It was a poor hold indeed that could not produce a guitar or at least pipes and a drum to liven winter nights and special occasions.

The meal was very good—though Iantine had to concentrate on tasting it. Most of his senses were involved in sitting thigh to thigh with Debera. She was quite volatile, talking to everyone, with a great many things to say about the various performances and the melodic lines that she particularly liked. Her cheeks were flushed and her eyes very bright. He'd never seen her so elated. But then, he knew he was feeling high with an almost breathless anticipation of the dancing. He'd have her in his arms then, even closer than they were now. He could barely wait.

He had to, for of course on First Day, ice cream, the special and traditional sweet, was available and no one would want to miss that. It was a fruit flavor this year, creamy, rich, tangy with lots of tiny fruit pieces, and he was torn between eating slowly—which meant the confection might turn sloppy since the Lower Cavern was warm indeed—or gulping it down firm and cold. He noticed that Debera ate quickly, so he did.

As soon as the diners finished, they dismantled the tables and pushed back the chairs so there'd be space for the dancing. The musicians, reassembling in smaller units so that the dance music would be continuous, were tuning up their instruments again.

When all was ready, K'vin led Zulaya, resplendent in the red brocade dress of her portrait, onto the floor for their traditional opening of the dance. Iantine caught himself wanting to sketch the distinguished-looking couple, but he'd hidden his pad in the pile of tables and had to content himself with storing the details in his mind. He'd never seen Zulaya flirt so with K'vin, and the Weyrleader was responding gallantly. He did notice some riders talking among themselves, their eyes on the two Leaders, but he couldn't hear what was said, and while the glances were speculative, it wasn't his business.

Next the wing leaders handed their partners out on the floor for three turns before the wing seconds joined them. Then Tisha, partnered by Maranis, the Weyr medic, whirled very gracefully in among the dancers. The first dance ended but now the floor was open to everyone. The next number was a brisk two-step.

"Will you dance with me, Debera?" Iantine asked with a formal bow.

Eyes gleaming, head held high and smiling as if her face would split apart, Debera responded with a deep dip. "Why, I was hoping you'd ask, Iantine!"

"I get the next one," Leopol cried, appearing unexpectedly beside them, looking up at Debera, his eyes exceedingly bright.

"Did you sneak some wine tonight?" Iantine asked, suspicious.

"Who'd give me any?" Leopol replied morosely.

"No one would give you anything you couldn't take another way, Leo," Debera said. "But I'll keep you a dance. Later on."

And she stepped toward the floor, Iantine whisking her away from the boy as fast as he could.

"Even for a Weyr lad, he's precocious," Debera said, and she held up her arms as she moved into his.

"He is at that," Iantine replied, but he didn't want to talk about Leopol at all as he swung her lithe body among the dancers and eased them away to the opposite side of the floor from Leopol.

"He'll follow, you know, until he gets his dance," she said, grinning up at him.

"We'll see about that," and he tightened his arms possessively around her strong slender body.

Will I dance when I'm older? Iantine clearly heard the green dragon ask.

Startled, he looked down at Debera and saw by the laughter in her eyes that the dragon had spoken to them both.

"Dragons don't dance," Debera said in her fond dragon-tone. Iantine had noticed that she had a special one for Morath.

"They sing," Iantine said, wondering how he was ever going to eliminate Morath from the conversation long enough to speak about *them*.

She'll listen to anything you say. Morath's voice, so much like Debera's, sounded in his head.

Iantine grimaced, wondering how under the sun he could manage any sort of a private conversation with his beloved.

I won't listen then. Morath sounded contrite.

"How long do you think you'll be at Benden, Ian?" Debera asked.

He wondered if Morath had spoken to her, too, but decided against asking, though he didn't want to discuss his departure at all. Certainly not with Debera, the reason he desperately wanted to stay at Telgar.

"Oh," he said as casually as he could, "I'd want to do my best for Lord Bridgely and his Lady. They've been my sponsors, you see, and I owe them a lot."

"Do you know them well?"

"What? Me? No, my family's mountain holders."

"So were mine."

"Were?"

Debera gave a wry laugh. "Don't let's talk about families."

"I'd far rather talk about us," he said and then mentally kicked himself for such a trite response.

Debera's face clouded.

"Now what did I say wrong?" He tightened his arms on her reassuringly. Her expression was so woeful.

She's been upset about something Tisha told the weyrlings yesterday. I know I said I wouldn't interfere but sometimes it's needed.

"You didn't," Debera said at the same time, so he wasn't sure who had said what, since the voices were so alike.

"But something is troubling you?"

She didn't answer immediately but her hands tightened where they gripped him.

"C'mon, now, Deb," and he tried to jolly her a bit. "I'll listen to anything you have to say."

She gave him an odd glance. "That's just it."

"What is?"

"You wanting to talk to me, dance with only me and—"

"Ooooh," and suddenly Iantine had a hunch. "Tisha gave all the riders that 'don't do anything you'll be sorry for at Turn's End' lecture?" She gave him a startled look. And he grinned back at her. "I've been read that one a time or two myself, you know."

"But you don't know," she said, "that it's different for dragonriders. For green riders with very immature dragons." Then she gave him a horrified look as if she hadn't meant to be so candid. "Oh!"

He pulled her closer to him, even when she resisted, and chuckled. All those casual questions he'd asked dragonriders explained all that she didn't say.

"Green dragons are ... how do I put it, kindly? Eager, loving, willing, too friendly for their own good ..."

She stared up at him, a blush suffusing her cheeks, her eyes angry and her body stiffening against the rhythm of the dance. They were about to pass an opening, one of the corridors that led back to the storage areas of the Weyr. He whirled them in that direction despite her resistance, speaking in a persuasively understanding tone.

"You're the rider of a young green and she's much too young for any sexual stimulation. But I don't think a kiss will do her any damage, and I've *got* to kiss you once before I have to go to Benden."

And he did so. The moment their lips touched, although she tried to resist, their mutual attraction made the contact electric. She could not have resisted responding—even to preserve Morath's innocence.

Finally, breathless, they separated, but not by more than enough centimeters to let air into their lungs. Her body hung almost limply against his, and only because he was leaning against the wall did Iantine have the strength to support them both.

That's very nice, you know.

"Morath!" Debera jerked her body upright, though her hands clenched tightly on his neck and shoulder. "Oh . . . dear, what have I done?"

"Not as much to her as you have to me," Iantine said in a shaky voice. "She doesn't sound upset or anything."

Debera pushed away to stare up at him—he thought she had never looked so lovely.

"You heard Morath?"

"Hmmm, yes."

"You mean, that wasn't the first time?" She was even more startled.

"Hmmm. She knows my name, too," he said, plunging in with a bit of information that he knew might really distress her, but now was the time to be candid.

Debera's eyes widened even more and her face had paled in the glowlight of the corridor. She leaned weakly against him.

"Oh, what do I do now?"

He stroked her hair, relieved that she hadn't just stormed off, leaving all his hopes in crumbs.

"I don't think we upset Morath with that little kiss," he said softly.

"*Little* kiss?" Her expression went blank. "I've never been kissed like that before in my life."

Iantine laughed. "Me neither. Even if you didn't want to kiss me back." He hugged her, knowing that the critical moment had passed. "I have to say this, Debera: I love you. I can't get you out of my mind. Your face . . . and . . ." he added tactfully because it was also true, ". . . Morath's decorate the margin of every sketch I draw. I'm going to miss you like . . . like you'd miss Morath."

She caught in her breath at even the mention of such a possibility.

"Iantine, what can I say to that? I'm a dragonrider. You know that Morath is always first with me," she said gently, touching his face.

He nodded. "That's as it should be," he said, although he heartily wished he could be her sole and only concern.

"I'm glad you do know that, but Ian . . . I don't know what I feel about you, except that I did like your kiss." Her eyes were tender and she glanced shyly away from him. "I'm even glad you did kiss me. I've sort of wanted to know . . ." she said with a ripple in her voice, but still shy.

"So I can kiss you again?"

She put her hand on his chest. "Not quite so fast, Iantine! Not quite so fast. For my sake as well as Morath's. Because . . ." and then she blurted out the next sentence, "I know I'm going to miss you . . . almost . . . as much as I'd miss Morath. I didn't know a rider could be so involved with another human. Not like this. And," she increased pressure on the hand that held them apart because he wanted so to kiss her for that, "I can't be honestly sure if it's not because Morath rather likes you, too, and is influencing me."

I am not, said Morath firmly, almost indignantly.

"She says . . ." Debera began as Iantine said, "I heard that."

They both laughed and the sensual tension between them eased. He made quick use of the opportunity to kiss her, lightly, to prove that he could and that he did understand about Morath. He had also actually asked as many questions about rider liaisons as discretion permitted. What he'd learned had been both reassuring and unsettling. There were more ramifications to human affairs than he had ever previously suspected. Dragonrider-human ones could get very complicated. And the green dragons being so highly strung and sexually oriented were the most complex.

"I guess I'm lucky she talks to me at all," Iantine said. "Look, love, I've said what I've wanted to say. I've heard what Morath has to say, and we can leave it there for now. I've got to go to Benden Hold, and Morath has to . . . mature." He gently tightened his arms around his beloved. "If I'm welcome to come back . . . to the Weyr, I will return. Am I welcome?"

"Yes, you are," Debera said as Morath also confirmed it.

"Well, then . . ." He kissed her lightly, managing to break it off before the emotion that could so easily start up again might fire. ". . . let us dance, and dance and dance. That should cause no problems, should it?"

Of course, the words were no sooner out of his mouth than he knew that having her so close to him all evening was going to be a trial of his self-control.

His lips tingled as he led her back, her fingers trustingly twined into his. The dance was only just ending as he put his arms around her, so they managed just one brief spin. Since he now felt far more secure, he did let Leopol partner Debera for one fast dance, lest he'd never hear the last of it from the boy. Other than that surrender, he and Debera danced together all night, cementing the bond that had begun: danced until the musicians called it a night.

He was going to hate to be parted from her, more now because they did have an understanding—of sorts—but there was no help for it. He had the duty to Benden Hold.

15

▼▼▼▼▼▼▼▼▼

NEW YEAR 258 AFTER LANDING; COLLEGE, BENDEN HOLD, TELGAR WEYR

On the first official day of the new year, 258 AL, Clisser had a chance to review the four days of Turn's End. Frantic at times, certainly hectic despite the most careful plans and the wealth of experience, the main performances—the First Day "Landing Suite," and Second Day Teaching Songs and Ballads—had gone very well: far better than he had anticipated given the scanty rehearsals available for some of the performers. Fort's tenor, for instance, had been a bit ragged in his big solo: he really should have held that final note the full measure. Sheledon glowered from the woodwind section: he'd've sung the part himself but he hadn't the voice for it. But then, the only solos that Sheledon wouldn't find fault with would be Sydra's, and she never failed to give a splendid performance. Bethany's flute obbligatos had been remarkable, matching Sydra's voice to perfection.

Paulin had been on his feet time after time, applauding the

soloists and, at the finale, surreptitiously brushing a tear from his eye. Even old S'nan looked pleased, also fatuous, but on the whole Clisser was relieved at the reception. He hoped the two performances had been popular elsewhere on the continent. A great deal of work had been put into rehearsals from folks who had little spare time as it was.

The Teaching Songs and Ballads had been just as well received, with people going about humming some of the tunes. Which was exactly what the composers had hoped for. Fortunately, honors were even between Jemmy and Sheledon for catchy tunes. He caught himself humming the Duty Song chorus. That had gone particularly well. He wouldn't have to deal with a laborious copying of the Charter once youngsters learned *those* words by heart. It certainly fit the bill. Copies of all the new songs were being made by the teachers themselves, who would then require their students to transcribe them, and that saved a lot of effort for his College.

Really, a printing press of some kind must be put high on the list of Kalvi's engineering staff. They'd managed quite a few small motor-driven, solar panel gadgets, why not a printing press? But that required paper, and the forests were going to be vulnerable for the next fifty years no matter how assiduous the Weyrs were in their protective umbrella.

One tangle of Thread could destroy acres of trees in the time it took to get a groundcrew to the affected area.

He sighed. If only the organics plastic machinery were still operating . . . but the one unit housed in the Fort storage had rusted in the same flooding that had ruined so much else.

" 'Ours not to wonder what were fair in life,' " he quoted to himself, "which is a saying I should get printed out to remind me that we've got what we've got and have to make do."

He couldn't help but feel somewhat depressed, though. There had been some high moments these last few days and it was hard to resume normal routine. Not every one in the teaching staff were back, though all should have checked in by late evening. He'd hear then how the performances went elsewhere. He'd have to wait to learn how the new curriculum was working. By springtime he'd know what fine tuning would be needed. He could count on Sallisha for that, he was sure. By springtime Thread would fall and the easy pace they had all enjoyed would be a memory.

Ah, that was what he had to do. He'd put it off long enough—write up the roster for groundcrews drafted from students over fifteen and teachers. He'd promised that to Lord Paulin and, what with everything else, never produced it. He pulled a fresh sheet of paper from the drawer, then stopped, put it back, and picked up a sheet from the reuse pile. A clean side was all he needed. Mustn't waste or he'd want soon enough.

Lady Jane herself led Iantine to his quarters, asking all the gracious questions a hostess did: Where had he been for Turn's End? Had he enjoyed himself? Had he had the opportunity to hear the splendid new music from the College? What instrument did he play? What did he hear from his parents? He answered as well as he could, amazed at the difference between his reception here and the one he'd had at Bitra. Lady Jane was a fluttery sort of woman, not at all what he would have expected as the spouse of a man like Bridgely. She must be extremely efficient under all that flutter, he thought, contrasting the grace, order, and appearance of the public rooms with those at Bitra, and seeing a vast difference between the two.

No low-level living for him here, either. Lady Jane led him onto the family's floor, urging the two drudges who were carrying the canvases and skybroom wood panels to mind their steps and not damage their burdens.

She opened the door, presenting him with the key, and he was bemused as he followed her into a large dayroom, at least ten times larger than the cubicle at Bitra, on the outside of the hold so that it had a wide, tall window, facing northeast. It was a gracious room, too, the stone walls washed a delicate greeny-white, the furnishings well-polished wood with a pleasing geometric pattern in greens and beige on the coverings.

"I do know that Artists prefer a north light, but this is the best we can do for you on that score . . ." Benden's Lady fluttered her hands here and there. They were graceful, small hands, with only the wide band of a spousal ring on the appropriate finger. Another contrast to the Bitran tendency to many gaudy jewels.

"It's far more than I expected, Lady Jane," he said as sincerely as he could.

"And I'm sure it's far more than you had at Bitra Hold," she said with a contemptuous sniff. "Or so I've been told. You may be sure that Benden Hold would never place an Artist of your rank and ability with the drudges. Bitrans may lay claim," and her tone expressed her doubt, "to having a proper Bloodline, but they have never shown much couth!" She noticed him testing the sturdiness of the easel. "That's from stores. It belonged to Lesnour. D'you know his work?"

"Lesnour? Indeed." Iantine dropped his hand from the smoothly waxed upright. Lesnour, who'd lived well past the hundred mark, had designed and executed Benden Hold's murals and was famed for his use of color. He'd also compiled a glossary of pigments available from indigenous materials, a volume Iantine had studied and which had certainly helped him at Bitra.

Lady Jane pushed open the wooden door into the sleeping

room. Not large but still generous in size: he could see the large bed, its four posts carved with unusual leaves and flowers, probably taken from Earth's botany. She pointed at the back to the third room of the suite: a private toilet and bath. And the whole suite was warm. Benden had been constructed with all the same conveniences that Fort Hold boasted.

"This is much more than I need, Lady Jane," Iantine said, almost embarrassed as he dropped his carisak to the floor of the dayroom.

"Nonsense. We know at Benden what is due a man of your abilities. Space," and she gave a graceful sweep of her hand about the room, "is so necessary to compose the thoughts and to allow the mind to relax." She did another complicated arabesque with her hands and smiled up at him. He smiled back at her, trying to act gracious rather than amused at her extravagant manner. "Now, the evening meal will be served in the Great Hall at eight and you'll dine at the upper table," she said with a firm smile to forestall any protests. "Would you care to have someone put at your disposal to help with your materials?"

"No, thank you most kindly, Lady Jane, but I'm used to doing for myself." Maybe he could have borrowed Leopol for a few weeks? There was certainly enough space for the boy to be accommodated in with him.

So she left, after he once again expressed his profuse thanks for the courtesies.

He prowled about the rooms, washed his hands and face, learning that the water came very hot out of the spigot. The bath had been carved out of the rock, deep enough for him to immerse himself completely, and sufficiently long to lie flat out in the water. Even the Weyr hadn't such elegant conveniences.

He unpacked his clothing so the wrinkles would hang out of his good green shirt and began setting up his workplace. And then sat down in one of the upholstered chairs, plunked his feet down on the footstool, leaned back and sighed. He could get accustomed to this sort of living, so he could! Except for the one lack—Debera.

He wondered briefly if Lady Jane would flutter while she posed for him. And how would he pose her? Somehow he must put in the flutter of her but also her grace and charm. He wondered what instrument she played with those small hands. If only Debera weren't so far away.

Iantine might not have been pleased to know that she was at that very moment the subject of discussion between the Weyr-leaders at Telgar.

"No," Zulaya was saying, shaking her head, "she has more sense than to jeopardize Morath. And I think Iantine would not risk his standing with the Weyr in an indiscretion. I understand from Leopol that Iantine wants to come back. Tisha wasn't worried about *that* pair. They may have danced till the musicians quit, but they were visible all the time. Then, too, Debera's hold-bred. Jule's the one I might be worried about, especially since she and T'red have been weyrmates."

"They're not now?" K'vin asked sharply.

"Of course not," and Zulaya dismissed his anxiety on that and then grinned up at him. "T'red's biding his time. He knows he'd better."

K'vin sighed and checked off another matter discussed with Zulaya. "Let's see—a tenth-month Hatching, so by this fourth month, the greens won't be flying yet."

"Oh, now, I'd say Morath might. If she keeps growing at the same rate, her wings'll be strong enough to test by late spring. But we don't need to include the latest Hatching in our calculations, K'vin," she said, and leaned toward him and the lists he was compiling. "They've got all the site-recognition training to do, the long-range flights to build wing muscle. If we don't need to force their training, let's not. We've got fifty years to use them . . ."

"Do we?" and K'vin tossed his pencil to the table, leaning back and sighing.

Zulaya reached a hand across to tap his arm reassuringly. "Don't fret so, Kev," she said. "That can't change events. I think that the group we're going to have trouble with is not the babies, but the elderlies. Those old riders're going to insist on being assigned to fighting wings, you know."

K'vin closed his eyes, shaking his head as if he could somehow lose that problem. "I know, I know," he said, all too aware that he couldn't avoid making a decision there. "They'll be more of a liability than the youngsters ever would—trying to show that they've lost nothing to their age."

"Well, the dragons won't have," she said, and then she, too, sighed. "But we can't baby them: that's not fair. And the dragons' reflexes are as fast as ever. They'll protect their riders . . ."

"But who'll protect the rest of the wing from slow reflexes? You know how close Z'ran and T'lel came to disaster yesterday morning?"

"They were showing off," Zulaya said. "Meranath chewed the two browns out as if they were weyrlings."

"We won't have time for that during a Fall . . ." K'vin rubbed the ache in the back of his neck. "I've called a safety-strap check for the entire Weyr."

"Kev," she said gently, "we had one last week. Don't you remember?"

"We can't have enough," he snapped back at her, and then shot her a look of apology.

"It's the waiting that's getting to you," Zulaya said with a rueful smile. "To all of us."

K'vin gave a snort. "So do we pray that Thread falls early?"

"I wouldn't wish that on us, but we could legitimately go south on an excursion . . ."

"*Not,*" he objected emphatically, "another Aivas expedition."

"No, no!" She laughed at his vehemence. "But we could check on the Tubberman grubs: see how much farther they have penetrated. We should do so soon now anyhow, since we're supposed to check on their spread. A trip away, out of this cold, would lift spirits. After the excitement of Turn's End, First Month is always a letdown. Who knows? We might even find some of those spare parts Kalvi's always whingeing about."

"Spare parts?" K'vin asked.

"Yes, ones lost in the Second Crossing storm."

"Now that's a real lost cause," K'vin said.

"Whether it is or not, it provides a training exercise in the sun, away from here and all of that," and she pointed at the disorder of lists and reports on the table.

"Where would we go?" K'vin sat upright in his chair, examining the possibility.

"Well, we should check the original site at Calusa . . ." She retrieved the relevant chart from the storage cabinet and brought it to the table. K'vin hastily cleared a space. "Then look along the Kahrainian coast where the Armada had a long stop for repairs."

"That's all been gone over so often . . ."

"And not much retrieved. Anyway, it's not so much what we find, but more that we went for a look," Zulaya said with a droll grin.

"The entire Weyr?"

"Well, the fighting wings, certainly. Leave the training ones here, give them responsibility . . . and see how they like it."

"J'dar had better be in charge," K'vin said, glancing to see if she agreed.

She shrugged. "J'dar or O'ney."

"No, J'dar."

Oddly enough, she gave him a pleased smile. He hadn't expected that, since she had specifically named O'ney, one of the oldest bronze riders. He tried to defer to her judgment whenever possible, but he'd noticed that O'ney tended to be unnecessarily officious.

"Now, this is as far as grubs had migrated on last winter's check," she said, running her finger along Rubicon River.

"How're the grubs supposed to get across that?" K'vin asked, tapping the contour lines for the steep cliffs that lined the river, gradually tapering down above the Sea of Azov.

"The Agric guys say they'll either go around or be carried across the river as larvae in the digestive tracts of wherries and some of those sport animals that were let loose. They have been breeding, you know."

Zulaya was teasing now, since she knew very well that Charanth had had to rescue him from a very large, hungry orange-and-black-striped feline. Charanth had been highly insulted because the creature had actually then attacked him, a bronze dragon! The incident was a leveling one for both rider and dragon.

"Oh, and don't I know it. I'll not be caught that way twice."

"It grew a mighty fine hide," she said, her eyes dancing with challenge.

"Catch your own, Zu. Now, let's see . . . should we check and see if any of the other Weyrs want to come? Make this a joint exercise?"

"Why?" she countered with a shrug. "The whole idea is to get our wings away for a bit for something besides Fall readiness. Meranath," and she turned to her queen, who was lounging indolently on her couch, her head turned in their direction and her eyes open, "would you be good enough to spread the word that the Weyr's going off on an exercise," and she grinned at K'vin, "tomorrow, first light? That should startle a few."

"Undoubtedly," and glancing at Zulaya for permission, K'vin made a second request of Meranath, "And ask J'dar and T'dam to step up here, please?"

The sun will be much warmer in the south, Meranath said, *and we will all like that, K'vin.*

"Glad you approve," he said, giving the gold queen a little bow. He was also considerably gratified that she was using his name more. Could that mean that Zulaya was thinking of him more often? He kept that question tight in his mind, where even Charanth wouldn't hear it. Did she really approve of his leadership? Zulaya never gave him any clues despite her courtesies to him in public: though he certainly appreciated that much. He didn't seem any closer to a real intimacy with her, and he wanted one badly. Would he ever figure out how to achieve that? Could that be why she had suggested this excursion?

"How long has it been since there was an update on the grubs?"

She shrugged. "That's not the point. We need a diversion and this makes a good one. Also, someone should do it for the Agric records. And we'll probably have to go down during Fall to see if the grubs really do what they're supposed to do."

"Do you want to put us out of business?" he asked.

Zulaya shook her head. "As long as Thread falls from Pernese skies, we won't be out of business. Psychologically, it's imperative that we keep as much of the stuff as possible *off* the surface of the planet. The grubs are just an extra added precaution, not the total answer."

The two Weyrleaders had forgotten to caution their dragons against mentioning the destination, and it was all over the Weyr by dinnertime. They were besieged by requests from

Weyrfolk to be taken along. Even Tisha was not shy about requesting a lift.

"Some of the bronzes would need to carry two passengers," K'vin said, doing some quick calculations.

"The weyrlings would have to stay," Zulaya said, that necessity causing a brief hitch to the euphoria. But she shrugged. "We'll make an occasion for T'dam to take them down once they are flighted, but they're Weyrbound this time."

"That wouldn't be until after Thread has started," K'vin said, looking doubtful.

"Sure, we know when it falls, north or south, and a day off for the auxiliaries is no big thing. Plan it for a rainy day, here," Zulaya said, "and they won't mind having the sun down south."

So that issue was settled.

The entire Weyr assembled, loading passengers and supplies for an outing that was now scheduled for three days. K'vin allowed they would need that long to make a diligent survey of grub penetration. He brought with him maps and writing materials so he could make accurate records.

The morning had its moment of humor: getting Tisha aboard brown Branuth had been a struggle, involving not only Branuth's rider, T'lel (who laughed so hard he had hiccups), but four other riders, the strongest and tallest.

Branuth, an extremely quizzical expression on his long face, craned his head around to watch and got a bad cramp in his neck muscles doing so. T'lel and Z'ran had to massage him.

"Stop that and get up here, T'lel," Tisha was yelling, her thick legs stuck out at angles from her perch between the neck ridges. "I'll be split. And if I'm split, you'll suffer. I never should have said I'd come. I should know better than to leave my caverns for any reason whatsoever. This is *very* uncomfortable. Stop that guffawing, T'lel. Stop it right now. It isn't funny where I'm sitting. Get up here and let's go!"

Getting Tisha aboard Branuth had taken so much time that everyone else was in place and ready to go by the time T'lel did manage to get in front of Tisha.

"Not only am I being split, I'm also being bisected by these ridges. Did you sharpen them on purpose, T'lel? No wonder riders are so skinny. They'd have to be. Don't dragons grow ridges for large people? I should have had K'vin take me up. Charanth is a much bigger dragon . . . Why couldn't you have put me up on your bronze, K'vin?" Tisha shouted across the intervening space.

K'vin was trying to preserve his dignity as Weyrleader by not laughing at the sight of her, but he didn't dare look in her direction again. Instead he swiveled his torso so he could scan everyone, pleased to see all eyes on him—rider, passenger, and dragon. He peered upward to the rim, where more dragons awaited their departure, poised well clear of the newly positioned Eye and Finger rocks. Now he raised his arm.

Charrie, they are to assume their wing positions in the air.

They know. Charanth sounded petulant, for this was a frequent drill. K'vin slapped his neck affectionately with one hand while he gave his upheld right arm the pump.

All the dragons in the bowl lifted, swirling up dust and grit from the Bowl floor with such a battery of wings, and then those on the rim rose, sorting themselves out in the air to form their respective wings. Zulaya and the other queens positioned above the others.

And in formation in jig time, too. Let's go, Charrie.

With a great leap, Charanth was airborne. One sweep of his wings and he was level with the wings, another and he was in front of the queens. Heads turned upward and Charanth dutifully angled himself earthward so that all could see the Weyrleader.

Inform the Weyr that our destination is the Sea of Azov.

I have!

K'vin pumped his arm in the continuous gesture to signal *Go between!* The entire Weyr blinked out simultaneously.

Steady, he cautioned Charanth, pleased with that disciplined departure. *Now we go!*

Three seconds he counted and then the warm air above the brilliantly blue Sea of Azov was like the smack of a hot towel in his face. Charanth rumbled in pleasure.

K'vin was far more interested in discovering that the ranks of the dragons, wing by wing, had arrived still in formation. He grinned.

Please inform the wingleaders to take their riders to their separate destinations.

One by one the wings disappeared, with the exception of T'lel's, which had picked the sea area for their excursion site. The queens started to glide toward the shore, too, for they carried quite a few of the supplies that Tisha would need to set up her hearths for the evening meal.

Let's wait and let them all get safely to the surface, K'vin told Charanth, although part of him wanted to see how Tisha managed to dismount Branuth. He was therefore somewhat surprised, and at first a little concerned, when he saw a brown dragon detach itself from the main wing and glide in a landing, on the water, just short of the shore. Charanth had his head down and was observing the effort.

Branuth says she ordered it. She's swimming free of his back. Charanth sounded amused, too, and K'vin chuckled.

That was much more dignified.

Branuth says it was easier on him, too, but he doesn't think he should do the same back at Telgar.

Not with the water that cold this time of year.

We can now land? Branuth says the sun is warm.

I thought you wanted to hunt.

Later. NOW I want to get warm all over.

Charanth's preference was almost unanimous as the dragons spread out over both the pebbled beach and the shore-line, which was covered with a shrub that, when bruised by large dragon bodies, gave off a rich pungent odor, not at all unpleasant.

Tisha had some of the Weyrfolk off finding kindling and stones to make campfires, and to see what fruits might be ripe, and another group to fish where boulders had tumbled down into the sea like a breakwater.

"I'm going for a long swim," Zulaya called out to him as he and Charanth glided to a landing. She was already stripping off her jacket. "Meranath wants one, too." She touched down long enough to strip off the rest of her clothing, which she left in a neat pile on a boulder before making her way to the water.

"What about the grubs?"

"They'll wait," she yelled over her shoulder, wading out until the water was deep enough for swimming.

We don't have to go find grubs now, do we? asked Charanth plaintively, and the eyes he turned up to his rider whirled with a yellow anxiety.

"No, we don't," K'vin said. "Grubs were an excuse to leave the Weyr for a few days."

He shucked his clothes, and dragon and rider joined the others in the warm Azovian waters.

It might not have pleased K'vin to learn that almost every rider procrastinated over the stated objective of the journey south: grubs were, in fact, probably the last thing on anyone's mind. Sunning, swimming in the pleasant waters, hunting for dragons, and food-gathering for humans took precedence—and space and time for absolute privacy.

P'tero and M'leng asked permission of V'last, their wing-leader, to take their dragons hunting.

"Remember what K'vin told you about the sport creatures down here," V'last said, serving the same warning to the other riders wishing to hunt their dragons.

P'tero and M'leng nodded obediently but, as soon as they left the clearing where their wing had landed on the Malay River, they laughed at the very notion that any creature could be dangerous to *their* dragons.

"It's really hot here," M'leng said, glancing back at the river.

"We'll be hotter after we've hunted the dragons," P'tero said. "But once that's done we really don't have to do another thing until dinner."

"So let's not come back here until just before," M'leng said, laughing recklessly. "Or we'll end up having to hunt or fish or gather it."

"There're enough Weyrfolk with us to do all that. And enjoy," P'tero said, rather condescendingly. "Let's get out of here."

He made a running jump and neatly vaulted onto Ormonth's blue back. M'leng simultaneously boarded green Sith.

"What game shall we go after?" M'leng asked.

"Whatever we see first," P'tero replied, and pumped his arm to send them both aloft. M'leng preferred him to be leader.

They didn't have far to go to see grazing herds of runner beasts, smaller than the ones they were accustomed to seeing in the holds. But when they also saw other dragons in the sky, gliding in to hunt, P'tero signaled M'leng to fly on, in a south-westerly direction. They hadn't gone very far before both found it necessary to strip off their flying jackets, and then their shirts, which were winter weight anyhow. P'tero admired M'leng's compact body. The green rider was small-boned, which had always delighted P'tero, with a surprisingly strong and agile wiry frame. He was also winter-white, right to his collar. P'tero giggled. He looked so funny, as if he had two different skins.

Then the blue rider became fascinated with the tropical terrain around them, subtly different from the North's warmer holds. Nerat was rain forests and vast tracks of almost impenetrable jungle except along the western side, whereas Ista was sharp hills and deep valleys, also densely vegetated. But here, a vast grassland, similar in some respects to the plains of Keroon, spread out in all directions, dotted by upthrusts of bare yellow rock, occasional copses of angular trees with fronds spilling from the crests, and large, wide-branched trees like islands. The dragons' flight over some of these caused flocks of wherries and other avian forms to debouch in frantic escape.

Can I eat them? Ormonth inquired of his rider, speeding up in case he was allowed to give chase.

What? Those tough mouthfuls? P'tero asked scornfully. Then he cupped his hands and shouted at M'leng. "Ormonth's hungry enough to eat wherries!"

"Sith wanted to, as well. We'd better feed them," M'leng yelled back. "Over there!" and he pointed to one of the rock piles. One of the spreading trees had grown right up against the pile, shading the long incline to the top.

P'tero thought the formation looked like the prow of a ship, with midships plunging into the sea of ground. And the tree a muchly misplaced mast.

M'leng nodded vigorously in approval and pumped his arm, kicking Sith into a wide curve so that they came up to the prow to land. A fine breeze blew against them from the south, cooling the perspiration on their bare torsos.

As soon as they landed, the two young men stripped off their heavy flight pants and boots. They had to put their socks back on for the rock was far too hot for bare feet.

M'leng, who had good distance vision, covered his eyes with one hand, peering to the west, where a long dark line seemed to be moving.

"Oh, good, herd beasts." He hauled Sith's head around and then pushed it in the right direction. "See? You can eat those. Much better than wherries. Off you go now!" And he gave Sith a thump of dismissal.

"Follow Sith, Ormonth," and P'tero shoved the blue's head to the right. "Hunt with him, and you can't get into any trouble that way. We'll watch from here."

Ormonth shifted weight from one diagonal to the other, his eyes whirling with a trace of anxious yellow.

"What's the matter with you?" P'tero demanded, wanting both dragons to be away so he and M'leng could have some real privacy. And if the pair were busy enough hunting and eating, they'd pay no attention at all to what their riders were doing.

Smell something!

"M'leng, does Sith smell anything?" P'tero was annoyed but you didn't ignore your dragon.

"Different smells down here, that's all." M'leng shrugged, his eager expression indicating that he wanted the dragons away as much as P'tero did.

"I'll keep my eyes open," P'tero assured Ormonth, and slapped him peremptorily to be on his way.

The two launched upward at the same moment, and P'tero watched with some pride the blue's elegant flight attitude as he made height before he would glide down toward his prey.

M'leng slipped in under P'tero's arm. "Oooh, your hide is hot. We'd best be careful not to burn in this sun."

"We'll be all right if we move a lot."

"And we will, won't we?"

They enjoyed each other's company so much that neither were aware when the breeze altered to the west. It still cooled their bare bodies, drying the sweat they had generated. They weren't even aware of much until two things happened at the same instant: Ormonth's angry scream reverberated in P'tero's skull and he was rammed down hard against M'leng so that he cracked his chin on the rock as sharp things tore into his buttocks.

"*ORMONTH!*" he shrieked mentally and vocally.

M'leng was limp under him as he writhed in agony from whatever was attacking him.

Help me! he howled, struggling to turn and see what was trying to eat him.

A dark shadow and the air pressure above him seemed compressed: a most hideous roar sent a carrion stink and hot breath across his bare back. The talons were ripped from his flesh, causing him to shriek again. Something heavy and furry was being hauled across his tortured legs and away. He caught a glimpse of green hide and then blue. And then something large and tawny that seemed to come from nowhere. A blue tail curled protectingly around him. Above his head he heard Ormonth roaring, which turned to shrieks of pain and anger, but mostly anger. He was mentally assailed by vivid images and emotions of revenge that were totally alien to a dragon mind.

As waves of almost unendurable agony gripped him, he realized that Ormonth and Sith were rending whatever had attacked him into shreds; showering blood and gobbets of hot flesh all over him. Then he realized that he was lying on top of M'leng, who was suddenly being pulled away. To his horrified eyes, he saw a great brown paw, dirty big yellow claws unsheathing and curling into his weyrmate's shoulderblade, blood welling up. Despite the pain in his legs and back, he lurched across M'leng and beat at the paw, struggling to lift the claws out of his lover's body.

More noise, more draconic roars, and suddenly there was space above him, letting in fresh air, and the sight of other dragons. Two were attacking the tawny lean creatures that were swarming up the rock outthrust. The dragons hauled them backward by their tails or hindquarters while the creatures writhed and roared and spat defiance, turning to attack the dragons. One had curled itself around a brown's forearm, slashing out at a dragon face.

"M'leng, M'leng, answer me!" P'tero cried, turning his lover's face toward him, slapping his cheeks.

Booted feet stopped by M'leng's head.

"Oh help us, help us!" he pleaded, clutching at the boots. "Help me! I'm dying!" The pain in his legs was so awful . . .

"Who's got the fellis? Where's the numbweed?"

As P'tero felt himself slipping into oblivion, he wondered how under the sun Zulaya had got here and if he was dying.

16

CATHAY, TELGAR WEYR, BITRA HOLD, TELGAR

P'tero didn't die, although for some days he wished he had. The shame of being attacked, of endangering M'leng, of being responsible for injuring nine dragons—when K'vin had particularly warned everyone to be careful—was almost more than he could bear. M'leng might say that P'tero had saved his life—although he had to have his shoulder wound stitched—but P'tero knew that was incidental in the sequence of the attack. Both Sith and Ormonth had suffered from the fangs and claws of the attacking felines, for the creatures had not been easily quelled. Meranath nursed a bite on her left forearm and a slash on her cheek. P'tero hadn't yet been able to look Zulaya in the eye. V'last's Collith's worst injuries were to his forearm, gashed to the bone by the powerful hind legs of the female attacking him. The dragon-lion battle had been fierce while it lasted, for the lions had no fear of the dragons and the entire pride of some fourteen adult beasts had joined battle with the dragons.

Meranath had reacted instantly to Ormonth's shriek; in fact, so quickly that she had actually left Zulaya behind. The Weyr-woman had been astonished: dragons simply didn't do that. Though later, Leopol told P'tero, she had laughed about it—since she'd been swimming and would not have appreciated being hauled dripping wet to companion her dragon. She'd followed, quickly enough, with V'last, K'vin, and others who answered the mayday.

"She was some put out, too," Leopol went on, relishing the telling, "because the dragons made a mess of good lion fur . . . well, what they didn't eat."

P'tero gasped. "The dragons ate the lions?"

"Sure, why not?" Leopol shrugged, grinning. "The entire pride attacked the dragons. But they let the cubs go, you know, though some folks thought they ought to get rid of all they could find. V'last said Collith said they were quite tasty, if a bit tough to chew. Waste not, want not. But Zulaya really would have liked a lion fur for her bed."

P'tero shuddered. He never wanted to see anything to do with lions ever again.

"You shoulda seen yourself brought in, P'tero," Leopol added, gesturing to the temporary quarters that had been set up to tend the badly injured riders. "Charanth himself carried you back in his arms."

"He did?" P'tero's chagrin reached a new depth.

"And O'ney's bronze Queth brought M'leng in. Your wing helped Ormonth and Sith back. Actually, they came in sort of piggyback on Gorianth and Spelth. They were pretty shaken, you know."

P'tero had heard echoes of that journey from Ormonth, who, bless his heart, had never once criticized his rider: another source of infinite distress to P'tero. The blue had been intensely grateful to his weyrmates for their assistance as he couldn't leave his rider out of his sight. It had been all the other dragons could do—although Leopol did not relate this—to reassure Ormonth and Sith that neither of their riders would die.

The Weyr had set up a hasty camp to tend the injured, for some, like P'tero and Collith, couldn't risk being taken *between* until their wounds had scabbed over. K'vin had sent to Fort for Corey to stitch the worst wounds. Medic Maranis was more than competent for the dragons' wounds, but he needed reassurance on his treatment of the two injured riders. Messengers had gone back to Telgar Weyr to reassure those whose dragons had reported the accident and to bring back more equipment for an extended stay.

The two young riders had, in their innocence, chosen a site just above the cave home of a pride of lions. P'tero had never even heard of "lions." Evidently he could thank Tubberman for their existence, for they'd broken out of Calusa and bred quite handily in the wild. They were, Leopol told him with great relish, some of the sport beasts that Tubberman had been experimenting with.

This was not much consolation to P'tero while he lay on his stomach to let the deep fang and claw marks heal.

He worried endlessly that M'leng would no longer love him, with such a scarred and imperfect body. M'leng, however, seemed to dwell so on P'tero's heroism in protecting him with his own body that the blue rider decided not to mention the fact that it had not been entirely voluntary. M'leng had been unconscious from the moment of attack and had a great lump and a cut on the back of his head as well as the wound on his shoulder.

Zulaya had arrived to see P'tero trying to remove the claws from M'leng's body, so there was little the blue rider could say to contradict the Weyrwoman's version.

Tisha, coming to give him fellis early one morning, found him in tears, positive that he had lost M'leng with such a marred body.

"Nonsense, my lad," Tisha had said, soothing back his sweaty hair as she held the straw for his fellis juice to his lips. "He will only see what you endured for his sake, to save him. And those scars will heal quite nicely, thanks to Corey's neat stitching."

The reference to the skill of the Head Medic almost reduced him to tears again. He'd caused so much fuss.

"Indeed you have, but you've livened things up considerably, young man, and taught everyone some valuable lessons."

"I have?" P'tero would just as soon not have.

"For one, dragons think they're invulnerable . . . and they aren't. A very good lesson to take into Fall with them, I assure you. Cool some of the hotheads, so certain that it's just a matter of breathing fire in the right direction. For another, the Southern Continent has developed its own hazards . . ."

"Did the Weyr ever find out about the grubs?" P'tero asked, suddenly recalling the reason for the excursion.

Tisha burst out laughing, then stifled it, though P'tero's tent was a distance from any others. "There, lad, you've a good head as well as a brave heart. Yes, they completed the survey faster'n any other's ever been done."

P'tero learned later that the grubs had infested yet a few more kilometers westward and southward toward the Great Barrier Range in an uneven wave of expansion. Their progress into the sandy scrublands east of Landing had slowed to a few meters, and the agricultural experts were not particularly concerned: they were more eager to have the rich grass and forest lands preserved.

"So the trip hasn't been a waste?" P'tero said, relaxing as he felt the fellis spreading out.

Tisha gave him more maternal pats, settling the furs and making sure nothing was binding across his bottom and legs.

"By no means, lovey. Now you go back to sleep . . ."

As if he could prevent that, P'tero thought as the fellis took over and blotted out conscious thought as well as the pain.

It was three weeks before P'tero's wounds had healed sufficiently for the trip back. The makeshift infirmary had more patients since there were other hazards besides large hungry and territorially minded felines in the Southern Continent: the heat, unwary exposure to too much sun, and a variety of other minor injuries. Leopol got a thorn in his foot which had festered, so he joined P'tero in the infirmary shelter until the poison drained.

Tisha and one of the Weyrfolk came down with a fever that had Maranis sending back to Fort for a medic more qualified than he in such matters. The woman recovered in a few days, but Tisha had a much harder time of it, sweating kilos off her big frame, to leave her so enervated Maranis was desperately worried about her. K'vin sent to Ista to beg a ship to transport her back North since he could not subject her to trying to climb aboard a dragon.

Her illness depressed everyone.

"You don't really know how important someone is," Zulaya said, having come down to reassure herself on the state of the convalescents, "until they're suddenly . . . not there!"

Her remark quite sunk P'tero's spirits. And Tisha was not there to jolly him out of his depression. M'leng was, and appeared in the shelter.

"How dare you be so self-centered?" the green rider said in a taut, outraged tone of voice.

"Huh?"

"Tisha's illness is *not* your fault. Leopol wasn't wearing shoes when he was told to and so his infected foot also isn't your fault. In fact, it isn't even your fault that we picked *that* rock out of all the ones we could have picked. It was *bad* luck, but nothing more, and I don't want Ormonth upsetting Sith anymore. D'you hear me?"

P'tero burst into tears. Just as he'd thought: M'leng didn't love him anymore.

Then M'leng's gentle arms went around him, and he was pulled into M'leng's chest and comforted with many caresses and kisses.

"Don't be such a stupid idiot, you stupid idiot. How could I *not* love you?"

Later P'tero wondered how he could ever have doubted M'leng.

When the convalescents did return to Telgar Weyr, they found Tisha once more in charge of the Lower Cavern. If her clothes were still loose on her frame, she was tanned from the sea voyage back from the mouth of the Rubicon and looked completely recovered.

Some of the green and blue riders in the wing had freshened up both P'tero's and M'leng's weyrs, with paint and new fabrics. The worn pillows had been replaced with plump ones.

"Because Tisha said you'd need to sit real *soft* for a while longer," and Z'gal giggled into his hand. "Lady Salda let us have feathers from the Turn's End birds."

Then Z'gal's lover, T'sen, brought an object from behind his back. P'tero stared at it, puzzled. It seemed to be a pad with very long thongs.

"Ah, what is it?"

Z'gal went into a laughing fit which annoyed T'sen, who scowled and kept pushing it at P'tero.

"To sit on, of course. It'll fit between neck ridges. We measured."

Belatedly but as effusively as he could, P'tero thanked T'sen for such a thoughtful gift. It wasn't so much his bottom that needed padding, but the muscles in the buttocks and down his legs that needed strengthening and massage to get them back in full working order. Of course, M'leng had been assiduous in the massage sessions, but P'tero was now concerned that he'd not be fit for fighting when Threadfall began. M'leng had been wounded in a much better site. He wouldn't miss a day's fighting.

There was wine, biscuits, and cheese for a small in-weyr party. M'leng capped the return celebrations by presenting P'tero with a flat wrapped parcel.

M'leng's eyes were shining in anticipation as P'tero untied the string, wondering what on earth this could be.

"Iantine's back, you know," M'leng said, breathlessly watching every movement of P'tero's hands.

The other riders were equally excited, and P'tero felt a spurt of petulance that they all knew what this was and were dying to see his reaction.

Naturally, the picture was picture side down when he finished unwrapping. P'tero was stunned silent when he turned it over, and his eyes nearly bugged out of his head at the scene depicted.

"But . . . but . . . Iantine wasn't even there!"

"He's so good, isn't he?" Z'gal said. "Did he get it all right? M'leng described it over and over . . ."

P'tero didn't quite know what to say, he was so bewildered. So much of it was what he would have given his right arm to have actually happened. The lion was clawing his backside, M'leng was sprawled under him, and there were more lions climbing up the rock, their vicious intent vivid in their posture, their open mouths showing fangs longer than a dragon's. P'tero was posed in an obvious act of defending his lover, his head turned, one arm upraised in a fist aimed at the attacking lion's head. But that wasn't the worst of the inaccuracies: both riders were fully clothed.

"P'tero?" M'leng's voice was quite anxious.

The blue rider swallowed. "I don't know what to say!"

Where am I? Ormonth wanted to know, evidently viewing it through his rider's eyes, as a dragon sometimes could.

"There!" and P'tero pointed to the dragons high up in the sky, wings straight up in a landing configuration, claws unsheathed, ready to grab the attacker, eyes a mad whirl of red and orange.

"Of course, I was unconscious," M'leng was saying, "but that's what Ormonth and Sith would have been doing. Wasn't it?" And he jabbed P'tero warningly.

"Exactly," P'tero said hurriedly. And it probably was, although he hadn't seen it, since he'd been looking in the other direction. "Everything happened so fast ... it's almost eerie how Iantine has got it all down in one scene!" The amazement and respect in his voice was not the least bit feigned.

"Now," and M'leng pointed to the wall, "we've even got a hook for you to hang it on."

"Wouldn't you rather have it?" P'tero suggested hopefully.

"I've a copy of my own. Iantine did two, one for each of us," M'leng said, beaming proudly at his lover.

So P'tero had to hang the wretched reminder of the worst day of his life on his own wall, just where he couldn't miss it every morning of his life when he woke up.

"You'll never know how much this means to me," he said, and that, too, was quite truthful.

No one thought it the least bit odd that he got very, very drunk on wine that night.

Lanath *comes,* Charanth told his rider.

"So Meranath tells me," Zulaya said before K'vin could speak. "He wants to know *all* about our trip south."

"I thought he'd given up on that notion to practice on the first Fall in the South," K'vin said. He tried to sound diffident.

Then Zulaya put a finger across her lips and pointed to the sleeping Meranath, a signal to K'vin to guard his thoughts to Charanth outside on the ledge. He nodded understanding.

"You don't fool me, Kev." She waggled her finger at him. "You and B'nurrin would give your eyeteeth to be in on the first real Fall—even if it does take place in the South where nothing could be hurt. Or, for that matter, saved."

"The grubs haven't spread across the entire Southern Continent, you know."

"That has nothing to do with *seeing* Thread for the first time in two hundred years."

He answered her droll smile with an abashed grin. "We don't need to have the dragons stoked up or anything," he said.

"Yes, but do you really want to have S'nan reproaching you for the rest of your career? That is, if you have one as a Weyrleader with this sort of antic in mind."

K'vin gave her a long look. "And don't tell me you like the fact that Sarai will be leading a queen's wing in the Fall before you will."

Zulaya rocked back in her chair just enough that K'vin realized he had made a palpable hit. She was honest enough to grin back.

"We don't even know that's what's on B'nurrin's mind," she said.

That's exactly what was on his mind, however, even after both Zulaya and K'vin enumerated the problems they'd had on that ill-favored excursion to the Southern Continent.

"In the first place," B'nurrin said, after repeating Zulaya's signal to shield their thoughts from their dragons, "we wouldn't be landing anywhere. And I don't mean for whole wings to go, Kev," he added quickly. "Not like it makes sense to fight the first actual Fall we do get—wherever *that* actually is . . ."

"And you're hoping S'nan doesn't go first," Zulaya said with a malicious grin.

"Too right on that," B'nurrin replied sourly. "He really gets up my nose, you know. I don't see any harm in having a look. I mean . . ." He paused, steeling himself a moment and staring straight into K'vin's eyes. "I'll be frank. I'm scared I'll be needing clean pants half a dozen times the first Fall I have to lead."

"I've wondered about that myself," K'vin admitted drolly. Out of the corner of his eye, he was surprised to notice a fleeting expression of approval on Zulaya's face. Surely B'ner had never mentioned that even as a remote possibility?

"So, I figure, if I get a good look at it *before* I have to act brave and unconcerned . . ."

"Anyone who isn't concerned about Thread's a damn fool," Zulaya put in.

"Agreed." B'nurrin nodded at her, grinning. "So, will you join me?"

"Because if two of us go, neither of us will be as much to blame?" K'vin asked, one eye on Zulaya's face.

B'nurrin scratched his jaw. "Yes, I guess that's the size of it."

"We're the first you've asked?"

B'nurrin gave a snort. "Well, I certainly wouldn't suggest it again to S'nan after the way he's clapped my ears back twice now. I figured you were more likely to than D'miel, though, you know, I think M'shall might come. If the weather's wrong at Fort and High Reaches, Benden's might be the first actual Fall we meet."

"M'shall might just be amenable at that," Zulaya said, "though he's the last one of the whole lot of you to doubt his abilities."

"That's true enough," B'nurrin said, then his enthusiasm got the better of him. "But look at it this way, even if old S'nan gets to fight this Pass's first Fall over Fort, we'll have been to one before him, so to speak." The Igen Weyrleader grinned with such boyish delight in the scheme that K'vin had to chuckle.

"How long is there between Southern's first and ours?" he asked. He was astonished to see that Zulaya was already unrolling Telgar Weyr's Thread chart onto the table.

"Roughly two weeks," she said.

"So we could go and see and not jeopardize the readiness of our own Weyrs," B'nurrin said.

"The first possible Fall over Fort is number seven. Number four is over the Landing site," Zulaya went on, tapping her finger on the various Thread corridors. "Five's no good, but six starts offshore of the mouth of Paradise River, not far from where we just were."

"What about the first three?" B'nurrin asked, craning his neck to see. "Oh, not really as good for safe coordinates, are they?" Then he looked up in a direct challenge at K'vin. "Will you join me?"

"I'd like to," K'vin said decisively, pointedly not looking in Zulaya's direction.

"I think I would, too," she said, surprising both men. When they regarded her in amazement, she added, "Well, queens' wings fly a lot lower into danger than the rest of the Weyr does. Makes it quicker for me to change *my* pants, but that doesn't mean I want to *have* to." Then, when they grinned with relief at her, she asked, "So, does Shanna want to come, too?"

Grinning even more broadly, B'nurrin said, "Only if you were going."

"At least one of you at Igen Weyr has some sense," Zulaya said. "Let's just sit on the idea for a few days. Just to be sure."

"Who will know, if we don't mention it?" B'nurrin asked, swiveling around to pointedly regard a sleeping Meranath.

Paulin took Jamson with him to Bitra Hold. The older Lord Holder was still furious with his son for voting High Reaches Hold in the impeachment. But he had been unable to fault his son's management during his two-month convalescence. This had indeed restored Jamson to vigorous health, if not tolerance.

The change in Bitra was obvious from the moment Magrith dropped to the courtyard and Vergerin hurried down the steps to greet his guests. He had been alerted.

S'nan had insisted on being allowed to convey the two Lord Holders, for he had been as stunned as Jamson by the swiftness of the impeachment.

"My word!" the Fort Weyrleader said, staring about him. Magrith was staring, too, and Paulin had to suppress a grin since the dragon was looking in one direction, his rider in the other.

The courtyard was neat, and the recent snow swept from the paving, which showed fresh cement grouting. The road, in either direction, was no longer bordered by straggling bushes and weed trees. The row of cotholds sported fresh roof slates, repaired chimneys, and painted metal shutters, all obviously in good working order. Although some of the hold's upper windows were already shuttered tight, the facade was no longer festooned with dead vine branches. Sunlight glinted off solar panels that had been cleaned and repaired.

Piled under a newly built shed were HNO_3 tanks, racked for easy usage and the hoses and nozzles hung properly on pegs. Kalvi had told Paulin that he'd been asked to deliver the Bitran consignment within a week of Vergerin taking hold. And the following week he had sent his best teachers to instruct in their use and maintenance.

Vergerin wore a good tunic over his trousers but they were made of stout material and he had obviously been working before his guests arrived. He greeted Paulin affably and re-sponded courteously to the introduction to Jamson, whose response was frosty.

"You've done a lot since you took over, Vergerin," Paulin said, giving the man the encouragement of his public support. "I wouldn't have believed it possible, frankly."

"Well," and Vergerin grinned in the most charming way, "I found Chalkin's hoard, so I've been able to hire in Craftsmen. Even the nearest holders aren't accustomed to me yet, and . . . shy?"

"Scared, more likely," Paulin said dryly.

"That, too, I'm sure, but I've done what I can to supply them with materials to make their own repairs. The hold was in an appalling state, you know."

Jamson grunted but his eyes widened as he saw the quiet order and cleanliness of the first reception room. S'nan made approving noises deep in his throat and even ran a finger across the wide table with its attractive arrangement of winter berries and leaves. A drudge, in livery so new the creases hadn't been lost, was hurrying across the hall with a heavy tray.

"My office is quite comfortable," Vergerin said, and gestured for them to enter.

Paulin noticed that the heavy wooden door gleamed with oil and the brass door plates were polished to a high gloss. The interior had been totally replaced, with worktops, tidy shelv-ing, and bookcases. A scale map of Bitra Hold was nailed up on the interior wooden wall: beneath that was the Northern Conti-nent and, oddly enough, the Steng Valley. Did Vergerin plan to reopen the mines there? A fire burned on the hearth, three upholstered chairs arranged cozily nearby, while a low table evidently awaited the tray. Polished metal vases on the deep window ledge held arrangements of bright orange berries and evergreen boughs: altogether a different room under Ver-gerin's management.

"There's klah, an excellent broth which I do recommend, and

wine, mulled or room temperature," Vergerin said, gesturing for his three guests to take the comfortable chairs.

"You've a new cook as well, Vergerin?" Paulin asked, and pointed to the steaming pitcher when Vergerin grinned. "I'll sample the broth, then."

Jamson didn't mind if he did, too, but S'nan wanted the klah.

"You remember the back staircase, Paulin?" Vergerin said, taking the broth as well and pulling up a straight chair for himself.

"I do. Was that where the marks were hidden?"

"Yes, in one of the steps." Vergerin chuckled. "Chalkin must have forgotten that I knew about that hidey-hole, too. It's been a lifesaver, both to return unnecessary tithings and to buy in supplies. One thing Chalkin did do correctly was keep records. I knew exactly how much he had extorted from his people."

Jamson cleared his throat testily.

"Well, he did, Lord Jamson," Vergerin said without cavil. "They hadn't even enough in stores to get by on this winter, let alone have reserves for Fall. I'm still unloading what we couldn't possibly use from what Chalkin had amassed." He gave a mirthless laugh. "Chalkin would have weathered all fifty years of the Pass from what he had on hand—but none of his people would have lasted the first year, let alone have the materials to safeguard what they could plant out. Bitra being established after the First Fall, there were no hydroponics sheds, although the tanks are stored below."

Jamson gave another snort. "And the gaming? Have you curtailed that?"

"Both here and elsewhere," Vergerin said, flushing a little. "I haven't so much as touched dice or card since that game with Chalkin."

"What about his gamesmen?"

Vergerin's smile was grim. "They had the choice of signing

new contracts with me—for I will not honor the old ones—or leaving. Not many left."

S'nan barked out a cackle of a laugh. "Not many would, considering the hazards of being holdless during a Pass. You have done well, Vergerin." He nodded an emphasis.

"You've had a second chance, Vergerin," Jamson said, waggling his finger. "See that you continue to profit by such good fortune." He had finished the broth and now stood. "We will go on a quick survey of the holds, if you please."

"Of course," and Vergerin rose hastily, pushing back his chair. "By horse—"

"No, no," Jamson dismissed that. "You've no need to accompany us. Better if you don't."

"Now, Jamson," Paulin began, for it was discourteous of the High Reaches Holder even to suggest Vergerin stay behind.

"Certainly, as you wish." Vergerin motioned them to pause at the map and indicated directions. "We've managed to complete all the necessary repairs on the holds adjacent or not far from the major link roads. Those high up have had to wait on supplies. I can't outstay my welcome at Benden Weyr, though M'shall has been far more obliging than I thought he'd be."

"It's to his advantage to oblige," S'nan said stiffly, at the merest hint of criticism of a Weyrleader.

Jamson had opened the door into the Hall and stopped so short, staring at the opposite wall, that Paulin nearly walked up his heels. Jamson muttered something under his breath and, pointing at the wall, turned to Vergerin.

"Why under the sun are you hanging his portrait *there*?" he demanded, almost outraged.

Paulin and S'nan peered in the direction indicated.

And Paulin had to laugh. "When did Iantine get a chance to . . . redo it?" he asked Vergerin, who was also broadly grinning.

"I got it yesterday." Vergerin walked across the Hall to stand beneath it. "I think the likeness is now excellent."

There was a moment of silence as they all viewed the portrait, now altered to an honest representation of the former Bitran Lord, including close-set eyes, bad complexion, scanty hair, and the mole on his chin.

S'nan sniffed. "Why would you want his face around at all, Vergerin?"

"One, to remind me to improve my management of Bitra, and two, because it's traditional to display the likenesses of previous Lord Holders." He gestured up the double-sided staircase, where hung the portraits of previous incumbents.

Jamson harrumphed several times. "And Chalkin? How's he doing?"

Paulin shrugged and looked to S'nan.

"He was supplied with all he needs," the Weyrleader said. "There is no need to exacerbate his expulsion by further contact."

"And his children?" Jamson asked, eyes glinting coldly.

Vergerin grinned, ducking his head. "I feel they have improved in health, well-being, and self-discipline."

"They stood in great need of the latter," Paulin said.

"They may surprise you, Lord Paulin," Vergerin said with a sly smile.

"I could bear it."

"As the branch is bent, so it will grow," Jamson intoned piously.

"Come this way," Vergerin said, putting a finger to his lips to indicate silence.

He led them down the corridor, toward what Paulin remembered as one of the gaming rooms. They could hear muted singing: Paulin instantly recognized the melody as one of the College's latest issues. As they got closer to the source he heard the words of the Duty Song. Jamson gave another one of his harrumphs and sniffed.

Carefully Vergerin opened the door on a mightily altered room. The students—and there were far more of them than Paulin had expected—were seated with their backs to the door. The teacher—and Paulin was surprised to recognize Issony back at Bitra—gave an additional nod to his head to acknowledge their presence as he continued to beat the tempo of the song.

Children's voices—even the ones who can't carry the tune—are always appealing: perhaps it is the innocence of the tone and the guilelessness in their rendition of the song's dynamics. Even Jamson smiled, but then the verse they were singing was about the Lord Holder's responsibilities.

"Which ones are Bitran Bloodline?" Paulin whispered to Vergerin.

He pointed, and only then could Paulin pick the children out in the front rows: the girls on the one side and the boys on the other. They were much better clothed than the others but no less attentive to their teacher, and singing lustily: the older girl had the most piercing voice. Somewhat like her mother's, Paulin thought.

Vergerin motioned for them to withdraw, grinning.

"Issony's been right that those youngsters needed competition. The holder kids need no incentives: they want to learn, and Chaldon is determined not to let mere holders get better grades than he. Oh, there's still whinings and pleadings and tantrums, but Issony has my permission to deal with them. And he does. Most effectively."

"Nadona?" Paulin asked.

Vergerin raised his eyebrows. "She's learning much the same lessons as her children, but she's not as quick a study, as Issony would say. She has her own quarters," and he inclined his head toward the upper levels. "She stays within."

"And leaves you to get along with the real work?" Paulin asked in a droll tone.

"Exactly."

"Hmm, yes, well, that's it here, I think," Paulin said, and then made much of fastening his riding jacket to indicate his willingness to depart on the inspection tour. "Do you agree, Jamson?"

Jamson harrumphed, but Paulin took the fact that he did not have questions as a good sign.

When they left the house, men and women were busy putting on the flamethrower tanks.

"I've scheduled a drill. Have to make up for lost time, you know," Vergerin said by way of explanation. Jamson and S'nan exchanged such fatuous glances that Paulin did his best not to laugh out loud. Vergerin caught his eye and winked. Then bade a polite farewell to his guests before he returned to the groundcrew.

"Well, he obviously learned a thing or two," Jamson said in a sanctimonious tone as they went down the steps to the waiting bronze dragon.

"Yes, it would seem he has," S'nan said and then frowned slightly. "Although I cannot like him turning loose Chalkin's gamesmen. They'll cause trouble at Gathers, mark my words."

"No more than they've always done," Paulin said, giving Jamson a discreet helping hand up Magrith's tall shoulder. "Probably less without Chalkin exhorting them to squeeze more out of innocent and guileless holders."

"No gambling should be allowed for any reason in a Weyr," S'nan said, as portentous as ever.

Paulin mounted silently, hoping that these two would see sufficient in a quick swoop to reassure S'nan about Vergerin's worth—and the wisdom of Chalkin's impeachment. The brief visit had satisfied him. Especially the sight of Chalkin's much improved portrait. He must send a message to Iantine at Telgar Weyr—Bridgely had said the artist returned there as soon as he was finished at Benden Hold—and inquire when he and his spouse could hope to have a sitting.

Paulin was well pleased he had taken the trouble to accompany Jamson. He hoped Lady Thea would be able to tell him that Gallian was off the hot seat.

"You are *not* saving the entire world from Threadfall by yourself, P'tero," K'vin said, glaring up at the young blue rider. He was nearly beside himself with rage at P'tero's utter disregard of common sense. "You are *not* going to impress M'leng. If this is how you see your role in Threadfall, I think you'll be a long time on messenger duty."

"But, but—"

"Furthermore," and K'vin pointed a finger fiercely under the boy's nose, "Maranis tells me that your wounds are not well enough healed for you to be back on duty."

"But . . . but . . ." and P'tero, eyes wide with fright, recoiled from his Weyrleader's fury, clutching the neck ridge before he overbalanced. The pad that T'sen had given him now slipped, the ties torn loose sometime during the exercises. Blood spotted it.

"Get down here," K'vin roared, pointing to where he wanted P'tero: on the ground. "Right now."

P'tero obeyed, as promptly as he could, but he was stiff from sitting so long during the day's maneuvers and from the barely healed flesh of his buttock.

K'vin caught him by the shoulder and whirled him around.

"Not only new blood, but old stains," he said, his voice trenchant with scorn and fury. "You're off duty . . ."

"But . . . but . . . Thread's nearly here!" P'tero cried in anguish, almost in tears with frustration and the fear of being unable to show M'leng just how brave he really was. Not mock-brave, like the lion attack, but real brave in selflessness in the air.

"And Thread'll be here for fifty years, young man. That's plenty long enough for it to fear you and Ormonth in the air! Report to Maranis immediately. You're grounded!"

"But I have to be in the first Fall wings," P'tero cried, anguished.

"That wasn't the way to get there. Get to Maranis!"

K'vin didn't wait to see if P'tero obeyed. He stormed across the Bowl, the temptation to shake sense into the blue rider so intense he had to put distance between them.

Ormonth tried to keep him from flying today, Charanth informed his rider.

K'vin halted, glaring up now at his bronze dragon, who was settling himself on his weyr ledge to get what sun remained.

Then you're as bad as the pair of them! K'vin had the satisfaction of seeing Charanth quail at his fury.

From now on, you are to report to me—instantly—when any rider, or his dragon, is not one hundred percent fit for duty. Do you understand me?

Charanth's eyes whirled, the yellow of anxiety coloring the blue. His tone was remorseful.

I will not fail you again.

If they had been in real danger, I would have warned them off, Meranath said, entering the conversation.

I didn't ask you! K'vin was so irate he didn't really care if he offended Meranath, or her rider. But he was *not* going to lose riders from foolish and vainglorious actions. There *were* fifty years of Thread fighting ahead of them, and he was *not* going to lose partners. Or risk their injuries due to some cockamamie notion of what comprises courageous actions.

If you think that I would jeopardize a single rider . . .

K'vin took the stairs up to the queen's weyr three at a time, trying to work out his rage before he had to confront Zulaya and explain why he thought he could speak to her queen in such a peremptory fashion.

I should be informed of ANY unfit rider or dragon, at any time, anywhere, Meranath, and you should know that or, by the first egg, why are you senior queen?

"Because I am her rider!" Zulaya came storming out onto the weyr ledge, her eyes sparkling with indignation. "How dare you address my queen?"

"How dare she withhold information from *me*?"

Zulaya stared at him, surprised, for K'vin had never reprimanded either her or Meranath, though she had to admit privately that he could have legitimately done so on several occasions she would be embarrassed to admit.

"Did you know about P'tero's condition?" he demanded, and she backed into the weyr, away from him. He was rather magnificent furious, eyes blazing, face stern, the epitome of indignation.

"Tisha remarked that Maranis wasn't pleased with him assuming duty. The scar tissue is thin . . ."

"And you said nothing to me?"

"He's only a blue rider . . ."

"EVERY ONE OF MY RIDERS IS IMPORTANT TO ME!" K'vin roared, clenching his fists at his sides because they wanted to grab something to release the pent-up fury in him. "Threadfall is two days away. I need to have a Weyr in full readiness. I need to be sure of everyone I ask to face Thread in two days time. I don't need secrets or evasions or—"

"K'vin," Zulaya began, reaching a hand out to him, "Kev, it's all right. The Weyr is ready—perhaps tuned a little too tight, but that's all to the good . . ."

"*All to the good?*" K'vin batted her hand away. "When we have unfit riders taking positions they couldn't possibly manage in their condition?"

He began pacing now, and Zulaya watched him, smiling with relief and pride. He was going to be a splendid Weyr-leader, much better than B'ner would have been.

He halted, just short of where she stood, his eyes, brilliant with his anger and frustration, fixed on her face.

"What on earth can you find to grin about right now?" he demanded, suspiciously, for there was a quality in her smile that he'd never seen before.

"That you're in full control," she said, leaving her smile in place.

"Oh, I am, am I?" Then, as she had always hoped he would, he took her in his arms and began kissing her with the full authority of his masculinity and his position as her Weyr-leader, without a trace of hesitation or deference. Just what she'd always hoped she'd provoke him to.

K'vin was still very much in complete control even very early the next morning, before dawn in fact, when Meranath told them that B'nurrin and Shanna were waiting for them.

"Waiting for what?" K'vin asked, pulling himself reluctantly away from Zulaya to reach for his pants.

It is time to go, Charanth added.

"Go where?" K'vin asked in a querulous tone of voice.

"Go where?" Zulaya asked sleepily.

South, they say, Meranath and Charanth echoed.

Suddenly K'vin remembered. Today was the day they would go see Thread. He said that very, very quietly in the back of his mind where Charanth might not hear it. Both dragons had been asleep when B'nurrin had made his visit. Which was just as well or the whole Weyr might have been privy to the notion of previewing Thread.

"B'nurrin wants us to join him," K'vin said, giving Zulaya a cautionary look.

She frowned for a moment, then her face cleared abruptly as she said "Oh." With a conspiratorial grin, she was out of the bed, trailing the sheet on her way to her riding gear.

When they passed each other once in the course of dressing, she pulled his head down to her mouth. "I could bring my flamethrower . . ."

"Might as well paint your destination on your forehead," he murmured back. "We're only going to *watch*."

"Yes, watch." Then she asked more loudly, "Where do we meet B'nurrin, Meranath?"

"We know that, too, remember?" K'vin said, grabbing Zulaya and giving her arm a little shake. Then he mouthed "Landing."

"Yes, how could I forget?"

If the dragon and rider on watch on the rim wondered why the two Weyrleaders were slipping away long before dawn, neither asked, and the rider gave a cheery swing of his arm as they passed over him.

Ianath says to count to three and then go, Charanth told his rider, still mystified.

Landing is where we're going, K'vin replied, glancing across the space between his dragon and Meranath. Zulaya showed him a thumb's-up signal to signify she had had the same message. Visualizing the arid sweep of desolate volcanic ash from Mount Garben down to Monaco Bay, K'vin nodded his head three times.

Go!

Abruptly, Charanth rumbled deep in his belly while his mind said in surprised shock *Oh!* K'vin felt him shift. Consequently he was perhaps not as surprised as he might have been to realize that the airspace around them, and Meranath and

Zulaya, was well occupied. With that extra sense dragons had, the two had averted a collision. In fact, as K'vin swiveled about to check, the only two Weyrleaders he didn't see were S'nan and Sarai, although they might well have been among those who winked out of sight *between* so as not to be recognized. K'vin caught flashes of blue, brown, and even one or two green hides in the southern sun before they disappeared. Nor was this meeting composed now only of Weyrleaders and dragons: some thirty or so bronzes and browns were present.

The sight was too much for K'vin's sense of the ridiculous, and it was a good thing that he was clipped into his safety harness. He was seized of such a laughing fit that he reeled back and forth against Charanth's neck ridges. Had every rider on Pern been possessed of the compulsion to come here this morning? Of course, the particular site of Landing was well known to all riders. But for so many to decide independently to come here . . . probably every one certain he or she'd be the only ones daring enough.

Nor was K'vin the only one laughing hard. Right now he was more in danger of wetting his britches from mirth, not fright at seeing Thread for the first time. Which reminded him why he was here. Again that realization became universal. Laughter faded as every dragon and rider irresistibly turned northeastward.

It was there, too, the much-described silvery gray haze on the upper levels of the blue sky. Not a dragon wing moved, not a rider recoiled as the silver stuff began to drop onto the sea. *Thread!* And so aptly called.

Thread!

The word seemed to rumble from dragon to dragon, and K'vin had to grab hold of the neck ridge as Charanth started to lurch toward what he had known all his life as his adversary.

I have no firestone! How can I flame it! What is wrong? Why have you brought me here where there is Thread and I have no fire to char it!

It's all right, Charanth. We're here to watch. To see.

But it is Thread! I must chew to flame. Why may I not flame when there is THREAD!

Glancing wildly around him, K'vin realized that he was by no means the only rider having the same difficulty with a frustratedly zealous dragon, rapidly trying to close the gap to Threadfall.

I've seen enough, Charanth. Take us back to Telgar.

But THREAD? And the bronze dragon's tone was piteous, confused, and horrified.

We leave. Now!

Leave? But we have not met Thread.

Not here or now or in this place, Charanth.

It took K'vin every bit of willpower and moral strength, and Charanth's faith in him, to overcome his bronze's impassioned protest. Then, all of a sudden, Charanth stopped flying toward Thread.

Oh, all right! The tone was that of a petulant child forced by a senior authority to follow orders totally against the grain.

What?

The queens say we must go to the Red Butte.

Then let us go there. K'vin did not question the order, being far too glad that one was given that the dragon would obey.

The Butte was a training landmark in lower Keroon, a laccolithic dome so difficult to mistake that it figured in all weyrling training programs. And there the would-be observers managed to get their dragons to land. Even the queens' eyes were whirling at a stiff red-orange pace; some of the bronzes were so distraught with anger that their eyes pulsed wickedly, whirling at incredible speed in their anger. K'vin was almost relieved to swing down from Charanth's neck. But he and the other Weyrleaders all kept one hand on their dragons' legs, shoulders, muzzles: some contact was maintained. In a wide outer circle were the brown and bronze riders, who had also been "rescued": they remained mounted, soothing their dragons, allowing their leaders the center for discussion.

It was M'shall who spoke first. "Well, that was one good idea gone awry," he said in a droll tone. "Great minds, all of us."

"Except for forgetting one simple rule," Irene added, pulling off her flying cap. Her face was still pale from fright.

K'vin glanced at Zulaya, who was wiping sweat from her face, so he knew none of the queen riders had had an easy time to get their queens to insist on the disengagement.

"Dragons know what they're supposed to do when Thread falls," M'shall said, nodding. And then he started to laugh.

K'vin grinned and, when he heard G'don's bass chuckle, saw no reason any longer to hold his laughter in. B'nurrin was howling so, he had to clutch at K'vin to keep his balance. Even D'miel looked properly abashed, and Laura's giggle was infectious enough to increase the volume. Beyond the inner circle the rest of the riders caught the joke on themselves and joined in the laugh. It was a good release from the fright that they had all just had.

"Did anyone happen to notice a Fort rider disappearing in guilty retreat?" M'shall asked when the laughter died down. He'd been checking the identity of those on the rim of this informal assembly.

"They'd be the last to admit coming," Irene said.

"I doubt that, Renee," G'don said. "S'nan runs a strict Weyr, it's true, but I'll wager there're a few renegades among his wingleaders."

"I know there are," Mari said, blotting her eyes, which were still merry from laughter. "It's just such a hoot that we all," and she ringed them with a swirl of her hand, "thought to come have a peek."

"It's not going to inhibit any of the dragons, is it?" Laura asked, turning pale at the sudden thought, "turning them off like that?"

D'miel wasn't the only Weyrleader to dismiss that notion derisively. "Hardly! It's increased rider credibility a hundredfold. They now know without doubt that what we've been telling them since they were hatched is true!"

"Oh, yes, it would, wouldn't it?" she said, relieved.

"I myself would like to thank the queen riders for exerting their powerful influence on our bronzes," G'don said with a formal hand over his heart as he bowed to the five queen riders.

"The advantage of having three very senior queens," Zulaya said, "and two very strong-minded young women."

Laura blushed while Shanna stood even straighter.

"All right, then," M'shall said, having taken note that most of the male dragons' eyes were resuming normal color and speed. He took a step toward the center of the sandy circle and cupped his hands, turning as he spoke. "All right, then, every one of you. This is a meeting that never happened and isn't to be referred to in any Weyr for any reason. Do you understand me?" The response was loud and clear. He nodded and stepped back toward Craigath. "We'll meet . . ." he said now to the other leaders, "where Thread first—officially—falls North."

"We've sweep riders out all the time," G'don reminded them.

"And we're all very sure that S'nan does, too," B'nurrin put in, grinning.

"So we'll know when and where to meet again."

"Wait a moment more, G'don," K'vin said. "Why don't we rotate the wings that meet that first Fall, wherever it is?" A little cheer from the outer circle gave instant approval to that suggestion. "That'll give even more riders a chance for at least a little experience before the individual Weyrs have to meet Thread on their own."

G'don paused at Chakath's side, looking around to check the reaction to that idea.

"In hourly intervals?" he asked.

"Make it two hours to allow wings to get properly into the routine," M'shall amended.

"It's not that we're green riders or anything," B'nurrin put in as protest.

"Two hours makes more sense than swapping around every hour . . ." D'miel said thoughtfully.

"I'd agree on two," G'don said. "We'll bring the matter up to S'nan. He deserves that much from us. I'll initiate the idea." He grinned again, since S'nan would listen to him as the oldest Weyrleader, where he would summarily dismiss a younger man. "I'll let you know when we'll meet to make the changes we've already agreed to."

Red dust swirled up in a cloud around the Butte as all the dragons leaped almost simultaneously from the ground.

17

▼▼▼▼▼▼▼▼▼

THREADFALL

Bitter cold weather and winds swept down from the icy poles of Pern on the day that S'nan set a meeting with the other five Weyrleaders to discuss the rotation of wings that G'don had suggested to him. Freezing weather was likely to do Fort Weyr out of its chance to be the first Weyr to meet Thread in this Fall.

That S'nan keenly felt deprived was obvious. Throughout the meeting he paced the floor, pausing to peer out the slanting corridor to the sleet falling heavily into Fort Bowl. He had only half his mind on the discussion. B'nurrin was all but laughing, only the kicks he received from K'vin under the table kept him from bursting out. Not that K'vin could blame the Igen Weyrleader, for the meeting was a charade: each of them giving soberly presented reasons for the two-hourly rotation while S'nan said little more than monosyllables. S'nan kept his expression blank. It was Sarai's petulant expression that was honest.

"She's been dying to get all of us under her wing," Zulaya whispered to K'vin when the Fort Weyrwoman's face was turned toward her anxiously pacing mate.

"Don't think she will, love," K'vin said, the endearment coming easily to his lips now. He sighed. "You know," and he moved his lips close to her ear. "I'm almost sorry for the old man."

Zulaya gave a little snort. "I'm not." Then she altered her expression to one of earnest attention as Sarai looked over at them for whispering.

Thread came down as black dust, sifted in with snow or sleet. Fort sweep riders brought buckets of it for S'nan to see and mournfully wave off. High Reaches were even more diligent in their efforts to locate live, dangerous Thread. Some riders even suffered frostbite, so earnestly did they watch for the reappearance of the old enemy, although one long piece of frozen Thread was brought for G'don to examine. The stench of it as it melted was enough for them to dispose of it completely.

By the time of Benden's First Fall—by the numbers, Ten—the weather pattern had shifted sufficiently on the East Coast to a warmer front so that a good deal of that projected Fall would be considered "live" and dangerous. The call went out to all the Weyrs of Pern.

K'vin and Telgar Weyr's two full wings of dragonriders reassembled in the upper-right quadrant of air above Benden Weyr, not a rider out of alignment. Below him the Weyr was ablaze with lights in this dark predawn time, lighting the bellies of the dragons in their ranks. He wasn't sure if the Telgar contingent got there before the units of the other Weyrs, but they were certainly all present and accounted for at the designated hour and in the assigned positions. Everyone would have preferred a daylight defense, but Thread didn't need to see to fall. And according to Sean's reports of early morning or late evening Fall, the silvery stuff would be luminous enough for the practical purpose of flaming it out of the sky.

This First Fall of the Second Pass would start across the high mountains, still deep with winter snows, and would thus fall harmlessly. Much would probably fall as black dust in the still frigid temperatures of that area, though quite likely, on other occasions, Fall would merely be observed until it moved inexorably down to habitable lands. Today was the exception.

The final decision by the Weyrleaders had been unanimous, when M'shall had made S'nan put it to a vote—to ride the entire Fall over the ranges, harmless or not, "to see it for themselves." Everyone was too keyed up over the first three "dud" falls to wait any longer to go into action. Of course, some of the peaks jutted at altitudes where oxygen had thinned to an unsustainable level even for dragons. But it could be seen in actual descent and the general aspect of this Fall judged.

The wings would be rotated after two hours, giving as many as possible a chance at the "real thing." K'vin briefly thought of P'tero's vain attempt to be included in the fighting force Telgar would launch. Maybe he should have put the blue rider in, sore ass and all, to prove that there was a lot more to fighting Thread than having the guts to do it. But to include P'tero would have been to exclude a perfectly healthy and less erratic rider. K'vin had not selected M'leng of the green riders chosen for the First Fall. That would ease discord between that pair: that one had gone and the other had not. Basically, they were good weyrmates, having a reasonably stable relationship ever since P'tero, who was the younger, had Impressed Ormonth.

Movement and a shift in air pressure caught K'vin's attention and he looked down at Benden's rim.

Craigath warns us, Charanth told his rider. *Three, two, one . . .*

GO!

The command came from many minds and many throats in the dark above Benden Weyr. The blackness of *between* was more intense but scarcely less cold than the atmosphere above the peaks where the wings reentered real space. K'vin was glad of the wool fabric across his mouth and nose, though it did not altogether warm the thin air he inhaled. Below, the snowy mountains gave off a curious light of their own. Belior was setting in the west, and K'vin looked around to the east and saw the baleful orb of the Red Planet, vivid amidst the stars.

Spits of fire blossomed in the darkness all around as eager dragons belched. Too full a belly of firestone, K'vin thought with professional detachment, but he could hardly fault rider or dragon for overpriming.

For two centuries they had waited for this moment: centuries of training and lives lived so that dragons—and riders—would be here, right now, waiting to defend Pern.

Yet this was a first, too. For Pern had had no dragons the first time Thread had fallen, and the planet had been close to total disaster before the first eighteen dragons had emerged from *between* above Fort Hold to flame the parasite from the skies and give hope to the beleaguered defenders. K'vin had always been struck by the courage of the despairing Admiral Paul Benden—he should make P'tero read those entries in the admiral's diary, made just prior to that magnificent triumph. Even in his most recent reading of that journal, his throat closed over as he read the words:

And then that young rogue had the temerity to salute and say, "Admiral Benden, may I present the Dragonriders of Pern?"

More spurts of fiery breath and every dragon head turned northward.

It comes, Charanth said, rumbling deep in his chest, a vibration that K'vin felt through his legs. He was aware then that the only warm part of him was what was pressing against his dragon's neck. His nose had no feeling of the fabric across it. Maybe they should drop down a thousand feet or so . . . and he looked toward the central block of the massed wings, where M'shall and Craigath waited. It was the Benden Weyrleader's call, not his.

Then he saw it, or rather the mass of something lustrous against the black of night, like a banner spread from some distant source in the sky, a banner that rippled and spun. The pace of his heartbeat picked up. He felt an odd coldness in his guts, but it could be because it was very, very cold at this altitude.

Charanth's rumble increased and a little spit of flame spilled from his mouth.

Steady, lad!

I'm not moving! It is! And I can flame this time!

K'vin could not reproach Charanth for that snide reminder. And, oddly enough, he also felt no fear as he regarded the advance. There was this sense of inevitability, that he would be here, at this moment in time, to observe this phenomenon, to be part of this defense.

Closer and closer the waves of Thread came as the massed wings watched. The leading edge was now falling visibly on the mountainsides. In this cold air not even the steam of its dissolution was visible.

Thread was falling in a steady stream, freezing dead in the snow. A steady stream, no tangles, no bare spots.

Craigath says we regroup at the second meeting point.

Agreed.

Oddly enough, K'vin did not like even to regroup, though there was nothing Thread could have done to harm the snowy mountainsides and it was foolish to waste time and flame here. But it *felt* like retreat.

Charanth had broadcast the order and took them *between*.

The air was noticeably warmer at the altitude of the new position. He rubbed at his nose and cheeks to bring blood to the surface. Even his fingertips felt numb from the cold.

False dawn began in the east, the Red Star paling slightly in the graying skies. And Thread suddenly looked more ominous. More dragons spewed flame and he told Charanth to warn them to conserve their breath.

Suddenly the wait was chafing. They had waited so long, hadn't they? Two hundred years! When would they begin?

But Thread fell on snow, and K'vin was close enough to Leading Edge now to see the holes it made in the whiteness.

NOW! Craigath's command reached K'vin's mind in the same moment that Charanth roared, full flame erupting from his mouth as he beat his wings to power his forward surge. K'vin clutched at the flight strap, felt frantically for the rope that tethered the firestone sacks to the neck ridge in front of him, and clamped his knees as tight as he could to his bronze. His right arm rose and pointed forward, as if any rider could have missed Craigath's command or the roars that emerged from dragon throats across the sky.

They were flying in ranks, Telgar being the second and slightly behind the uppermost wings, which were from High Reaches. There was sufficient air between the two layers of dragons so that flame from one level would not interfere with another: and a corridor for maneuver as well. Every Weyr had drilled its wings for this strategy until it was instinctive to stay within the plane assigned them.

The moment when Charanth's breath sizzled up descending Thread was a transcendental experience for both partners. Charanth sustained his flame magnificently, crossing this cordon, and then they were out, beyond Thread's Fall and turning. K'vin spared a glance at the rest of his wings and saw them pivoting simultaneously, all those long, long hours and years of practice resulting in a perfect maneuver. His heart was like to burst in his chest with pride. Below and above him other wings were turning, all now flaming to catch the next band of falling Thread. And the next. And the next.

Meranath and the others are here, Charanth announced, dropping his head to peer far below.

They are? Turn. K'vin looked below and saw the unmistakable arrow of golden bodies in their low-level position, the flamethrowers that the queen riders used spouting here and there as they disintegrated stray strands escaping the higher ranks.

Does Meranath fly well?

Meranath flies very well, Charanth said proudly.

Tell the wings it is time to execute the first change-over, K'vin said. He swiveled his body around to watch that maneuver, holding his right arm up high, sweeping his eyes across Telgar's wings. He dropped his arm and counted nine or ten dragons still flaming. Then they, too, went off. He counted to five and suddenly full wings flew behind him. He raised his arm high in recognition of their arrival, which was all he had time for because the wall of Thread advanced to flaming distance and Charanth was ready with his fire. So far he could find no fault with the performance of Telgar's wings.

It seemed no time after that when he realized his sacks of firestone were empty. He had Charanth call for more. It surprised K'vin to notice that they had flown from night into day, for the sun slanted right into the eyes as they flew east again. There was good reason to use tinted glass in the goggles.

Z'gal and blue Tracath made the drop, swooping in neatly just above his head and depositing the new sacks across Charanth's neck. K'vin pulled the release knot of the empty sacks and saw Tracath swivel and dive beneath Charanth, Z'gal deftly catching the limp ones and disappearing instantly *between.*

Tell Tracath that was well done, K'vin said.

They were over the northernmost edge of Benden now, above pasturelands, forests, and small farming holds. The need for accuracy and complete destruction of Thread was more crucial now. The queens' wing was more visible, gold against the dark green or brown of fields not yet verdant with spring growth.

Sacks had to be replenished again. He called in the second change-over of wings, only then realizing that he was beginning to tire.

Are you all right, Charanth?

I flame well. My wings beat strongly. We are together. There is no problem.

The calm, strong tone of his bronze was like a tonic. Yes, they were together, doing what they had been bred and maintained to do.

Meranath says we are over Bitra Hold now. They were turning west again, back for another run. K'vin did notice that there seemed to be less Thread falling now, even gaps between the sheets of it. *This Fall is nearly over?*

K'vin wasn't sure if Charanth was pleased, surprised, or disappointed. He, for one, was enormously relieved. He had survived the ultimate test of the Weyrleader.

They did one more pass eastward and then there was no more Thread visible above. A cheer echoed from rider to rider, and all those within K'vin's range pumped both arms in jubilation.

We should land at Bitra Hold, in case we are needed for burrows that might have escaped us, K'vin told Charanth. *Tell the wings well done and all but J'dar's may return. He will wait with us for the all-clear. It is M'shall's pleasure to tell us that! Any casualties?*

That was the traditional Weyrleader's query, though reports would also be made to him during the Fall so that he could assess what replacements might be needed.

Today only some minor burns from char. Nothing bad enough that anyone cared to report to you.

K'vin wasn't that pleased that news had been withheld, but he could understand the reluctance of any rider in today's Fall to retire for a mere char burn. Now he noticed that he had quite a few black spots on his own riding leathers, but nothing had penetrated through to his flesh. Would that every Fall be so trouble-free! And the next one that Telgar flew would show up the foolhardy. He'd have to give the entire Weyr a hard bollicking to prevent the cocksure from disaster.

Today the queens' wing would join the wingleaders at Bitra Hold, though traditionally they stayed aloft to assist groundcrews.

Zulaya sought K'vin as soon as she was on the ground and embraced him, seeking his mouth to kiss him with enthusiasm.

"We did it. We did it."

"This time," K'vin said, hugging her tightly. He could almost have thanked P'tero for getting him so angry. It had done the world of good for his relations with Zulaya. The way she looked at him, the way she had to touch him . . . well, they were truly weyrmates now.

M'shall was moving among the riders, slapping one on the shoulder, thanking each Weyrleader for participating in this almost scatheless Fall, a wide smile plastered on his face.

"I'd say that this was a normal Fall," S'nan was saying portentously.

"How can we possibly tell?" G'don said.

"The records, man, the records," S'nan said, glaring. "It's exactly as Sean described Fall number 325, in his records of Fifty-eight A.L. Exactly."

"Oh, Fall number 325?" B'nurrin asked, his eyes dancing. "Myself, I felt it was more like number 499 in Sixty A.L."

"B'nurrin?" and M'shall's raised eyebrows suggested that

the irrepressible young Igen Weyrleader should stop baiting S'nan.

"We got off much too easily," D'miel of Ista said, shaking his head. "I mean, we were all on a high. I for one was expecting far worse . . ."

"Isn't it nice to be disappointed?" K'vin said, but he agreed with D'miel. Everything had gone too well.

"Nonsense," G'don said. "We were all flying our best riders. We've been keyed up for weeks and nervous. And I don't mind admitting I was," he added, glancing around him, but he winked at K'vin and B'nurrin. Others nodded agreement. "So we were very cautious. It's when we're so accustomed to the menace that we're liable to be careless, to take unnecessary risks, to stop watching out of the backs of our heads."

A murmur of agreement and nods greeted that observation.

"We must never relax our guard during Fall," S'nan said, again sententious. "Never!"

"We'll have to be doubly cautious during the second Fall over south Benden and Keroon," Zulaya said softly to K'vin.

"Well, I for one was pleased with the way the wings performed. Not much got through," he repeated. "Between the upper flights and the queens' wing, only four incidents of burrow, and those were handled with great dispatch. Thanks to Vergerin . . ."

The Bitra Lord Holder was directing the distribution of Hegmon's sparkling wine to those crowding in his courtyard.

"Only think what might have happened if Chalkin was still here!" Irene said, raising her glass toward Vergerin.

"Who *wants* to think what might have happened?" Laura of Ista Weyr demanded, laughing with exaggerated relief.

"For one thing, we wouldn't have this champagne," Irene replied. "That's for damned sure!"

"How'd you get the sparkly out of Hegmon, Vergerin?" G'don wanted to know, cradling his glass lovingly.

"We're old friends, you might say," Vergerin replied with a droll grin.

"Did any wing report injuries?" M'shall asked, his expression turning sober.

"Nothing above char burns in mine," K'vin said. And that was what the other wingleaders reported one after another.

"Well, we're fragging lucky if that's all. Though I shudder to think how careless the average rider can get," M'shall said. "We'll have to keep them on their toes."

"And on their dragons," his weyrmate replied.

"Look at it this way," B'nurrin said, grinning from ear to ear, "we've only 6,649 more falls to attend, give or take a few, before it's all over for another two hundred years."

There was a moment of dumbfounded silence as that fact was absorbed, and then B'nurrin ducked away before the wrath of his peers could descend on him.

"But Fall has begun," K'vin said softly to Zulaya, standing proudly beside him, "and we have met the enemy again."

"What a time to be alive . . ."

"And riding a dragon!"

And thus began the Second Pass of Thread on Pern!

ABOUT THE AUTHOR

ANNE MCCAFFREY shuttles between her home in Ireland and the United States, where she picks up awards and honors and greets her myriad fans. She is one of the field's most popular authors.

In 1967, the Dragonriders of Pern were introduced to the world in a short story called "Weyr Search," which appeared in the October issue of *Analog*. With the publication in 1997 of the newest Pern novel, *Dragonseye*, Del Rey® Books is thrilled to celebrate the 30th Anniversary of The Dragonriders of Pern! If you would like to send Anne McCaffrey a personal congratulatory message, we would be happy to forward it to her along with our own. Send all messages to:

Del Rey Books
Pern 30
201 E 50th Street
New York, NY 10022

or e-mail us at:
delrey@randomhouse.com

Please limit messages to 500 words. If you include your return address you will be added to our mailing list. The first 100 people who sign up for our mailing list will receive a bookplate autographed by Anne McCaffrey.